Emiko

Emiko

CHIERI UEGAKI

tundra

Tundra Books, an imprint of Tundra Book Group, a division of Penguin Random House
Canada Ltd., 320 Front Street West, Suite 1400, Toronto, Ontario, M5V 3B6, Canada
penguinrandomhouse.ca

Published simultaneously in the United States of America by Tundra Books of Northern
New York, an imprint of Tundra Book Group, a division of Penguin Random House
Canada Ltd., P.O. Box 2040, Plattsburgh, NY 12901, USA

Tundra with colophon is a registered trademark of Penguin Random House Canada Ltd.

The authorized representative in the EU for product safety and compliance
is Penguin Random House Ireland, Morrison Chambers, 32 Nassau Street,
Dublin D02 YH68, Ireland, https://eu-contact.penguin.ie

*Publisher's note: This book is a work of fiction. Names, characters, places and incidents either
are the product of the author's imagination or are used fictitiously, and any resemblance to
actual persons living or dead, events, or locales is entirely coincidental.*

Library and Archives Canada Cataloguing in Publication

Title: Emiko / Chieri Uegaki.
Names: Uegaki, Chieri, author
Identifiers: Canadiana (print) 20240432339 | Canadiana (ebook) 20240432347 |
    ISBN 9781774885734 (softcover) | ISBN 9781774885741 (EPUB)
Subjects: LCGFT: Romance fiction. | LCGFT: Novels.
Classification: LCC PS8591.E32 E45 2025 | DDC jC813/.6—dc23

Library of Congress Control Number: 2024942386

Edited by Tara Walker with assistance from Ashley Rhamey
Cover designed by Gigi Lau
Production edited by Ashley Rhamey
Typeset by Kianna Mkhonza
The text was set in Minion Pro, 12pt.

Printed in Canada

1 2 3 4 5   29 28 27 26 25

To all my friends and family

1

Wedding Day

I am a matchmaking GENIUS.

I repeat this to myself, owning it à la Beyoncé, as I help my Aunt Mitsuko get ready for her wedding, the wedding I can most definitely take nearly one hundred percent credit for.

"Emiko." My aunt interrupts my inner strutting. "Is my flower crown crooked?"

I walk up behind her and look at her reflection in the mirror; there's a tiny crease of worry between her eyebrows and I'm sensing some actual jitters, so I adjust the circlet of ranunculus and roses a fraction to make her feel better. "There," I assure her. "It's perfect."

She smiles back at me, her cheeks rosier than usual. "I can't believe I'm so nervous," she says as her hands flutter around her neckline.

"I think that's pretty normal. Unless you feel like sneaking out and running away on a horse?"

"Oh, no," she says quickly. "Not at all."

There's a gentle tap on her door, accompanied by my grandfather's voice. "Knock-knock. Mitsuko, Emiko, are you almost ready? We do not want to be late today."

"Thanks, Ojiichan. We'll be right down," I say, and wait till I hear him pad down the hallway.

Mitsuko lets out a contented sigh as we pick up our hand-tied bouquets. "Alright, Emiko, this is it," she says to our reflections. "I'm getting married today." Her voice is soft and filled with awe.

"You are." And even though I'm beyond happy for her, and we both look amazing, the fact that this is the last day she'll call this place home is a big, fat smudge on an otherwise perfect picture. But I mentally wipe it away and give her a matching smile. "Ready?"

She nods.

"Okay, then." I exhale deeply as I open the door. "Let's do this."

* * *

After the most beautiful service ever, sixty or so guests gather at our house.

Ojiichan insisted on hosting the afternoon reception, going all out hiring decorators, caterers, even a jazz manouche quartet (because who doesn't love an accordion?). He initially had mixed feelings about Mitsuko and Seiji, thinking they were rushing into things. But when it became obvious that the two of them looked at each other with cartoon hearts for eyes, Ojiichan got on board and did everything he could to fulfill Mitsuko's wish for an intimate, laid-back wedding.

I'm sure part of his early reluctance also came from the fact that, like me, he simply didn't want to deal with not having Mitsuko around. We were a tight little family unit, a perfectly balanced three-legged table. As thrilled as I've been since the engagement, if I'm honest, I've spent more than a few nights awake at the thought of my aunt no longer sleeping down the hall from me.

I mean, I know I can always talk to her, anytime I want. Unlike my best friend, Meeta, Mitsuko isn't leaving the Golden Coast. And thankfully, she and Seiji are staying in the village, so I can easily walk or bike to their house. But things are going to be different now. Things *are* different now.

"You'll be going away yourself after this year," she'd said one night. We were in my bathroom experimenting with hairstyles for the big day. She'd been attempting a crown braid for me, but my super-straight hair kept slipping loose.

"Maybe." I showed her another inspo photo on my phone, hoping to distract her. "How about something like this instead?"

She stuck a few bobby pins in her mouth and squinted in concentration as she tried again to secure the braid. "What do you mean *maybe*, Emiko?" she asked, giving my phone a quick glance. "Aren't you excited about graduating and going off to university next year?"

Thankfully, her own phone rang before I had to answer, and since it was Seiji, she took the call. No kidding, they're like hand-holding otters, so cute I almost can't stand it.

I wonder if my aunt noticed how I didn't answer her question that day.

Or how skillfully I've deflected every conversation since — with her or Ojiichan — about my plans for after graduation. The thing is, grad is a LONG way away — like, almost a whole year. What IS the rush? (I say this to my aunt and grandfather, too, in my head.)

By the time the toasts and speeches are over and the party is at peak volume, I'm ready for a bit of quiet time to sort out some thoughts. I skirt my way downstairs, slipping out the patio sliders, and steal over to the viewing pavilion; it's one of my favorite spots on the property because you can see not only the house and the garden but the water, too.

As I make myself comfortable on one of the bamboo benches, I automatically scan the strait for signs of marine life. Over the years, Ojiichan and Mitsuko have had multiple sightings of orcas as well as humpbacks and grays, but I've only seen whales in the wild once, a pod of orcas when I was nine. Seals are common, popping their heads out of the water like aquatic gophers, and every summer a raft of sea lions spends about a week in our bay, barking like dogs in a kennel. Whales, though, are elusive.

I'm literally inhaling the peaceful vibe along with the cedar-scented air when the sound of my grandfather's laugh makes me glance towards the house. I smile when I see Kenzo Sanada, my lifelong friend and neighbor, coming down the stairs and walking towards me; I sit up when I note he's carrying three plates.

"Hey, Em," he says when he reaches me. "Figured I'd find you here." Sitting on the bench, he sets the plates down between us. "Thought you might want some cake."

4

"Ha." I can take or leave sweets, even strawberry cream wedding cake. Instead, I go straight for the plate I know Kenzo brought especially for me, the one heaped with the adzuki bean sticky rice our family serves at every special occasion. "Good sir, you read my mind." I pop a forkful into my mouth and make a happy humming sound.

Kenzo takes his own fork and digs into a piece of cake. "Wow," he says as he goes in for a second bite. "This is insanely good."

"Same," I say, lifting my plate. He grins, and as we continue to eat cake and pink rice, I give a slow mental nod at how he looks today with his shoulder-length hair neatly tied back, dressed in something other than his usual tees and year-round shorts. I mean, a dandy he is NOT, so I appreciate the effort. And I did notice earlier, but this being the first chance we've had to talk all day, I brush aside the urge to tease him a little and focus on a more important subject.

"So . . . what'd you think of the wedding?" I ask. "And be effusive, Sanada. I promise I won't let it go to my head." Last summer, after throwing Meeta a boffo farewell party, Kenzo claimed all the roses people threw at my feet made me obnoxious.

"Uh-uh. I told you, I'm no longer contributing to your problem. I want you to be able to walk without tipping over."

"Come on. It's been a year," I say.

"No."

"One light pat on the back — a kudo or two — that's all I ask."

"I'm just looking out for you, Em. Concussions are real."

"That cake wouldn't exist if today hadn't happened."

This makes Kenzo pause, a laden fork halfway to his mouth. "Did you bake the cake?" he asks.

"No. But I helped pick it."

"Doesn't count. And I already told you what I think of the cake." He grins before the fork completes its journey.

"That's fine. *I don't really care, but Mitsuko will be sad to hear you had nothing to say about her special day.*" I wait, eating my rice while I keep him in my peripheral vision.

"It was nice," he says, finally, with a shrug. A shrug!

"*Nice?*" I parrot as my eyebrows lift. "That's it? That's your review? *Nice?*" I shake my head in disbelief. "*Au contraire, mon frère.* I've been collecting compliments all day and the consensus is pretty much unanimous that this wedding was more than *nice.*" I realize I'm letting him rile me up, something he's been doing since preschool.

Kenzo laughs. "Okay, first, *not* your brother. And second, alright . . . you can tell Mitsuko I thought the wedding was more than nice. It was, I don't know, how about *magnificence incarnate? Spectacular squared?*" He makes these suggestions with a straight face. "*Beyond sublime?*"

"Ha ha. You're funny. And such a butt." Our favorite childhood insult only cracks Kenzo up, so I try pushing him over, but he's like a human Weeble. "Seriously, you realize this wedding might not have happened without me?"

"And you realize that repeating a thing over and over doesn't make it true, right?"

"Mitsuko and Seiji *both* said so in their speeches." I flash back to when they met, just six months ago, in her café. In movie terms, theirs was a total meet-cute. I couldn't have scripted it better if I tried.

"She fell off a stool and he caught her. I'm pretty sure they would have figured things out without you."

"They were both in shock, and she was mortified. I calmed them down, made them sit, and eat, and talk."

"So, basically, you waited on them."

"It was more than that! I set the stage for all of this." I wrestle with the temptation to smush cake into his tanned, skeptical face, but settle for muttering "You're impossible" instead.

Clearly, he doesn't understand that sometimes people are too distracted or embarrassed or just plain blind to the possibilities and don't know when something great is right in front of them. It's like having an eye for putting together a fabulous look — you either have it or you don't. Luckily, I do, and because of it, here we are.

I get ready to explain all of this again to Kenzo when he asks what happened to Seiji's son, Jun. "I thought he was flying in to be best man," he says, stabbing his cake.

"He was. But he had to cancel last minute."

"Did he say why?"

I shake my head. "I was super disappointed, too. I was really looking forward to meeting him."

"Must have been something big to bail on his own dad's wedding."

Something in Kenzo's tone makes me feel compelled to defend Jun. "I'm sure if he could have, he would have come," I say.

Kenzo makes a noise.

"Did you just 'hmph' me? You sound like Ojiichan." I lean back on my hands, thinking. "Maybe it was his mom. Mitsuko says Seiji's ex doesn't exactly encourage the relationship."

"Well, being a no-show on a day like today isn't going to help."

"Or there was an emergency."

"Right."

"We don't know," I say. "And he did try to video call them."

Kenzo makes another dismissive sound.

"What? The time difference with Tokyo is confusing!"

"Sure." He gestures to the second plate of cake. "Are you even going to try it?"

"Go ahead."

"Last chance." He picks up the plate and waves it in front of me. "No backsies."

I roll my eyes. "No backsies."

We sit there, quiet and comfortable as we look out at the water. I can hear the waves lapping the shoreline but, beyond that, the water's glassy surface is barely rippling.

"Looks awesome for a paddle," Kenzo says eventually.

"I was thinking the same thing. I can't remember the last time we went kayaking."

"It's been a while. We should go out soon."

"We should."

More quiet minutes tick by and I'm as relaxed as a well-fed cat until Kenzo finishes his cake and asks, "Now that the wedding's over, what else you got planned for the summer?"

I know Kenzo doesn't mean it this way, but his question is like a Slip 'N Slide into a mud pit full of questions regarding my future-with-a-capital-F. Since I'm not ready to go there yet, I remove the pins and elastics from my hair.

Separate them into neat piles beside me.

And slowly shake my braid loose.

As I comb it out with my fingers, I tell him what I know for sure, trying my best to add breaking-news energy to my voice. "I've got my volunteer work at the rescue. And I'll be helping out at the café as much as Mitsuko needs me."

Kenzo doesn't say anything, probably lulled to sleep by the sound of crickets accompanying my answer. It'd be different if Meeta were still here. Not because we'd have anything extraordinary planned, but I'd be excited because I'd know she and I would be having fun, making the most of our last summer as high schoolers.

Now, with Mitsuko married and moved out — I mean, I always have things to do, I have a lot of interests. Hobbies R Me. But for some reason, none of them seem quite enough anymore. What I need is to come up with a new project, fast.

Which makes me think, if I can't figure out what I want to accomplish in the next two months, how can I know what I want to be doing a whole three hundred and sixty-five days from now?

"I still don't understand how you haven't already brought home a pack of dogs . . . or even one," Kenzo says, like I haven't flaked out of our conversation; clearly, my face isn't a billboard for what's happening inside my head.

Dogs I can talk about. "Trust me, I've come close. But — even though I think he secretly is — Ojiichan swears he's not a dog person. And with Mitsuko gone now . . ." I shrug.

"And I guess if you're going away for school next fall . . ."

"Mm-hm. Yeah." Feeling myself tense up again, I stick some bobby pins in my mouth. "What about you, what are your plans?" I mumble as I gather my hair and manage a messy bun.

Kenzo's eyebrows quirk slightly but he doesn't push it. "Working, mostly," he says. "I've been getting slammed with calls since spring."

When he was thirteen, Kenzo started cutting lawns to save up for his first truck, and because he doesn't do anything by halves, it's morphed into a proper business.

"I had to hire another guy," he adds.

"Oh, yeah? Who?"

"Will Rivers. He's going into tenth grade. I play hockey with one of his cousins."

"Cool." I try to place the name. "Does he have a sister a year behind us?"

"Yeah, Arlo."

"Right. She ran for student council."

I run through the faces of ninth-graders I remember from last year but come up blank.

"Nope, can't picture Will."

"Well, he's solid," Kenzo says.

I fist-bump his shoulder. "Look at you, all entrepreneurial."

He smiles, looking a little embarrassed.

"I mean it," I continue. "Being a boss, that's like proper grown-up stuff." It's also the sort of thing that makes Kenzo seem more than just a year older than me.

"Emiko!" I hear my grandfather calling and see him beckoning from the veranda, clearly in need of my help. It hits me then that, as of today, I am now Ojiichan's go-to person in the family.

"Duty calls." Standing up, I wave at my grandfather, who nods and heads back into the house.

"Wait up." Kenzo stacks the empty plates, folding them around the forks. "Wanna race?"

We did this all the time as kids, any chance we could, and I suddenly really want those seconds of thinking about nothing but beating him. So, instead of answering right away, I pretend I'm going to remove my flats, and at the very last second, before he can even blink, I take off running, laughing all the way.

2

Meeting Harumi

After yoga on the covered deck, Ojiichan and I are almost ready to sit down for Sunday brunch. Normally, Ojiichan eats a traditional Japanese breakfast of rice, miso soup, grilled fish, and homemade pickles. But because our housekeeper, Mrs. Yoshimatsu, and her husband, our caretaker, get weekends off, I'm in charge of cooking today. Which means I've also come up with the menu.

I turn the heat off under a mushroom and Gruyère frittata and finish prepping a salad of baby greens and berries Ojiichan picked earlier from the garden. With jalapeño cheddar corn muffins baking in one wall oven, a sheet of bacon crisping in the other, and a pan of garlicky salt and lemon kale waiting on the stove, my mouth is already watering from all the delectable smells that fill the kitchen.

"I ran into Satomi-san yesterday in the village, outside the café," my grandfather says as I flip the bacon.

"Mm-hm?" Satomi Natsugawa is the assistant to the principal at my school and lives in upper Otter Creek. "How's she doing?"

"That is what I asked her. She says she has gotten very busy because her niece has come to live with her."

"Oh?"

"I think she said the girl's name is Haruko," Ojiichan continues. "She is going into eleventh grade."

"Really? That's a tough year to start a new school. I wonder why she'd come here to do that."

"I did not press for details, but Satomi-san did mention that Haruko needed a change of scenery."

"Where's she from?"

"She was born in Osaka. However, I believe she has been going to school in Toronto."

People from Osaka tend to love their food, so I already have a good feeling about her. "Is Osaka where her parents are?" I ask, assuming she's one of those kids who get sent overseas to learn English.

"No . . ."

Something in the way he answers makes me turn to look at him. "What is it?"

Ojiichan pulses some coffee beans in his grinder; Sundays are the one day he'll treat himself to an espresso he makes in his ancient Bialetti. One thing about my grandfather, there's no rushing him for anything, so I have to wait until he's turned on the burner before he continues.

"She did not tell me too much, but she did explain that it is Satomi-san herself and a network of relatives who have cared for Haruko since she was a baby."

"Oh. That sounds like me."

"Yes, I thought this, too. And since you and Haruko are the same age, we thought it would be good for you both to meet."

"That'd be great." As I say this, I realize how true it is. I'm not bragging when I say I'm popular, it's just a fact. But since Meeta and her family moved to the U.K. last summer, and my other school friends live in communities outside Otter Creek, there's no one within walking or biking distance that I can easily hang with. Which, until recently, didn't matter because I had my aunt, who was always up to do anything with me.

Of course, there's Kenzo.

His mom, Abby, says the first time my mom brought me to their house, Kenzo commando-crawled over to me in my carrier and wouldn't leave my side for the entire visit. We've literally grown up together, so he's an important friend — practically family, really — but it's not like when we were younger and played all the time.

Which leads me back to my excitement at the possibility of making a new friend, an actual *girl* friend, who lives in the Creek.

"Have you invited them over yet?" I ask.

"Not yet, no."

I check the clock, noting there's plenty of time to bake something. "Do you want to call Satomi-san and see if she and Haruko would like to come by for tea later?"

Ojiichan smiles. "I will call her right after we eat."

The timer for the muffins goes off, and I grab some oven mitts to take them out. They look exactly how I'd hoped — caramelized cheese on top of golden domes of cornmeal and jalapeño goodness. While they cool on a rack, I put the rest of the food out buffet-style on the island and hand Ojiichan a plate.

As I help myself to a bit of everything, I take a moment to enjoy the variety of food I've assembled. All the colors are gorgeous together; I swear it's art on a plate as far as I'm concerned. I add a ripe cherry tomato just off center before sitting down at the table.

Once Ojiichan joins me, we bow our heads, say "Itadakimasu" in appreciation for the food, and dig in.

As we eat, we talk about the movie we watched last night. Ojiichan's a huge film buff, which makes sense given his acting career, and we've been working through his massive DVD collection for years. Right now we're in a Billy Wilder phase, and I tell him again how much I loved *Sabrina*, especially Audrey Hepburn's wardrobe.

"I'm still not convinced she should have ended up with Linus, though," I say, referring to Humphrey Bogart's character. "The younger brother was way more dashing."

"I agree initially he appeared so. However, did you not find Linus's actions more impressive than David's words?"

I think about it. "Maybe. But Linus looked old enough to be her dad."

Ojiichan chuckles as he pushes his empty plate away. "That I cannot argue with. Another excellent meal, Emiko-chan. Gochisousama deshita."

"Osomatsusama deshita," I reply.

Neither of us has mentioned how much we're missing my aunt's presence in the house. I've seen Ojiichan pull out the big teapot when all he needs now is the single-person size, and the evenings are quieter without her shouting answers at the TV during the game shows we usually watch together after dinner.

Even the fact that there are still so many corn muffins on the plate hits differently now. I mean, in the past, I'd be like, *Yay, leftovers!*

Anyway, after we tidy up, I decide I need a walk on the beach, while Ojiichan heads over to the Otter Creek Library to pick up some books. Satomi-san and Haruko aren't expected for hours, so I have time for an endorphin boost before getting back into the kitchen.

I love our beach. During high tide we have our own private stretch, and when it's low, it expands to the point where Otter Creek flows into the sea; depending on the time of year, I can jump across the stream and carry on for almost a mile before the shoreline gets too rocky. Up the coast, I can go a couple more before hitting an impassable rock bluff.

Either way, it's incredible, and I've spent thousands of hours here beachcombing for smooth rocks and sea glass and sun-bleached oyster shells.

Right now, the water's ebbed enough to reveal a shore dominated by boulders and massive outcrops. With no one in sight in either direction, I don't hold back as I give myself fifteen minutes to scramble as far down the beach as I can. Moving from sand and pebbles to giant rocks and silvery white logs, I bound from point to point in some places, so that I'm breathing hard by the time I have to head back.

But before I do, I squint towards the horizon, hoping, as always, for a whale.

Her name is actually Harumi, not Haruko, and she is *absolument adorable*, like a living doll with to-die-for long, curly hair and a smile that dimples her round cheeks.

After introductions, her Aunt Satomi and Ojiichan go out onto the veranda with a tray of refreshments while Harumi and I stay in the kitchen. I pour her a glass of iced mugicha and set out honey cake as well as black bean hummus and pita chips.

Harumi was quiet when she first arrived, but as she takes a seat at the island and looks around the room, I can see her shoulders relax. "Wow," she says, completing a full 360 on her stool. "This place is like something out of the movies."

"Thanks. The architect my grandfather hired is kind of famous." I push the plates of food towards her. "Is this your first time to the coast?"

Shaking her head, she takes a slice of cake. "I was here once when I was five, and again when I was ten, for summer camp." She looks out towards the garden. "I'd never seen so many big trees, and the woods seemed so dark, I was always scared I'd get lost, like Hansel and Gretel."

"Well, there are definitely things you need to watch out for."

"Like witches in gingerbread houses?"

"More like cougars and bears."

Her eyes go round when she sees I'm not kidding. "Cougars AND bears?"

"Mm-hm. Although you'll probably never see a cougar — they're stealthy. Bears are around, though, unless they're hibernating. But it's easy enough to avoid them. You have to be aware, that's all."

She shudders. "Ugh. Bears." She pops a piece of cake into her mouth and chews thoughtfully as she looks out the window. "Honestly, they're more scared of you than you are of them. Unless it's a garbage bear."

"What's that?"

"One that's used to eating garbage instead of foraging like a wild bear," I explain. "They're dangerous because they're usually not afraid of people. But everyone around here's good about getting rid of attractants."

"That's okay. I'm going to stay indoors until winter."

I laugh as I stand up. "So, do you want a tour of the house?"

"I'd love one," she says, jumping off the stool.

I lead Harumi down to the walkout basement to show her the family room, home theater, and guest suite. We return to the main level, which, except for Ojiichan's study, is mostly public spaces, and finish upstairs, where the last room I show her is mine.

"This is me," I say as I open the door.

Harumi takes a couple of steps before coming to a standstill. "Whoa," she says.

When Ojiichan let me do a room makeover for my sixteenth birthday, the first thing I did, besides change the paint color, was trade in my white childhood bedroom suite for a mixture of new and vintage pieces. Then, I used as many of my collections as I could to decorate, so that the end result was a space that fulfilled my maximalist dreams.

Since his room skews more Zen retreat, when I did a reveal for Kenzo, he just shook his head; I'm pretty sure he still thinks my choices are interesting, though. Now I try to gauge what Harumi's reaction will be.

"I LOVE this chair!" Harumi squeals when she spots my dark orange recliner. The emerald velvet daybed grabs her attention next, and she reaches out to run a hand along the arm. "Oh my god, I LOVE this, too. SO. MUCH."

"Have a seat on either," I say as I stream some music from the computer on my MCM desk.

"I will. Ooh, where'd you get that?" Harumi points to the art piece above my bed, a weathered metal box spring fitted with old chicken wire that's been hung with vintage Christmas baubles.

"I made it. It's supposed to look like a spiralized rainbow," I tell her.

"That's so cool! I can totally see it. You're *so* artistic." She continues walking around, checking out my bookshelves and a trio of old cameras, before stopping in front of an alcove of photos. "Who's that?" She points to one of the largest ones.

"That's my best friend, Meeta." It's a blowup of a selfie we took together at her farewell party. "She moved to England last summer."

"She's really pretty," Harumi says.

"She's crazy smart, too. Like, cure-a-disease smart."

"Wow." Her gaze shifts to another of my favorite photos.

"That's me and my mom and dad," I tell her before she asks. Ojiichan took the shot at the Otter Creek Pier a few months before they died in a car crash.

She doesn't respond right away but continues studying the photo. "My aunt told me . . . Do you miss them?"

It's been a while since I've been asked that, so it takes me a moment to answer. "I guess. I mean, I was barely two, so really, my memories of them are all secondhand. But, yeah. I wonder what they'd be like now. How different my life would be if they were here."

I'm about to ask Harumi about her parents, but thinking back to what Ojiichan told me this morning makes me hesitate, and then the moment passes because she nods, says, "You're lucky to have pictures like this," and moves on to a mounted display case full of kokeshi dolls.

"Where are these from?" she asks.

"My grandfather made them. One for every birthday."

She leans in for a closer look. "They're beautiful."

"I think so, too. Unfortunately, I used to play with them like Barbies until I realized I shouldn't. That's why some of them are a little dinged up."

"Does he sell them? I have some from my grandma but I've never seen any that look like these."

I open the glass door, inviting her to take them out. "Well, he's self-taught, so they're his own design. And yeah, he sells some at the Creek gift store."

Harumi turns my thirteenth doll in her hands before carefully replacing it and closing the door with a click. "That's super cool."

After she's gone around the room, she makes herself comfortable on the daybed while I settle into my lounge chair.

"So, you're going into eleventh grade?" I ask.

"Yup. You too?"

I shake my head. "Twelfth."

"I thought we were the same age!"

"We are, but I skipped fourth grade."

"My aunt said you were really smart."

I shrug. "I know how to write tests."

"I wish I could graduate early," she says enviously. Before I have a chance to understand her eagerness, she perks up like someone's flipped a switch. "Hey, what's the boy situation around here? I haven't met *any* my age yet."

"Well, most of the ones I know are working or away this summer," I say. "Did your aunt mention our Obon party next month? There might be a few guys there."

"No! I love parties! Should I dress up?"

"I usually wear a yukata. Do you have one?"

She purses her lips. I'm learning that Harumi has a very expressive face — all her feelings are right there out in the open. "My aunt might."

"Don't worry about it. I've got you covered." I go to the cedar chest that holds all of my mom's silk kimono, flat in their original wrappers. Besides being too heavy and fancy for a summer event like Obon, I'm saving those for another day, so I leave them aside and reach for my cotton yukata. I choose a few I think would be flattering on Harumi and fan them out on the bed.

"They're sooooo pretty!" she says, clasping her hands in excitement.

"Borrow whichever one you like. I've got loads of accessories, too," I add.

Her eyes dart back and forth over the selection before she points to a blue one with showy purple and pink peonies on it. "Ooh, yes, please."

21

I take the yukata and hold it up in front of her. "Mm, no," I say. "The pattern's too big. It's overwhelming you." I test the others before deciding on one with vertical stripes and stylized chrysanthemum heads.

"Follow me." Leading her to my full-length mirror, I drape the yukata over her shoulder and step back so I can see her reflection. "That's it. That's the one."

While Harumi tries various poses with it, I return to the chest.

"Are you sure it's not too, I don't know . . . plain? I mean, it's nice," she adds quickly. "But it's not as splashy as the other one."

"That's the point." I place a large box of obi belts and ties on top of the chest before disappearing inside my walk-in closet. "It's more elegant," I call out.

"Oh, okay. Why not?" I hear her giggling before she asks, "What's next, then?"

I return, grinning, with an armload of boxes. "Shoes."

3
Meeting Gareth

Mitsuko and Seiji are finally back from their honeymoon and are expected for a welcome-home dinner at our place tonight, but I can't wait till then. Two weeks is the longest I've ever gone without seeing my aunt, so here I am at their house. I'm sweaty from my bike ride, but Mitsuko doesn't care.

"Emiko! I'm so happy you came," she says, giving me a squeezy hug.

"You sure you're not too tired?" I ask again, although, if she said yes, I'm not sure I'd leave.

She shakes her head. "The jet lag will probably hit me later, but that's alright. Come in, tell me what's new. It feels like it's been months!"

"You first. How was Italy? The photos were amazing."

We head into the kitchen and, over tea and Tuscan can-tuccini, spend the next two hours talking about the trip and all the drool-inducing food she and Seiji ate and brought back as souvenirs and gifts; seriously, based on what's spread out on the counters, they could open a pop-up shop.

I'm admiring some squid ink pasta when Mitsuko hands me a package wrapped in marbled paper. "I found this in Florence and it had your name on it," she tells me. "Go ahead, open it."

It's a backpack, made of rich blue leather, that folds almost flat but opens up to hold way more than you'd think possible. "What a cool design," I say, trying it on.

"Isn't it? I immediately pictured you wearing it around some university campus next fall." She beams so proudly at the idea that I have to turn away so she doesn't see my face.

"Everyone's going to ask me where I got it," I say, as brightly as I can. "Thank you, Mitsuko. I love it." I model it for a few more moments before shrugging it off and placing it with the other gifts.

"So, who's this new friend Ojiichan mentioned?" she asks as she refreshes our tea.

"Yeah, Harumi. She's really sweet. I'm having fun showing her around. I'll bring her by the café so you can meet her."

"Oh, speaking of meeting — wait, Seiji, tell Emiko the news," she says as Seiji walks into the room.

"Hi, Seiji. Welcome back." I give him a hug; he's not a natural hugger like Mitsuko, but he's getting better. "What news?"

"It's about Jun. Since he missed the wedding, we thought we'd invite him to come visit us before the summer ends. And just today, he said he would." Seiji gives Mitsuko a tender smile. "He's looking forward to finally meeting my beautiful wife. And you, too, of course, Emiko," he adds. "I've told him all about you."

"He sent me the sweetest card," Mitsuko tells me. "He was so sorry about everything. And now he's coming!"

I feel an actual frisson of wedding-level excitement travel down my spine at the thought of Jun's arrival. "Will he be here in time for Obon?" I ask.

She smiles. "We're hoping so. I'll tell you as soon as his flight's confirmed."

✳ ✳ ✳

A few days later, I'm at the café helping out while Mitsuko catches up on business with her staff.

I've been here since opening. Usually, there are two of us out front, but I'm doing fine on my own so far.

Working the espresso machine, a chrome beauty of a beast, making all that steam and noise, is maybe my favorite part of the job. I also enjoy the chance to practice my abstract latte art which, IMHO, adds a lot to the hot beverage experience.

"Here you go, gentlemen." I slide over a couple of prime examples to Albert and Walter, two longtime customers. "One cloudy and one snow-capped latte. How many specials should I add to that?"

While Albert and Walter pretend to think it over, I plate two haskap berry Danish, and bag up a loaf of milk bread for later.

"Emiko, darling, as usual, you've read our minds," Walter says as Albert pays. "Haskap! Only at Mitsuko's."

"Honestly, we should buy shares." It's Albert's routine parting joke.

I know I can get what another regular calls "charmingly pushy" when it comes to the baked goods and savories Mitsuko is renowned for. But because I've taste-tested every item on the menu, I'm confident no one will ever be disappointed with anything I recommend. Proof? No one's ever come back to tell me I was wrong.

After replenishing the display case — gaps irk me — I go around wiping down the counters and tables. There's a new rotation of local art hanging for sale on the walls, so I'm checking that out as well when the front door creaks open and a guy about my age walks in.

He looks like a catalog model — tallish and clean cut, with short, dirty-blond hair and faux-nerd glasses perched on his nose. I've never seen him before, and I'm surprised to see that he's wearing a café T-shirt. He flashes very white teeth at me.

"Hi. I'm Gareth. Is Mitsuko in?"

I nod, smiling. "Sure. Back in a second." Ducking through the noren hanging in the kitchen doorway, I find Mitsuko.

"Oh, dear." She checks the clock when I tell her she has a visitor. "I knew I forgot to mention something important — I think part of my brain is still in Italy." She gives me an apologetic smile. "He's a new hire, this is his first day. And I was hoping you could help with his training."

"Of course," I say as we walk out. Given that I practically wrote the staff handbook, I can't believe she'd even doubt it.

I hang back as Mitsuko greets him.

"Gareth, welcome. Sorry to keep you waiting, I totally lost track of time." She waves me over. "Emiko, this is Gareth

Tolman." Gesturing to me, she continues, "And this is my niece, Emiko Kimori."

"Nice to meet you," I say.

"Likewise."

"Gareth is going into twelfth grade too." Mitsuko stops suddenly. "Oh, I have paperwork! I'll be right back." She returns to the kitchen, leaving Gareth and me alone.

"She might have jet lag," I say after an awkward pause. "So, where did you enroll?"

He nods. "Cedar Grove. We figured I should stick with the school in Pebble Bay since Mom's new job is with the town hall."

"Oh?"

"Yeah. She got a job in the planning department. That's why we're here."

"Well, even if I didn't go there, I'd tell you Cedar Grove is a *great* school. Where'd you go before?"

He names a school in a Vancouver suburb. "Go Woodpeckers!" he cheers suddenly, making me jump.

While we wait for Mitsuko, I find out Gareth's dad lives in Whistler, that his older sister goes to university in Seattle, and that he speaks fluent Japanese.

"I've got relatives in Honshu that I visit a lot," he explains. "And I take lessons."

"Reading and writing, too?"

"My hiragana and katakana aren't bad, but my kanji is pretty basic."

"That's impressive." I can speak my first language well enough, but without any close family in Japan (other than a great-aunt in Kyoto who mails us the most gorgeous

27

calendars every year), I don't have much reason or opportunity to practice reading or writing in any form.

Mitsuko finally returns with a file folder, and while she and Gareth move to a table, I decide to tidy under the counter. When I straighten up, I'm startled to find our local librarian standing there.

"Oh. Taka-san." Maybe it's from working where she does, but Taka Kobayashi moves like a ninja; I swear I didn't even hear the door open. "How are you?" Then I bite back a groan, because that's not a question to ask if you have things to do. But since she and my family go way back — Ojiichan visits Taka-san at the library every week, and she and Mitsuko are both rabid pickleballers — I take a breath and settle in.

"I'm very well, very well, thank you, Emiko-san," she starts, and then she's off, listing everything she's done today, and everyone she's bumped into so far. Unfortunately, Mitsuko and Gareth are still talking, and there's no one behind her, so I'm trapped.

"And did I tell you the latest news about Chisato?" Taka-san's eyes light up as she mentions her niece.

"No." I give the spotless counter another wipe. I met Chisato, who's the same age as Kenzo, back in my preschool era during one of her infrequent visits to the Creek. Because Ojiichan, Mitsuko, and Taka-san are all such good friends, I've always felt this expectation that Chisato and I would be, too. Even though it's obvious to me that we're like the same pole on a bar magnet, and any efforts to try and stick us together are pointless.

"You won't believe it, but she won another award for . . ."

As Taka-san starts listing the usual litany of accomplishments, I'm barely listening, because Chisato Ishi is a classic overachiever. And, frankly, it's boring to hear about her perfect grades, and first prize for whatever, and accolades for I don't even know what, over and over again. We get it. Every little thing she does is magic.

I mean, good for her, but if you ask me, Taka-san going on like she does, it's a little braggy. So, when Mitsuko and Gareth come walking towards us, I interrupt her. "Excuse me, Taka-san, but have you met Gareth?" As soon as he gets close enough, I grab his hand, barely noticing how clammy it is, and drag him over for presentation.

"No, I haven't." Her voice delighted, she gazes up at him.

"He's new, and there's so much I need to teach him." I give Gareth a dazzling smile. I'm so relieved to have him as my buffer, it even takes me an extra second to drop his hand as I tell him, "This is Taka Kobayashi. She runs the library up the street." I turn back to her. "Do you think Gareth could take your order, as part of his training?"

"Of course, of course! I'll finish telling you about Chisato another time."

"Can't wait."

"You're very lucky you get to work with Emiko. I've known her since she was a baby," Taka-san tells Gareth as I haul a tray of dirty dishes to the kitchen. When I return, she's still talking.

It takes a few more minutes, but after Gareth hands Taka-san her food and Mitsuko arranges a time to drop off treats from Italy, Taka-san finally leaves.

"Word to the wise," I say as the door shuts behind her. "Don't ever ask her how she is if you value your time."

"Noted," he says.

Mitsuko gives me a quick disapproving look (which I pretend not to notice) before she says, "I'll go through how to close up later, Gareth, but for now, Emiko will help you, okay?"

"Happy to," I say, and Mitsuko heads back to the kitchen.

Gareth winks. "I'm in your capable hands."

At first, the customers trickle in, so it's easy to show him the ropes, but as we get closer to noon, the door creaks almost constantly as customers flow in and out. Thankfully, Gareth's past coffee chain experience kicks in, and by the time the rush is over, it's like he's been here for weeks.

By the time the next lull comes around, I can no longer ignore my growling stomach. Since Gareth's proven he's a quick study and has the kind of confidence where if he didn't know something he'd fake it convincingly, I figure it's safe to take a quick fifteen.

"Did Mitsuko mention you can have anything you want on your breaks? And any house drink?" I ask while grabbing a mushroom puff and an iced rooibos. "She likes staff to be able to make recommendations."

He nods. "I've been eyeing the tapenade rolls all morning."

"Oh, those are killer." I tilt my head towards the kitchen. "I'm out back if you need me."

"Got it," he says, giving me another wink with a finger pistol on the side.

I let Mitsuko and the other staff know Gareth's flying solo, then head out the screen door to the employees-only garden behind the café. Sitting down at the shaded picnic table, I take out my phone.

As I scroll through my contacts, I think about Gareth and see a glimmer of possibility. Not for me — as much as I love a good romance, *obviously*, they seem to take up a lot of time and energy. And at this point in my life, with Ojiichan, and school, and all the other things I have on my dance card, a boyfriend doesn't really fit into my lifestyle. It's kind of like how I feel about heels — I love the look of them, but the idea of running around in a pair every day is a hard pass. That doesn't mean they wouldn't work for someone else, though. Like Harumi.

And, clearly, she's got boys on the brain. Which is why, when she asked me about the local situation, I didn't have the heart to tell her that most of the available boys I know are available for a reason.

It's also possible that my standards are too high, but growing up around my grandfather, and Kenzo's dad, Mas, and now, even Seiji, well, it's not my fault if I'm a little spoiled. And I'm not just talking about looks, although presentation helps — even a bag of peanuts tastes better if you make the effort to pour it into a nice bowl.

No, what I'm talking about is that *je ne sais quoi* that sets someone apart from the crowd, and I know it when I see it. And while I don't see it in Gareth (his damp palms and winking tic aren't helpful), for *Harumi*, Gareth may be quite right. Like, I can picture them together, in the same way I can mix and match two clashing yet complementary patterns.

But I need to strike now, while he's still new and likely hasn't met anyone. Once school starts, it'll be too late. He'll be like a french fry to a flock of seagulls.

I take a deep breath — it feels good to have a sense of purpose — and text Harumi, figuring she's across the road, working her new job at Re: Gifting in the heart of the village.

ME: What time are you done work?

HARUMI: It's my day off! 😃 Why? What's happening?

I think for a minute.

ME: Are you near the café?

HARUMI: Yes! Collecting rocks to paint with Auntie S.

ME: By the pier?

HARUMI: Yup.

I grin and take a bite of my puff.

ME: Feel like a snack at Mitsuko's? Around 3?

HARUMI: Always! See you soon!! 😋 🎁 🍰

Back behind the counter, I try not to smile too much. Gareth is at the add-in station, wiping up spilled cream and sugar.

"Hi," I say. "How was it?"

"Uneventful." He heads to the sink to rinse the cloth. "I sold a dozen pistachio bars, though."

"Good job." I look around to make sure no one's in earshot. "So, I know we've just met, but random quick question."

"Go for it."

"Do you have a girlfriend?"

Gareth looks startled, but before he can answer, the door opens and Kenzo walks in.

"Hey, Em." He approaches the counter, pulling off his work gloves and baseball cap and tucking them under his arm.

"Hi, Kenzo." He's obviously hot, so I pour a large, iced oolong and slide a couple of his favorite peanut-butter oatmeal cookies into a paper bag for him. "How's it going?" I ask as he makes his payment.

"Great. Been looking forward to this all day, though." He takes his order, then looks over at Gareth, who, I realize with a start, has sidled up beside me.

"Oh, yeah. Kenzo, this is Gareth. He's going to be in our class. It's his first day on the job. Gareth, Kenzo, one of my oldest friends."

"Good to meet you," Kenzo says with a lift of his chin.

"You too, man." Then, for some reason, Gareth goes in for a fancy handshake that gets weird when he realizes Kenzo's hands are full. "Uh, yeah. So, cool." He steps back, crossing his arms as his head bobs like a parakeet. I have to work really hard to keep a straight face.

Kenzo is a far nicer person than I am because he smiles politely. "Guess we'll see you around, then."

"Sure, sure, cool. Cool. Cool." Gareth copies the chin-lift thing Kenzo did earlier, but on him, it looks stiff and unnatural.

Kenzo nods, then, looking at me, raises the bagged cookies. "Thanks. Say hi to Ojiichan and Mitsuko for me."

"Will do." I smile and watch as he holds the door open for a customer before heading out and across the street to his truck.

Gareth seems to snap out of whatever trance he's in and helps the customer without issue. After she walks away, Gareth turns to me. "So, Kenzo's in our grade?"

"Yeah, why?"

"He looks older."

"Does he?" I think about it. "Maybe it's just his size. Although he is pretty mature for his age. Even before he became one, he's always had older brother energy."

"He grow up here too?"

"Yup. Across the street from me." I wave in the general direction of our houses. Gareth follows my sightline and, after blinking a few times, he turns back to me, his eyes wide.

"Wait, which side of the road are you on?"

"The water side."

"The house on the corner?"

"Mm-hm."

"So, like, Akiro Fuji's house?"

It's clear from the way Gareth says his name that he knows who Ojiichan is. Or was, I guess, would be more accurate. "He's my grandfather. You're a fan?"

"My cousins got me hooked on his movies — that blind detective trilogy? I mean . . . wow. He's your grandfather?"

I've met other fans before, but they're not usually people my age, since Ojiichan, who started acting in his teens, made his last hit movie — a samurai period piece, at that — more than twenty years ago. I wonder if this is going to get weird.

"Sorry," he continues, with a sheepish grin. "I mean, he's kind of a legend, you know. Talk about range. I read that he lives on the coast, even found an old article about the house. But I never thought —" He stops, and gives a nervous chuckle. "I promise, I'm not some kind of stalker."

I laugh, not in the least bit worried. "That's a relief."

❈ ❈ ❈

Before I know it my shift's over and on the dot, Harumi walks into the café. "My friend's here," I tell Gareth, giving her a wave.

"Oh, hey, uhm, before you go . . ."

"Yeah?"

He gives me a sidelong look. "The answer is no."

It takes me a beat to figure out what he's talking about. "Right!" I give him a quick smile as Harumi approaches. "Great, good to know. Thanks."

"I'm so glad you texted, Emiko," Harumi says, draping herself on the counter. "It's scorching out there and I am TOTALLY dehydrated. Please, please make me something cold and sweet. Please?"

"Well, since Emiko is officially off the clock, let *me* take your order." Even though there's no one else waiting, Gareth holds up a marker. "Can I get a name?"

"Harumi," she says with a giggle. I take off my apron and watch the two of them exchange smiles.

"*Harumi, friend of Emiko.*" He writes this on a cup and sneaks me another wink before turning back to her. "I'm Gareth. What can I get you today?"

While Harumi decides, I catch her eye, mime going into the kitchen, and leave as Gareth runs through the drink menu.

I find my aunt at her desk inside the dry goods storage area. "That's it for me today," I tell her.

"Thanks, Emiko. I have one more call to make, then I'll be out front to help Gareth."

"No rush. He's good. See you tomorrow."

Instead of going out right away, though, I peek through the noren to see how Gareth and Harumi are doing. As I'd hoped, there's still no one behind her so they're chatting away. It sounds like they're comparing notes on the coast and Otter Creek, and it's obvious Gareth is having a much better first meet with Harumi than he did earlier with Kenzo.

After what I feel is a suitable amount of time, I walk out and step behind the counter to grab a couple of asiago-prosciutto straws and a cold Lapsang Souchong. I don't let Mitsuko pay me for working here; instead, I get to help myself to whatever I want, whenever I want, working or not.

"So, you guys getting acquainted?" I ask before biting into a straw.

Harumi nods. "Can you believe? Gareth and I have the same favorite okonomiyaki restaurant in Osaka. Ooh, thank you," she says as he hands her a cup. She takes a sip of her vibrant drink, stops, takes another, and then stares at Gareth with an awestruck look on her face. "What IS this?"

"Well, you said surprise me, so it's a little special something I like to whip up for VIPs," he tells her with, yes, another wink. But I don't care because I think I'm getting the same buzz I felt the day Mitsuko met Seiji, and it's thrilling.

As Harumi blushes and fiddles with her straw, I turn to Gareth with a discreet thumbs-up and mouth "Good job." Based on his expression, my approval of how he's treating Harumi seems to make him really happy, which just further validates my hunch about these two.

I wish I could capture all of this on camera somehow, to show Doubting Kenzo and prove that Mitsuko and Seiji weren't a fluke.

I won't jinx things by saying it out loud, but I can't wait to see how well this goes.

4
Obon Party

It's the morning before Obon, and Ojiichan, Mitsuko, and I are going over our to-do lists one last time. I'm only half-listening though because I'm also trying to figure out what to do about Harumi and Gareth.

Since last month, they've met at the café at least twice a week, but only when both Gareth and I have been working, so, not ideal, I know. As a result, even though the summer is whizzing by, things between them have progressed at the pace of a starfish.

I had thought I'd be able to invite Gareth to Obon as a guest, but, unsurprisingly, Mitsuko already had him down for one of the food stations. So, I'm stuck at the very beginning, which is not a very good place to be.

My grandfather clears his throat, bringing me back to the present. "Emiko," he says. "Status report, please."

"Right." I refer to my clipboard. "Uhm, including neighbors, the final head count is ninety-eight. And Kenzo asked if he could bring a friend. I said no problem." Ojiichan and Mitsuko nod in agreement.

"Games are en route, the prizes are ready, and all the water-balloon yo-yos are —"

At this, Mitsuko gasps. "Oh, no. The watermelons."

"What?" both Ojiichan and I ask.

"No, no, no, no, no." She flips through her notebook and runs her finger down a page before looking up, a panicked expression on her face. "The watermelons. I can't believe I did this. I forgot the watermelons."

"Yikes." It slips out before I can stop myself, and I feel bad because my aunt looks really upset. But, holy Fruit Ninja, watermelons are a biggie. *Everyone* loves the watermelon splitting game. It's tradition, and no summer party is complete without it.

Ojiichan is already heading to his study. "I will call the grocer to see if she can reserve fifteen for us."

"Twenty!" I call after him. "Get twenty!"

Fortunately, by late afternoon, we've got all the watermelons we need, and after supper Mitsuko and I are out on the deck giving them each a wash, our last task for the day.

"It's looking good, isn't it?" Mitsuko says, handing me another melon.

I nod. Down on the lawn, Ojiichan, Mr. and Mrs. Yoshimatsu, and some family friends are setting up tables and umbrellas.

"It's too bad Jun doesn't arrive until next week." I feel a little conflicted as I say this, because, on the one hand, even if it turns out he's only half as handsome as his dad, I suspect Jun Morimoto in a yukata might be something to behold. But, on the other, with the Harumi-Gareth situation pressing on me, I don't need the distraction.

All day, I've been working on how to get the two of them together as much as possible. Their first meeting was a good start, but just as an appetizer needs a couple more courses to make a full meal, the instant chemistry I witnessed that day doesn't matter if there's no satisfying follow-up.

"Emiko."

I realize my aunt's been talking and I haven't heard a word she's said. "Sorry, Mitsuko. Daydreaming."

"I was saying I think we're done."

"Wow, yeah." Somehow, we've gotten through the pile of watermelons and I'm holding the last one.

Later, after everyone's gone home, I wander around the yard, still trying to come up with an idea that doesn't get tossed back like an undersized crab, but there's no getting around the fact that Gareth is going to be busy tomorrow. And as much as Harumi likes food, she can't spend the entire day lining up at his station for something to eat.

I briefly consider asking Harumi for suggestions, but then I'd have to tell her what I have in mind for her and Gareth. After her initial encounter with Seiji, I didn't explicitly tell Mitsuko what I was up to when I arranged "chance" meetings between them, and that worked out, so I'm reluctant to mess with my methods.

Besides, knowing might make Harumi uncomfortable, and she's such an open book, even a rice grain's worth of self-consciousness would show on her face. So, no. It's up to me to mark the trail, provide directions, send them off with a full picnic basket, and hope they don't get lost along the way.

Neither Ojiichan nor Mitsuko is particularly religious, and we don't go to a temple, so I'm not an expert on Buddhism. But during Obon, especially, there are customs and rituals we follow to honor our dead.

Before breakfast, I start by adding an offering to the fresh fruit and greenery already placed in front of the butsudan we keep in Ojiichan's study. I light a joss stick next and insert it into the sand-filled incense pot, as fragrant smoke wafts past the photos of my grandmother, my mom, and my dad.

"Ohayou gozaimasu." Gently striking the small standing bell, I close my eyes and bow my head in prayer.

No one's ever told me if there's a proper way to do this, or any particular words I should use. I just talk to them in my head, hope they're happy wherever they are, ask them to keep watch over us all. This year, I throw in an extra request, asking them to send me a sign when the time comes for me to make some of the decisions I have ahead of me. Obviously, I don't get an actual reply, but I savor the sense of calm that comes over me.

That's the last quiet moment I have for a while because, despite all the careful prep, there are always last-minute details to deal with.

However, after greeting the taiko drummers from Vancouver, and making sure all the kids' game stations are properly set up, I check in with Mitsuko.

"We're almost ready," she tells me. "I'm just going to feed the crew before everyone starts arriving."

Over by the food stations, I spot Gareth putting canned drinks into a barrel of ice. He's got a hachimaki tied around his forehead and he's wearing a happi coat, café tee, and shorts, the uniform for all of Mitsuko's staff today.

He must feel me staring because he lifts his head and looks right at me before I can shift my gaze. He's too far away for me to hear him, but basic lipreading tells me he's saying hi, so I smile back before turning to Mitsuko.

"How long is Gareth working today?" I ask.

"Till eight," she says, checking her watch. "I'd better get going or I won't have time to change. I'll see you in a bit."

As Mitsuko walks away, Harumi arrives and waves at me from the house. Heading up to meet her, I continue running scenarios for her and Gareth through my brain, hoping that, unlike Dr. Strange, I won't have to rip through fourteen million of them before I come up with the one that works.

Now that we're dressed in our yukata and Harumi's helped with my updo, I sit her down at my dressing table and consider her hair. Worn down, it's naturally curly and glorious, but I think today calls for something sleeker, to give Gareth a different image of her.

"How about two buns?" I suggest.

"Like Princess Leia?" she asks with a slight frown.

"No, more like this." I gather half her hair in a ponytail and hold it at the most flattering point. "Picture them here, like round Hello Kitty ears."

She turns her head, checking the angles. "I love it!"

When her hair is how I want it, I add rosebuds and baby's

breath from a bouquet on my desk before taking her to my full-length mirror. "There. What do you think?"

She studies her reflection and pats her hair as the grin on her face grows. "It's *meccha* kawaii, Emiko! Thank you. For the yukata, too. Are you sure you don't want it?"

"Absolutely. It looks way better on you than it ever did on me." Then, sensing an opening, I ask, "Did you happen to see Gareth outside?"

Still admiring her reflection, she shakes her head.

"He was asking about you." Just because this occurred days ago and had to do with some leftover cronuts doesn't make it irrelevant; the fact is, she was on his mind. "He's going to flip when he sees you."

Harumi giggles nervously as her cheeks turn pink. "You think so?"

Noting these obvious signs of interest, I smile. "Of course," I say. "Why wouldn't he? We should make sure we get a photo of you two looking so cute." I let her sit with that possibility while I go to my desk.

"What about you?" she asks after a moment. "Are you wearing flowers too?"

I shake my head and pick up a lacquered box I'd set out earlier.

"What's that?"

"My mom and grandmother's kanzashi collection. Ojiichan gave it to me when I turned thirteen." I lift the lid to show her the contents.

"Oh, Emiko. How gorgeous."

I nod, sorting through the variety of hair ornaments, and find — according to Mitsuko — one of my mother's favorites, a long gold coloured pin topped with tiny dangling bells and metal strips. I slide it through my hair so that it sticks out at a flattering angle and shake my head to test how it feels and sounds.

Just then, we hear the booming sounds of the taiko drummers; they must be practicing because it's not quite time for the party to start. A thunderous volley of drumbeats fills the air, and suddenly my heart's echoing the rhythm, and a big smile takes over my face.

"Let's go," I say, and with a final check in the mirror, Harumi and I head downstairs.

I figured I'd lead her over to say hi to Gareth, or do a slow-mo sashay past him before it gets too crowded, but when she spots the kids' games area, Harumi goes rogue and veers to where our caretaker, Mr. Yoshimatsu, is running the yo-yo fishing pool.

"Wait, Harumi —" I start.

"OMG, I haven't played this in years. Am I allowed?"

"Of course, of course!" Mr. Yoshimatsu says, handing her a hook attached to a paper string.

While Harumi tries to snag a water balloon yo-yo before the paper line breaks, I hear two excited voices calling my name and turn to look behind me.

"Emiko! Emiko!" Kenzo's nine-year-old twin brothers, Takeo and Tomio, come barreling towards me. They're dressed in matching short jinbei and are beyond adorable.

"Hi, guys." I reach out to muss their hair; they're growing

so fast, I probably won't be able to do this much longer. The thought causes a funny ache as I try to imagine what else will have changed by this time next year. As it is, when Takeo gives me an annoyed look as he smooths back his hair, I have to fight the urge to give him a smothery hug. "Did you just get here?" I ask instead.

Tomio nods, his eyes darting towards the games.

"Why don't you show Harumi how good you guys are at fishing?" I suggest, seeing that Harumi has lost her hook and is getting another one from Mr. Yoshimatsu.

"Come on, Tomio," Takeo says, and the twins rush past me to join her.

When I turn back to look for the rest of the Sanada clan, I'm in time to see the crowds parting, as if for royalty, as they walk towards me. Even dressed in their casual worst, the Sanadas are an impressive family. Now, seeing Kenzo with his parents — Abby with her auburn hair, elegant in a dark green yukata, Mas, in his charcoal gray, and Kenzo himself in patterned indigo . . . it kind of takes my breath away.

And the details! The bamboo fans both Kenzo and his dad have tucked into their low-slung obi, Abby's golden sash wrapped high on her waist, all of them wearing geta on their feet — it's perfection.

The phrase *kimochi ii* floats through my mind as I continue to enjoy the picture this family makes. The word, at its simplest, means something that feels good, but, as with so many Japanese words, there are nuances that don't have English equivalents. The closest I can come to explain what I mean is that the way the Sanadas look together today, well, it makes my spirit feel at ease.

Abby reaches me first and folds me into a hug. "Aren't you a vision, Emiko." She leans back to get a better look at my yukata, a burnt-orange one I paired with a teal and gold obi. "That fletching pattern is so striking." Her eyes land on my hairpin and she gives me another affectionate smile.

"You look amazing too," I say, before turning to Mas.

"Emiko-hime." Mas's pet name for me, "*hime*," always makes me feel so special; not even my grandfather calls me "princess," preferring "little one" as a now occasional endearment. "How's my favorite girl?"

"'Alive and Kicking.'" I grin, going in for my hug. With our shared love of '80s music, Mas and I try to work in at least one reference whenever we meet.

"Good one," Mas says.

"Oh my god." Abby's head swivels as people walk by with plates of food. "Is that yakitori I smell?"

I nod. "Mitsuko made five kinds."

"Well, that's it, kids. Looks like we're going to have to 'Keep On Movin'' and get some grub," Mas says.

"You two . . ." Kenzo groans. "Dad, please stop."

Mas chuckles as Abby grabs his hand and starts dragging him over to the grill station. "Bye, ducklings," she calls over her shoulder.

While I watch his parents tease each other as they get in line, Kenzo clears his throat.

"Uhm, you look nice," he says, even though he's not looking at me.

"I'm sorry — what?"

He sighs. "You're turning this into a thing, aren't you?"

46

"Oh, this is diary material. 'Today, Kenzo *finally* broke down and paid me a compliment!' But, wait . . ." My brow furrows with mock concern. "Is it 'cause you've had too much sun? Do you need a cool compress?" I lower my voice. "Should I get your mom?"

"I take it back. You're hideous."

I grin. "Uh-uh. No backsies."

"I'm ignoring you now."

"But how can you? When I look . . . nice." I preen, I'll admit, obnoxiously, while Kenzo keeps his eyes trained on something above my head. I'm about to ramp things up, because this is fun, when I notice he's done something different with his hair. This feels like a teachable moment.

"By the way, I really like what you've got going on there, coif-wise."

Kenzo gives me a baffled look.

"That half-up, half-down situation you're rocking? It makes your profile pop, which, no kidding, would look good stamped on a coin."

"Okay. Thank you?"

"Yes, it's a compliment, Kenzo. I mean it sincerely."

He narrows his eyes at me. "Why does it feel like you don't?"

"I have no idea. Now, come on." I loop my arm through his. "Let's go rescue Harumi and grab some food."

By the time we've sampled almost everything and put ourselves at real risk of falling into food comas, Ojiichan announces that Momiji Taiko is about to perform. I steer Kenzo and Harumi towards the temporary dais.

"It's probably not good for our long-term hearing," I tell Harumi as we settle down on the grass, "but being up close when they go all out — just wait."

Ojiichan, dignified in his black linen yukata and silvery striped obi, steps onto the low platform and turns on a wireless mic. "Good afternoon, everyone." Around us, the crowd quiets. "I am so happy you could join my family and me today, to enjoy these festivities with our loved ones, and to honor and remember those who have passed."

His eyes meet mine and we give each other a small smile. I see him searching the crowd for Mitsuko, and I can tell when he finds her because his face softens. Following his eyeline, I see her standing, leaning into Seiji, and though I'm too far away to know for sure, her eyes look overly bright. I turn back before she notices I've seen her, and I let out a breath.

"You okay?" Kenzo asks quietly.

I nod. "I am. Thanks." He knows me well enough not to point out that my eyes are kind of shiny, too.

"So, please," Ojiichan continues. "Eat. Have fun. Children, play all the games you wish. And everyone, I hope you will join us later for the suikawari and dancing. Do not be shy! Now, with great pleasure, I am honored to introduce . . . Momiji Taiko." He walks backwards off the dais, while we applaud as seven men and women wearing braided headbands, dressed in red and black sleeveless happi coats and shorts, run up and take their places behind their drums.

The gathering falls silent; all you can hear is the constant

48

sound of waves in the background, leaves rustled by the breeze, and eagles keening overhead.

The drummers strike a ready pose, legs braced, arms up, batons poised. It would be dramatic anywhere, but with the trees and water as their backdrop, the group looks spectacular. Beside me, I can feel Harumi trying to repress shivers of anticipation while I hold my breath, my hands clasped together in front of my mouth.

Seconds tick by, and I can almost see the energy coiling up before me. Then, just when I feel like screaming from the tension thickening the air, the lead drummer lets out a sudden, loud, gut-felt kiai, a battle cry that makes the hair on the back of my neck stand up. Then, in perfect synchronization, the troop unleashes a pounding, rhythmic wave of sound that rolls off the stage, shaking me to my core, and drowns out, for a little while, all the questions and worries clamoring for attention inside my head.

5
Obon Evening

"Wow," Harumi says, sounding dazed. "I've never seen taiko up close like that. I'm still vibrating." She holds out her hand to show me.

Feeling a little off-kilter myself, I nod as Kenzo scans the dispersing crowd. "Are you looking for your family?" I ask him.

He shakes his head before suddenly waving his hand in the air.

A couple of minutes later, a lanky redhead in a faded Canucks tee, basketball shorts, and sneakers emerges. As he gets closer, looking flustered and sweaty with his hair sticking to his forehead, a relieved smile takes over his face. "Kenzo," he says.

"Will, I was starting to wonder about you. What'd you do, run here or something?"

"My bike got a flat." He leans forward, hands on his hips, and draws in some deep breaths.

"You should've texted. I would have come to get you."

Will's face gets even redder. "I did."

Frowning, Kenzo reaches into his obi and pulls out his phone. "Sorry, Will," he says as he scrolls through his messages. "I didn't hear them during the concert."

Will shrugs. "It's okay. It wasn't that far."

"Where'd you leave your bike?"

"It's over there." When he turns to point behind him, he finally seems to notice Harumi and me and swallows hard. "Oh, uh, hi."

"Right. Introductions." Kenzo nods at me. "This is Emiko, this is her house, and this is Harumi. Emiko, Harumi, this is Will. He's the friend I mentioned."

"Of course." I smile at Will, who stammers hello again; he's got a baby face and a cowlick on the crown of his head. "I'm glad you could make it, although you missed a great show. You must be starving after all that extra exercise."

Will's eyes light up. "Food would be really good right now."

Harumi steps forward before I can say anything. "I'll take him, Emiko." She smiles up at Will. "Follow me. Have you ever had Inarizushi? It's one of my favorites. And yakisoba? That's good, too."

Will stammers, "Sounds, uh, great," as a flush creeps up his neck, and he nods at everything else she suggests as the two walk away.

I give Kenzo a look. "This is the Will who works for you?"

"Yeah," Kenzo says. "He's a good kid."

"I'm sure he is."

"Harumi's new here, I thought she might want to meet some people."

"Yeah, but not to babysit. I mean, how old is he? I thought I heard his voice crack."

"Emiko."

"What? I'm serious." Actually, I'm not. But it feels better to focus on how tadpole-ish Will Rivers is than to point out that he dresses like he simply grabs whatever's on top of the laundry pile, in the dark. And I'm not saying everyone needs to be fashion-forward — to be fair, except on certain occasions, Kenzo is hardly a clotheshorse either. It's just that Will's whole vibe is so . . . sub-basic. Which wouldn't have registered at all if I hadn't seen that spark of interest in his eye when he saw Harumi, and the returning flicker in hers.

Now, if Will were a popular senior, like Kenzo, then he could potentially get away with his anti-fashion stance, and he and Harumi could possibly work. Or, conversely, if Will dressed with any demonstrable sense of style, then him being a younger-looking tenth-grader maybe wouldn't be as noticeable, and he and Harumi wouldn't feel so unlikely. But he can't be both a baby-faced sophomore AND cosplay Shaggy from Scooby Doo and not be anything but a detriment to her entrée into high school society.

Anyway, I watch Harumi and Will, who are now at the front of the food line, and see Gareth serving them. Even from here, I can see how much attention Gareth's paying to Harumi, and when whatever he's saying makes her laugh, I relax a little.

"Come on." I nudge Kenzo's elbow, still eager to get closer and eavesdrop. "Let's go get some dango." Can I just say that anything made with mochi is all good as far as I'm concerned? Skewering tiny balls of it on a stick? Yes, please. Kenzo grins. "You're on."

By the time we get our treats, Will and Harumi are at a table with empty plates in front of them.

"Hey, Emiko, guess what?" Harumi says as Kenzo and I sit down to join them. "I've met Will before."

"Really?" I say slowly, mind on high alert.

"Yeah, crazy, right? His sister, Arlo, was at the same summer camp I went to, the one I told you about, remember? With all the big trees, when I was ten? We were in the same cabin, and Will came with his mom and dad on Visitors' Day."

"Huh. Interesting." I note Harumi's excitement over this.

"I can't believe I might see Arlo again! She was so nice to me back then. Too bad you didn't invite her, too," Harumi says to Kenzo.

"Yeah, too bad." I sneak a closer look at Will, who's listening intently while Harumi chatters on.

Just then, Kenzo leaps from his chair and runs over to the dais. We all turn to see why, and right away I spot the problem.

While Mas and Seiji are helping Ojiichan get ready for the suikawari, off to the side Takeo and Tomio are play-fighting with a couple of bokken, which is basically Step One in "How to End Up in the ER."

As Kenzo grabs the wooden swords from his brothers seconds before they make contact, Will takes in the entire set-up on stage and asks, "Why are there so many watermelons?"

"It's for the suikawari," Harumi explains as we stand. "Aka 'watermelon splitting,'" she continues. "It's like the watermelon's a piñata, and you use one of those bokken to break it open while wearing a blindfold, and then everyone eats it."

"Oh. Now I feel dumb for asking," Will says.

Harumi giggles. "Wait till you try it. It's super fun."

We're in front of the dais now, and while we can't hear what he's saying to Takeo and Tomio, based on their expressions, Kenzo is clearly in lecture mode.

Kenzo sees us, and after handing the bokken back to Seiji he steps down onto the grass. "Split skulls averted," he says.

"For now," I joke, just as Mas calls my name. I walk over to meet him. "What's up?"

"We need one of you to get the game going."

"No problem." I turn around. "Alright, who wants to go first?"

When Harumi sticks her hand up right away, Will copies her and raises his as well.

Kenzo chuckles. "I'll go after them."

"How about we start with the newbie." I beckon a nervous-looking Will onto the platform. "Come on. It's really simple."

While Takeo sets a watermelon on a low, plastic-covered table, I have Will stand on the duct tape marking the starting point. Then I ask Takeo to give Will a demo with the bokken.

Grinning, Takeo plants one end of the heavy stick on the floor and rests his hands and forehead on the other. "Now, do this," he says, and starts spinning like a human top.

Tomio goads him from the sidelines to go faster and faster until I grab Takeo by the waist to stop him. He manages a couple of wobbly steps before toppling to the floor, laughing with Tomio as he tries to stand up.

"You don't have to go that far," I assure Will, passing him

the stick. "But spin around a few times. I'll make sure you're facing the right way before you start walking. Ready for the blindfold?"

Will nods, and after checking that he can't see from under the tenugui tied behind his head, I tell him to listen to everyone's tips to help steer him into position. "Then you have one shot. Got it?"

"Got it."

"Alright, here we go." I face the crowd that's gathered now. "Okay, everyone. Let's help Will split a watermelon!"

After three spins, I shift Will over a step and pat his back to signal he can go. People immediately start shouting encouragement and "Hot" or "Cold" as he veers off center, stumbling left, then right, till, somehow, he manages to correct his course.

When he reaches the strike zone, both Takeo and Tomio yell, "Stop!" and he freezes.

"Come on, Will," I hear Kenzo say.

"You've got this!" Harumi cheers.

The crowd hushes as Will stands there, holding the bokken like a golf club. He takes several deep breaths, as if trying to catch the watermelon's scent, then swings the bokken straight up overhead — so suddenly that people gasp — and then, after the briefest of pauses, brings the wooden staff back down in a whistling blur straight into the heart of the watermelon with such force that it detonates like a bomb. After a moment of stunned silence, the crowd erupts into hoots and applause.

"Whoa," the twins say as Will pulls off his blindfold. Staring at the shattered mess, eyes agog, Takeo adds loudly, "Guess no one's eating *that* melon."

Ojiichan takes the bokken and blindfold from Will. "Well done, young man. Well done." He pats him on the shoulder before he walks away, chuckling.

Will rubs the back of his neck as he looks at me. "Sorry. I didn't think it would explode like that." His face flushes as he watches Mas clear the table for the next player.

"Don't apologize," I say. "That was fantastic."

Harumi goes next, surprising us when she attacks her watermelon like a caveman, while Kenzo's approach is textbook and he cracks his open like an egg. His technique sets the tone for almost everyone else, and soon Abby, Mitsuko, and Mrs. Yoshimatsu are serving up huge metal bowls of frosty-looking fruit.

Even with the surrounding trees and the breeze off the water, the late-afternoon heat is fierce, so Kenzo, Harumi, Will, and I take our cups of watermelon and find some shade under a Douglas fir.

"Oh my god," Harumi says after her first piece. "This is *so* good."

We all nod in agreement as we eat what might be the perfect summer refreshment.

After laughing so much during the suikawari, everyone seems loose and relaxed, even Will, and I'm keeping an eye on him and Harumi, when Kenzo announces he needs a nap and lies back on the grass.

"Here? Now?" I ask.

"Half an hour. That's all I need," he says before closing his eyes.

"Well, I want to play some more games." Harumi maneuvers herself up as Will collects their cups and forks.

"Wait . . ." I start, but when they look at me expectantly, my mind goes blank. "You . . . nothing. I, uh, never mind." Harumi and Will having more time on their own is definitely not a scenario I'd envisioned, and my suddenly sluggish brain fails to come up with a legit reason to make them stay.

"Aren't you coming too?" Harumi asks.

I want to, I want very much to be a third wheel, but then I look over and realize I can't abandon Kenzo. If he were up at the house, or on the deck, without hesitation I'd go. But out here, it doesn't feel right to leave him.

"No." I do my best not to sound annoyed. "I'd better stay." There's no denying, though, that as I watch Harumi and Will walk away, laughing together, I feel like I'm stuck in a giant pool of sap.

It also doesn't help that I have to be mindful how I sit and move. I unfold my legs and straighten them out, making sure my yukata is properly arranged, before I lean back on my hands and try to figure out what to do next.

I should be thrilled Obon is going well. But I'm not, and I'm starting to think I would have had more fun if I hadn't invited Harumi. Then maybe Kenzo wouldn't have invited Will, and then I wouldn't have cared that Gareth had to work today, and around and around goes my hamster-wheel brain.

"Emiko."

My eyes snap open at Harumi's voice. I realize I'm curled up on my side, my hands a pillow under my head, and after remembering where I am and what I'm wearing, I carefully get myself upright.

Harumi passes me a cup. "Here. You're probably dehydrated."

"Thank you." I take a long swallow of iced mugicha. "I can't believe I fell asleep. What time is it?"

"Time for some dancing," Harumi singsongs, gently nudging Kenzo's foot. He sits up immediately. "One for you, too," she says, holding out another tea.

"Thanks, Harumi." Kenzo drains his cup in one go, then stretches his arms over his head before springing to his feet; unlike me, he doesn't seem the least bit disoriented. "Okay, what's next?"

Will clears his throat. "Apparently, we're dancing," he croaks out.

"Just watch me." Harumi smiles. "It'll be fun."

A nap usually leaves me feeling refreshed, but watching Harumi continue to explain Bon-odori to a captivated-looking Will, my skin prickles with frustration, and I try to think of a way to get the Harumi-Gareth train back on track.

"You guys go ahead," I say, suddenly, as the music starts. "I just remembered something I need to do. I'll come find you." And with that, I turn and jostle my way through the crowd to the food stations, where Gareth is packing up coolers.

"Hey," I say.

"Hey, yourself."

"I know you're still working, but I was thinking —"

He grins. "About me?"

I'm so caught off guard by his direct question that I blurt out, "Yes," before I can stop myself. I pretend that the pause that follows is more surprised than awkward and continue. "If you have time, why don't you come find Harumi and me after you're done?" I could be imagining it, but his smile seems to grow when I say Harumi's name. "I mean, it's too bad you can't join us for the dancing. But we could hang out later."

"Hang out with you . . . ?"

"And Harumi."

"Harumi, sure." He nods. "Yeah, I could make time. Sounds great."

I smile, happy with the baby step I've made. "We'll see you later, then."

"With bells on."

I find Harumi, Kenzo, and Will near the front of the dais again, their attention on Ojiichan and a couple of ladies as they give a short demo of some of the dance steps. We then form two concentric circles and wait for Mas to turn the music back on.

From speakers all around us, traditional Japanese folk music fills the air, and even though it's a little bumpy at first, eventually most everyone finds their groove and the circles move forward, and back, and forward on repeat.

As muscle memory takes over, I look around. Even those who don't know exactly what they're doing, like Will, are having fun. Harumi is shining, her dancing smooth, hands and feet graceful in their movements.

In the inner circle, I see Abby and Mas, and Mitsuko and Seiji, aglow with happiness.

Behind me, I hear Kenzo trying to coach Takeo and Tomio. It's pointless, of course, because every time I turn around, the twins grin and — much to the amusement of everyone around them — throw in a trendy TikTok move, somehow managing to sync it with the music.

By the time the last dance is over, signaling the official end of the festivities, the sky's a dusky blue, and portable bonfires are lit up around the yard. There's just a scattering of people remaining, and as Kenzo, Harumi, and Will help themselves to refreshments that have been put out on a table, I look towards the food stations that have long been dark, wondering what's happened to Gareth.

6
Five's a Crowd

"You coming, Kimori?" Kenzo asks as I continue to stand there, scanning the darkened perimeter for signs of movement.

"In a sec," I say, taking my cell out from my sleeve. Pulling up Gareth's number, I send a quick text.

ME: Just checking. We still on?

Then, I turn my attention back to the snacks and put a few things on a plate before hurrying over to where everyone's settled in camp chairs around one of the bonfires.

Since I wasn't quick enough to prevent Harumi from sitting next to Will, and there's no room between him and Kenzo, I do my best from her other side to monopolize Will's attention until Gareth arrives.

"So, how'd you like your first Obon party?" I ask him.

I only half-listen as the possibility that Gareth has forgotten occurs to me — which would be *very* surprising, but given how much time has flipped past, I'm starting to think he has. I debate texting him again when Kenzo coughs and, looking up, I realize I've missed Will's answer. My face warms.

"Sorry," I tell him. "Could you repeat that?"

"Uhm, I said everything was epic. But the watermelon game was bonus. You do this every year?"

"Yeah, although at first it was just a barbeque with Kenzo's family. What were we, three? Four?"

Kenzo nods. "Sounds right."

"It grew a bit every summer as we got to know other families locally, until it became the unofficial Obon festival for the coast. This year's probably the peak, though —" I stop abruptly mid-sentence when I see Gareth approaching from behind Will. Harumi notices and follows my gaze.

"Gareth! You're here, finally!" I spring up, sounding way more enthused than I need to.

"Yeah. I just saw your text," he says, grinning.

His belated arrival is explained by hair that looks freshly styled and a wardrobe change. Indicating his designer-logo sweatshirt and ironed-looking jean shorts, he continues, "I changed at the café. I didn't want you to think I only had work clothes."

"Oh, we wouldn't have cared, would we, Harumi?"

Harumi giggles, and if I weren't already on my feet, I'd give Gareth a standing O for his extra effort.

"Anyway . . ." I continue. "Look, everyone. It's Gareth! Kenzo and Harumi, obviously, you know. But this is Will. He works with Kenzo."

I don't hear what Kenzo and Will say, but Harumi gives him a cheerful welcome.

"How was your yakisoba?" Gareth asks her. "Did I add enough beni shoga for you?"

Harumi grins. "Exactly enough, thank you."

"And extra aonori?"

"Oh my god, I can't believe you remembered that, too!"

"Well, you *are* kind of a preferred customer." He turns and gives me a quick wink as he says this.

"Gareth speaks fluent Japanese," I say to Will.

"Oh." Will looks at Gareth.

"Impressive, right? He can read and write, too. Japanese, I mean." Kenzo gives me a look, as if to say "Seriously?" which I ignore. "And he's going to be a senior this fall." I step forward. "Here, Gareth, have a seat."

"No, I can get —"

"I insist."

Gareth takes my chair next to Harumi and gives her a smile. "I think I just got the best seat in the house," he says to me as Harumi giggles again and, if I'm not mistaken, blushes, too.

Feeling pretty cheerful, I plop another chair between Gareth and Kenzo, liking how well Harumi and Gareth are vibing. But then, despite tossing conversation starters into the air like confetti, things inexplicably flatten out after that.

Maybe everyone's just tired, or maybe we're all hypnotized by the flickering flames, but as the silence around our fire continues, I'm actually relieved when I see Taka-san walking towards us.

"Emiko-san." She waves her hands in a "sit, sit" motion when both Kenzo and I get to our feet. "Forgive me for disturbing you and your friends. Oh, Kenzo, don't you look handsome! And Harumi-san, so stylish! Your hair!"

Taka-san spreads the love to Gareth, too, on his food service, and even Will gets a compliment on his dancing attempts before she circles back to me again.

"Anyway, Emiko-san, I wanted to thank you. I've already thanked your ojiichan and auntie, but what a wonderful Obon that was! So much fun, and all the *food*. I was talking to Chisato the other day — she called me, which is tricky, you know, with the time difference — and I told her how much I was looking forward to today."

"Well, we're glad you could join us," I say.

"How's Chisato doing?" Kenzo asks.

Outside of when Taka-san town-cries all about her, I don't generally give Chisato Ishi much thought, so it takes me a second to remember that Kenzo has known her since we were little, too.

"You're so kind to ask, Kenzo. She's well, thank you. Very busy with her studies. I worry sometimes, she works too hard all the time. Always winning awards. But so modest! I tell her, 'You need to take breaks' — all that screen time — 'and maybe try eye yoga' —" Something behind us distracts her and she stops. "Oh, Mitsuko is waving at me. I must go." After a couple more compliments and another thank-you, Taka-san finally leaves.

I flop back into my chair and stare into the bonfire as we listen to actual crickets in the garden.

"So, Gareth, are you working at the café again tomorrow?" I ask when it finally gets to be too much.

"Yeah, the morning shift."

"Well, maybe Harumi and I will stop in. Pick up a scone."

"For sure. I'll put one aside, special."

"Harumi loves scones, don't you, Harumi?" I prompt.

"What?" she says, and I see she's been distracted by something Will must have said to her.

"Scones. You love them." I flare my eyes at Harumi, subtly tilting my head towards Gareth, to get her to talk instead.

Harumi nods quickly. "Oh, yeah. I love scones. So much."

I turn to Gareth. "It's a date, then." And I can't help smiling at his pleased expression.

Unfortunately, we hit another deep dip, and my mind pretzels as I try to think of a way to get a photo of Harumi and Gareth without it seeming completely random. I'm usually so much quicker on my feet. Maybe *I'm* the one who got too much sun. Maybe I should just say, "Hey, let's get a photo of you two, looking so nice, all dressed up."

Struck by the simple brilliance of this last idea, I'm about to open my mouth when a loud burst of EDM fills the air.

"That's me." Gareth pulls a phone from his back pocket and checks it. "Yup. It's my ride."

"Shoot, already?" I get up from my seat, frowning when I catch Kenzo grabbing Harumi's attention with a cookie.

"Yeah. Early shift, remember?"

"Right. But we'll see *you* tomorrow," I remind him, waving my left hand behind me, out of Gareth's sight, to try and catch Harumi's eye. I give up with a sigh when his phone goes off again. "Well," I say, as he texts a reply, "thanks for all your help today."

"No problem. Tottemo tanoshikatta desu." He gives me a final wink, grins at Harumi, and blanket waves at the guys before he trots off. "Oyasuminasai!" he says.

Harumi watches him leave. "It's so cool that he can speak Japanese. Doesn't he have the cutest accent?"

"He does," I say, but before I can come up with another virtue to extol, Will abruptly stands.

"I think I should go, too," he says, tossing his paper plate into the fire.

"I'll drive you," Kenzo says as he does the same.

Will clears his throat and looks at me. "Uhm, thanks for letting me come to the party." He turns to Harumi. "It was nice meeting you, again, Harumi. Thanks for . . . showing me around. And explaining all the food and stuff."

"No problem. It was nice meeting you, again, too. Tell your sister I said hi, if she remembers me."

"I will."

"Come on, Rivers." Kenzo smiles at Harumi and says good night in a way that just barely stretches to include me.

"Good night, Will. *Kenzo*," I say pointedly.

Harumi waves them off, her mouth now full of cookie, while I sit back down, feeling like an unplugged holiday inflatable.

"Mmm, that was good." She pats her mouth with a napkin. "Thanks for everything today, Emiko. It was meccha fun."

"Really?"

"Of course! I had a blast." She stifles a yawn.

"Well, I'm glad." While I believe some progress — in the form of tomorrow's *scone-devous* — was made, I want to try to hit a higher note for Harumi. "And you certainly made a good impression."

"I did?" She looks around. "On who?"

"Harumi! On *Gareth*! Didn't you notice how he was acting?"

"How did he act?" She looks genuinely perplexed, like she's completely forgotten what I said earlier in the day. Seems like the idea I planted hasn't taken yet.

"Come on. He was totally flirting with you. I mean, I thought there was a connection when you two first met. But tonight? 'Preferred customer'? Extra pickled ginger? And now he's going to save you a special scone?"

She sits back, palming her chin, and I decide to leave her with that thought. As with a dough, you have to be careful not to overwork things.

Shortly after that, Harumi's Aunt Satomi says it's time to leave, too, which basically ends the party for me. I text Ojiichan and Mitsuko, who are still visiting with Taka-san and some other friends, to tell them I'm going to bed.

Instead of falling asleep, though, I stare at the ceiling as I run through the day in my head. I've been trying to build a foundation for Harumi and Gareth, but it feels wobbly, like Jell-O, when what I really want is something sturdy, like a hot water crust. Maybe I could put the Jell-O *inside* the crust. It isn't wholly appetizing but I play around with the concept, considering ingredients and variations until, eventually, I lull myself to sleep.

7

Phosphorescence

A few days later, after another round of texts assuring Harumi that her unofficial micro-date with Gareth at the café was a success (as proven by the biggish sour-cherry-chip scone he saved her), I walk into my closet to consider my wardrobe. With school starting in a couple of weeks, I want to get a jump on styling some outfits so I'm not scrambling those first mornings back, and I am deeply contemplating a kilt when my phone chirps.

Kenzo: It's dark out.

I've been so focused, I hadn't even noticed. One look confirms it: there's no moon to be seen, and the garden, the trees, and the beach have all melded together, a thick, tarry night.

Me: You are correct, sir.

Kenzo: Got the kayaks out. Conditions optimal. Wanna go?

We both got kayaks a few summers ago and, as with any new toy, we used them a lot for the first while, but we haven't taken them out once this year. So, I don't hesitate to answer.

Me: Meet you in 20.

I find Ojiichan in the living room, reading in his chair. He doesn't even lift his head, just gives me the okay sign when I tell him where I'm going. I run back upstairs, change into a bathing suit, toss on a sweatshirt and board shorts, and collect a flashlight from a kitchen drawer before heading down to the beach.

Kenzo's there, ready and waiting. "It looks perfect out," he says, and I can hear the smile in his voice. After I strap on my life jacket, we each grab a paddle and carry our kayaks down to the shoreline.

As soon as our feet and kayaks disturb the water, silver-blue light shivers across the surface, and it scatters in all directions as we settle into our seats. This is the reason to go out tonight — the water is alive with phosphorescence.

Kenzo is right, this is the perfect night for a viewing. The air is warm and the velvet sky stretched overhead is teeming with stars. It always surprises me how dark it gets during a new moon, and how bright and infinite the stars are when they don't have any competition.

I could happily go lie on the beach and stare up at the sky until midnight. But then I hear the water lapping the shoreline, and the gentle wash of rocks tumbling back and forth in the waves, and I cast my eyes downward.

"Wow," I say under my breath. The water is so beautiful

it's almost overwhelming. You don't know where to look, what to focus on, there's so much to take in. For a few minutes, Kenzo and I just float, our heads on swivels as we try to catch everything happening in this natural light show that surrounds us. Even the water dripping off our paddles sparkles as if it's salted with diamonds.

It's enough to make me giddy, and I gasp when a school of neon-lit fish swims past in the water between us, fluorescent streaks that bunch and swell and swirl nonstop. Then, just as suddenly, like shooting stars, they're gone.

"Watch this, Em." Kenzo dips his paddle into the water, then whips it out, spraying luminous liquid silver across the surface. He does it quickly, over and over again, creating a cascade of light that's like something out of *Fantasia*, when Mickey Mouse commands the water.

I'm so entranced by this display that when he changes direction and starts tossing illuminated water over the bow of my kayak I don't realize Kenzo's intentions until it's too late. Thankfully, my mouth is closed when he ambushes me with a wave that leaves me spluttering and coughing.

"Prepare to die," I manage eventually.

"Bring it, Montoya," he says.

Swiping my face, I stare at him, silhouetted against the eerie bright, moving water. For several moments we sit poised, gunslingers at high noon. I steady my breath and slow my heartbeat as I listen for a creak or a shift, a clue that he's about to strike, but all I hear is a pounding in my ears.

As time turns elastic, I feel the tension in my body ratchet up; maybe it's contagious and Kenzo feels it too, because somehow, at the exact same second, we both burst into action and thrash the water with our paddles, aiming for volume and force as we engage in an all-out water war.

It goes on for minutes as we churn the sea like sharks in a feeding frenzy. I keep my face turned away, splashing at him blindly. We're both trying to be quiet but we can't help the screams and shouts of surprise as we drench each other completely. We're probably disturbing the neighbors, but it's so much fun, we don't stop. I'm soaked through, and my kayak is filling up, but I keep going, ducking my head, doing my best to avoid the worst of the water coming my way.

Then, I hiccup my timing and get a faceful. Drenched, I hear Kenzo chuckling to my left, and though my eyes are squeezed shut, I quickly dip my paddle as far back as possible, pull it forward fast and hard to bring up as much water as I can, and blast it towards him.

A shocked yelp tells me I've hit my target. "Ha!" I steer around so that I'm facing him. Our kayaks drift against each other as the water calms and, other than a few neon shimmers, remains dark. I can barely make Kenzo out, but I sense his solid presence there, like a black that's denser than the black around us.

"Truce?" I ask.

"Truce," he answers.

Even though it's a warm night, a breeze triggers goosebumps up and down my arms and I suddenly can't wait to get dry. Kenzo must feel the same because he aims his flashlight at the beach and suggests we paddle back. "Just leave your stuff above the tide line," he says as we step out of our kayaks. "I'll put everything away in the morning."

"Okay. Thanks," I say. "Then come over for breakfast after."

"Deal."

On our way home, Kenzo takes the lead, citing bears. "I'm bigger," he says as we navigate the path, shining our flashlights ahead and all around. "But make some noise if you want."

"You have to help, though."

"Fine."

"Name three animals that start with the letter A."

"Aardvarks, alligators, and anteaters."

"Nice. Now three dog breeds that start with B."

We work through the alphabet and manage to make the game last until we arrive at the kitchen slider. "Last one," I say. "Ready?"

"Hit me."

"Three foods that start with Z."

Kenzo finally looks stumped. "Zucchini. And . . . ziti . . ."

"And . . . ?"

He stares at me, as if the answer is written on my face.

Rubbing my arms, I offer a hint. "A type of bread."

He reaches over and slides the door open. "No clue. Just tell me, before you catch cold."

"Zwieback." I grin. "Also, zimtsterne, zeppole, zarzuela —"

"Show off." He smiles. "Thanks for tonight."

"Yeah, same." I step into the kitchen and turn to face him. "We shouldn't wait so long to do it again."

As I say this, I'm struck by the idea of somehow getting Harumi and Gareth to go on a night kayak like Kenzo and I just did, and I wonder how I could arrange it. I mean, under the right circumstances, this would be pretty romantic.

"Just say the word," he says. "See you tomorrow, Em."

"See you tomorrow."

He waves his flashlight before heading towards the driveway while I step back inside, my mind racing with possibilities.

Since Kenzo's coming over, I get up an hour early and, after washing up and getting dressed, head downstairs to turn on the kettle. I've been experimenting with non-coffee drinks and am about to make my current go-to, a matcha latte, when Ojiichan comes in from the deck.

"Ohayou, Emiko-chan."

"Ohayou gozaimasu," I greet him in return. I scoop powdered green tea into a rustic matcha bowl and whisk in enough hot water to make it frothy. Then I add some heated oat milk and a dash of almond extract before pushing the bowl towards Ojiichan. I make a second bowl for myself.

"Mmm," we both say after our first sips. It's such a great way to start the weekend.

"So, what time will Kenzo be here?" Ojiichan asks as he opens up the local weekly.

"In about an hour and a half," I say as a text comes in. "This is probably him now."

Turns out, it's not.

"Oh no."

Ojiichan looks up. "Is everything alright?"

"It's Mitsuko. Jun's visit's been cancelled," I tell him, surprised by how let down I feel by this.

"That is unfortunate news."

"I have to call her." Mitsuko picks up on the first ring. "What happened?" I ask. "Two days ago, everything was still a go."

"It's not Jun's fault. Seiji received a text from Jun's mother this morning. Jun's grandmother's health has worsened, so Kana wants to take him to Fukushima to see her. Obviously, we can't complain, but it's very disappointing."

"*Quelle* bummer. I mean, I hope his obaachan is okay and everything, but . . . *quelle grande* bumm-*aire*."

"Yes, it is," she agrees glumly.

"Seriously, Mitsuko. I'm really sorry Jun's not coming . . ." I think but don't say *again*. "But, maybe there's a silver lining. Like, maybe this means when he *does* finally come for a visit, it'll be for a good stretch of time, instead of for what basically amounts to a long weekend."

"That'd be nice. It's just . . . we've been waiting. And I was so excited . . ."

"I know. It'll happen, don't worry."

Mitsuko sighs. "I hope so."

Hearing the disappointment thick in her voice, I get it. It's as if we all got tickets to the hottest show of the year only to be told, the day of, that the headliner's plane is stranded in, like, Winnipeg, and there's no mention of rescheduling a new date, just an offer for a boring refund.

I think for a moment. "Do you want to go by Senior Dogs later? A couple of sweet old pups arrived this week and they need hugs. Seiji can come if he wants. Safiye won't mind. Maybe Ojiichan will join, too." I check to see if he's listening, and, sure enough, he's shaking his head.

"That's tempting." It wouldn't be the first time we've turned to canine therapy. "Maybe some other time. Thanks, Emiko-chan."

By the time Kenzo arrives, breakfast is on the table. It's possible I've gone overboard.

"Good morning, Akiro-san," Kenzo says as he comes in through the slider.

Ojiichan walks over and claps him on the back. "Ah, Kenzo." Ojiichan beams at him before turning to me. "It is almost like old times, is it not, Emiko? If only your aunt were still here."

"Ojiichan," I say, "Mitsuko hasn't moved to the moon."

Kenzo smiles, then notices all the food I've made. "Wow, Emiko. You throwing another party?"

"I couldn't decide what I wanted," I say, "so, I made everything." Everything includes buttermilk biscuits, ham and sweet potato hash, a three-cheese onion frittata, and a sorrel and cucumber salad from the garden.

"This looks incredible," Kenzo says as he and Ojiichan take their seats.

"There's dessert, too, so leave room."

One of my favorite moments of a meal is at the start, when everyone (hopefully) takes a breath to appreciate the food before them. Like, even if it's just toast . . . that anticipation before you actually taste something, followed by that satisfied *mmm* when you do — it sets a tone. So, I'm happy to hear that hum of excitement as everyone fills their plates.

There's not a lot of chatter at first, but as food gets eaten, the conversation picks up. Ojiichan asks Kenzo about his business, and Kenzo asks Ojiichan how his bonsai are doing. "I will show you later, if you have time," Ojiichan says. He pushes his empty plate away and settles back in his seat. "Now, tell me. Are you looking forward to school, Kenzo?"

"I am. It's going to be a lot of work, but I think it'll be a good year."

"Have you thought about what you might do after graduation?"

"University, for sure, although I haven't picked a top choice yet."

"Really?" Even though this isn't a topic I want to discuss myself right now, I'm piqued by his answer. "I thought it'd be Western B.C., for sure. Like your parents."

Kenzo takes a forkful of food and chews thoughtfully. "UWBC's on the list," he says after a moment. "But there are other possibilities." He grins, aware this isn't nearly enough info.

Ojiichan looks far more accepting and only says he looks forward to hearing what Kenzo decides.

"What about you, Emiko?" Kenzo asks.

"Ah, yes, perhaps she will tell you. She always distracts me with food whenever I ask this question." My grandfather, the traitor, tries to hide his smile behind a teacup.

I stand, pretending I didn't hear him. "Did I tell you Jun's had to cancel his trip again? It's too bad, his visit would have been a fun way to cap the summer."

"Huh," is Kenzo's only response. Then he says, "So, Em?"

"So, what?" I say, with a side of stink eye.

"Which schools are you thinking about?"

I know there are decisions to be made in the next few months, and that there will be meetings with my guidance counselor. But right now I don't want to think about it, and I busy myself with plating the cinnamon rhubarb muffins I baked for dessert.

Because I can feel them waiting, though, I give the answer I know Ojiichan wants to hear. "I mean, obviously, I'll apply to Cascadia U."

"Your parents would be delighted to see you attend their alma mater, Emiko. Although UWBC is also a most worthy institution," Ojiichan adds, nodding to Kenzo. "What an exciting year you both have ahead of you."

"Yeah," I say as enthusiastically as I can.

Kenzo looks at me like he's expecting more, but I press my lips together and give a subtle head shake. He nods and asks Ojiichan about pruning rhododendrons.

After breakfast, Kenzo loads the dishwasher while I put the food away. As I wrap up the muffins and biscuits he'll bring home for the twins, I hear Ojiichan calling Kenzo from the yard.

"You'd better go," I say, passing him the care package. "He's missed your visits."

"I know. So have I." Kenzo goes out onto the deck and tells Ojiichan he'll be right out, then turns back to me. "You good in here, Em?"

I nod. "Oh, yeah, I'm almost done."

"Well, thanks for breakfast. And the extras. See you later." He grins, then slips on his shoes and sprints down to the garden.

It's fun how much they enjoy each other's company. Ojiichan is pointing things out on a rhodo, leaning in to clip branches, and stepping back, as if to look at the whole picture. But as I watch him hand his pruners to Kenzo, I realize how rarely this sort of thing happens anymore, with Kenzo already too busy to visit as much as he used to. Fast-forward to this time next year and, well . . . I chew the inside of my lip thinking about how different things might be.

8
Harumi and Will Meet Again

"Tell me again why we're going so early?" Harumi asks as we ride our bikes to the Otter Creek Farmers' Market.

"For a loaf of bread." What I don't mention is that yesterday I told Gareth, more than once, that Harumi and I would be at the market right at opening, implying that this would give him time to maybe bump into us before his shift at Mitsuko's. But also, I'm not kidding about the bread.

"Is it bread disguised as cake?" she asks, huffing a little.

"Trust me. You'll be mad you haven't tried it already."

We're within sight of my old elementary school, where the Saturday market takes place, when Kenzo drives by and honks before turning in to the parking lot.

"Hey, that was Will in the truck with him!" Harumi says, and she surprises me with a burst of speed.

"Hold on," I call after her, switching gears to try and catch up.

It's a steady incline, so by the time we reach them, both Harumi and I are out of breath.

"Hi." I lift my water bottle and take a long drink. "What are you guys doing here?"

Kenzo points to his truck bed loaded with trays of tomatoes, plums, and pears. "Helping out Will's folks," he says, as he stacks two on top of each other.

"Really?" I turn to Will with genuine interest. "Which stand?"

Will looks at the ground and mumbles something.

"I'm sorry?" I say, and, given the way he keeps staring at the ground, I start to wonder if maybe he's lost a contact.

But then he lifts his head and tries again. "Uhm, my parents have a stand."

"Right. I was just wondering which one."

Will, who's now busy sneaking glances at Harumi, doesn't reply. Harumi doesn't notice, though, because she's absently fixing her outfit as she looks towards the market.

"Rivers' Farm Organics, under the red canopy." Kenzo gestures to the rows of mostly white tents.

I don't need to see it to know exactly which one he means. Besides fruits and vegetables, Rivers' Farm also carries the most glorious cut-flower bouquets on the coast. "No way. I didn't make the connection."

I'm about to compliment Will on his family's business when he says something to Harumi that I miss, and she's blushing as she smooths her hair. I frown and give her a "what's going on?" look. When she blinks rapidly but doesn't speak, my expression shifts to "knock it off."

Before I can do anything more, though, Kenzo abruptly turns his baseball cap around and lifts the double stack of laden trays like they're filled with packing peanuts.

"Come on, Rivers," he says. "We've got things to do."

"Someone's bossy," I tease.

I expect Kenzo to laugh it off, but instead his eyes widen, like he can't believe me, to which I'm, like, *what?* Then he shakes his head as he starts stalking away.

"See you around, Harumi," he calls over his shoulder. I barely get a chin bob.

"Kenzo?" I'm totally baffled by his behavior, but I get nothing more.

Will hoists a couple of trays too, but instead of leaving, he turns back to Harumi. "Uhm, so, maybe see you around?"

"I hope so," she says with a smile.

Will's goofy look lasts until Kenzo comes back and bumps him with his trays. "Let's go," he says, still ignoring me.

Will nods and gives Harumi one last smile before he turns and scurries to catch up with him.

I have no idea what's gotten into Kenzo, because that was just rude, but I need to deal with Harumi first. I move so I'm standing in front of her, noting the faraway look in her eyes.

"Hey," I say.

"Hm?"

I wave my hand in front of her face. "Harumi. Over here."

"What?" she says when she finally notices me.

"What are you doing? What was all that about?"

"Nothing." She gives me a pouty look. "He's cute."

"He's also going into the tenth grade."

"I know."

I turn and walk towards the chain-link fence where we'll secure our bikes. Harumi follows silently behind me.

81

"Look. It's not just his age." I click my lock in place. "You're new. So, you have this chance to set the tone for your last years of high school. With my help, it could be pretty spectacular, but . . ." I pause, trying to come up with a useful analogy. "Think of it as being the star of your own movie."

She nods, listening.

"Well, if you want it to be a blockbuster, you have to choose the right co-star to be your leading man. And I hate to say it, Harumi, but Will is not leading man material. At best, he's background."

"But —"

"Whereas Gareth . . . remember him? The camera-ready guy who's already interested?"

"I don't . . ."

I stop, waiting for her to finish her sentence.

"Nothing," she says after a moment, and she locks her bike up, too.

"I mean, ultimately, it's up to you. You don't have to listen to me. But wouldn't you like to have the most fun possible these next two years? Be part of a hit movie — a hit couple?"

I realize I may be overselling the allure of Gareth Tolman, but it seems to be working. Harumi looks like she's gazing into the future and liking what she sees.

I let my words sink in while I stop by Queenie B's, the coast's only source for blackberry honey. One of the few sweet things I crave, it smells like flowers and has this unique taste that elevates buttered toast and tea to a level I never thought possible.

The QB herself is working today, dressed in a mango yellow jumpsuit with her braids tied up in a vivid headscarf.

"I'm loving all the color, Queenie," I tell her, handing her some cash.

"Thank you, sweetness. And how is life treating you today?"

"Never better."

She passes back my change and a big jar of molten gold. "You say hello to that handsome grandfather of yours for me. And tell him the propolis is almost ready."

After thanking Queenie, I check on Harumi, who's gnawing on her thumbnail. I put the honey in my backpack and keep walking.

"You really think Gareth might like me?" she says finally.

"I do."

Before we can get into it further, we arrive at Me-Want-Cookie Bar, home of the comically oversized cookie. While Harumi pores over the selection, I search the growing crowd in an increasingly frustrating game of *Where's Gareth?*

"Sorry," Harumi says after finally paying for her baker's dozen. "I couldn't decide, they all looked so good!"

I nod as I check the time, and I shove my phone away when it confirms that Gareth's window to stop by before work has slammed shut. Feeling a pinch of irritation that the possibility of an "accidental" meeting is now gone, I just want to get my errands done and go. But since Harumi wants to check out the crafts section, I suggest we split up and meet back at Dough!, the bakery with the craveable sourdough that not even Mitsuko can replicate.

"Ten-fifteen," I remind her.

"Ten-fifteen," she agrees, and we take off in opposite directions.

It takes me longer than expected to pick up Ojiichan's favorite tisane at Teas Please Me and halibut cheeks for dinner from Sirens' Sea Chest, so by the time I get in line at Dough! with the other breadheads, I'm surprised Harumi's not already there waiting for me.

It's almost half past by the time I get my loaf and there's still no sign of her. I check my phone but there are no messages, either, so I send a text asking where she is. When I get no answer, I start searching for her, even walking back to where our bikes are, and I'm about to send another text when I spot her standing under a bright red canopy. The Rivers' Farm Organics stand.

As I get closer, I see Harumi handing a pen back to the familiar-looking girl standing behind tubs of lush bouquets. She's wearing a denim sundress and she has a multicolored cast on the arm she uses to pass Harumi a vibrant bunch of dahlias and peonies.

"Hi," I say as I come up beside her. "I was starting to worry about you."

Harumi smiles when she sees me, but then her expression drops. "Oh, no! You're here! I'm sorry, I completely lost track of time." She looks at her phone. "I was talking so much, I missed your texts."

"That's okay. What've you got there?"

She holds up her bouquet. "I couldn't resist."

The girl behind the flowers holds out her good hand. "Hi," she says. "You must be Emiko."

"And you're Will's sister, Arlo. I recognize you from school," I tell her.

She smiles broadly. "The one and only."

"What happened to your arm?"

"Oh, it's so stupid. I tripped over our goat and landed wrong. Broke it in three places."

"Ouch."

Arlo shrugs. "It happens, although it sucks that I have to wear this for, like, another month. But it's also why I'm working the market today so, yay me!"

"It's the first time I've seen her in the Creek, so we were just catching up," Harumi says.

"Right. You two went to camp together."

"I couldn't believe it when Will told me Harumi had moved here," Arlo says to me.

"*I* couldn't believe it when he recognized me after all these years." Harumi touches her hair and starts giggling. "I mean, I had a boy cut!"

"Aw, it was cute." Arlo leans forward. "Plus, I think he had a crush on you."

"Really?" Harumi squeaks.

"Well," I say before Arlo can reply, "I hate to break up the reunion, but I've got seafood that needs chilling." I hold up my backpack as proof. "Harumi?"

"Oh, right. I guess we'd better go." Harumi turns to Arlo. "I'm so glad I ran into you. Hopefully, I'll see you at school?"

"Or here. Or wherever. Just keep an eye out for this," Arlo says, grinning, and she raises her colorful cast.

I think I'm in a quandary.

As we return to our bikes, my mind is spinning with what to do about Harumi and Will and Gareth.

As far as Harumi's concerned, I don't think Will on his own is any kind of threat to Gareth. Yes, he's cute, but so are puppies. And as I always tell people who show up at the rescue looking for one, puppies are a LOT of work.

But, Will plus his sister, Arlo? That could be a problem. Obviously, I'm thrilled Harumi has reconnected with an old friend. OBVIOUSLY. Because she seems nice, and the more nice people you know before you set foot in a new school the better. So, it's not like I don't want Harumi to be friends with Arlo.

Except, being friends with Arlo means Harumi will likely spend more time with Will, and that extra time might be what tips the scales in Will's favor. Arlo's a complication I didn't anticipate.

I'm unlocking my bike before I realize Harumi's been trying to catch up to me.

"Emiko." Huffing, she secures her cookies and flowers on the rear rack. "Are you mad about something?"

"What? No," I say, and stop as I remember that while Gareth may not have Arlo, he does have me.

"Are you sure?"

"I just want to get home before the fish spoils."

She looks unconvinced, but I don't say anything more as we get on our bikes and ride off. I decide to take a different route and lead her down a side street. After a couple of blocks, I brake and step off my pedals.

Harumi rides past before realizing I've stopped, and she walks her bike backwards until she's standing beside me.

We're in the middle of an intersection but there are no cars anywhere, and the neighborhood is quiet.

"I'm not mad," I say. "But I am confused."

Harumi's eyebrows peak together. "Why?"

"Are you not interested in Gareth? Because you seemed to like the idea back at Obon, and earlier, I thought we were on the same page. Now, I'm not so sure. And I don't want to waste time helping you two get together if you're not, because I *definitely* have other things I could be worrying about instead."

"I'm sorry, Emiko." She kicks a pedal. "I'm confused too. I guess I don't believe Gareth would really like me that way."

"Well, can you believe *me* when I say he does? He just doesn't know how much yet." I start walking my bike and she follows. "Look," I say after a few moments. "All I want is for you to have the best time possible at Cedar Grove. To do that, it helps if you're sitting at the big kids' table. Being with someone like Gareth will get you there. Dating a tenth-grader will not."

I pause, checking that Harumi's still listening. She doesn't speak, but she's worrying her lower lip. "I know t t sounds mean . . ." I say.

She shakes her head. "No, no, you're right." She takes a deep breath and gets a determined look in her eye. "Yes, that's what I want. I want Gareth. I want *Gareth*."

"I promise you won't regret this." Saying this, though, brings a slight tickle of unease, like there's a pine needle stuck in my sweater. But I mentally shake it off, remind myself I know what I'm doing, and get back on my bike. "Alright, now let's go. Dinner's melting."

Harumi's face relaxes and she laughs as she hops onto her bike, too, and we ride, standing up on the pedals like we're little kids chasing after an ice cream truck.

9
September

"EMIKO KIMORI, get yourself over here A-STAT."

Laughing, I run in for a bear hug from Tayjon King, my locker-buddy since ninth grade. "How was New York?" I ask when he finally sets me down.

"Most epic summer of my life, E. Crazy busy, but in the best way."

"I can't wait to hear all about it. But first, I want you to meet a new friend, Harumi." I wave her over from the other side of the hallway and watch as she skillfully Froggers her way through the streaming crowd to join us. "This is Tayjon," I tell her.

"Hi, there," she says, hoisting up her backpack.

"Hello, new friend Harumi." Tayjon turns and brings a Nikon out of his locker. "Since this is your first day at Cedar Grove, you have to let me take your picture."

"I do?" she asks, her eyes wide.

Nodding, I move to give them space. "Tayjon is a magician. He'll make you look fabulous."

"Correction: I'll *capture* your fabulous. Like this." Tayjon turns his camera around to show Harumi her photo.

"Oh, wow. Could I get a copy of that? To show my family?"

"With plezh. And here, I'll get one of you and Emiko together."

Harumi and I lean in and Tayjon shoots a few more before he's happy. He and I are discussing which one's the keeper when I hear a familiar scream and someone runs up behind me and covers my eyes with their hands.

"Guess who!" they say.

"Liv?"

"Oh my gosh, how do you always know it's me?"

The hands drop from my eyes and, blinking, I turn around to find Liv Soo, looking genuinely disappointed. "Because you're the only one who ever does that," I say as I go in for a proper hug.

"Missed you in Tofino! You should have come — surfing or fishing on the daily. I caught a halibut!"

"Liv's family owns a cottage on Vancouver Island," I tell Harumi.

"You would have died, it was *sooo* good."

"I promise. I'll make it out there one day," I assure her. "Here, this is my friend, Harumi. Harumi, Liv Soo, cheer captain and future Nobel Prize Winner —"

"For Literature, capital L," Liv interjects, before giving Harumi the once-over. "You look bouncy. Ever cheered before? Tryouts are next week. It's great cardio. You should come."

Harumi looks briefly dazzled — as much as I love her, Liv's energy can do that to you — but then blurts out, "I AM bouncy!"

"*Knew* it. Next Tuesday, after school, in the gym. Shorts and grippy shoes." Just then, someone yells Liv's name from down the hall. "I'LL BE RIGHT THERE," Liv yells back. "Sorry," she says at normal volume. "Jeremy. The boyfriend. 'Kay, lovelies, I'll check you later."

By the time Harumi and I head to our first classes, she looks exhausted by all the introductions I've made so far. "We can do a review with the yearbook later, if you want," I say.

"Yes, please." She lets out a big breath. "I mean, everyone seems so . . . friendly. And kind of amazing?"

"It's a really good school." Just then, the warning bell rings, and you can feel the energy surge as everyone starts funneling towards class. "Okay, you know where you're going?"

"I think so."

"Remember, it's a square doughnut. We're at the bottom. Cafeteria's on the left."

"Got it."

"See you at lunch. Good luck!"

"What IS this?" Harumi asks, her eyes circles of wonder.

It's already the first day of fall, and it's still warm enough to sit outside under the giant cedar tree in the school's central courtyard. Harumi's just had her first spoonful of chili-pepper-pineapple froyo.

She takes another taste and closes her eyes to savor the flavor. "And can I buy it anywhere else?"

"Sadly, it's another limited-edition cafeteria exclusive, courtesy of Culinary Arts." I've told the department heads, our principal, my guidance counselor, even the student council that the school really needs to market and share their bestsellers with the outside world. They'd make a fortune.

Anyway, it's been a hectic morning, and this is my first chance to eat so I'm really enjoying my mezze plate. I'm about to dig into some muhammara when Gareth walks by.

"Here are my two favorite ladies," he says, sitting down at our table. He snags an olive from my plate without asking and pops it in his mouth, chewing as he makes himself comfortable. It doesn't escape my notice that he took the last big green one.

"How are you today, Harumi?" he asks, after spitting the pit out onto the ground.

"Fine." She draws the word out like taffy and smiles. "How are you?"

"Stellar, now that I've seen you." He winks at Harumi who, on cue, blushes and giggles, before he turns to me. "So, Em —" he starts.

"— iko," I finish, arching my brow. I don't mind a select few people using a nickname for me, but Gareth is not one of them.

He swallows. "Right. Emiko."

"Yes?"

"Er, I was wondering . . . is there any chance you'd be up for starting a study group for French? I really need help — Monsieur Adomako is way tougher than my last teacher."

I look at Harumi, and when her face brightens, I make a snap decision.

Since that day at the farmers' market, Harumi hasn't mentioned Will Rivers once. And for the rest of the summer, if I wasn't at the shelter or the café, and she was free, and Gareth was on shift, then she and I were at Mitsuko's, occupying our now regular table.

I did my best, giving her styling advice, setting her up to tell stories about herself, laughing at all her jokes. Gareth was always attentive, popping over between customers, and they seemed to get along really well. But so far, Gareth hasn't taken the next step of asking her out.

It's frustrating, but my current theory is that it's because he really hasn't had any time alone with her. And all of their conversations have been broken up into little bites, spaced out over days. I mean, imagine trying to eat a complete meal that way. You'd probably give up and just grab a bánh mì or something.

I also think we're up against the fact that most guys can't multitask the way girls can. I read an article once that said some teenage boys literally cannot chew gum and walk at the same time. They'll actually trip if they try. So, they have to decide what's important to them, and focus on that one thing. What we need is to create a controlled environment with no distractions where Gareth can focus on Harumi.

With a guidance counselor meeting looming over me like an old-growth fir, figuring out how to do this is exactly the kind of distraction I need.

Which is why I exaggerate *un peu* and tell Gareth that Harumi and I have already been reviewing lessons every week. With Harumi taking French 11 and me, 12, it makes total sense. I give Harumi a look and she catches on and plays along.

"Even better," he says, smoothly. "Any chance you'd let in a third?"

I pretend to think about it, but inside, I'm happy-dancing. "I think we can do that. I'll let you know when we're meeting next."

Gareth stands up, brushing back his hair. "Excellent. I can't wait. Until then . . . then," he says, his smile faltering.

I get the feeling that's not exactly the line he wanted to exit on, but he does his best to go with it, and he performs a little turn on his heel before he tries sauntering away.

Harumi watches, rapt, as he gets swept up in the stream of students heading in through the double doors. Once he's out of sight, she turns to me and squeals. "French study group?" An incredulous smile spreads over her face.

"*Mais oui, bien sûr,*" I say.

After lunch, I head down to see my guidance counselor. Mx. Galloway has known me since ninth grade, and is one of the coolest people I know, with maybe the best hat game in town. But I'm still not looking forward to our session.

"*Hai, douzo,*" they say after I knock on their door. Mx. G. makes an effort to learn the basic niceties in every language their students speak. Last year, they told me they were up to twenty-three, not including English and French.

"Hi, Mx. G." I close the door behind me and set my backpack on a varnished tree stump by the wall. My stomach is fluttery with nerves and I exhale as quietly as I can as I sit down on the beanbag chair waiting on the braided rug.

"Emiko, *irasshai*. It's nice to see you. What can I get you — Oolong, Darjeeling, or genmaicha?"

"Genmaicha, please." As they move to their refreshment trolley, I look at all the plants placed around the room. Their office gets a ton of indirect light so everything grows green and lush in here.

Soon, they pass me a mug full of fragrant, hot tea. I place it on the table beside me and slip off my shoes before settling cross-legged on the squishy chair.

"Now then," they say, as their own beanbag rustles beneath them. "How've you been? How was your summer?"

"Really good. How was yours?"

They pass me a framed photo. "George and I took a road trip to P.E.I. so he could meet my family. That's him in the Atlantic." George is Mx. Galloway's eight-year-old Newfoundland-Lab cross — one hundred plus pounds of slobbery canine love. I'd invited them to an adoption blitz we were having at the shelter last year and, on a hunch, set them up to meet George. As I watched them take a get-to-know-you walk around the property together, I knew Mx. G. wouldn't be driving home alone that day. I consider it my first successful match.

"Aw." I hand the photo back. "I love his Mohawk."

"That was my nephew's idea. But it works for him," they say fondly, putting the photo back on a side table. "So, your aunt got married, right?"

I nod, picking up my mug. "Yeah, and it was a pretty fabulous wedding, if I do say so myself."

"How's it been since she moved out? You and your grandfather doing okay?"

"Oh yeah. We're fine. Although we still sometimes think Mitsuko's coming back at some point, that she's just on vacation somewhere." I mean to say this like it's a joke, but then I have a sudden image of Ojiichan sitting alone in the house, and my throat closes up. I swallow hard and take a quick sip of tea, burning the roof of my mouth in the process.

"I'm glad to hear that, because that's a significant change — she's been a big part of your life, so to suddenly lose that can be challenging."

I shake my head. "Nope. Totally good."

Mx. G. looks at me for a few moments — direct eye contact is one of their signature moves, and normally I'm okay with it. But today, I'm feeling a little bit like Montgomery, an old Shiba Inu at the shelter who squeezes his eyes shut if you stare at him too long.

Thankfully, I must be convincing, because they blink and sit back in the beanbag. After sliding on a pair of glasses, they take my file off a side table and open it up.

"How are your classes?"

"Brilliant, all my teachers are great. I have nothing to complain about there."

They nod, tapping a pen against their chin as they flip through some papers. "Good extracurriculars, with your ongoing volunteer work at the shelter — three years, now, right? Photo editor for the yearbook, again. And I take it you'll be continuing your excellent work with the decorating committee." They check another page before looking up. "And you're all set as far as university requirements go."

I carefully take another sip of tea as my stomach backflips onto a trampoline. "Yup."

"So, assuming you maintain your grades," they look up over the rims of their glasses and give me a smile that's somehow a warning and encouragement at the same time, "then all that's left is to decide your top three choices and start preparing your application packages."

"Right."

"Are you sure you don't want to apply for any scholarships? You really have an excellent shot at quite a few."

I shake my head. "I don't need the money," I remind them. I don't like to talk about it, for obvious reasons, but somewhere in my file is a note about the trust fund I have as a result of the insurance payout after my parents' car accident, one that's grown significantly thanks to Ojiichan's shrewd investing.

"Of course." After a moment, they continue. "Did you want to try for early admission anywhere? Cascadia, maybe?"

I feel myself tense, and I press a point on my inner forearm with my thumb. "Uhm, sure," I answer automatically.

"You don't have to." They frown slightly as they notice I'm giving myself acupressure.

"Uhm, sure."

Mx. G. closes my file and puts it aside. I can feel another direct stare coming on.

"Emiko, is there something you'd like to talk about?"

I turn to look out the window; from where I'm sitting, I can see the treetops silhouetted against the cloudless sky. The trees are so still, they look photographic.

"Emiko?"

I turn back to Mx. G., who isn't smiling, but is emitting an energy that makes me feel like they are; like, if I wanted one, they would walk over and give me a hug.

My arms fall by my sides and I breathe in and out slowly, repeating the cycle until my breathing steadies. I nod. "Yes," I say.

"Whenever you're ready, then." Mx. G. sits back and waits.

"I don't know if university is what I really want." The words spill out in one go and I wait for a reaction, but the expression on their face doesn't change. They just nod.

At first, I try not to be that person who can't resist filling a silence. I've read how people will do that, not speak right away if they want the other person to keep talking. But then I remember Mx. G. isn't the one here trying to figure out what they want to do with their life — I am.

I try again. "I don't think university is what I want."

Pause. Nothing.

"I don't think I want to go to university."

When they still don't acknowledge anything I've said, I try one more time. "I don't want to go to university."

I thought it would feel good to say this out loud, in front of someone, but the enormity of it hits me, and I fall back, groaning as I turn and bury my face into the beanbag.

After a few moments, I hear Mx. G. get up and refill their mug. "Oh, Emiko," they say. I can't tell if they're mad, or disappointed, or what. So I don't respond, feeling as wrung out as a dishcloth.

Eventually, I restack my spine, sweep the hair off my face, and sit up properly.

Mx. G. has my file open on their lap again. "So."

"So."

"You're not keen on university anymore?"

I sigh. "I don't know if I ever was. I mean . . ." I shake my head. "No, I shouldn't say that. I'm not against the idea of university. But it's kind of like if you asked me if I wanted to go to, I don't know . . . Niagara Falls for the first time. I'd say yes, because most people would, but it wouldn't be my top choice. It's what my grandfather expects, though, and my aunt. Even though neither of them went, or got degrees. Just my parents."

"Is there something else you'd like to do post graduation?"

I flop back into the beanbag. "That's my problem, Mx. G., there are *so many things* I want to do." I sigh loudly and stare up at the ceiling. "But . . . do I have to move off coast to do it? I mean, I love food and baking — maybe I could apprentice with my aunt. I already help at the café. I could be more hands-on, learn in the real world how to run things."

"Mm-hm." Mx. G.'s pen scritches as they write something in my file. "What else?"

"I love photography and art and fashion . . . and I love music and books and movies. Making things with my hands. Dogs, especially the old ones we get at the shelter. And organizing. I love organizing things. I know I'm really good at that."

"Mm-hm." They pause before asking, "Does the idea of leaving the coast concern you?"

I blink. Mx. G. sits quietly while I think about their question. "Not really. But, maybe sometimes."

"How so?"

My head feels like a dryer, full of a mixed load of thoughts all tumbling together into a blurry mass. I try to pinpoint the one that stands out enough that I can identify it. "It's just that, with my aunt moving out, I wonder if me leaving, leaving the coast, too . . ." My eyes suddenly feel hot and I stop.

"You're worried about your grandfather."

I nod. "A little. Not because he's said anything." I sit up quickly. "It's just . . . Mx. G., I've looked at everything from arts institutes to the Ivies. But none of them feel compelling enough to make leaving him — and what is empirically a pretty terrific life in Otter Creek — worth the effort. And shouldn't it? Otherwise, why bother?" I cup my chin and drum my fingers against my cheek, thinking.

"I don't disagree with you." They pause. "Did you consider any business schools?"

"What? No," I say, like it's the most absurd idea I've ever heard.

"Maybe you should." Mx. G. flips a few pages. "On your Strong Interest test last year, you scored almost fifty-fifty on Artistic and Enterprising. Usually, people skew definitively one way or the other. I don't often see these two particular interests match up so closely."

"But business school?" I can't help but make a face. "I don't know."

Mx. G. shrugs. "It's a thought. From what you're telling me, and your test results, I'm not surprised by the list of things you're passionate about. I also think you're very persuasive, and if you believe in something, whether it's an object or an idea, you'd probably be remarkably good at selling it to others."

I nod as Mx. G. and George, Mitsuko and Seiji, and Harumi and Gareth come to mind. This test is kind of uncanny. I mentally add professional matchmaker to my list of potential careers.

Mx. G. glances over at the driftwood clock on the wall. I can't believe I've been here almost an hour.

"Before you go, Emiko, I'd like you to do me a favor."

"Sure," I say.

"Don't make any hasty decisions, okay? Don't close your mind to any possible opportunities until you have to. I respect that the idea of university isn't sparking a fire for you right now. But you're smart, and capable of earning the grades that would get you into any school you want. So, how about we continue down this path and see what happens? Just because you're accepted somewhere doesn't mean you have to go — but at least you'll have the option, should you want it. Okay?"

"Okay."

"Good. Thank you."

Mx. G. stands while I slip on my shoes. Following them to the trolley, I finish the rest of my cooled tea before putting the mug on a tray.

"Thanks a lot, Mx. G." I grab my backpack, and before I even put it on, I notice something different. "Is it weird that this actually feels lighter now?" I say.

"Not at all." They open the door, and as I step into the hallway, where another student is waiting on a bench, they add, "I look forward to our next meeting."

I smile. "Me too."

"Ah, *hallo*, Henrick," Mx. G. says as I head to my next class. "*Kom binnen.*"

10
Kokeshi Doll

With everyone's schedules being so packed, it took Cirque du Soleil–level juggling to organize it, but we're finally having our first French study session tonight.

The scene has been set: chilled bottles of sparkling water and white grape juice sit next to a colorful charcuterie board, a crusty baguette, and a basket piled high with still-warm madeleines. There's French pop playing in the background, and I'm singing along to it when Gareth and Harumi arrive.

This is only the second time Gareth has been to the house. On his first visit, he was here as Ojiichan's guest, after Mitsuko told Ojiichan how big a fan Gareth was. The two of them spent most of that meeting in Ojiichan's study or out in Ojiichan's workshop.

This time, while Harumi hangs up their coats, he strolls into the kitchen and does a slow turn as he checks everything out. "Pretty swanky, Emiko. Pretty swanky, indeed."

Harumi comes in and goes straight for the table. "I thought

I smelled baking." She leans over and takes in a deep breath. "So yummy."

Since I have the strongest foundation in French, I went ahead and prepared some lesson plans. While the two of them help themselves to the food, I open my folder.

"So, I wrote these scripts." I hand them each some paper. "I thought we could start with some dialogues, to practice pronunciation and work on our conversational skills."

Gareth nods as he and Harumi flip through their pages. "Sounds good."

I suggest we do a couple of run-throughs with the script first, then see if we can go off book, for fun. As they review their lines, I fix myself a white grape sparkler and a small plate.

"*Vous pouvez commencer*," I say. And, holy *calamité*, they do.

If French is to language what ballet is to dance, then listening to Gareth and Harumi read their lines is like watching them grand jeté across the stage in humungo wooden clogs, drunk.

When they finally finish, they turn to me, expectant smiles on their faces. And I don't know what to do except ask them to try it again, because I have this fleeting hope that maybe I just imagined what I just heard.

Non, it turns out. A thousand times *non*.

Harumi begins. "*Vooley-voose aller ow cinema avec mwah seh swhawr? Sest oon programmay doobel.*"

"Don't forget, some letters are silent," I remind her.

"Oh, yeah. Which ones, again? I'll highlight them."

Now, this is how Gareth's supposed to reply: "*Avec plaisir! Et nous pourrions faire une promenade après. Ou aller prendre un café.*"

What he says instead is this: "*Aveck playzzeerrrgh! Ay nu poo-rrrheeon fehrrr-uh oon prrr-aahmenahd aprrr-aay. Ooh, al-laay prrr-hond-rrrha oon caffay.*"

"Uhm, about your *Rs* . . ." I say.

"I know, I watched a video on YouTube." He looks at Harumi. "You keep the tip of your tongue behind your bottom teeth while you say it, so it gets nice and guttural."

I do my best, I really do, even leaving the room at one point for twenty minutes to recover and give them both "space to practice without an audience." But finally, my body rebelling, I stand up and close my folder. "Why don't we move on to some grammar worksheets?"

"Are you sure?" Harumi says. "These dialogues are really fun."

Gareth nods. "Yeah, very realistic scenarios."

"Thanks." I paste a smile on my face. "But you both mentioned having trouble with the verb tenses, so let's focus on that instead."

I manage to hang in for two more Wednesdays before I give up, take the after-school shift at Senior Dogs, and let our study group die an unnatural death.

Which means I'm back to trying to get Harumi and Gareth some quality face-to-face time together. The trouble is, they don't share any split-grade classes. Lunch hours are out because Gareth has joined so many clubs — to look well-rounded on his university applications, he said — that he rarely makes it to the cafeteria. And weekends are hopeless since they both have jobs.

It's a problem I chew on while I review my list of potential universities, until I recall something Gareth said at our last study session, about my grandfather's kokeshi dolls. That gives me the inspiration I need, and it takes me to Ojiichan's workshop.

The smell of the space transports me back to when I was four and obsessed with Kenzo's pet hamster, Pikachu. I'd pleaded with Ojiichan for a hamster den of my own, so he found a gigantic cardboard box, filled it with the biggest wood shavings he could make, duct-taped a water bottle and a bowl of Cheerios to one wall, and let me climb in. The only thing missing was a child-sized running wheel.

I spent hours in that box, burrowing into the shavings, living my best hamster life, until Mitsuko found me napping in it and declared the whole thing a health hazard. She still talks about how long it took her to comb all the bits of wood out of my hair and pluck them from my clothes.

Since then, Ojiichan has taught me how to use the wood-working tools, and though I've tried making my own dolls, honestly, they were all just an excuse to use the lathe. Holding one of Ojiichan's chisels and turning leftover wood until I'm left with a drumstick and a pile of curly shavings that look like katsuobushi — I can't tell you how satisfying that is.

But today, I'm determined to start — and finish — my very first kokeshi doll.

I switch on the dust-collection system, put on my safety gear, and power up the small lathe to work on a practice piece, turning it into a smooth, knuckly spindle.

Once I'm warmed up and feeling confident, I take the length of maple Ojiichan left for me and get it centered and secured in place. Then, using a rough sketch as a template, I pencil marks on a guide piece to remind me where I want to gouge the wood.

Kokeshi dolls usually consist of a head piece that fits onto the body, but some makers carve one-piece dolls, which is what I'm going to do. I turn on the lathe, pick up the roughing gouge, and take off the squared edges until I have a smooth column of wood.

Next, after changing tools, I shape the head, rounding the top, and carve out a small section to create the neck before pulling the gouge back to curve the shoulders. I leave the part that makes up the body, but I shave some wood near the bottom to create a gentle bell shape, inspired by a particular dress.

When it's as clean as I can make it with the tools, I take varying grades of sandpaper and run those over the turning wood, polishing it free of any unwanted bumps or ridges.

Painting the doll while it spins is tricky because watching paint go on is so spellbinding, it's really hard to stay disciplined. Like, you know how when a potter pulls up wet clay on a wheel, it looks so cool? Well, if you've ever tried throwing a pot, you know how tempting it is to keep pulling that clay up or out as far as you can. But if you overdo it, then the clay collapses in on itself. That's kind of how it feels to put a paintbrush to a piece spinning on the lathe; I want to keep it there, and move it along the guide, watching the paint line grow until the whole thing is one solid color. But, as hard as it is, I resist the temptation and focus on sticking to my design. And in no time at all, I successfully paint a series of different-colored rings around the torso.

When that's done and dried enough, I paint the rest of the details freehand.

It takes me the weekend, but when I put the finished result on the table before me, I can't help but feel absolutely delighted with myself. It's exactly what I'd pictured in my head, what I'd rough-sketched out, and it's the key to my new plan.

I invite Harumi to a late lunch at the café on a day I know Gareth is working. I've picked what's usually a slower time, and with the place barely half full, I'm confident we can get Gareth to spend a few extra minutes with us.

After we've ordered, I wait till I see Gareth coming out of the kitchen with our food before I reach into my bag and bring out a colorful furoshiki-wrapped bundle.

Harumi's eyes light up. "What's that?"

I slide it across the table to her. "It's a just-because present — I was feeling creative and I got this idea, so I made this for you."

"Ladies," Gareth says in that way he has. "Oh, is it someone's birthday?" He tilts his chin towards the gift.

Harumi shakes her head as Gareth puts down our Golden Coast bowls. "No. Emiko made me something."

"Really?" Gareth looks at me as he lays down our cutlery bundles. "Well, color me curious."

I smile at Harumi. "Go ahead, open it."

She unties the cloth and lets it fall away to reveal the doll inside.

Just then, the door opens and, *oh chou-fleur*, of course it has to be Kenzo and Will who walk in. Kenzo's eyes meet mine and he says something to Will before they both head over to our table.

"Gentlemen." I'm almost always glad to see Kenzo, but right now, I'm telepathically yelling at him to take Will and go away so Gareth and Harumi can have this moment alone.

"Hi," Kenzo says, showing no sign of hearing me. Will mumbles a greeting too, while trying to look at Harumi without being obvious. Thankfully, she's too preoccupied to notice.

"What's that?" Kenzo indicates the doll.

"Emiko made it." Harumi holds it up. "Isn't it adorable?"

"Actually," I say, since it appears no one has noticed, "it's a Harumi-kokeshi. I designed it to look like you." Harumi looks at me with a perplexed expression on her face. "In kokeshi form," I add, noting the growing silence I wasn't expecting.

Harumi looks at the doll more closely. "Oh." She turns it over and examines it from multiple angles. "Yeah, I can sort of see that now. And the black and white and pink and yellow stripes —"

"Are Hello Kitty colors." Honestly, I'm astonished that she, of all people, didn't pick up on this.

Kenzo moves next to Harumi and peers down at the doll. "It looks like a bowling pin with a face."

My mouth drops open and I glare up at Kenzo. "It does not," I say through gritted teeth.

Harumi's eyes widen and dart back and forth between me and Kenzo. Will stares at the floor, but he's biting his lip, as if he's trying not to laugh. I inhale and exhale loudly, and think about kicking Kenzo in the shin.

"Well, I think it's outstanding," Gareth says, and he puts his hand out towards Harumi. "May I?"

Harumi blinks up at him as if she's waking up from a dream, and after a moment she places the wooden doll in his palm.

Gareth handles it like a precious artifact. "Unbelievable. I don't know how you did it, Emiko. I wish I could have watched your process, but I think this is, well . . . it's obviously not a *realistic* rendering of Harumi. But in a way, it's almost better. More an expression of you, and how *you* see her spirit so perfectly. So clearly."

He places his hand on his chest, like he's overcome, which is, like, okay. I mean, my doll isn't THAT good. But, whatever, it's working. Harumi melts into her chair and eyes him as if she's Lady AND the Tramp and he's the giant plate of spaghetti.

She sighs. "Do you really think so?"

"I do." Gareth smiles at me, and I smile back encouragingly. *Keep going, Gareth*, I think to myself. This is going so much better than I'd expected.

Suddenly, Gareth straightens up, reaches into his back pocket, and pulls out his phone. "In fact, it's so good, I'm going to share it with my followers."

Kenzo snorts. "And that's our cue to leave. Let's go, Rivers." They turn without even saying goodbye and walk to the counter to place their orders with my aunt.

I cross my arms, feeling Mitsuko's eyes on me and pretending I don't notice. I try to ignore the guys, too, but I'm totally aware of Kenzo looking back at me and shaking his head as he walks out of the café, Will close behind him.

Gareth glances towards the counter and nods at Mitsuko before he quickly leans down between me and Harumi while holding up the doll. "Come on, Emiko. Harumi, too," he says as he puts his camera arm around me.

"No." I shake my head as Harumi makes kissy lips and leans sideways towards Gareth. "That's a weird angle." I duck under his arm and move away. "It's better with just you two."

"But you're the artist —"

"And she's the model," I say. "Go ahead, before Harumi falls off her chair. And our lunch gets cold."

"It's salad."

I don't budge.

"Fine," Gareth says as Harumi scoots closer, refreshing her pout. "Ready, Harumi?"

"Mm-hm."

Gareth adjusts his phone angle and takes the selfie.

"Ooh, show me, show me," Harumi says, as Gareth checks the image.

He holds the screen up to her.

"Will you send me a copy?" she asks.

"Of course. What do you think, Emiko?" He turns his phone towards me.

"Nice job," I say. It *is* a great photo, my kokeshi in the middle bringing the two of them together just as I'd planned. I keep my expression calm, but inside, I'm throwing my pom-pom-holding hands up in the air and high-kicking like Liv Soo at a championship final.

Harumi taps her number into Gareth's phone and he

gives us one more grin before returning to the counter. Harumi watches him go, while I catch my aunt's eye and give her an apologetic shrug.

As she swivels around to face the table, Harumi lets out a tiny squeal. "Oh my god, Emiko!" she stage-whispers as she unwraps her cutlery. "Oh my god." She takes a deep breath and leans forward. "Did that just happen? Did I just give Gareth my number? Oh, I should look."

She digs into her bag and pulls out her cell. Her disappointment as she checks it is quick. "Oh, well." She places her phone on the table. "He's working."

"Exactly. I'm sure he'll send it as soon as he can."

She picks up her fork and skewers a chickpea, then stops. "Oh, Emiko, I'm so sorry. I didn't thank you properly for the doll. I love it! It's almost like being a Funko Pop!"

I smile. "I'm glad you like it."

"It's honestly the nicest present I've ever gotten. I can't believe you did that, 'just because.'"

"Mm-hm," I say absently, as I watch Gareth behind the counter. I lower my voice. "Okay, don't turn around, but *someone's* staring at his phone, and while I can't be a hundred percent sure, I'll bet that someone is zooming in on *someone else's* face."

"What?!" Harumi stamps her feet in excitement. "Really?"

I nod, nearly bursting with glee at how things are going. Now I wish Kenzo *was* here, to witness this moment of triumph.

"Oh my god, I'm so glad you invited me to lunch," she says.

I dig into my bowl, grinning. "Me too, Harumi. Me too."

11

Trick or Treat

I finally ripped off the Band-Aid and started the application process for three universities — Cascadia, Western B.C., both on the mainland, and Royal Victoria on Vancouver Island. Now I just want to forget about it for a while and concentrate on prepping for the first big event on the school calendar, the All Hallows' Eve Dance. I'm extra-buzzy about it because I also have this gut feeling that the dance is where Gareth and Harumi's relationship will take a giant leap forward.

Earlier in the week, Gareth had mentioned he was preparing something special for the occasion, and when I asked him if it involved Harumi, he paused, like he didn't want to give anything away, which *totally* means that it does.

All day I've been trying to imagine what Gareth's surprise will be, but now, as I get ready, my mind wanders to Halloweens past, and all the costumes Kenzo and I have planned together.

The first year, we were six and seven, and we went as Jessie and Woody from *Toy Story*. In tenth grade, I was Angelica

Schuyler and Kenzo was Alexander Hamilton, from the musical. Last year, I dressed as the mutant Yukio and Kenzo was Wolverine.

Since that day at the farmers' market, things between Kenzo and me have felt a hair off, as if someone brushed against our photo and knocked it just out of level. So neither of us had mentioned anything about pairing costumes again this year. Fresh off the success of my kokeshi idea, though, I decided to be the bigger person, and I sent him a text to nudge that picture back into place.

ME: Hey. What are we doing for Halloween?

KENZO: Who is this?

ME: Ha ha. Still a butt.

KENZO: And still no idea who this is.

We went back and forth like that until Kenzo admitted he had been thinking about it too. When he told me his idea, it took me a second to love it. But now I'm really excited that, for our last Halloween in high school, we're going to surprise each other.

I went to my bookcase for inspiration, and thanks to a thrift store wedding dress, a box of brown fabric dye, and Mitsuko's tailoring skills, I am going as Anne of Green Gables, dressed in a glossy silk dress with the puffiest of puffed sleeves.

I've just put on my braided auburn wig and am about to draw on my freckles when the doorbell rings. Ojiichan is driving Harumi and me to the dance, and though I told her we'd pick her up, when I open the door, I'm half expecting to see her there.

Instead, I find three Totoros on our doorstep.

I burst out laughing. Each of the Sanada boys is wearing a full-on Totoro onesie — Kenzo is wearing the gray one, Takeo, the blue, and Tomio's is white. Kenzo's also carrying a black umbrella, while the twins have subbed a monstera leaf for the butterbur leaves used in the Miyazaki film. The look has been nailed.

"We're your *Neighbor* —" starts Takeo.

"*Totoros!*" finishes Tomio.

Kenzo smiles down at his brothers. "They wanted to do a team costume this year." He reaches out with his free arm to put Tomio in a mock headlock. "What could I do?"

"Well, I love it. Come on in."

"We won't stay long. Dad's going to take them out. They just wanted you to see us all together."

"You look nice, too," Takeo says.

"I like your hair," Tomio adds. As he's the quieter twin, I'm extra happy to get his compliment.

"Do you know who she's supposed to be?" Kenzo asks.

"An old doll?" Tomio guesses, while Takeo shakes his head.

"Nope. Remember that miniseries Emiko made you watch last year at Christmas? *Anne of Green Gables?*"

Both boys nod, staring at me.

"That's who Emiko's dressed as. Right?" Kenzo smiles at me.

"You two are lucky your brother is so much smarter than he looks. And since he guessed correctly, everyone gets a prize." I walk to the console table where I put their goody bags. "You saved me having to drop these off."

"Thanks, Emiko!" they say, cracking the bags open.

"And yours." I hand Kenzo one, too.

"Thanks, Em. Okay, guys, let's go." He steers his brothers towards the door. "See you at the dance," he says.

I smile. "See you at the dance."

Ojiichan drops Harumi and me off at the school entrance, and once we're inside the doors, I take a moment to adjust her Hello Kitty ears and make sure my wig is in place. Then, linking arms, we turn left, heading towards the cafeteria, as spooky sound effects fill the air around us.

Even though I'm on the decorating committee, I'm still excited by what's to come. As Harumi and I continue down the darkened hallway lined with flickering jack-o'-lanterns, I start pointing out details Harumi might not have noticed when we're ambushed by a Lego Man and a tube of Kragle.

"BOO!" they yell, waving their hands in our faces.

Harumi drops her Hello Kitty purse and we both scream, which, of course, makes Lego Man and Kragle howl with laughter.

"Oh my god, you guys." Once I recover, and because I now recognize our assailants, I give them each a whack on the arm with my homemade reticule. "Harumi, this literal boy toy is Jacob Austin, and the Krazy Glue is his boyfriend, Darcy Jang. Way to make a first impression, you two."

Darcy bends down to pick up Harumi's purse. "Sorry," he says, still chuckling as he hands it to her. "We couldn't resist."

"Come on, Emi-K," Jacob adds, slinging his arm around my shoulders. "What's Halloween without a little scare?"

"Point taken." We start walking again, Darcy and Harumi already chatting like old friends behind us.

We get in line outside the cafeteria, and the three Powerpuff Girls ahead of us turn around. It's the Triple As. "Fine costumes, people," says Blossom, a.k.a. Astrella Hadi, our school president.

"Same to you three," I say. "Especially the wigs."

Jacob studies them, then looks back at Astrella. "Wait, my sister loves all of you. Let me guess. You're Bubbles?"

"*I'm* Bubbles," says Ani Labrecque. "God, this line is taking forever. Emiko, you know people, can't you do something?"

"I wish," I say, as we move up a step.

"Harumi, right?" says Alix Eliot, who's dressed as Buttercup. She holds out a bag of candy. "Hi-Chew?"

As Jacob and Harumi dip into the sweets, I ask Darcy, who's the tallest in our group, if he can see Gareth anywhere in the line.

"Negatory," he says after a few moments. "I see Kenzo way at the back, though, in what looks like a very fetching costume."

"Okay, thanks for checking."

Finally, Astrella reaches the check-in table, and within minutes the rest of us have our hands stamped and we're inside the gym.

Harumi grabs my arm and shakes it. "I'm so excited, Emiko! Do you think Gareth's already here?"

"If he is, he'll find us," I say.

We walk farther into the room and I take in how unreal it looks under all the colored lights flashing and spinning in time to the music. The theme we chose this year is a mashup of Tim Burton's *Beetlejuice* and *Miss Peregrine's Home for Peculiar Children*, and everything looks fantabulous, creepy yet funny at the same time.

"Come on." I tug Harumi's hand. "Let's beat the rush and hit the photo booth."

I'd asked Tayjon to take the assignment for the yearbook, and I grin when I spot him, dressed as T'Challa.

"At last. Models!" Tayjon greets us as he steps off his stool.

His assistant, a tenth-grader in full zombie garb, grins and jumps up to take their place by a table. While Tayjon checks his camera, Harumi and I get comfortable against a painted backdrop of a haunted Cedar Grove.

"You ready to have some fun?" he asks.

"Ready," we say, and for the next few minutes we're nearly blinded by all the flashes as Tayjon calls out a string of directions.

"Blue Steel!"

"Charlie's Angels!"

"Avengers!"

By the time Tayjon gets to prompts like "Celine Dion!" and "marmot!" our poses are getting sloppier and sloppier and we are crying with laughter.

When I finally hold my hand up in defeat, I straighten up to find we've attracted an audience. Harumi looks embarrassed, but I wave at everyone before walking over to Tayjon, who's uploading the shots onto a laptop.

As Harumi fills out the order form, I watch the people flowing in through the doors.

"Don't worry, E.," Tayjon says, mistaking the reason for my frown. "It's early, things will pick up. And if they don't, I'll go around and get some candids. Like this." The flash goes off in my face just as I turn towards him. Smiling, Tayjon looks down at the display screen on his camera. "That's a keeper."

"Tayjon! Let me see." I hold my hand out for his camera.

"Uh-uh," he says, though he shows me the image.

Honestly, *Teen Vogue* would be lucky to get him. "I'll want a copy of that, *s'il vous plaît*." He really is a magician.

Harumi joins us then. "I couldn't decide which ones I liked best, so I ordered them all."

As Tayjon predicted, people are now flocking to the photo booth, so, after promising to check in later, Harumi and I continue our lap around the room. As we near the far end of the cafeteria there's still no sign of Gareth, so I suggest grabbing a table that gives us a view of the entrance and dance floor.

Harumi nods as she stands on tiptoe in her red platforms. She's scanning the crowd, her gaze sweeping back and forth like a searchlight, when she grips my arm hard. "Oh, I think I see him, Emiko."

After Gareth finally sent Harumi the photo from the café, they traded what I would objectively classify as subtle, but flirty, texts. For Harumi, though, they were as potent as love notes written on parchment.

"Ouch, okay," I laugh, gently prying her fingers off me.

"Ooh, sorry. It's just," she turns to me with a helpless look in her eyes, "he told me he was dressing up as a *vampire*,

Emiko. A *vampire*. You know what that means. What am I going to do?"

Harumi has a SERIOUS vampire problem. It's more of a *What We Do in the Shadows* problem than a Team Edward / Team Jacob problem, though, which I totally approve of because, honestly, *WWDITS* is a masterpiece. Now that I think about it, I'm surprised she didn't dress as vampire Hello Kitty. I make a note to mention it to her later, when she's not hyperventilating.

"Hey."

I turn to find Kenzo standing beside me. He lifts his chin at Harumi and smiles. "Hello, Kitty."

"Hi, Kenzo," she says, barely looking at him. Then she does a double take, and he does a slow-mo three-sixty for her. "Oh my god!" she squeals. "That's SO *kawaii!*"

"And comfortable. I can go straight to bed in it."

Harumi laughs, but then her attention slings back to Gareth. "Oh, no, he's coming over, Emiko." Kenzo notices the near-panicked expression on her face too, and we both turn to see what her eyes are laser-locked on.

Looking like something out of an '80s music video, Gareth emerges from the crowd, dry ice fog billowing up around his feet, as pulsing lights illuminate his path. His hair is gelled spiky, his eyeliner is heavy, and instead of the traditional caped costume, he's gone biker, wearing a studded leather vest with torn black jeans and lug-soled boots.

"Hi, Gareth." Harumi almost sighs his name.

"Good eeev-ening," he says in a cheesy accent, and he starts posing for us, which just about kills Harumi. It's amusing until he goes on far longer than necessary. But, smirking like he's got a secret, he keeps swiveling left and right, flexing his wiry arms bodybuilder style, until we finally notice the tattoo.

"Ooh, can I see?" Harumi reaches out and Gareth stops, holding up his left inner forearm. It's not bright in here, but it's clear, at least to the three of us, what Gareth's got inked there.

Harumi makes a funny noise. "Is that my kokeshi?" she asks, staring up at Gareth.

"You bet it is." He looks at me. "What do you think, Emiko? Cool, right? I showed the photo of your carving to a makeup artist I know in Vancouver and told her I wanted an exact replica on my arm."

I'm beaming. I mean, first, coincidence or not, he comes dressed as a vampire. Now this visual tribute to Harumi — if this isn't worth a thousand words, then I don't know what is. Harumi must agree, because she looks ready to launch herself into his arms. The kokeshi is surrounded by intertwined vines and roses, and while I'm not a fan of the flower myself, there's no doubt Harumi thinks Gareth's fake tattoo is the most romantic thing she's ever seen.

"It looks just like her," I say.

Right on time, Kenzo the party pooper makes his presence known. "Except it doesn't."

I give Kenzo my best *stop-talking-now* glare before I turn back to Gareth. "Ignore him. I think it's phenomenal."

Harumi is holding Gareth's arm now. "I really need to see this under a light."

Gareth gives me a look, like he's asking for permission. "Go ahead," I say. "I'll wait here."

Gareth hesitates, but then Harumi starts dragging him over to a better-lit table across the room. As I watch them leave, I resist the urge to literally pat myself on the back and make do with clasping my hands together with glee. Another match made? Check, check, and check!

"Emiko . . ." Kenzo's mouth is right by my ear when he says my name, and I jerk away in surprise.

I turn to look up at him. "What?"

His gaze flickers to where Harumi and Gareth are now sitting, her fingers hovering over his inner arm while Gareth talks and talks and she listens with a dreamy expression on her face. Kenzo's eyes narrow slightly as he turns back to look at me.

I keep my face as neutral as possible as I meet his eyes. He says something else but, thankfully, the music seems a lot louder than when we first came in, so I shrug and mime that I can't hear him.

Shaking his head, he grabs my hand and takes me behind a column where the sound is muffled enough to have a loud conversation.

"What are you up to, Kimori?" he says.

My eyebrows disappear under my fake bangs. "What are you talking about?"

"I'm talking about whatever it is you've been trying to make happen between those two." He lifts his chin towards where Harumi and Gareth are still sitting.

"I'm not trying to make anything happen. It's happening all on its own."

"Those two are not a good fit."

I stare at him, flabbergasted.

"I'm sorry," I finally get out. "Did we just *Freaky Friday* each other? Are you now her closest friend?" I poke him in the chest, which is a mistake because it's like jamming a finger into a tree. "News flash, you're not. And, FYI, she and Gareth are perfect together."

"Do you even know Gareth?"

I make a dismissive sound. "Do you?"

"Well enough."

"Well, I worked with him all summer —"

"For what, like, a month?"

"He was at Obon! He's been to the house. We have classes together." (Okay, one. And we're not allowed to speak English in it.)

Kenzo closes his eyes and pinches the bridge of his nose. Then he takes a deep breath, and exhales slowly. "Look, Harumi is a nice girl. She's not a doll for you to play with, to make do whatever you want. And Gareth Tolman is not the guy for her."

"Of course she's not a doll. And what is your problem with Gareth?"

He sighs. "I know he's charming and helpful at the café, and he dresses nicely. But I've heard him when he's with just the guys, Em. He's a climber. And a snob."

I don't respond, still smarting at Kenzo's crack about me treating Harumi like a doll.

"All he cares about is status and money, and he will never ask a girl like Harumi out."

"What is THAT supposed to mean? 'A girl like Harumi'?" Now I'm fuming, and Kenzo seems to recognize this, because he holds up his hands, like he's worried I'm about to breathe fire.

"Emiko, I'm trying to help."

"Right, that's exactly what it sounds like you're trying to do here." I peer around the column so I can see Harumi and Gareth, only now, Harumi's sitting by herself, looking, I assume, in the direction Gareth's gone.

Suddenly, another tall vampire and a T-Rex approach Harumi from behind. While the Jurassic wingman hangs back, the vampire walks up beside her, his back to me, and he must say something because Harumi starts in her seat before turning to look up at him.

At first, she seems almost glad to see him. But she must sense that she's being watched, because she glances over to me before responding to the vampire. Then Gareth reappears with bottles of water and some snacks.

Harumi says something to Gareth, and then again to the other vampire, and I see the guy's shoulders slump a little before he nods and turns to leave, followed by the T-Rex. That's when my suspicion is confirmed, and even with his shiny black wig, undead makeup, and prominent plastic fangs, I recognize Will Rivers.

I turn to look at Kenzo, who has also been watching the little scene across the room. "Is this about your boy, Will?"

"Whether it is or isn't is irrelevant. But Will is a good kid."

"Exactly! He's a kid! And why do you even care? I mean, you're meddling —"

"*I'm* meddling —?"

At this, I put my hand up in front of his face and we stand there glaring at each other. I can feel people gawking, but I don't care.

"You don't know Harumi the way I do. And whatever you've heard about Gareth —"

"I haven't heard anything *about* him. I've heard it directly —"

"— I believe what I see, and as *you* can see, she's NOT interested in Will."

Kenzo shakes his head. "If Harumi thinks she wants Gareth, then fine, let's see how this plays out. But it's not going to pan out the way either of you want, Emiko. Trust me on this."

"I guess we'll find out," I say. "Now, I'm going to go join my *friends*."

I turn to leave, but a part of me feels bad about how we're ending this. I mean, Kenzo is my oldest friend. And other than childhood scraps over toys or food, we've never really fought.

This feels like our first real fight, and I don't like it. I slow my steps, hoping he'll say something first, before I get too far away. But he doesn't, so I keep going until I reach Harumi and Gareth. Then, after cracking open the bottle of water Gareth offers me, I take a sip, pretending I'm not looking for Kenzo.

But I am. And he's gone.

12
Christmas Decorating

Since the Halloween dance, Kenzo sightings have gone from "often" to "rarely." It's unlikely a casual observer would notice, though, since Kenzo still says hi and all when we bump into each other at school. But he's making no effort to talk to me between classes or at lunch; our text stream has dried up; and he's completely stopped popping by the house whenever. And I have no idea what to do about any of it.

Thankfully, term practice-finals are approaching. And even if I don't know what I'm going to do with them, as a point of pride, I intend to get the best grades possible. So, focusing on my studies turns out to be the perfect reason to forget trying to suss out whatever Kenzo's deal is.

Unfortunately, we're also approaching Abby Sanada's favorite holiday of the year, which means, this weekend, Kenzo and I are going to be in the same room together.

For me, Christmas is synonymous with the Sanadas.

It started before I was born, when, a few years after Ojiichan retired here, my parents left the big city and came to settle in Otter Creek too. Their first Christmas, instant BFFs Mas and Abby invited them and Ojiichan over for turkey dinner, and when Mom and Dad brought a hangiri of chirashi sushi, a new culinary tradition was born. And even after my parents died, my family continued to join Kenzo's around their enormous dining table every December 25. For me, that moment, when we're all sitting together before a feast of Canadian, Scottish, and Japanese dishes, is always a highlight.

But the magic actually begins right after Remembrance Day, when Abby kicks off her annual decorating marathon. And watching her open the first bin of decorations of the year — it's like witnessing the first time a dog sees snow. That pure joy is something, and she does her best to spread that bliss to everyone else.

Which is why I'm here today to help. It's part of the tradition.

"Oh, hi."

I look up from taking off my shoes and see Kenzo standing in the living room next to a stack of full clear bins.

"Hi. I didn't bother knocking," I say, pointing into the air. From now till the end of December, Abby plays nothing but Christmas music of every genre, and right now, Kelly Clarkson is singing about being underneath some mistletoe. This song must be a favorite, because it's on pretty loud.

Kenzo nods, then looks towards the kitchen. "Mom," he calls. "Emiko's here."

Almost immediately, the music volume goes down a bit and Abby comes out. She's wearing one of her many ugly Christmas sweaters, and gives me a hug. "Thanks for coming, love. Now, the fun really begins!"

Conscious of Kenzo standing nearby, I try, for Abby's benefit, to sound eager. "I can't wait to get started. What should I do first?"

"Oh, okay. Well, I guess there's no point in dawdling." She gives both Kenzo and me a quick look. "Why don't you help Kenzo bring the rest of the bins upstairs from the basement?"

"Sure," I say, though I'm groaning on the inside; I'd hoped she'd ask me to unpack the ones already in the room, alone.

"Great. I'll leave you both to it, then."

As Abby returns to the kitchen, Kenzo heads towards the stairs. "Come on," he says over his shoulder.

We walk in heavy, uneasy silence, and I can feel my chest start to squeeze in on itself. It gets so bad that by the time we enter the storage room, I'm contemplating telling Abby I feel sick and going home.

But then Kenzo sighs and turns around, a resigned expression on his face. "Emiko —" he starts.

"I'm sorry," I blurt out. I glance at the ceiling, aware that Abby is somewhere above us, but the Christmas music is playing throughout the house, so I'm pretty confident she didn't hear me.

"You are?" He looks surprised.

I nod. "Yes. I mean, you're still wrong about Harumi and Gareth —" He huffs a little here so I put up my hand. "No. You are, Kenzo. But if you'll agree to disagree on this, then we can forget about it and move on."

Kenzo crosses his arms. "And if I say *you're* still wrong about Harumi and Gareth?"

"We can agree to disagree." When he doesn't respond right away, I grin, *Chicken Run* style, hoping it'll lighten the mood. "Please? Because I really would like to stay and decorate your house."

After a moment, Kenzo laughs and shakes his head. "You know I'm only agreeing because I don't want to help Mom by myself?"

"Agree to disagree," I reply as I walk past him to pick up a bin.

The day gets a thousand times better after that. Under Abby's direction, we hang garlands around the front windows and doors, and set up a forest of artificial trees, ranging from tabletop to ten feet tall, throughout the main floor. Mas has his own assigned tasks, which include keeping the excited twins outside installing lawn ornaments and string lights.

"Hey, Mom," Kenzo calls as I open up bins marked "Village." "Are we putting garlands on the handrails, again?"

Abby comes out from the kitchen where she's setting up her baking-themed vignettes. "I'm sorry, how long have you been my son?" she asks.

"Never mind." He picks up two luxurious-looking garlands. "Spruce or pine?"

"Which feels nicer to the touch?"

Kenzo gives Abby a look but runs his hands over each one, while I press my lips closed so I don't burst out laughing.

"Well?"

"The pine is softer," he says grudgingly.

"That's because it's called *cashmere* pine, son o' mine." Abby's eyes twinkle with amusement as she smiles before heading back to the kitchen.

"What?" Kenzo asks as he drops the rejected garland back in the bin.

"Nothing. You two are funny, that's all. It's nice."

Kenzo doesn't respond, but as he heads up the stairs, garland and Velcro wrap in hand, I catch the pleased half-smile on his face.

Most of Abby's decorations are vintage, including a bunch made in Japan, from the 1950s and '60s. The Putz houses — sherbet-colored cardboard houses dusted with sparkly mica powder — are my favorites; basic and cute, they come with a hole in the back so you can place a string light bulb inside and make the cellophane-covered windows glow. And for the past few years, Abby has given me the honor of using them to set up a village on the mantel.

I try something different every year, and I always start by using books, boxes, even empty cans to build the underlying landscape. It takes some rejigging, but once I'm satisfied with the lay of things, I cover it all with a snow blanket and begin placing the houses.

It's a good thing the mantel is as long and as wide as it is because there are almost three dozen houses to work with. I'm about halfway done when Kenzo comes into the living room.

"How's it going?" he asks.

I step back to survey the whole thing. "You tell me."

Kenzo studies my work, planting his socked feet apart on the floor and crossing his arms in front of his chest. "It's okay," he says finally.

"Could you be more specific?"

"It's neither awful nor outstanding."

"That's not helpful at all."

"You've done better."

"Alright, thank you. You're dismissed. Please feel free to go hang things."

He laughs, unbothered, as I wave him away. The boy is annoying, but he's not wrong; it's not clicking for me yet, either. I redo my bun and play around some more.

Eventually, it comes together. As I shift the houses back and forth, an idea starts to form and, suddenly, I'm moving them around with purpose. Everything is flowing — my hands know exactly what goes where — and when I'm done, and all thirty-three houses are in place, I stand back to compare what I see before me with what I pictured in my head.

"I like it."

Kenzo might as well have thrown a banana slug at my head, I yelp so hard. I turn and glare at him, my hand on my pounding chest.

"Could you please wear a bell or something? You just about gave me a heart attack." Cranky from being yanked out of my zone, I wave my hands around to indicate the whole house. "Seriously, don't you have more halls that need decking?"

"It was interesting, watching you work," Kenzo says, and I think he's being sincere until he adds, "Plus, I thought I smelled smoke, so I came out to see if your hair had caught fire." His mouth twitches but he manages to contain his smile, probably because he can tell from my face that I am not in the mood.

"Ha ha," I say stiffly.

I take a deep breath and return my concentration to the village. The next step is to lay out the string lights and tuck a bulb into the back of each house. This is trickier than it sounds because the wires get twisted from being coiled up all year. I'm on the floor, straightening out two strings, when Kenzo's feet come into view as he steps closer to the mantel.

"I like how you've arranged the houses by color so you have this cool rainbow ice cream effect going on."

I tilt my head up to look at him.

"Except for that one." He points to the green house I've placed among the pink ones.

"It's the leaf on the pathway," I say.

The way his eyes flash, I know he remembers one of the lessons Ojiichan taught us in the garden years ago. We had been raking leaves and, after a lot of work, had them heaped around the yard, ready to be bagged.

I had been especially proud of clearing the gravel pathways and rock garden of any fallen debris and wanted Ojiichan to come admire them in their pristine state. He came over, Kenzo following, and, after praising my diligence, shocked me by taking a few colorful leaves from a pile and scattering them on the ground.

I remember being really mad when I asked him why he'd littered on the gravel I had spent so much time clearing. He knelt down beside me and explained how the leaves enhanced it, because, without them, the gravel would look perfect, and that would be boring. Then he picked up the leaves to show us the difference they made. The leaves, he said, were the point.

"I like it," Kenzo says again. I prime my eyes for rolling, waiting for the inevitable jokey comment. But when he lets his simple compliment stand, for some reason my face gets a little bit warm. I turn away just as Abby walks into the room.

"What do you like?" She stops in front of the fireplace and takes in the display. "Oh, Emiko, that's looking good."

I jump up and shake my hands out, hoping that'll get rid of this sudden zappiness running through my system. "Thanks. I still have to add the trees . . ." From the corner of my eye, I see Kenzo moving away.

"Well, don't let me stop you." Abby turns around. "Kenzo, honey, can you bring in the big ladder, please? I'd ask your dad, but he's up a tree right now and I want to get started on my mobile."

As he heads towards the back door, Abby tells me about her plan to suspend her grandmother's embroidery hoops above the central landing in the stairway. "Then, I'm going to hang baubles from them to make an upside-down tree shape." Somehow, even though I'm still unsettled, I manage to take in all the details.

"I've made the frame," Abby continues, as I sort through some bottle-brush trees. "But I couldn't figure out how to pre-hang the balls. That just felt like an accident waiting to happen. I think it'll work fine if I attach them in place." She grins and claps her hands with excitement when Kenzo returns with the ladder.

While I finish planting flocked trees around my village, Kenzo and Abby work on placing the ladder without dinging any walls. As they complete their setup, I start organizing the boxes of ornaments Abby wants to use by color on the dining table, as she's asked.

"Okay, this is going to be a three-person job," Abby says, fastening her tool belt. "I need Kenzo to hold the ladder, so, Emiko, could you hand me the balls as I need them?"

"Of course." I'm happy to have something to do that doesn't require me to think too hard.

"Great, then, here we go."

Abby gathers her hoops and climbs the ladder as Kenzo keeps it anchored. After several tries, she manages to attach the frame to the ceiling, and I hold my breath as she slowly lets it drop free, reminding me of mid-century mobiles I've seen online.

"You alright there, Kenz?"

"All good, Mom."

"Now the fun part." Abby climbs down a few rungs and holds out a hand. "Red, please, nurse."

I pass her box after box of different colored balls, and she hangs each one with metal hooks from her tool belt. None of us is especially chatty, but with Abby singing along to every song and carol, it's not uncomfortable. I'd even say it's relaxing, which is a relief after whatever was going on with me earlier.

And, to be honest, I'm also enjoying Abby's process. I have to agree with what Kenzo said earlier — it *is* interesting to watch someone at work, especially when it's on something so creative. Unfortunately, this also reminds me of my odd reaction to Kenzo being nice earlier. Maybe I just need something to eat. Shaking my head, I do my best to focus back on Abby.

Eventually, every hoop is hung with vintage glass balls that shimmer in a way new ornaments just can't. After a final inspection, Abby hands me back the last box. "I think we're done here," she says, all smiles.

While I repack the bin, she climbs down, and once the ladder is out of the way, the three of us gather on the landing to look up at Abby's creation. It's simple, beautiful, and fills the space with a joyful, festive energy.

"Alright, I think we've all earned some pizza." She looks at her watch. "I'll order it for six o'clock. That'll give us time to tidy up."

Kenzo goes down the stairs first, carting the ladder straight out the front door to the workshop, while I follow Abby into the living room.

"Is there anything else I can do, Abby, other than stack the bins?"

"Thanks, Emiko, but I think we're good. You both did great today — all the big stuff is done." She goes over to the mantel and switches on the string lights. "I love these little houses so much."

She turns to look at me, a gentle smile on her face. "Everything okay with you, sweetheart?"

I try not to look too startled. "Who, me? I'm fine. Why? Do I look like I'm not okay?"

Abby shakes her head. "No, it's not that. It just feels like . . . like your light's a little dim today, a little flickery."

I don't want to lie to Abby, and even if I did, I'm not sure I could. But I also don't know what to tell her. "I'm okay," I say. "I think I'm just tired. I've been hitting the books really hard." This is true, and sounds reasonable to me, so I hope it does to Abby, too.

Abby studies me a few moments longer, but just when

I think she might want to say something else, Kenzo walks back into the house.

"Hey, Mom. I think we'd better get that pizza sooner than later. Dad says the twins are getting hangry."

"Well, we can't have that," she says. "I'll make some snacks."

Kenzo's eyes dart from me to his mother, then back to me again. "Everything alright?" he asks.

I smile, mustering up my own festive energy. "Absolutely." I look at Abby. "And snacks and pizza will make things even better."

13
December Days

After my last practice-final for the semester, I find Gareth leaning up against my locker.

"Hi," he says, stepping aside so I can open it. "How'd it go? Geometry, right?"

I nod. "Well enough. I think I'm more than ready for the real thing next month. What'd you write?" I ask as I take out my coat.

Before he can answer, Nisha Janssen, school treasurer and the best soccer goalie in Cedar Grove's history, returns to her locker as well. "Hey, you two." She punches in her combo. "You ready for winter break?"

"Like, *beyond*," Gareth says. "In fact, I'm heading to my dad's in Whistler tonight."

"You are? I didn't know that." I frown. Now that exams are over, I had been planning on setting up a "date" for Harumi and Gareth at my house, since he still inexplicably hasn't made the move to ask her out. I was going to call it a fête for the *solstice d'hiver*. I guess I can *oublie* that now.

"Yeah," he says, mostly to me. "The snow report's insane this week."

"Lucky you," Nisha says. "Wish I were going."

"Well, that's too bad." My response is automatic as I think about Harumi — unfortunately, I'd mentioned I had something special in the works for her. Looks as though I'll need to come up with a fun alternative *tout de suite*.

"I'm sorry, Emiko," Gareth continues. "I debated it, you know."

"For real? Why? It's Whistler, dude." Nisha pulls on a toque before shutting her locker. "A bunch of us are hitting Shawarma Guys. Wanna join?"

"I could eat," I tell her.

"Cool. See you soonish. Later, Gare."

As Nisha walks off, I turn to Gareth. "When are you back?"

Gareth smiles. "In time for the mochitsuki, Emiko, I promise. There's no way I'd miss it."

"That's something, at least." I purse my mouth, thinking. Harumi's helping that day, so that gives me one more chance before New Year's to get these two off the sidelines and onto the dance floor. As I ponder this new wrinkle, I grab my backpack and swing the locker door shut. For some reason, when I turn around, Gareth's standing so close I have to press back against the door to avoid a collision.

"Uhm, excuse me?"

"Do you need a ride?" he asks, barely moving. "I've got my mom's Camry."

"No, I'm good," I say, frowning at this discovery that he's a close talker.

"You sure?"

"Yeah. Kenzo's got me." I turn my head at the sound of footsteps. "There he is now."

"Oh. Okay." Gareth takes a quick step back and I see his throat move as he swallows. "Yo, Kenzo." He bobs his chin as Kenzo approaches. "What shakes?"

"Not much," Kenzo says, slowing to a stop. He looks at Gareth, who retreats another step, before turning to me. "You ready, Em?"

"More than." Relieved to have some breathing space, I slide into my coat and swing my backpack wide to put it on so that both Kenzo and Gareth have to make room or risk getting whacked. "Have fun in Whistler," I say to Gareth, but don't wait to hear his reply.

Our walk to Kenzo's truck in the parking lot is quick and quiet. But as he backs out of his spot, he asks, "So what was going on there with you and Tolman?"

"Hm? When?"

"At your locker."

"At my locker . . ." I stop and think about it. "Nothing. He told me he's going to Whistler."

"That's it?"

"Yeah. Oh, and Nisha invited us to go for shawarma. Sound good?"

Kenzo looks over at me and grins. "You're on."

"And we are *done*." I set the last batch of cranberry butter tarts on a cooling rack and take a seat at the kitchen island.

"Okay, present time!" Grinning, Harumi slides a gift bag towards me. "You first."

Since Harumi and her aunt are heading to Vancouver until the 27th, we're exchanging gifts early.

"This feels heavy." I give her a look. "You stuck to the rules, right?"

Our family doesn't do expensive presents anymore, not since I started high school. We trade small gifts, though, making it fun by setting a spending limit and choosing a different theme or challenge every year. When Harumi started talking about Christmas last month, I suggested she and I do the same.

Harumi nods. "Totally."

"Good." I remove some tissue and look inside the bag. "What . . . oh, Harumi." I take out a vintage-looking jar and turn it slowly to take in the contents.

"It's a dry snow globe," she explains. "I got the idea while unpacking a bunch of these fancy ones at the shop. You wouldn't believe how fast they sold out. Do you like it?"

"I *love* it." She's cut our figures out of a photo Kenzo took at Obon and attached them to the bottom of the jar with some moss so that it looks like we're standing in a field. Behind us, there's a backdrop of individually cut out photographed trees, and from inside the lid, she's suspended tiny origami lanterns and stars. "It's like a 3-D version of our photo."

"That's what I was going for," Harumi says. "I was so happy with how it turned out, I made one for — uh," she stammers and her face flushes. "Uhm, for my aunt, too."

She's a terrible liar. "Harumi . . . ?" I nudge.

"Okay. Don't laugh." She bites her lip and I wait. "I made one of me and Gareth, too. From a picture Tayjon took at the Halloween Dance. With fake spiders and cobwebs." She drops her head onto the counter. "I know. I'm pathetic."

"You're not."

"I am," she continues, her voice muffled. "It's just, we had so much fun that night. And you know, he's always so nice to me, remembering what I like to eat at the café, and like you said, he's SO cute. Those glasses . . . ! I just want to smudge them! And . . . nothing." She looks up, misery caked all over her face.

"Don't give up yet, Harumi." I try to keep my annoyance at Gareth out of my voice, but please . . . why is he being so *obtuse*? "It's only been a couple months —"

"It's been FIVE."

"I meant since Halloween." I prop her arms on the counter so she has to sit up. "Come on, Harumi. Don't —"

She snaps upright and I back off. "I'm calling it. It's never going to happen."

"No." I lean forward. "Don't give up yet. I still have a good feeling about you two."

"Really?" She eyeballs me. "Why?"

I open my mouth to speak, then close it abruptly, floundering. "Well, because . . ."

"See?" Harumi slumps back into her seat. "You don't have an answer."

"No, wait. I do." I grab the snow globe and hold it up. "You don't see things the way I do because you're *in* it, like this. That's you inside, and I'm out here, seeing the bigger picture

140

that you can't. And from what I've seen, Gareth likes you. He's just . . . a lot shier than I expected."

Harumi looks unconvinced.

"I mean, he got a tattoo of you on his arm."

"A fake one."

"It still meant hours sitting in a chair. You know how antsy he is. That took commitment. Isn't that worth being patient for, a little while longer?"

After a few moments, she sighs and gives me a small nod. "I guess."

"I bet he'll love the globe," I add.

"When would I give it to him? Christmas will be over."

I think fast. "How about at mochitsuki. As a New Year's present."

"I don't know, Emiko." I can see she's contemplating the idea. "Wouldn't that be weird?"

"Maybe? But memorable."

"Forget it. I'll wait for his birthday or something."

"Are you sure?"

Harumi nods, her mouth a firm line.

"Fine." I leave it for now and push a washi-wrapped box towards her. "Okay. Your turn. Merry, merry."

Harumi shimmies in her seat as she unwraps and opens the box. "No way!" she says in an excited voice. "Is this Hello Kitty?" She holds up the clay sculpture I made in art class. "It's a Hello Kitty!"

"I know she's more wabi-sabi than normal." Which, given the lack of bright colors and slightly lopsided head, is an understatement. "The first couple exploded in the kiln, so I was really relieved when this one came out intact."

"Well, she's going right onto my nightstand, so I can look at her every day," Harumi says, her good nature restored. "Thanks, Emiko."

With a rare dump of snow on the 23rd and temperatures staying below zero, it's a white coast Christmas this year.

Kenzo, the twins, and I have already had a snowball fight, made snow angels, and built a ginormous standing snow bear in the front yard. Now inside, we're warming up in front of the gas fireplace, watching vintage Rankin/Bass holiday specials.

All the adults are sporting ugly Christmas sweaters, and both twins have elf hats and ears. I'm wearing what I would call a pretty Christmas cardigan: soft pink cashmere embellished with silver stars and beading. Kenzo is wearing a creamy shawl-collared cable knit with dark jeans, and he looks quite cozy.

"I'm actively coveting that sweater, Sanada," I say. "Can I borrow it some time?"

"No way. You never give them back."

"Well, you've never asked me to."

"Okay. Please return my sweaters."

"Why? You hardly ever wear them. I give them life. Let me give that one life, too."

He shakes his head. "Don't think so. This one's a keeper." He pulls at the hem. "Besides, you'd drown in this."

"Come on." I bump him with my shoulder. We're sitting on the floor, leaning against the sofa where the twins are arguing over whether Heat Miser or Snow Miser would win in a cage fight. "I can't help it if you have excellent taste in knitwear."

"Fine. But only if I can borrow yours." He looks at me, a challenging glint in his eyes.

My jaw drops in horror. "This is *vintage*."

Kenzo shrugs the shoulders that would absolutely ruin my sweater. "It's your choice."

Crossing my arms, I try to figure a way around this ridiculous condition. "It's such a waste. You keep that sweater in storage for practically the whole year. It deserves to be seen."

"You know what you have to do."

"You're actually committing a fashion crime, holding that poor sweater hostage."

"Do you want to borrow my hat, Emiko?" Tomio asks in his quiet voice. He's still watching the show but clearly he's been listening to Kenzo and me. "I don't mind sharing."

I smile and pat his foot. "Thanks, Tomi-chan. But I think it suits you way better than it would me. It's super nice of you to offer, though." He flashes me a quick smile before returning his gaze to the TV. "At least someone in this family has some manners," I mutter as I shift to face front again.

Kenzo's mouth quirks. "What can I say? I set a good example."

"That good example, I'm sure, would be your dad." And at that moment, as if summoned, Mas walks into the living room and announces that dinner is ready.

While Mas and Abby stand at opposite ends of the laden table, Takeo, Ojiichan, Mitsuko, and Tomio take one side, and I sit between Seiji and Kenzo on the other. Once settled, we join hands and bow our heads as Abby says grace.

Then, after popping Christmas crackers and putting on paper crowns, we pass around the mouthwatering dishes before us, and fill our plates to a soundtrack of appreciative comments.

"So, is it true about Jun? That he's coming to the coast?" I ask Seiji after the first scrumptious bites. "Mitsuko mentioned he was trying again to get over here."

Seiji takes a sip of wine. "We're discussing the possibility, but nothing has been confirmed yet. And there are some . . . difficulties right now."

"Oh. That's too bad." I note the look he gives Mitsuko. "Well, I hope things work out — it feels like we've been teased with a visit from him forever."

"Yes, I'm sorry for that," Seiji says, with an apologetic nod.

"No, no, I didn't mean — I wasn't trying to —" Feeling my face warm, I stop to gather my thoughts. "I just meant . . . I'm really looking forward to finally meeting him. You know, like, seeing him here, in actual living color. That's all." As I say this, I feel a kick of excitement rush through me.

Seiji smiles. "He says he can't wait to meet you, too, Emiko." Seiji glances at everyone around the table. "We've told Jun all about Otter Creek. He's very eager to come visit."

I hear Kenzo mutter something like "Yeah, right," but when I turn to look at him, he's asking Mas to pass the gravy.

"Keep your fingers crossed, Emiko. He could be here as early as the New Year," Mitsuko says.

"That soon? Well, I'll cross my toes, too, because that would make for a most excellent start to the year," I say — extra cheerfully to compensate for Kenzo's lack of enthusiasm — and pop a Brussels sprout in my mouth.

14
Mochi, Mochi

When Ojiichan immigrated to Canada, he shipped over a container full of furniture, art, and heirlooms, including a heavy wooden usu that's been in the family for five generations. For nearly twelve whole months, this big, heavy mortar sits in storage, until it's time to bring it out for the annual mochitsuki.

Mochitsuki, when we make the rice cakes integral to a proper New Year's Day meal, will take place this year on December 28, at Otter Creek Hall. We opened this event to the community a few years ago, giving mochi-making demonstrations and sharing samples of the many ways to enjoy the pillowy, chewy, sticky cakes.

But first, the usu has to make it to the hall in one piece.

"Watch the wheels." The snow-crusted ground is proving to be a challenge, and I shout warnings more than once as Kenzo and Mas push-pull the usu on its dolly to the driveway. When a wheel gets stuck between the flagstones and the usu teeters, I shout, "It's tipping!"

"It's NOT tipping," Kenzo says, grunting as he rights the dolly.

Eventually, the usu makes it to Mas's truck and I clap my hands as Kenzo and Mas lift it into the bed. "Thank you so much," I say as I load in the mallets and the water basins. Kenzo wipes his brow. "Totally worth it for Mitsuko's ozoni."

"Grab the steaming trays, and you, sir, may have a bucketful."

"Don't think he won't, Emiko," Mas says. "You should see how much this boy eats these days. In fact . . ." Mas pauses, "you *could* say he's 'Hungry Like The Wolf.'"

As Mas waits for my reaction, Kenzo groans. "Dad. Come *on*."

I stifle a giggle and pretend to give Kenzo the once-over. "You know, I knew there was 'Something About You,'" I say slowly, and without skipping a beat Mas and I raise our hands and give each other a solid high-five.

Kenzo shakes his head. "I am *so* earning my mochi this year. I'm embarrassed for you both," he tells us, and escapes back to the storage room.

The next morning, we're at the hall by eight. The public event doesn't start until three, but we're going to need all that time because there is a lot of mochi to make.

Mitsuko, Mrs. Yoshimatsu, and a couple of ladies are already in the kitchen steaming presoaked sweet rice in wooden box steamers. The usu is set up on a tarp in the middle of the main hall, ready for the first batch of fresh, hot rice.

Ojiichan and Mas take the first shift; they've been doing this for years and have their rhythm down to the split second. As soon as Mitsuko drops the cooked rice into the usu, Mas brings the kine down like Thor, while on the upswing Ojiichan darts in to sprinkle the rice with water, or give it a knead, or lift and turn it to keep it from sticking to the bowl.

POUND, sprinkle — POUND, knead — POUND, turn — each move is punctuated by Mas or Ojiichan counting out loud "ichi," "ni," "san," "shi" on repeat. It's hypnotic and knuckle-biting at the same time, because one wrong move and Mas could smash the mallet onto Ojiichan's hands.

When the rice is a sticky, smooth mass, Ojiichan gathers it up and drops it onto the plastic-wrapped table that's been powdered with potato starch.

Next comes the team of obasans — women I've known since I was little — who take over and get busy tearing off balls of hot dough with their Teflon hands and rolling them quickly in the starch to make small, flattened, circular cakes that are as soft as a baby's cheek. Once cooled, the mochi cakes will be bagged, ready for distribution.

I'm getting in on the action too, but first, I check to see if Harumi has texted. Like me, Harumi is a serious mochi addict, and she was supposed to be here by now. Plus, as promised, Gareth's coming later. But there's no sign of her. With no missed messages, I fire off a quick "Are you okay? Where are you?" before washing my hands and joining the fun.

By noon, I still haven't heard from Harumi, and it's time to enjoy the fruits of everyone's labors. I like my mochi savory, Isobeyaki style, with straight soy sauce and a nori wrapper. I take my plate over to join Kenzo and the twins at a table. They've gone the sweet route, and they're rolling theirs in kinako powder and sugar.

Later, we'll have to toast the mochi to soften it before it's eaten in any form, but today, we get to enjoy it fresh. Dipped in soy sauce, mine is soft and chewy and salty, with the nori adding a touch of crispness. "Sooo good," I say, inhaling the first of many.

Once everyone's eaten, we tidy up and resume making more batches, because the public mochitsuki always takes longer and we want to have enough ready for people to sample.

Hearing a bleep, I check my phone again, happy to finally see a text, just as Gareth walks through the back doors and makes his way towards me.

"Hi-de-ho, Emiko." He's all chipper until he notices my frown. "What's wrong?"

"It's Harumi. She had to have emergency dental surgery this morning. Wisdom teeth. She's just waking up now and she feels like death, so she's not coming."

"Oh well. That's too bad. Guess that means more mochi for us," he says, his tone perky. He correctly reads my expression, though, because he quickly drops his smile. "But, we should, uh, you know, save some for her, for later."

"Mm-hm."

Thankfully, Mitsuko comes over just then and asks Gareth to help set up more tables. I stare after him, not sure how to take his lack of disappointment and concern for Harumi.

Maybe, I tell myself, it's a personality quirk, and he's one of those people who laugh inappropriately whenever they hear bad news.

Fortunately, Ojiichan and I are on greeter duty, so once the doors open I'm too busy to stew about Gareth. Which is good, because until then it felt like every time I turned around Gareth was right there, getting in my way.

Besides the Creekers and Coasters eager to experience the joy of mochi, friends from school show up, too, including Tayjon and his new girlfriend, Skye, followed by the Triple As, and Jacob and Darcy. Liv Soo and Jeremy come with their families, and even some teachers and Mx. Galloway stop by. I can't chat with anyone for long, though, because the lineup is steady.

Eventually, the flow of guests slows to a trickle, so Ojiichan goes back to mochi-making while I handle the door on my own. Then, just when I think I can leave the entranceway, I feel a tap on my shoulder.

"Emiko-san! I was hoping to see you! I wanted to tell you how much I enjoyed your butter tarts. With cranberries!" Taka-san shakes her head in disbelief. "Such a refreshing twist! I was so happy when your ojiichan stopped by to deliver them. I intended to save some for New Year's but they were too tempting!"

"I'm glad you liked them," I say.

"Yes, they were such a treat. And also, I wanted to share some wonderful news. Chisato's coming to Otter Creek!"

I'm saved from having to respond because walking in behind Taka-san are Will and Arlo and two people I assume are their parents.

"Isn't that exciting?" Taka-san continues. "I was surprised when she asked if she could stay with me, but of course I said yes. It's been so long since her last visit. You remember, of course."

"That's great," I say, only half listening.

Taka-san finally notices we're not alone, and she turns and smiles at the Rivers family before thanking me again for the baking. "Now, I will go find your aunt and ojiichan, to let them know about Chisato as well."

As she leaves, I turn to Will and his family. "Hi. Welcome to our mochitsuki."

"Uhm, thanks," Will says. "Harumi told us about this. We've never tried mochi, so she said we should come." As I process this nugget of info, he continues, "So yeah, this is my sister, and my mom and dad."

Arlo lets out an easy laugh. "Oh my god, Will. We all go to the same school. Emiko and I have met." Arlo grins, holding up her left hand. "Although we haven't spoken since I got my cast off."

"I guess we haven't," I agree, as I admire her chunky scarf.

"So, is Harumi inside?" Arlo asks before I can compliment her on it. "She said she'd be our guide. I'm really looking forward to having a shot with that wooden hammer."

I smile. "It's called a kine, actually. And unfortunately, she couldn't make it."

"Oh, nuts." Will's shoulders sag in obvious disappointment, and I can't help but compare his reaction to this news to Gareth's.

"Yeah, I know. But don't worry. Go see my grandfather," I say, pointing him out to Arlo. "Tell him I sent you. He'll make sure you get a chance to try."

As his parents and sister head into the hall, Will hangs back. I suspect he's going to ask about Harumi, but instead, he says, "This is really cool. Your family always does nice stuff. Thanks." Then, he gives me one of his quick, shy smiles before joining Arlo and his parents.

I stand there, surprised, watching him walk away. I have to admit, given another year or two, and with a complete makeover — Will Rivers has some real potential. And he really is sweet.

It's almost eight by the time Gareth and I are ready to leave the hall and take what needs returning to the café. But first, I need something to eat.

In the kitchen, Mitsuko is still loading the dishwasher, so I try Mrs. Yoshimatsu, who has finished sweeping the floor and is — like my aunt — usually a reliable source for snacks.

"Please tell me there's a leftover Isobeyaki mochi in here somewhere. Even a plain one will do."

"Oh, Emiko-chan," Mrs. Yoshimatsu says. "Everything's packed up already. I have some kakipi in my purse, though, if you like?"

As much as I enjoy the spicy peanut mix, I shake my head. "Thanks, Mrs. Y. I'll wait till I get home. I need *food*-food."

Kenzo pokes his head through the pass-through. "We're heading out soon, Mitsuko. Do you need any more help before we go?"

She shakes her head as she turns on the dishwasher. "Thanks, Kenzo. We're nearly done here."

I walk Kenzo to the truck to say good night to Mas and to tell Ojiichan, who's catching a ride with them, that I won't be much longer.

Kenzo nods towards Gareth, who's packing the last of the boxes into his mother's sedan. "You going to be okay with him?"

"Of course. He's fine." I wish I could tell Kenzo how much I'm bothered by Gareth's apparent lack of concern for Harumi today. But, remembering our disagreement about them at Halloween, I decide to hold off, in case I'm simply misreading Gareth, and *not* just because it might prove Kenzo right. "We're not going to be long," I add, stamping my feet to warm them up.

"Sorry, Em. Go inside. I'll see you soon."

Too chilled to speak, I give a final wave and hurry in behind Gareth, back into the kitchen where he gets the café keys from Mitsuko.

"We have a couple more things to do," Mitsuko tells us. "If you finish before we get there, just put the keys in my desk and leave the back door unlocked."

"We're just dropping off, right?" I'm happy to return to the café tomorrow to help properly unpack, but tonight, I want to get home and eat something filling as soon as possible. I curse myself for not mochi-loading earlier.

"Yes, don't worry about anything else."

"Sounds good, Mitsuko," Gareth says. "Oyasuminasai."

I hop into the passenger seat and buckle up, shivering as Gareth starts the ignition. The day was so much busier than we expected and he and I haven't talked much, except in passing. It makes me think I should give him a chance at a do-over, to confirm that I'm just overreacting to his *under-reacting* to Harumi's news. Because maybe, when it comes to his feelings, he's more of a silent, stoic kind of guy than I realized. Which would explain a lot.

Blowing into my cupped gloved hands, I consider everything that's happened till now from this new angle as Gareth drives us slowly down the road to the café.

15
Realizations

After unloading everything at Mitsuko's, Gareth asks if he can make a quick stop before taking me home. I don't really want to because I'm tired and cold and so hungry it sounds like the Tasmanian Devil's hiding under my coat. But given the no-time-for-chitchat vibe inside the café — Gareth seemed preoccupied with getting the car unpacked as quickly as possible — this might be my opportunity to mention Harumi again.

So I shrug. "Sure, why not."

Grinning, instead of turning right at the stop sign, he drives through the intersection and down the road till he's parked facing the ocean at the Otter Creek Pier. It's a cloudless night, so cold everything is frosted with sugar, and the moon looks like a half-eaten cookie.

"It's just for a few minutes." He turns off the engine and unclips his seatbelt before turning towards me. "I thought it'd be nice to sit and talk. You know, decompress."

I give a grudging nod and then we sit there in silence,

except for the several times Gareth clears his throat. I turn my head to look over towards my house; through the bamboo fencing, I can make out the kitchen lights, and there's enough beach exposed that, if I wanted to, I could get out of the car, cross the public footbridge over the creek, and be home in minutes.

Facing forward again, I sigh. I'm not sure what Gareth wants to talk about, but as the seconds drag on, I decide I might as well take control of the situation and bring Operation Redemption into play.

"Wasn't it too bad Harumi couldn't make it today?"

"Mm-hm. Mm-hm. Yeah. Hopefully she feels better soon."

It's a pretty generic response, so I try again.

"I bet she'd feel a lot better if you took her over some mochi tomorrow."

"Emiko, look at that moon. Doesn't it make you feel, like, such awe?" He leans forward so he can stare at it through the windshield and exhales loudly. "It makes you think, too, doesn't it?"

My eyebrows rise in disbelief. Not only did he brush Harumi off again, but he also completely ignored my suggestion. Now I'm just too hungry to deal, so I give up. I tell myself I can regroup tomorrow, and I start thinking about our take-out dinner from Perogy Hut last night. Hopefully, there'll still be some sour cabbage rolls left by the time I get home.

". . . and New Year's, well, it's a time to look back and ask yourself, did you meet your goals? And what are your dreams for the future . . . ?"

As Gareth goes on, my stomach actually starts to hurt, and the temperature is so low I can see my breath. I cup my hands together and blow into them again to try and warm them before I turn to ask him to take me home. That's when I realize he's stopped talking and is staring at me.

"Sorry, what?"

Gareth gives me a crooked smile. "I just wondered if you felt the same."

I have no idea what he said other than something about goals; it seems a safe enough subject, so I answer, "Yeah, I guess."

He pushes up his glasses. "I knew it," he says, like he's won a bet.

Then — have you ever seen that clip about this Australian octopus that hunts prey OUT of the water? I saw it on BBC Earth, and it was one of the most intense scenes I've ever witnessed. The octopus uses its suckers to pull itself in and out of tide pools, and you see this crab scuttling across the rocks, minding its own business, probably wondering where its next krill is coming from, when suddenly, the octopus *hurls* itself out of this tiny pool and — WHAM! — lands on the unsuspecting crab.

I am the crab.

Gareth launches himself at me and I react instantly, crisscrossing my arms in front of me like Wonder Woman.

"Oh my GOD, Gareth!" I yell, pushing back as hard as I can. "Get OFF me!" Thankfully, his mouth doesn't come close to landing anywhere, and the volume of my voice makes him freeze. "What are you DOING?" I glare at him as he flops back into his seat.

He rakes his hand through hair so full of product it springs back into place. He takes a couple of deep breaths but doesn't look at me. Even in shadow, I can tell his face is red.

"Seriously, what is wrong with you?" My voice is still very loud.

"What's wrong with *me*?" He's not quiet either. "What's wrong with *you*?"

"Excuse me?"

"You've been flirting with me for months!"

"I *what*?" My eyes widen.

"Yeah, you," he says, finally turning to look at me.

I have no words, but my mouth opens and closes like a guppy's as I try to process what he's saying. "Why would I flirt with you? You like Harumi," I manage eventually. "You like Harumi," I repeat, like it's a statement of fact.

Gareth glowers at the windshield.

"You got a fake tattoo . . . of her kokeshi doll."

"That *you* made. I was being supportive! Even though it was, hands down, the dumbest piece of woodworking I've ever seen." He shakes his head like he can't believe what he did.

"But, you were so nice to her." I must look as stunned as I feel, because Gareth eyes me and I can see him trying to calm down.

"Come on, Emiko," he says, his voice thawing. "*Of course* I'm going to be nice to Harumi. She's your friend. And I know some girls need their friends to sign off on guys before they'll go out with them."

My brain short-circuits as I flashback to all the times I've seen Gareth and Harumi together since the summer. Nothing is making sense right now.

When I don't respond, he huffs and crosses his arms. "And why would you think I'd even go out with someone like Harumi?"

My face flushes. "What is *that* supposed to mean?"

"Can you *seriously* see me with her? She's not exactly on the university track, is she? And she dresses like a cartoon!"

"Oh my god." I groan and slump into my seat, palming my face as I realize just how wrong I've been, and how much Kenzo wasn't. I feel like I'm trapped in a blizzard, blind to my own hand in front of me.

Without another word, I get out of the car. I'm tempted to slam the door, but I don't want to risk the sound carrying to our house, so I leave it wide open and trek home across the beach. Thankfully, the moon is bright enough to light my way, but honestly, I could probably walk this beach with my eyes closed, I know it so well.

Behind me, I hear Gareth swear, and I glance back to see him jump out of the car and slip, nearly falling, before he runs around to shut the passenger door. Then he gets back into the driver's seat, turns on the ignition, and races out of the parking lot, skidding on the icy surface as he goes.

My grandfather is still up, reading at the kitchen island, when I come in through the sliding doors. He looks at me over his glasses, a questioning look in his eyes.

"Boys suck. Good night, Ojiichan."

"Good night, Emiko," he says.

I give him a hug before I head upstairs.

I don't even turn on the lights. I just walk over and drop, face down, onto my bed. I'm not even hungry anymore, and I'm too angry to cry, but my face feels hot and there's pressure building under my eyes from tears waiting to fall at any second.

I cannot *believe* Gareth. I replay everything he said to me, tell myself he's wrong, as I think back to all the times I spoke to him about Harumi.

Harumi.

My stomach twists as her face looms before me like a friendly ghost. I groan into my duvet cover as I realize I have to explain all of this to her, and soon. As much as I'd like to forget about the whole mess, I can't let her go on thinking Gareth likes her. Especially not after he basically said she wasn't good enough for him.

Idiot.

I flop over, starfish out, and stare at the ceiling. Some matchmaking genius I'm turning out to be.

✳ ✳ ✳

The next day the roads are clear, so after lunch, once I've checked that she's up for a visit, I bike over to Harumi's.

"Emiko!" she says when I enter the living room. Only, because she's trying to talk without moving her jaw, it sounds more like "Enny ho!" She clicks the TV off and sits up on the couch against a mound of pillows, a colorful striped quilt tucked around her. "Ow arr yoo? Ow as . . ." then she mimes what I take is her idea of pounding mochi.

I sit in a chair near her and smile as normally as I can. "It was great. I brought you a bag. Maybe your aunt can make you some plain soup or something to eat it with."

Harumi, giving chipmunk with her swollen cheeks, had

159

texted that she was on a soft-food diet, and she nods enthusiastically, adding two thumbs up.

Stalling, I look around the room. There are still some Christmas decorations up and I can see a half-finished puzzle on the dining room table. Her Aunt Satomi sounds like she's in the kitchen, talking on her phone.

"Erryhin ohay?" She must sense something's up because she sits forward and hugs a Hello Kitty plushie to her chest.

"Enny ho?" she prompts when I don't respond.

I take a deep breath. "I have to tell you something."

I feel like I'm about to take that first swim of the year, when you have to choose between plunging into the cold water and getting it over with, or easing in slowly, step by step, till you feel comfortable enough to dunk in over your head. I decide to plunge.

"Gareth Tolman is a colossal jerk."

Harumi's brows knit in startled confusion. Clearly, more details are required, so I swallow before continuing. "We . . . he . . . was supposed to drive me home after the mochitsuki, but he wanted to go to the pier first. So I said okay, and while we were there, he . . ." I let my voice trail off, hoping she'll figure out the rest.

She looks at me like I've asked her to solve a physics problem.

"He talked . . . And basically, he made it clear that he's not in love. With you." I watch for her reaction, and at first there's nothing. Then her lower lip starts to tremble and her eyes well up and a very soft "Oh" comes out of her mouth, so soft I could've imagined it.

"Oh," she says, louder this time. "I she." She hiccups and holds her breath, and for a brief moment, I think maybe this isn't such a big deal and she's going to be okay. But as soon as that thought crosses my mind, the tears spill over, and then she's crying and it's awful.

"I'm sorry, Harumi." I hand her a tissue box from the coffee table. "This is all my fault."

"Whah?" She looks up at me, her confusion obvious. "Whah ahr you hawkin' awout?" It clearly hurts her to talk, so I point to her phone. Nodding, she picks it up and her thumbs fly across the screen.

HARUMI: Why your fault? You didn't do anything. Of course he'd like you more than me. Look at you. Look at me. Why would anyone like me?

As I read her text, she starts crying harder, and I sit there feeling helpless as she starts tapping again.

HARUMI: What was I thinking? Gareth so outta my league I knew it . . .

She stops to blow her nose.

"Oh, no, don't even start," I say. "Gareth is a shallow, arrogant, Grade-A status hound. I'm so sorry. I wish I'd seen it earlier. But you know he has to be dumber than a sponge because you are amazing, and he would have been the luckiest guy in the world if he had seen that. That's the truth."

She hiccups as she grabs another tissue.

I lean forward and wait till she looks at me. "That's the truth, Harumi. Okay?"

She nods, sniffling, and picks up her phone again.

HARUMI: Thanks. Better this way. To find out now. Glad I didn't give him snow globe.

She manages a trembly smile before leaning back into her pillows and staring at the crumpled tissues in her hand.

"You need to rest. I should go," I say after a few moments.

Shaking her head, she makes a sit-down motion.

I stand and pick up my backpack. "There's some daifuku mochi Mitsuko made as well. If I cut it into tiny pieces, do you think you can manage some, maybe with some tea?"

Harumi nods, smiling till she winces. She cups her hands over her puffy cheeks and nods again as she struggles to get up. "Yesh hease."

"No, stay. I'll make it," I say before I walk to the kitchen. "And we can finish that puzzle, if you want."

Every January 1, we host an open house where people can come to enjoy some osechi-ryori and help us welcome in an auspicious new year.

Mitsuko is in charge of the food, of course, and while the café is closed for the holidays, for the next two days, she — along with Mrs. Yoshimatsu and the team of obasans who helped at the mochitsuki — will be there making the traditional foods that symbolize everything from abundance to a zest for knowledge.

The star on the menu for me, though, is the ozoni, the soup that's served with grilled mochi. Mitsuko's version brims with chicken and vegetables, including daikon and carrots and spinach, and it's not New Year's without it. When I walk through the back door of the café, it's clear from the umami-rich smells and the variety of cooked food everywhere that Mitsuko, Mrs. Y., and the obasans have already been hard at work for hours.

"Konnichiwa," I say, prompting a chorus of greetings in return. I grab an apron from the shelf and, like most of the women here, wrap a cotton tenugui around my head to keep my hair back. "So, what can I do?" I ask Mitsuko, sneaking a peek at the simmering pot of soup before taking a pair of chopsticks to sample some spicy lotus root.

"How is it?" she asks.

Mouth full, I give her a thumbs-up. Mrs. Yoshimatsu's been cooking for us forever, and Ojiichan and I continue to eat well under her care, but I still miss the flavor of my aunt's food. Weekly dinners with Mitsuko and Seiji at their home help, but sometimes it's not enough.

Mitsuko smiles before gesturing to all the various dishes on the counters. "You can help fill the jubako," she says. "Take the kuromame."

With a small spoon and the pot of sweetened black soybeans in hand, I look for a gap in the assembly line going around the island. Now that everything's been made, it's time to divvy up the food into the fancy stacking bento boxes. I step in beside Mrs. Watanabe, remembering too late that she's a bit of a gossip.

Right away, she leans over and, in a low voice, says, "My granddaughter, Nicki, saw you and Kenzo at the hall the other day. She asked if you two were finally dating . . . ?"

She gives me a sidelong look as she doles out rolls of fluffy omelette.

"What?" I fumble my spoon, barely managing to catch it before it lands on the floor. "No. No, no, we're just friends," I say, wishing Mitsuko had given me something less spilly to work with.

"That's what I told her, but she wanted to know for sure."

"Yeah, no. Definitely just friends."

Mrs. Watanabe nods. "Nicki will be very pleased to hear that. Kenzo's always been so sweet to her, you know. Maybe I'll bring her by the open house, then, if she's not already busy."

"Of course," I answer automatically as I scoop more soybeans. It's totally not weird that Nicki might be at my house, for the first time in years, to see Kenzo.

Suddenly, Mrs. Watanabe makes a loud *tsk*-ing sound, her attention shifted from me. "Okabe-san! You're overfilling again."

While Mitsuko mediates the situation, I continue with my task, keeping my head down as I try to figure out why I'm so unsettled by Mrs. Watanabe's questioning. It's not a secret. I mean, we *are* just friends, Kenzo and I.

Normally, I love spending time with Mitsuko in the kitchen. It's always been our thing, ever since I was old enough to stand. Learning from my aunt, enjoying the results of our labors, or commiserating over a culinary disaster — the bulk of my favorite childhood memories are made up of those moments.

Right now, though, this particular kitchen is suddenly the last place I want to be. I just want to go home.

But I can't. There's too much to do and I can't let Mitsuko down. Sighing, I empty my last spoonful and put the dirty pot in the sink. Then, I take a deep breath and turn around to face the room.

"I'm done," I say, as breezily as I can. "What's next?"

16
New Year's Day

"Happy New Year, Ojiichan."

"Akemashite omedetou gozaimasu, Emiko-chan," Ojiichan says in return.

"What's it like out there?" I ask, noting the tree branches swaying outside the kitchen window.

"Much more hospitable than last year."

I turn and give him a smile. "I'll go get changed."

Rain or shine, one of our family customs is to head to the beach to do our version of an annual cleanse. We invited Mitsuko and Seiji to join us, of course, but Seiji likes to start the year with a hike along Otter Creek up to the falls, so it's just the two of us today.

Last year it was stormy, and icy rain lashed our faces red. This year it's dry, so things are already off to a better start, but it's still blustery, and the waves crashing on the shore are dark and foamy.

In a few hours, there will be a crowd of spectators cheering on die-hard Polar Bear swimmers down by the pier, but right now, it's Ojiichan and me for as far as the eye can see. We pick out a big heavy log and climb up.

"Akemashite omedetou gozaimasu!" I shout into the wind, my hair whipping around my head. "Happy New Year!"

Ojiichan does the same and, grinning, we stretch and twist and bend to get the blood flowing, breathing in the bracing salty air that flows nonstop off the Salish Sea. It's beyond invigorating as I imagine every cell in my body sloughing off the old year and emerging shiny and new.

When Ojiichan suggests it's time to move on to the next part of our ritual, we jump down and start searching for the first wishing stone that catches our eye. Before long, I spy an egg-ish blue one ringed in white, while Ojiichan shows me his pick, a flat greenie with a thin vein of quartz running through the middle.

As we move closer to the shoreline, I scan the horizon. It always amazes me how different it can look, how it changes depending on so many variables. Like, there are times when Vancouver Island is so clear, you'd swear it was close enough to paddle to; other times, you wouldn't even know it existed. Today, the Island is a graded wash in the distance, more suggestive than real.

"Emiko, shall we sit for a moment?"

I look at Ojiichan, surprised by his question. Normally, this is where we'd be making our wishes, but I nod and we settle ourselves on the nearest log. I keep my eyes on the water, searching, but against all the different grays and the choppy water it's impossible to tell a whale blow from a whitecap.

"Is everything alright?" I ask when he remains quiet.

"Very alright. I just wished to enjoy this time with you a little longer. I hope you do not mind."

"Oh, no, of course not." And it's true, I don't, but I'd be lying if I didn't admit to feeling a bit discombobulated by this change in our program. I play with the woven elastic on my wrist, letting my windblown hair hide my face. "I wish Mitsuko could be here, too," I say after a few moments.

"Yes." Ojiichan nods slowly. "Yes. Today and other days, I wish that as well. But I am also happy she is not, for what a year she has had. What a year we have *all* had."

I hold my hair back so I can get a good look at him, but he's shading his eyes, squinting off into the distance. "I guess," I say, but hearing how ungrateful that sounds, given how much I have to be thankful for, I add, more emphatically, "No, you're right."

"It is all very exciting. And what a year we have to look forward to." We sit there for a few more minutes, not speaking, until he pats me briskly on the knee. "Now then," he says, getting to his feet. "Shall we make our wishes?"

I think about what he's said, and what I think he's trying to say, as I follow him to the water's edge. We stand with our eyes closed, and I know I'm supposed to make my heart's wish, but my heart can't decide what to focus on. So, instead, I stick to the same old same old and ask whoever's listening for some really obvious signs to help with all the decisions that are coming my way as relentlessly as a tidal wave.

Then, when I feel ready, I open my eyes, glance over at Ojiichan, who's there patiently waiting for me, and together we cast our stones into the sea. I usually feel exhilarated when I do this, relishing the sensation of throwing something as hard as I can, but this year, there's a swirl of nerves in the mix. After a few more cleansing breaths, though, Ojiichan and I exchange smiles and head back home.

The open house is not going well.

Correction: Ojiichan's in the living room with a mixed group of our friends, laughing and exchanging stories, while in the kitchen, Abby, Mas, Mitsuko, Seiji, and a bunch of other adults are mixing up cocktails using some fancy liquor Seiji brought back from his latest business trip.

People are eating, almost everywhere I look a good time is being had, and I think I've hit the sweet spot between comfy and chic in my black and white houndstooth shift dress. I should be happy.

Except I'm not. *So* not.

First, Harumi. Her cheeks are back to normal, and even though she told me she was looking forward to the party, I keep catching her getting teary-eyed over Gareth. The house is like a minefield of reminders, and, unfortunately, I can't remember where they're all buried.

It started with the kitchen chairs. "I keep picturing him sitting there, asking me to go to the movies with him in French . . ."

Then, the platter of Mitsuko's to-die-for yakisoba: "Extra ginger . . . !"

Even the mochi isn't safe: "He helped make this, didn't he?"

I do what I can, in between hosting duties, to cheer Harumi up, but nothing's working. Thankfully, the twins talk her into playing Bouzu Mekuri with them, and that seems to keep her distracted.

Then, there's Nicki, Mrs. Watanabe's granddaughter. When she showed up, all glitz and glam, in full hair and makeup and a feather-trimmed sequin dress, Kenzo was talking to some of his hockey teammates by the kitchen island. Nicki left her grandmother with Mitsuko and homed right in on him, giving him a big hug, all "Hey, Kenzo" and "It's been too long" and "When are you coming to Vancouver again?" in her drawly voice.

"Who's that?" Liv Soo asks as she peruses the vegetarian sushi.

I turn my attention back to the dining table. "Just a girl we've known since elementary," I say, rearranging some food.

"Huh. Need me and the squad to run some interference?" Liv jerks her thumb towards the cheerleaders trying to teach Ojiichan and a couple of his friends some moves.

"Nice touchdown, Mr. Fuji!" I hear Jeremy yell.

"What for?"

"*What for?*" Liv glares sideways at Nicki, who is now running her vividly manicured hand along Kenzo's arm like he's been upholstered. "*That.*"

I shake my head and force a laugh. "Oh, no. There's nothing going on there. She's an old friend."

Just then, I see Kenzo turn from Nicki and look towards the entrance; whoever he sees there makes his face light up, and after a brief word with Nicki, he starts walking towards the new arrival.

"Sorry, Liv. I've got to go." I give her a quick smile and wind my way through the crowd, stalling when I see not only Taka-san standing there, but her niece, Chisato Ishi, too. I vaguely recall Taka-san saying something to me — when was that? — about her visiting the Creek, but I'd assumed she meant later in the year, like during Spring Break, or the summer.

"Chisato!" Kenzo greets her as he bends down to give her a hug. "I didn't think you'd make it tonight."

"Hi, Kenzo." She has this husky voice which always surprises me, because she's a tiny thing. The pixie cut is new, but she's still favoring her year-round wardrobe of gloom.

I step forward, putting on my best hostess face. "Hi, Taka-san. Chisato. Happy New Year. Can I take your things?"

After putting their coats and bags away and thanking Taka-san for the box of senbei, I lead them to the living room, where Ojiichan stops to welcome them before waving Taka-san over to join him.

"When did you get in?" Kenzo asks as the three of us continue to the kitchen.

"Yesterday morning." Chisato bobs her head in greeting as most of the older guests recognize and call out to her. From working at the library, her aunt probably knows more people than Ojiichan. Also, Chisato is always quiet and well-behaved and studious, so, naturally, adults love her.

"How's the jet lag?" Kenzo stops by the dining table. "You hungry? Thirsty?"

Chisato shrugs. "It's okay, except I feel like I'm having a minor out-of-body experience." She gives Kenzo a smile that fades a little as she takes in the bounty before her. "Wow. This looks . . . extravagant," she says, which feels like a criticism.

I push a plate into her hands. "Well, it's a party." Chisato's pale face flushes. "It's just, I'm vegan. This is all so fancy, it's a little hard to tell what I can eat." I feel my own cheeks warm. "Oh. Of course." Fortunately, I see a half dozen options for her and point them out. "And we have some sweets that are vegan," I tell her, by way of apology.

After Chisato picks up a few bites, we take her over to where Harumi and the twins are still playing cards.

"Harumi," I say as she stands for the introduction. "This is Chisato Ishi. She's visiting from Tokyo. You know her aunt, Taka-san, from the library?"

To Chisato, I say, "This is Harumi Natsugawa, originally from Osaka. Her aunt, Satomi-san, works at our school. And you remember Takeo and Tomio?"

Chisato nods, looking at the boys. "I do, but you guys probably don't remember me. You must be around ten now?"

"Almost," Takeo says proudly. As the twins go back to counting their cards, Harumi and Chisato murmur *nice-to-meet-you*s as they bow their heads slightly.

"How long are you staying?" Harumi asks as she sits back down.

Chisato shifts on her feet. "Uhm, for a while."

"Really?" I look at her. "What's 'a while'?"

"I transferred to Cedar Grove. I'm going to finish high school here."

"That's great, Chisato," Kenzo says.

Harumi brightens up. "Oh, another new person! I just finished my first semester. It's a really good school. Everyone's super nice. Where did you go before this?"

As Chisato tells Harumi about the international school she went to, my mind fills with questions. Why is she here now, with one semester left before graduating? I think how hard it must have been for Harumi, even Gareth, to uproot themselves and start over at a new school in their grades.

I can't imagine what it would be like to change schools halfway through my final year, let alone move to another country to do so.

While Kenzo and Harumi continue chatting with Chisato, feeling restless, I get up. Harumi is busy telling Chisato about her wisdom teeth, so she doesn't notice, but Kenzo sees me and gives me a questioning look.

"Bathroom," I mouth.

Kenzo nods and rejoins the conversation.

I head down the hallway, but instead of going into the powder room, I keep walking until I come to my grandfather's study. I knock to make sure it's empty, then go in, closing the door so I can lean back against it.

Ojiichan's study is the most serene space in the house. It's an actual tatami room, complete with a tokonoma where Ojiichan displays a rotation of heirloom scrolls and fresh flower arrangements. We were here earlier in the day, paying our respects at the family shrine, and I can still smell a hint of incense in the air.

Ojiichan's immaculate desk sits below the shoji screen window, and opposite that is a wall of bookshelves which, along with books, is full of DVDs, CDs, vinyl, and photo albums. There's a closet concealed by sliding doors, and in the middle of the room is a low table surrounded by zaisu chairs.

I'm about to sit at the table but, at the last second, I undo my ponytail and slide down flat onto the floor instead, fanning my hair out around me. Tatami is naturally warm when it's cool, and cool when it's warm, so I'm very comfortable as I close my eyes and breathe in its faint grassy scent. I run my hands across the smooth woven surface and suddenly I'm five again, moving my limbs as if I'm making a snow angel. It's all very calming, so I stay there until I hear a faint knock on the door.

My eyes pop open. "Yes?" I say as I scurry to stand up.

The door opens and Kenzo peers around the edge. "There you are. You alright?"

I nod, smoothing my hair. "How'd you know I was in here?"

"I didn't. After I found the bathroom empty, I checked the garage and worked my way back." He swings the door wide and steps in. "This room hasn't changed."

"I know."

"So why are you hiding?"

"Wanted a breather, that's all. It's been a busy day."

Kenzo walks over to the bookshelf and tilts his head to read the titles on the DVDs. "I might have to borrow some of these."

"I'm sure Ojiichan would be happy to let you."

"Yeah." He runs his finger across the spines, then turns to look at me. "So. Feel ready to go back out there?"

"Mm."

"What?"

I hesitate, but he's known Chisato as long as I have, and there's no one else I can ask.

"Don't you think it's weird about Chisato? I mean, who transfers in the middle of senior year?"

Kenzo shrugs. "I'm sure she has her reasons."

"Yes, but what are those reasons?" I look at Kenzo. "Seriously, they'd have to be really significant."

"Why don't you ask her, then?"

"Because I doubt she'd tell me," I admit.

"Then it's really none of our business."

A part of me agrees, but when I don't acknowledge him right away, Kenzo folds his arms across his chest. "I don't think I realized until now how much of a busy-body you are."

"I am NOT."

"I think you are."

I flick my hand in his direction. "Whatever."

"Harumi and Gareth would probably agree with me."

I freeze. There's no way he knows about Gareth and how badly I misread things. I wasn't planning to tell Kenzo, because who wants to hear "I told you so"? But I realize that, as soon as school starts, he's going to figure it out. It's best, I decide, to get ahead of the story.

"Uhm, yeah. About that."

Kenzo looks at me.

"It turns out that you may have been right. About Gareth."

"May have," he repeats.

"May have. Definitely. Been right."

"Huh. And you know this now because . . . ?"

"Let's just say . . . I have no doubt that Gareth's, uhm,

feelings . . . are directed elsewhere." I lift my eyes to Kenzo's and can see he's thinking about this.

"What happened when you found out where his feelings were directed?"

"I made sure that they were deflected. Very sure."

"And you're okay?"

I give him a reassuring smile. "Totally."

He gives me such a searching look in return that I almost blush. But just when I'm about to pull a Montgomery and close my eyes like that old pup, he smiles back.

"So, I was right," he says, and I almost pull a muscle in my eye, they roll so hard. "I think I need a minute here, Em."

"Gaah." I shake my head. "Let's go."

As we walk back to the party, Kenzo stage-whispers behind me as he closes Ojiichan's door, "I was right."

"Shut it, Sanada." Smugness — *so* unattractive.

In response, Kenzo pokes me in the back three times and I can tell he's mouthing each word as he does.

"I know what you're doing!" I say, and his laughter follows me into the living room, where it appears most of the adults have migrated as another annual tradition, a popular Japanese singing competition show, plays on the flat screen.

In the kitchen, I wish Happy New Year to more friends who've arrived, and see Nicki now deep in conversation with the hockey team captain, Dev Chowdhury. Chisato is still sitting with Harumi, along with Mitsuko, who stands as I approach.

"Well, we're all looking forward to seeing you around the Creek, Chisato," Mitsuko says. "Aren't we, Emiko?" she adds.

"Of course." I turn to Harumi. "Do you have a sec? I have

some mochi ice cream to bring out," I explain to my aunt before we walk away.

While I pull out boxes of the dessert from the freezer, Harumi grabs a serving dish and tilts her head towards Chisato. "She seems nice. Quiet, but nice."

"Sure." I watch Ojiichan join Mitsuko and Chisato and wonder what my grandfather thinks of his friend's niece, given that she's not much fun to talk to. I mean, unless you're big into soliloquies.

"She can't eat these, can she?" Harumi says as she plates the mochi ice cream. "Too bad. I'll eat her share. Don't judge!" Trailed by the twins, she leaves to deliver the dessert to the now crowded table.

The fact that Harumi finally appears to be having fun tonight should make me happy. But as I stand there, breaking down the packages for recycling, I can't pretend that Chisato Ishi's presence — now a long-term one, at that — doesn't ruffle me.

When we were younger and she visited, Taka-san, Mitsuko, and Ojiichan were always setting us up on playdates that were more awkward than fun. And my aunt was always reminding me to be kind. "She hasn't been as fortunate as you," she'd say.

I've never understood what my aunt meant by this. Yes, it's a sad coincidence that we were both orphaned at a young age; that doesn't automatically make us BFF material, though. And Taka-san always bragging about another accomplishment or a new award Chisato's racked up doesn't make me think she's being kept in a dungeon. But my aunt's words are a constant echo in my head whenever I hear her name.

So, over the years, I've tried. Like, I'm trying now. I just never get the sense that she appreciates my efforts. Eons ago, Meeta described Chisato as an iceberg, because she keeps so much hidden below the surface. I think Meeta meant it as a compliment, but to me, icebergs are something to steer clear of.

Unfortunately, now that she's living in the Creek, and going to my school, and generally being embraced by everyone like some kind of returning heroine, she'll be unavoidable.

I sigh loudly and lean back against the counter as I look out at the party going on before me. I don't make New Year's resolutions, but I do believe in trying to start the year the way I want it to go. And since I have enough to worry about this year, I guess, in the interests of minimizing the stressors in my life as much as possible, I will be friendly and kind to Chisato Ishi.

Great.

17
Birthday Sleepover

I don't know what happened to January, but it was like everyone at school agreed to work double-time to make up for the holidays, so the last month of the semester zipped by with the speed of a hummingbird. It's actually alarming, because as I get into the groove with my new semester's teachers and classes, I can feel graduation rushing up behind me on Mothra-sized wings.

Thankfully, February brings a welcome distraction.

"Knock knock."

It never gets old that Ojiichan adds a verbal "knock knock" to accompany the gentle taps on the door itself. "Come in," I say, getting up from my desk.

He enters my room carrying a tray with a cup of sencha and a small, furoshiki-wrapped object. This is how he always starts my big day, with something hot "to wake you up" and special delivery of my gift.

"Ohayou, Emiko-chan. I wish you a very happy birthday. And I hope you will enjoy this new addition to your collection."

"Thank you, Ojiichan." I set the tray on my desk, then pick up my gift and undo the knot, letting the fabric fall away. I let out a deep sigh when I see my seventeenth doll for the first time. "It's beautiful." It's always the best surprise, and this year's model glows pale golden under its varnished coat.

"Dogwood," he says before I have to ask.

He's tried a new silhouette this year. Instead of a column-like body, he's made the torso more of a cone, which makes the doll very different from all of the others in my collection.

"I like this." I place her on my desk so I can admire her as I pick up my tea. "She won't fall over if I bump into the display case."

"Yes, I think it is a good design."

"Thanks for the tea, too," I say, before sipping the comforting brew.

"You are welcome. Now, I will let you get ready for school."

As he turns to leave, an uncomfortable thought hits me. "Ojiichan?"

He stops at the door. "Yes?"

"What happens next year?"

"What do you mean?"

I suddenly feel embarrassed by what I'm about to ask but I kind of need to know. "Uhm, I just — will I still get a kokeshi next year?"

He looks a little confused by my question, which I'm starting to realize might sound silly. But then he nods. "Ah. You are getting too old for dolls."

"No! No. No. That's not what I meant. No. I mean . . . what if . . . what happens, if I'm not here?"

"I do not understand."

"Well, what if I'm not here, next year, on my birthday?" I can feel my heart starting to race, and I pull on my braid for something to hang on to.

"Then the doll will be here, waiting for you until you are." Ojiichan smiles and takes a step towards me. "Whatever happens, Emiko, next year and beyond — wherever your decisions may take you — as long I am able, my intention is to make you a doll to mark each year that you grow."

"Okay. I'm glad."

"And you understand this is also a gift for me? That I have this wonderful reason to continue practicing my craft. Because I do not think I am imagining that with every year, I am also getting much better at it."

"Yeah, you are." I sniffle as I pick up my kokeshi again. "Kenzo would never say *your* dolls look like bowling pins."

Ojiichan chuckles. "He has never seen the ones that do not leave my workshop."

I walk over to my grandfather, and as we hug, he pats my back. "Do not worry, little one. Though, perhaps I should not call you that anymore?"

"You can," I say, my voice muffled against his shoulder. "You can."

Last year, for my sixteenth birthday, we rented out Otter Creek Hall. Ojiichan hired an on-the-cusp local band called the Boat Rockers, Mitsuko created an epic board of finger foods and mini desserts that ran the length of a wall, and everyone, from the Triple As to Zera Oxley — who made me an actual robot — came to help me ring in my personal new year.

It was memorable in every good way. But it was also a lot. So, this year, I'm doing a complete one-eighty. I asked for dinner on the weekend with Ojiichan, Mitsuko and Seiji, Kenzo, his family, and Harumi. And a sleepover afterwards — something I haven't had since Meeta moved away — with Harumi.

Because I also don't want Mitsuko to have to cook, we've ordered a feast from Narmada's, one of the best restaurants in the Creek. Narmada herself, and one of her staff, have come over to set up the buffet.

"Dear girl," Narmada says when I walk into the kitchen. She gives me a big kiss on both cheeks. "Look at you, all ready for your party. Happy birthday."

"Thank you. And thank you so much for this wonderful dinner."

"It's my pleasure. Ash and the girls also send their best wishes," Narmada says, as she and her helper gather up their things.

Ojiichan joins me in seeing them off, and then we hurry back into the kitchen, drawn by the mouthwatering smells. I lift the first lid of the half-dozen chafing dishes lined up on the island and inhale the spicy-savory scent of chicken biryani. Besides the hot food, there's an array of salads and sides and chutneys that I peek at as well. Checking the clock, I'm grateful people are arriving soon, because all of a sudden I am starving.

"Narmada has outdone herself," Ojiichan says as he slowly

walks past the food. Like me, he can't resist, and he tilts open a lid. "Ah, okra."

In addition to my seventeenth kokeshi doll, now displayed on the counter, there's an enormous bouquet from Mitsuko and Seiji, cards and jokey heart-themed gifts from my friends at school, and a photo of Sir David Attenborough from Meeta, which I've framed, that's "signed," "*To my darling Emiko, Let us save the planet together. Love and kisses, Davey A.*"

Mitsuko and Seiji are the first to arrive, and after hugs, Seiji and Ojiichan go into the living room, while Mitsuko continues on into the kitchen to put my cake in the fridge and my birthday sekihan on the counter.

We've left the front door unlocked so, as Mitsuko tells me about her day, I hear Takeo and Tomio's excited voices before they tumble into the kitchen and zoom up to me like gangly puppies.

"HAPPY HEART DAY, EMIKO!" they shout as loudly as they can, and for the next few minutes it's like trying to put fireworks back in their paper tubes. Eventually, Abby calls for a time-out and the twins go into the living room to play video games until dinner.

Abby and Mas greet me with more hugs and flowers. I get a hug from Kenzo, too, but he barely has time to wish me happy birthday before Harumi bursts into the house.

"Hello, everyone!" she calls as she drops her overnighter by the stairs. There's a soft, shuffling noise as she does a little run and slides into the kitchen on her socked feet.

"Hey, Harumi." The way Kenzo smiles at her reminds me of how I smile at the twins.

They give each other a quick embrace before Harumi turns to me and offers up a small, square package. "I can't wait," she says. "Please open it!"

"Now?"

She gives a vigorous nod. "I just want to see your face . . ." She crosses her fingers and holds them up against her mouth. "Sorry, I know this is a lot of pressure, but I really hope you like it."

"I'm sure I will," I tell her.

It's a framed portrait of the two of us, done in cross-stitch, which is Harumi's latest crafting obsession. She's based it on another photo from Obon, a close-up this time, but the Hello Kitty ears and bows on our heads are an added touch.

It's hilarious, and I start laughing so hard I'm crying. As people turn to look at me, I show them the portrait, and the laughter spreads, as Harumi watches us all with a proud grin on her face.

"Oh my god, Harumi," I finally manage as I give her a thank-you hug. "This is one of the best, most original birthday gifts ever."

Soon afterwards, everyone's seated with full plates in front of them, passing around baskets of pillowy naan and crisp papadums, as they discuss which dish they're going to taste first.

After his third trip up to the island, Kenzo pushes his plate away. "Last year's birthday was fun, but I think I like this one better," he says.

"I think I could live off this food," Harumi declares as she swipes a piece of naan through some eggplant bharta. "Is this on Narmada's menu? I don't remember seeing it."

I shake my head. "It's a special request."

Harumi's shoulders sag, but then she perks up. "In that case, I'm going to get one tiny scoop more while I can."

As Harumi revisits the buffet, I sit back and watch everyone relaxed and enjoying themselves around the table. "I think I agree with you, Kenzo," I start to say, and I turn to find him smiling at me. "What?" I tuck my hair behind my ear. "Do I have something in my teeth?" I give him my best teeth-baring grin.

This usually cracks him up, and he's never shy about telling me if I resemble a jack-o'-lantern. But this time, he shakes his head and leans back in his chair. "You look happy."

"But of course. It's my birthday." For some reason, I say this in a really hammy French accent, just as the twins start a foot fight that rattles the dishes.

"Hey." Kenzo turns away to put a hand on Tomio's shoulder. "Maybe you could go get Emiko's present now."

"I'll get it," Takeo says as he bolts from his chair.

"No, me!" Tomio says, giving chase.

While Mas follows after them, Harumi and Kenzo help me clear the table to make room for Mitsuko's cake, a matcha and chocolate chiffon filled and frosted with chocolate whipped cream. It's actually challenging my preference for adzuki bean rice.

"Ooh, cake time," Harumi sing-songs as Mitsuko inserts number-shaped sparklers into the top.

"Yes," Ojiichan says as he flicks the lights off. "Everyone, sit down please." Once we're all seated, he gives Mitsuko the signal to light the sparklers and then leads everyone in an energetic rendition of "Happy Birthday," as she carries the cake over and sets it down in front of me.

As the last "you" fades away, I close my eyes to make my wish, opening them again in time to watch the sparklers fizzle and burn out.

"What'd you wish for, Emiko?" Takeo asks.

I shake my head and pull out the blackened 17. "No telling if I want it to come true."

When most everyone is close to finishing their cake and I'm considering another spoonful of sekihan, Takeo and Tomio push back their chairs and walk over to me. Takeo hands me a gift bag while Tomio lays a card on the table.

"That's from us," Takeo says.

"It was my turn to pick the box," Tomio adds.

Even though I receive a variation on the same gift every year, I'm still excited as I reach into the bag.

It started on my third birthday. Kenzo had spotted a heart-shaped box of chocolates in a window and, knowing I was a Valentine's baby, wanted to give me one. Since that first birthday without my mom and dad, the Sanadas have also kept up a tradition my parents began when I was born by giving me a tiny charm that I can wear on a necklace or a bracelet.

This year's heart is polka-dotted and tied with a red satin ribbon. "It's beautiful," I say to Tomio. "You picked well, thank you." He grins as I pull the ribbon loose and open the box.

Inside, tucked in the middle of the shiny chocolates, is a tiny blue velvet box. I pluck it out and lift the lid, holding my breath, because the Sanadas always choose the perfect charm.

"Oh, my." I pull out the tiny silver Totoro and hold it up, grinning as I remember the three Totoros from Halloween.

Harumi cranes her neck. "Can I see? Can I see?" I put the charm back in the box and pass the whole thing to her. While she admires my gift, I go to Mas and Abby.

"I love it," I tell them. "Thank you so much."

Mas pats my back. "You're welcome, Emiko-hime."

"It was Kenzo who picked it out," Abby whispers as she gives me a hug.

"Really?" I draw back in surprise.

"Really. Has done for years." She kisses the top of my head before moving away and picking up the teapot. "I need a top-up. Anyone else for a refill?"

I stand there, speechless.

I'm not sure why it's never occurred to me that Kenzo might be the one choosing the charms. I don't know if I should say anything, let him know what Abby's told me. I sneak a glance at him, relieved he's busy teasing Takeo about something, and wonder what else he's not telling me.

It's almost eleven by the time Harumi and I say good night to Ojiichan and go upstairs.

I'm a mixture of tired and wired, as is, I think, Harumi. She goes into the hall bathroom to get ready for bed and I head into my en suite to do the same. A half hour later, I'm PJ-ed up, feeling like I've got my second wind. When I walk into my room, Harumi's already under her covers, sitting up on the daybed; she looks more awake, too.

"Do you want to watch a movie?" I ask.

"Sure."

"What do you feel like?" I open up my drawer of DVDs. "Classics? '80s? Rom-coms? Docs?" I run through all my various categories and we decide on *Roman Holiday*, definitely one of my top three Audrey Hepburn films. Harumi loves *Funny Face* but she hasn't seen this earlier film, so we settle in to watch it.

At about the part where Gregory Peck takes Audrey on the Vespa tour, Harumi suddenly says, "My mom's in Rome."

I hit pause and turn to look at her.

She's staring at the TV screen but her eyes dart over to me, as if she's checking to see if I heard her. I did; I just don't know what to say. Mitsuko, who's known Harumi's Aunt Satomi almost as long as Ojiichan has, told me months ago that Harumi's mother wasn't in the picture — and not to ask Harumi about it, because apparently no one in the family talks about her mom, ever.

So, I wait.

Harumi swallows as she fiddles with the edge of the blanket. "She was fifteen when I was born," she says.

I nod.

"I try to picture . . . what if that was me? I mean, that's younger than I am now. I think I would totally freak out, because who wants a baby when you're still trying to figure out what to wear to prom?" She laughs, but it's not light or bubbly. "So, I'm pretty sure she didn't want me. But she had me, and then I guess she went back to her life like nothing happened."

She pauses, staring off into the distance for a bit, before continuing. "When I was old enough to ask, my grandma told me my mom had died, and no one knew who my dad was. That part's true, by the way." She glances at me quickly when she says this. "I was surprisingly okay with that, though, because I had my grandparents, and all my aunts and uncles — they all helped raise me. Still do."

She flexes her fingers a few times before she speaks again. "I didn't even know she WAS my mom until I was twelve. I thought she was another aunt, just one who didn't spend much time with me."

"Oh, Harumi."

"No, it's okay." Her jaw tightens and she nods as if she's just given herself a pep talk, or permission. "I was snooping through my grandma's closet, looking for my birthday presents, and I found a small suitcase I'd never noticed before. I opened it and found a bunch of papers, including my birth certificate. That's how I found out. She was already living in Italy by then."

I shake my head as I try to understand how that must have felt.

"I must have gone into shock or something, 'cause I just sat there for the longest time. And then my grandma came in and found me, and she knew." Harumi lets out a deep breath. "I know I'm really lucky to have her and my ojiichan, and all my aunts and uncles. I mean, they're the reason I'm here."

Harumi stares blankly down at her lap.

"I had a couple of bad years after that," she says after a little while. "But I got help, and everyone's been super supportive. Aunt Satomi's the best."

"She is," I say, thankful it's true.

Even though I was so young when they died, if my mom and dad *were* still alive, I know — like, in my bones, *know* — that neither of them would ever leave me by choice. As I try to absorb everything Harumi's told me, I realize how lucky I am to have that certainty, which I see now is like gold.

And if I have any pain at all when I think about them, it's from an understandable sense of loss. Which I think might not hurt as much as such outright rejection.

After a moment, I ask, "Is she — your mother — is she aware? That you know?"

Harumi nods. "She wrote me a letter, kind of explaining her side of things. But she's not really a part of my life." Harumi wipes her eyes and laughs. "I'm sorry, I didn't plan on telling you any of this tonight, Emiko. I mean, it's not exactly a fun birthday topic."

"Maybe not. But I'm glad you did." I sit down beside her and give her a long hug. "I'm really sorry, Harumi."

She doesn't say anything, but she hugs me back tighter, shuddering as she cries from a deep place, into my shoulder. Eventually, she stills, and sniffles.

"Are you alright?" I ask, rubbing her back the way Mitsuko used to when I was little and needed soothing.

She nods and slowly releases her hold. "I think so." I bring her some tissues, and when she takes one, she lets out a sudden snortle. "Actually, I think I'm also kind of hungry now. Crying really takes it out of you."

I smile and look at my alarm clock. It's nearly two in the morning but we throw on our hantens and slippers and creep down to the kitchen.

"How about some toast?" I hold up a loaf of sourdough. "And hot cocoa?"

"And cake?" she asks, hopefully.

"And cake," I say.

18
An Invitation

After hours of cleaning kennels at Senior Dogs, I stop by
Safiye's office to chat, and I'm snuggling a portly but ener-
getic Yorkie cross named Peppy when Harumi texts to see if
I'm free.

> ME: Just finished shift. What's up?

> HARUMI: Can we meet at 3? By the shop?

> ME: Everything ok?

> HARUMI: I need help!!!

> ME: I'll be there.

"That's all the pup-time for me. Hopefully, I won't see *you*
again, miss," I tell Peppy. I put her back on the bed beside
Safiye's desk before asking if there's been any interest in her.

"We've had several calls," Safiye says. "Someone's actually coming later today to meet her. Those new photos and the updates you made to the bio pages have really helped."

"It was probably the flower on her head," I say, modestly. Although, of course, I'm overjoyed to hear this. "It's all about the accessories."

Safiye smiles. "Well, the doggles and scarf definitely worked for Frisby."

My heart leaps with excitement. "Was it the woman on the motorcycle? With the sidecar?"

"How'd you know?"

"Yes!" I allow myself a double fist pump at this fantastic news. "I saw her outside before she came in and I had this . . . almost like a vision of the two of them. So I said, 'Check out the terrier mix with the bent ear.' Told her his theme song could be 'Born to Be Wild' and that he was *def-initely* looking for adventure."

Grinning at the image of Frisby riding shotgun into the sunset with his new person, I mentally add him to my "Matched" column and head out with a wave as Safiye's phone rings again.

My walk home takes about half an hour, giving me time to drop off my backpack and change out of my grubby clothes before I continue up the road towards the heart of the Creek. As I get closer, I wonder what could be going on with Harumi. She seemed fine yesterday at school, and we'd traded texts last night after dinner as usual.

By the time I reach the gazebo in the village green, semi-circled by shops, Harumi is already waiting on a bench.

"Sorry, am I late?"

"No," Harumi says as she chews her thumbnail. "I just got here."

I sit down next to her. "So, what's going on?"

She stares down the road, across the street, at the café. "He's working today."

"Oh," I say, and remember something Mitsuko told me recently about Gareth. I didn't bother to share the intel with Harumi because she hasn't mentioned him much since New Year's and I assumed she was properly over him. But the look on her face tells me she isn't. Which makes me feel terrible for not having noticed, and now I'm not sure what to do with what I know.

We sit for a few minutes while Harumi keeps glancing back and forth between her phone and the café. Finally, I ask her if there was something in particular she wanted my help with. "Your text made it sound like you did," I say.

Harumi thrusts her phone at me. "I need you to delete all of his texts."

I try not to look too surprised as I take the bedazzled phone, but the second I do, her fingers flex nervously and she holds out her hand again. "No. I need to do it. It has to be me."

I place the phone in her palm and she clasps it to her chest. Then, with a tight smile, she taps and swipes the screen, bringing up the selfie with the kokeshi doll. "Look at how happy we were," she says.

"It *is* a great photo."

She stares at it wistfully before shaking her head. "I'm keeping the kokeshi, Emiko. But I got rid of all the photos from Halloween, and last week, I took apart the snow globe. Now, all I have left are his texts."

Then she sits up and, before I know it, she's reciting them from memory, like she's at a flash poetry slam.

"*Here you go. Hope you like it.*"

"*No problem.*"

"*Nope, that's it.*"

"*Ha ha, funny.*"

"*What?*"

"*Hi.*"

"*Hi.*"

"*OK.*"

"*How many?*"

"*OK.*"

"*Sure.*"

It's not *un*-interesting, but as Harumi continues, hearing Gareth's words out loud, I recognize now how delusional I was to think there was even a single flirtatious syllable in the lot.

"*What time did she say?*"

"*Need a lift?*"

"*No problem.*"

"*Nope, not here.*"

"*No.*"

"*No.*"

"*Thanks, you're sweet.*"

"*OK.*"

"*Not telling.*"

"It's a surprise."

"You'll see."

"Bacon cheese."

"Sold out."

As she goes on, all those moments when I misinterpreted Gareth's interest flash through my mind, and I wish she would put us both out of our misery and get to the end.

"Cran-apple."

"How many?"

"OK."

Harumi sighs heavily and looks off into the distance.

"Are you okay?" I ask.

She nods.

"Alright, then," I say, and wait.

After a few more moments, she exhales deeply. "Here I go." She taps the trash icon and then "All Messages."

"Seventy-seven tick marks," she notes somberly. "Definitely not my lucky number." Sighing, she hits delete, and then delete again, and with a cheery *bloo-eep*, her screen clears. "Goodbye, Gareth Tolman," she whispers.

After a moment of silence, I ask, "Are you keeping him in your contacts?"

"Oh. Do you think I should? For, like, emergencies?"

"Like, if an asteroid hits Earth and he's the last man standing?"

She giggles. "Yeah, something like that."

"Then, no, not in the least."

As Harumi wipes Gareth completely from her phone, mine chimes and I pull it out of my pocket.

MITSUKO: Jun's coming! Welcome party Saturday. Open to all. We want Jun to meet everyone!

I quickly reply "YES!" and turn to Harumi. "Guess what you're doing next weekend!"

So far, my efforts to be friendly and kind to Chisato Ishi have not been very successful.

Since school started, I've looked for her at lunch to ask if she wants to join me and my friends, but she must bento-box it because I rarely see her in the cafeteria. And if I do, she grabs and goes before I can stop her.

I would have expected to bump into her in the Creek, given that her aunt runs the library and she apparently volunteers there, but I've yet to catch a glimpse of her. And Mitsuko says she hasn't been at the café much, either, just a handful of times, and always with Taka-san.

I even went so far as to invite her and Taka-san to join us for my birthday dinner, only to be informed that she was busy.

So, with Jun's party coming up, I'm trying again, determined to talk to her in our lone class together, English Lit.

The problem is, I sit up front because this is one of my favorite subjects, and our teacher, Dr. Velasquez, and I both appreciate a good scarf. And Chisato, as I suspect she does in every class, sits in the back corner mimicking a houseplant.

When I enter our classroom, I manage to catch her eye and say hello, but that's as far as I get before Dr. Velasquez wheels in and starts her lesson on Victorian poets.

I make another attempt when the bell rings, but somehow, even with the extra distance she has to travel, she manages to slip out the door before me. With no idea what the rest of her schedule is, I realize I'm going to have to hunt her down at lunch.

Since it's warm enough to eat outside, Harumi and I join the group gathered at the sunny tables by the cedar. Kenzo and Dev move over, making room on the bench seat, when they see us.

"Hey, Kimori." Dev gestures to my bento box. "What's on the menu today?"

I take off the lid to show him my chicken katsu sandwich. "Does anyone know where Chisato Ishi hangs out at lunch?"

"Why?" Kenzo asks.

"I want to invite her to Jun's party . . . What? Mitsuko asked me to," I clarify, when Kenzo looks surprised. "I'm supposed to invite as many people as I can."

"Who's Jun, again?" Alix asks.

"My aunt's new stepson. It's his first visit to the coast. Are you all coming?"

"Only if he's cute," Jacob says, prompting Darcy to give him a playful shove. "No, seriously, is he?"

I think about the school photo Mitsuko showed me awhile back. "As a matter of fact, he's quite cute."

"We'll be there," Ani says.

"So will we," Jacob adds.

Darcy's eyebrows arch. "Will we, though?"

"It's so cool you're finally going to meet him," Harumi says, picking up her onigiri. "After all this time."

"I know. I mean, talk about buildup. And I honestly can't tell who's more excited about it, me or Mitsuko. Anyway, Chisato . . . anyone know her whereabouts?"

"Later, guys." Kenzo gets up so abruptly that the bench bounces, making me almost drop my food. Before I can say anything, though, Harumi pipes up.

"Oops, sorry, I meant to say, she's probably in the library — I see her there a lot. Either that, or the music room. Oh, BRB," she tells me, and runs over to where Arlo and a couple of other girls are about to sit.

I've seen her with both Will and Arlo more often lately — since Arlo's in three of her classes this term, that makes sense — but since the Gareth debacle, I've stopped worrying about Will. I still don't think it would do Harumi any favors socially to date him, but given that the vibe, on her part anyway, feels very much like "just friends," I'm not concerned anymore. Plus, as Kenzo says, I do think he's solid.

Anyway, since Harumi is chatting with her girlfriends, I give Dev the rest of my lunch and go follow my leads.

I start with the music room since it's the closest, but when I find only drama kids inside rehearsing for the school musical, I turn around and climb the stairs to the second floor.

Our library, which is already an extraordinary space, features windows with immense views of the northern mountains that normally draw me in like a tractor beam; today, I ignore them and focus on the students sitting at desks lined up along the wall.

Unsurprisingly, Chisato is not there. A prowl through the open area in the middle of the library, with its cluster of large worktables, is also a bust, so I start searching the corners.

It's not till I get to the multimedia section that I finally spot the newly dyed electric-blue streak in her hair, and find her tucked away in a carrel, bent over an open notebook. She's wearing headphones, so she doesn't hear me approaching. I don't do anything right away, just stand beside her, waiting, as Chisato writes like she's on a deadline. Suddenly, she stills and slowly raises her head.

"Oh," she says when she sees me. After a few moments, she pushes one headphone off her ear.

"Hi." I smile. "Sorry to interrupt, but I was wondering, are you doing anything special this Saturday?"

She stares at me, her face a Noh mask for all the reaction my question gets. As several seconds tick by, she must realize she's being borderline rude because she swallows and lets out a barely audible, "No."

"Great. So, you know my Aunt Mitsuko? Her stepson, Jun, is visiting, and we're throwing him a welcome party." My voice is chirpy and upbeat. "We'd love it if you and your Aunt Taka could join us. Jun's planning some kind of entertainment so I'm sure it'll be fun."

Chisato closes her notebook, turning her body so that it's hidden on the desk behind her, and purses her lips. I continue to smile at her. In response, she clicks her pen a couple of times and stares at a spot just above my shoulder.

If anyone else ever took this long to accept an invitation, I'd turn around and leave, but Mitsuko was uncharacteristically insistent. "Taka-san's worried Chisato's not making friends," she'd told me the other night at dinner. "All she does is study in her room, so please do your best to get her to agree."

As I wait for Chisato to answer, I glance at my watch, a vintage Seiko that belonged to my dad, and see I have ten minutes to get to World History on the other side of the school. "So . . . do you think you and your aunt might come?" I prompt.

Chisato looks thoughtful, then stands, nearly tipping her chair over in the process. She rights her headphones and starts shoving her book and pencil case into her messenger bag. "I'll let you know," she mumbles. "I'm going to be late."

As she brushes past me and practically runs out of the library, I take a step to follow her, but it's as pointless as chasing a spooked deer. So I stop, and then I keep getting bumped from behind until people realize they should just move past me like water around a rock while I try work out what just happened.

I'll be the first to admit she and I aren't best friends, but I'm beginning to think that Chisato Ishi doesn't like me much. Which makes no sense because, objectively, I've been nothing but nice to her.

I find myself sifting through our history, which literally goes back years, searching for the glint of a clue, when the warning bell rings and snaps me back to the present.

"No running," one of the librarians reminds me as they wheel by with a cart.

I nod, giving them a tight smile, and race-walk till I get through the doors before launching into a sprint.

The buzz around Jun's visit is real, but there's also some confusion as to why he's suddenly here in Canada. Jun, who's lived in London, England, and New York City, had been attending a private school in Tokyo. But now, he and his mom are unexpectedly living in Vancouver, and he's apparently enrolled in an exclusive all-boys school there.

Jun's mother, Kana, is a famous visual artist, so there's some thought that her art is what's brought them to the west coast. But neither Mitsuko nor Seiji has been able to get the whole truth from either mother or son, so basically, it's all dish, no dinner. All I really care about is the fact that Jun's living a short ferry ride away, so we can expect to see more of him in the coming months.

I'm imagining our first meeting as I walk home from Yoga Yurt, where Harumi and I just finished a Vinyasa class. Even though the party's not for hours, I'm eager to shower and get ready for tonight, so I'm taking the shortcut behind the OC General Store. It's a trail for locals that cuts through the greenbelt and the easement that runs along Kenzo's, down to the side of the road across from my house.

The path is usually peaceful, but today I hear the obnoxious sound of something motorized coming towards me, and it's a good thing I'm so limber because I have to leap sideways to dodge some helmeted moron on a flashy dirt bike.

"Hey!" I yell. "Watch it, butthead!"

I genuinely don't expect the biker to hear me, let alone stop, but they skid on the dirt just before a bend and turn to look back at me. I can't see their face clearly through the visor, but I *can* make out a big grin, which completely douses my yoga-glow.

"It's a FOOTpath," I say indignantly as I step out of the undergrowth. "For pedestrians? People on their feet?" I look for the hand-painted "No Bikes!" sign that used to be nailed to a nearby alder, before remembering it rotted off years ago and hasn't been replaced.

"Noted," a muffled male voice says. "I'll remember for next time."

"*Next* time?"

The guy grins again, then flashes me a peace sign before riding off.

I gawk after him, shaking my head as the sound of his bike diminishes to a mosquito's whine. "Still irritating," I say to myself. For some reason, though, despite being really annoyed, I find myself fighting a smile all the way home.

19
Karaoke!

Mitsuko and Seiji's house is lit up, and I can hear music and people laughing as Ojiichan, Harumi, and I make our way up the steps. Mitsuko must have been watching for us because the broad front door swings open even before we reach the landing.

"Welcome!" she says. "Come in, come in."

We follow her into the kitchen which, along with the dining and living rooms, faces the humungous view of the water. We're not late, but there's already a good crowd out on the deck. Chisato and Taka-san are expected tonight, but I wonder if seeing this many people here will scare Chisato off.

"Seiji," Mitsuko calls as she helps me unpack the appetizers I brought. "Emiko's here."

While she puts Harumi's flowers in water, I take my temari sushi over to the dining table and nearly drop them on the floor when someone reaches out and grabs one before I've even set the platter down. I look up, ready to politely say *WTH?*, only to lose the power of speech when I find a *very* good-looking stranger grinning at me before he pops the sushi ball into his mouth. Even his chewing is attractive.

"Ah, Jun." Seiji suddenly appears, wearing a similar grin. "You've found Mitsuko's niece." He turns to me. "Emiko, I'd like to finally introduce you to my son, Jun."

Holy boy band, is he *cute*. And I immediately understand why I didn't recognize him from his school photo — it's like he's two different people. The unsmiling boy with his neatly combed black hair and school uniform is like the Clark Kent version of the boy in front of me.

Jun IRL is tall and lean, with broad shoulders under his white T-shirt and black suit vest. His hair, which is short on the sides, has a floppy layer of dyed silver on top that is so perfectly styled you'd think he stopped in after a cover shoot.

"It's nice to meet you." I'm aware that I'm staring, but it's hard not to. Thankfully, he seems not to notice.

"You too," Jun returns. And when he grins at me again, I gasp.

"It was you!" I say, rearing back.

Jun puts his hands up in mock surrender. "Guilty as charged."

"Have you two met before?" Seiji asks, clearly confused.

"Mm-hm." I give Jun a look before turning to Seiji with a wide smile. "Just this morning, in fact."

He nods. "We, uhm, ran into each other near . . ."

"The General Store," I tell Seiji. "But I didn't realize who he was."

Jun tries to appear solemn but his eyes are bright with mischief. "And now that she does, hopefully, she's not terribly disappointed."

"It's really too soon to tell." I'm grinning, because whatever it is that we're doing, I'm having fun.

"You know, they say not to bet everything on a first impression."

"Do they?"

"Oh, yes, I'm certain I've heard that."

Seiji watches us, a bemused expression on his face, but our exchange ends when Harumi joins us. After more introductions, Seiji leaves to find Mitsuko, and the three of us start towards the deck, when we hear a pretty warbling sound.

"Sorry," Jun says as he pulls out his phone. "I've been waiting for this. Go on ahead. I'll meet you outside." He gives us a quick smile before heading down the hall, presumably to his room.

I shrug, and as Harumi decides she wants to get some food, I end up walking out onto the heated deck on my own. I'm not alone long, though, because the first people I see are Abby and Mas.

"Emiko!" Abby gives me a big hug. "You're looking well, sweetheart."

"You are too." I turn to Mas and go in for another hug. "Where are the boys?"

"Well, 'At This Moment,' the twins are downstairs," he says, the air quotes apparent in his voice, "and Kenzo's over there." He lifts his chin, indicating the far end of the deck.

"Hm," I say thoughtfully. "Well, now I don't know what to do. 'Should I Stay or Should I Go'?"

Mas chuckles and we bump fists as I cock my head in Kenzo's direction. "I'd better check in."

As his parents head inside, I drift over to where Kenzo's standing, elbows on the railing, looking out at the view. "See any whales?" I ask as I come up beside him.

"Not without binoculars." He straightens and turns to look at me. "Hi."

"Hi." We haven't hung out much since my birthday, and I'm about to ask him about his hockey team when Harumi's loud "No way!" catches my ear. Looking over, I see her and Jun sitting together, laughing and chatting like they've known each other for years.

I also spot Chisato and her aunt standing just inside the sliding doors. Chisato's stony air as she checks out the other guests confirms my suspicion that accepting the invite was more Taka-san's idea than hers, which is reinforced when Taka-san encourages her gently to step over the threshold.

Mitsuko is there immediately to meet them, and Chisato's shoulders ease a little, so my eyes go back to Jun and Harumi, who've been joined by Mrs. Watanabe and some of the obasans who helped us at New Year's.

"What do you think of him?" I ask, since Kenzo's observing them, too.

"I think exactly what he wants me to think."

"Which is?"

"You first."

"Fine." Maybe it's reverse jet lag, but I've never met anyone so animated. "He's definitely not shy. A bit of a showman," I say as Mitsuko leads Chisato and Taka-san over to the group. He greets them as he has everyone so far, like they're his new best friends. "And . . . he's charming."

Kenzo makes a noise.

"Come on, he's even got the obasans smiling." Mrs. Watanabe and her crew are not easily won over, yet, within minutes, Jun's got them cackling.

"He cares a lot about his hair."

"Oh my god," I say, laughing. "Someone's judgy."

He frowns. "I'm not judgy."

"Okay, you're just *acting* judgy," I tease. "Anyway, he's Mitsuko's family now, so he's not going anywhere. And I think he's interesting." I turn back to Kenzo and get on my tiptoes to look him in the eye. "Seriously, be nice. He's probably trying to be a good guest of honor."

Kenzo doesn't comment and continues watching Jun, who's now talking to Taka-san. Then he nods towards the house. "What'd you bring?"

"Go look. Your favorite."

He smiles. "Meatballs?"

"Among other things."

"Sometimes you're kind of the best, Kimori. You coming too?"

"In a minute," I say, because I see Jun approaching. I look at Kenzo. "I'll be there in a minute."

Kenzo's gaze flicks to Jun and he lobs a "Hey" as they pass each other.

Taking Kenzo's spot, Jun leans back against the railing. He tosses his head to get his floppy hair out of his face and gives me an openly flirty grin. I have to admit, whatever game we're playing, I'm enjoying it quite a bit.

"Thanks for earlier, Emiko," he says. "For not ratting me out to my father. I wasn't sure if I needed some kind of license, but I thought I'd be fine if I stayed off the roads, and all your trails here are so tempting. I didn't know that one was for walking."

I barely know the guy, but for some reason I find myself nodding, like I'm totally okay with him breaking the rules like this. "As long as it was just this once," I clarify, laying down the law.

"I knew you'd understand."

"That's me. Miss Understanding." I'm also Miss Very Distracted by his accent, which is a disarming blend of posh English and casual American. I feel like I could listen to him talk for hours.

Due to the short notice, fewer than ten of my friends have made it to the party. But by the time everyone's eaten, and the sky's darkened to indigo, there's a decent cross section of the community here when Jun climbs onto a stool and waits for the chatter to die down.

"Thank you, everyone, for this warm welcome. It's lovely to make new friends," he scans the crowd, and, no lie, his eyes linger an extra second on me, "but I'd like to take things a little further, if you don't mind, to really bond us together." Here, he gives a grin worthy of the Cheshire Cat. "But to do that, I need you to bring your glasses and follow me."

"Who is this guy?" Darcy mutters behind me, but he's shushed by one of the Triple As as Jun leads us into the house and down a floor to the spacious family room. As people find seats at the bar lining the back, on the sprawling leather sectional, or on one of the many chairs scattered around the room, we turn our focus to Jun, who's waiting on a small stage in front of a screen.

"Welcome to karaoke night!" Jun announces as he gestures to the setup on a table beside him. The volume in the room instantly rises.

I LOVE karaoke. I'm a halfway decent singer, but even if I weren't, singing along to my favorite songs *anywhere* is a surefire way to cheer myself up and get my blood pumping. Harumi looks as thrilled as I am. "Oh my god," she whispers as Jun explains how the machine works. "I haven't done karaoke in ages!"

"And," Jun continues, "you can pick literally any song you like." He holds up a wireless mic. "Who's brave enough to go first?"

Harumi's hand shoots up and she gets things going with a boppy, if slightly pitchy, rendition of "Shake It Off." It's a steady stream of participants after that, everyone here for fun, and the evening bounces along to an up-tempo beat. I've already sung "Roam" by the B-52s, and I'm ready to do another if no one else will, but really, I'm waiting for Jun to go up.

Finally, after almost everyone else has had a turn, he takes the mic, and I swear, somehow there's a spotlight shining on him. He picks "Hey There, Delilah" by Plain White T's, and I know it's a cliché, but it truly feels like he's singing those lyrics to me.

And yes, I remind myself, we've just met, but when he looks at me during the chorus, I feel like I'm at the beginning of my own rom-com, and I start thinking about things like love at second sight, and soulmates, and other ideas that I always felt were great in theory but not for me, like bangs.

I'm so in my head that I don't realize Jun's finished until everyone starts clapping. Since no one's waiting for the mic, he looks around — I'm guessing for anyone who hasn't gone up yet — then walks over to where Chisato's sitting with her aunt.

He leans over and says something to her before straightening up and holding out the mic. I had watched her earlier and got the sense she'd been reluctantly enjoying herself, so I'm sure this is just Jun trying to make her feel a part of things. But now, obvious panic spreads across her face.

I can't hear what Jun says next to Chisato, but Taka-san seems to be agreeing with him, while Chisato keeps shaking her head, and frankly, it's getting awkward. Then, Taka-san says something, and after a few moments, Chisato finally stands and follows Jun to the stage like a kid being sent to the principal's office.

"Everyone," Jun says, his voice excited, "it took a bit of convincing, but Chisato is going to sing for us now."

There's a bit of restless shuffling in the audience as Jun brings her a stool and the guitar I noticed earlier on the stand in the corner.

I knew Chisato played the piano, but I had no idea she sang. Or that she played the guitar. I'm even more surprised when I see how completely at ease she looks when she picks up the instrument.

She strums it a few times, adjusting the tuning pegs, before she settles, holding the guitar loosely, her hands poised. The room is so quiet I can hear her take a couple of deep breaths. Then, without a word, she launches into the intro.

I immediately recognize "Barely Breathing" by Duncan Sheik, and when she starts singing, I feel a shiver, and goosebumps erupt up and down my arms. Her voice is a shock, pure, but with a hint of a rasp. I can't take my eyes off her. I don't think anyone can.

And the lyrics, the way she sings them — a word I learned in English last year, *plangent*, comes to mind. It's the ache in her voice and the melancholy. I can feel my throat tighten and my eyes well up, but I blink the tears away before they blur my vision, because I don't want to miss a second of her performance.

When Chisato sings the last word, her voice bends a little, then breaks, and as the final strums of the guitar fade away, there's a moment of stunned silence, followed by spontaneous applause from everyone. Except Taka-san, who bursts into sobs.

Chisato, looking stricken, puts the guitar down and rushes to her aunt's side.

"Oh, Chi-chan," I hear her aunt say.

Mitsuko goes to Taka-san as well, trying to console her, although I don't think she's unhappy, just overcome. If so, I totally get it.

I mean, what just happened? That was Chisato, who barely speaks to any of us, who apparently spends all her time in the school library, writing in her notebook. Is she writing songs? Poetry? Where did she learn to sing like that?

Jun's back on the stage, a slightly stunned expression on his face as well. But he recovers, and in a cheery voice he says, "Wow, Chisato. That was . . . brilliant. Brilliant." He looks around the room. "Do you think she'll give us an encore? Maybe if we ask nicely?" He tries to get everyone to clap, and I'm surprised at how insensitive he's being, since it seems obvious that she's still dealing with her aunt. I mean, give the girl a moment.

"Come on, Chisato," he cajoles her.

But then, just as the silence on her end gets cringey, Kenzo walks past me and strides up to the front of the room. He grabs the second mic, startling Jun, and leans over to say something to him. Jun, to his credit, doesn't ask questions and types something on the keyboard.

"It appears we're getting an encore performance from Kenzo, instead. Enjoy, everyone." Jun steps off the stage and goes and stands beside a much calmer Taka-san, while Chisato, now seated, holds her hand.

Kenzo looks around the room and catches my eye. I give him a thumbs-up, grateful he's taken the heat off Chisato and her aunt. He flashes back a quick smile before he shakes his head and arms like he's warming up before a game. And then he stops, plants his feet apart, his hands clasped loosely in front of him, and lets his head drop as we wait for the music to start.

Another hush falls over the crowd, but this feels different from when Chisato was up there. Having seen Kenzo once already, backing up Takeo and Tomio in a crowd-pleasing rendition of House of Pain's "Jump Around," you can feel the eager buzz of anticipation for more. Behind him, the screen fills up with images of a storm, dark clouds, and flashes of lightning, and I think I can guess — oh . . . I *know* which song he's chosen.

No one's there to perform Jay-Z's rap, but it doesn't matter, because as soon as Kenzo opens his mouth, channeling his inner-Rihanna, and starts singing "Umbrella," we're done for. Like, on the floor, done.

In no time at all, he's got us in the palm of his hand. And when Kenzo nears the end of the earworm-y chorus and turns the mic towards us, bobbing it in time with the beat, everyone — the obasans, Taka-san, even Ojiichan — joins in and sings along. The energy in the room is so high, so light and happy, that my cheeks hurt from smiling.

After the song ends too soon, Kenzo takes a short bow, hands the mic to Jun, and jumps off the stage. He makes his way over to me and I can't help it, I punch him on the shoulder. "You *killed* it," I say.

"It was fun," he says, but when he looks over at Chisato, his forehead furrows.

"What?"

"Nothing."

"Come on," I say.

"Chisato still looks upset. That Jun . . ." He shakes his head.

A part of me understands Kenzo's feelings, but just like when Jun missed the wedding, I feel compelled to defend him. "Maybe he did her a favor."

"How do you figure?"

"Well, now the secret's out, and we know how talented she is."

He frowns. "Maybe that was a secret she wanted to keep."

"I honestly think he was just trying to make her feel included," I say as I watch Jun talking to Seiji. The karaoke seems to have run its course after Kenzo. It's understandable — his would be a tough act to follow.

Kenzo looks like he wants to keep arguing, but behind him, Mitsuko's beckoning me. "Gotta go," I say, and follow her upstairs.

No one formally announces that the party is over, but as people make their slow exits, I help Mitsuko bundle up food for them to take home. As I parcel out sweets onto paper plates, she leaves me for a few minutes. When she returns, she nudges my arm and whispers, "Look."

Turning, I see Kenzo talking to Chisato in the foyer. She's gazing up at him with a shy smile on her face. Taka-san is smiling too, and she puts her hand on Kenzo's arm, as if she's thanking him for something.

"Wasn't that so good of Kenzo? Poor Chisato." Mitsuko shakes her head. "All that attention must have been so overwhelming for her. That *voice*, though."

"I know. Mind-blowing," I say as Kenzo heads our way.

"I'm going to drive Chisato and Taka-san home now, Mitsuko, so I wanted to say good night."

"I appreciate that, Kenzo," she says.

He gives me a quick nod. "See you, Em."

"'Night."

As Kenzo walks out the door with Chisato and Taka-san behind him, Mitsuko chuckles softly.

"What's so funny?" My aunt is acting super weird.

"Oh, I don't know. I was just thinking, maybe Kenzo's finally found a girl."

"What?" I look around, glad no one's in earshot, because that came out way louder than I expected. "What?" I repeat, only in a more nonchalant, less-interested tone.

Mitsuko looks at me, surprised. "Oh, come on, Emiko. You saw him."

"I'm lost." Honestly, I am. I start shoving fruit salad into a plastic container, squishing it down harder than necessary.

"We may have witnessed the start of a little romance, that's all. And maybe I helped it along." She gives me a wink — a *wink!* — and carries some dishes to the sink, while I process what she said.

It takes a few seconds for me to connect the dots. But when I do, and I realize my aunt has just tried her own hand at matchmaking, I stare after her, standing gobsmacked (another word I learned in English) beside the leftovers.

20
Prom Dress

Back in September, when Astrella Hadi, our school president, announced that the winning theme for senior prom was "Blooming '80s," I'll admit, I squealed.

Cedar Grovers traditionally lean into their chosen themes, and last year's "Enchanted Forest" prom brought out a lot of Maleficent and Snow White–influenced gowns, as well as a runway's worth of Middle Earth Elven-wear. I took my inspiration from the *Amanita muscaria*, the iconic mushroom of fairy tales and gnome lore, and paired a billowy red-polka-dotted blouse from the thrift store with a white tube skirt I found way back in Mitsuko's closet.

"This year, I know most people will go for vintage or celeb-inspired looks, but I'm taking the remake route, you know, as an homage to *Pretty in Pink*." I look over at Jun, who has surprised us with a weekend visit, as we walk around the Creek village shops. "You do know the movie, right? John Hughes classic? Era-defining soundtrack?"

"I am going to confess something, Miss Emiko." He comes

to a stop and blows his two-toned hair out of his eyes. "I've never watched it. I know some of the music, though — love it, in fact," he adds quickly when he sees my face.

"Oh, Jun." My disappointment isn't real, but I have fun acting like it is. "And I DO know how big a deal senior prom is. Which brings me to a question . . ."

Since the gazebo is already taken, I lead Jun over to a bench outside Re: Gifting, where a peek through the window tells me Harumi's busy with a customer.

"Okay." I sit down. "Sounds serious."

Jun remains standing, and looks away, as if embarrassed. "I was wondering if you would let me . . . go as your guest? And escort?" He says this last part with a cheeky grin — the words he uses sometimes!

I smile, surprised but flattered. "Really? You want to go to prom with me?"

"Well, I've never been to one. But I'd love to, if I could. And I know I can't just buy my own ticket so, if you're still free . . ." He shakes his head. "I'm mucking this up, aren't I? You probably already have a date, don't you?"

In fact, I do not. And my mind goes to the person I *thought* I'd be going to my own senior prom with — strictly as friends, of course. But ever since Mitsuko's completely-out-of-nowhere disclosure, I've been too preoccupied watching for signs that her matchmaking attempt has taken to also worry about who my "prom date" might be.

The problem is, I so rarely see Chisato anywhere outside our one class that I really have no way of knowing anything for sure. And it's made me weird around Kenzo.

Just then, because the universe also sometimes lets inch-worms catch in my hair, Kenzo's truck pulls up and parks across the street. Slumping back into the shadow to avoid detection, I watch him get out and go straight into the Otter Creek Library, where I'm pretty sure Chisato is helping her aunt today.

"Emiko?"

"Oh. Jun." I sit up and tell myself to focus. "I'm sorry. I just . . ." In that moment, I shake my head and decide, what-ever does or doesn't happen between Kenzo and Chisato, I'm not going to wait around to find out, not when such a fabulous option has presented itself. "You know what? I'd love it if you escorted me to prom."

"Thanks, Emiko. You've no idea what this means to me."

"Judging from the smile on your face, I think I do."

Then, noting her customer leaving, I stand. "Let's go tell Harumi," I say, hustling him into the shop. And then I keep him there, one eye on the road, showing him Ojiichan's kokeshi dolls, until I see Kenzo get back in his truck and drive away.

I wait a week before I decide to tell Kenzo about Jun. Even though, truth be told, I'm a little peeved that prom is barely a month away and he STILL hasn't said anything to me about it. I mean, it's our *last* prom. (I wave away the sugges-tion that maybe it's because he's made other plans and get back to the task at hand.)

Fiddling with my braids, I try to figure out the right tone to take. I think something upbeat, like I'm so carefree and this is no big deal, will suit.

ME: Hey! Guess what? Jun's never been to prom. So he asked if he could go with me.

It takes him a minute to reply.

KENZO: I know. Harumi told me.

For some reason, this makes me feel like I've done something wrong. I bite my thumb, wishing I had told Harumi not to say anything to anyone. Then I get another text.

KENZO: I'm going with the team. Should be fun.

I let out a breath, feeling confused and relieved at the same time. I don't know how I expected Kenzo to react to *my* news, but I do know his going with Dev and the guys and *not* Chisato Ishi is a wonderful idea. And that Mitsuko has no clue what she's doing.

ME: That's terrific. Do I get to vet what you're going to wear?

KENZO: No.

Before I can respond with a bit of faux-outrage, he follows up with:

KENZO: 😉

Winkers in emoji form I can handle, and even though I would love to give my opinion on his intended look,

I figure, in this case, it's best if I take a *laissez-faire* approach, and I text him back a smile.

Bringing my dress idea to life is only possible because I'm not doing it on my own. After barely managing a C-minus in ninth grade Home Ec, I've accepted the fact that I'm not going to be awesome at everything. So I've asked Mitsuko, a sewing whiz, to help me with my Spring Break project. And by *help me*, I mean *do most of it.*

We're starting today. I haven't told her much, other than that I want to turn one of my mom's kimono into a dress. But when she walks into my room and sees which one I've picked, her hand goes to her chest and her eyes fill with tears.

"Oh, no," I say, taking her free hand in mine. This is *so* not the reaction I was hoping for. "I'm sorry, Mitsuko. I'll choose another."

She shakes her head, and from her expression and the way she's gripping my hand, I can tell she's good.

Relieved, tears prick my eyes, too, and I laugh as I brush them away.

"She'd be happy, Emiko." My aunt walks over to the kimono hanging on the wall and gently touches a sleeve. "So happy."

This is the kimono my mom wore to her Coming of Age Ceremony. In Japan, in the year you become a proper adult — it used to be at age twenty, before they lowered it to eighteen — young people mark the occasion at annual mass celebrations across the country. It's a big deal, and young men may choose between wearing the traditional kimono or Western-style formal wear, and they look great either way, but the stars are the young women dressed in their finest kimono, bought or rented especially for the occasion.

My mother's kimono is pink and white silk embroidered with stylized peonies, chrysanthemums, and koi. I've thought about keeping it intact for my own twentieth birthday, but that's three more years away and it hasn't been worn in over two decades. I want to make something that I can wear now, and often, for years to come.

We carry the kimono to Mitsuko's old suite, which still has the table she and I spent hours at, doing arts and crafts and playing games. While she unpacks her sewing machine and sewing basket, I put together her dress form.

Then, after laying down a table pad, Mitsuko removes the kimono from its special hanger and spreads it out, while I pour us tea.

"Here you go." She hands me a stitch ripper and we each take a sleeve to begin picking the kimono apart, when she suddenly stops. "Oh, no," she says, dropping her sleeve on the table. "Wait."

"What? Why?"

"We need a picture of you wearing this. Properly, the way Mineko did. We need a record of that, before we change anything."

I let out a breath; I can't believe the thought didn't occur to me. Because we have so many photos of my mom wearing this. And yes, I want to wear it like she did, and have a photo to look back on.

So, after turning my Dutch braid into an updo, with my aunt's assistance, I dress in my mother's coming-of-age kimono.

Mitsuko first helps me secure the thin under-robe, then holds up the kimono so I can slip it on. She adjusts the collar until it sits properly, and while I hold the kimono closed and off the floor, she grabs the first of the three parts that form the obi. After tying each one, Mitsuko corrects how the kimono hangs, where it's folded, where it tucks.

Then, I slip on a pair of white tabi socks before stepping into the dress geta I picked out from my small collection.

The last thing I do to complete the look is take out the same kanzashi my mom wore and slide it into my hair.

When I'm done, I turn around to face my aunt.

"Oh, Emiko." She comes up to me, all weepy, and because she's so petite, her head tucks easily under my chin. She wraps her arms around me, and even though she's crushing the beautiful bow she tied behind me, we hug for a long time. Then, she lets me go so she can find her phone.

"Alright, that's good, let me take some photos now."

We go outside and she snaps some on the deck with the water view behind me. We take more in the garden, and we're debating whether or not I should change my shoes before heading down to the beach when Ojiichan comes around the corner, back from his daily walk.

When he sees me, he comes to a complete standstill. And when he doesn't say anything right away, I grin and do a little 'Walk Like An Egyptian' move to try and keep things light, but I can see he's getting misty, too.

I was so young when they died that I don't have actual memories of either my mom or my dad, just those shared by Ojiichan and Mitsuko, Abby and Mas, and other friends who knew them. And because the hole my parents left behind has been filled to overflowing, I've never felt a lack of anything, so it feels almost greedy to want more.

For my grandfather and my aunt, though, I know it's different. Their loss is bigger than I can understand.

"Emiko-chan." Ojiichan approaches slowly, his smile happy and sad at the same time. "You look just like your mother."

"Thank you, Ojiichan."

Mitsuko motions for us to get closer. I link my arm in his and smile as she takes photo after photo.

Then, Ojiichan takes over and captures just as many of me and my aunt.

Then, it's my turn, and I manage to get us all in frame for a series of selfies, including some deliberately bad ones that make us laugh.

"Okay, I think we've taken enough." I spread my arms out so the furisode sleeves hang like banners. "Time to transform this into the best prom dress in the history of Otter Creek." When I catch my grandfather's expression, I drop my arms. "Ojiichan, would you rather I didn't use this one?"

He shakes his head, and I almost tear up at the pride in his eyes. "I am happy for you to do as you wish, Emiko. I think your mother would be as well, knowing you are taking something of hers and making it your own."

I hug him a long time for saying that, a moment my aunt captures, and then she and I head back upstairs to take the kimono apart.

When I first began to think about my prom dress, I removed everything from the white corkboard above my desk and started a vision board.

There is, of course, a picture of Molly Ringwald as Andie, patron saint of refashioned prom dresses, at the top. I put up photos of Audrey Hepburn in her most iconic looks, kimono-remake ideas from Japanese magazines, sketches from costume designers like Dinah Collin, Ruth Myers, and Alexandra Byrne.

I've also included ideas for hair and accessories, song lyrics and poetry that put into words the mood I'm aiming for, and drawings of silhouettes and details I think might work.

After we deconstruct the kimono into pieces of fabric, Mitsuko and I go over everything on the board. She asks me questions, and we talk about what's most important to me, not only in how the dress looks, but in how it will make me feel.

Somehow, she distills all that information down and roughs out some designs that capture what I want — so quickly, it leaves me in awe.

She then makes a muslin sample which gets tweaked after a couple of fittings, and by the Friday before school starts, there on her mannequin is my dream dress.

"Thank you, Mitsu-Obachan," I say, using my childhood name for her. "It's exactly what I hoped for."

"You're welcome, Emiko," she says, and we stand there for a long time, arm in arm, admiring her work.

It's sleeveless, very simple — the interest coming from the rich fabric — with a V-neckline that mimics the way you wear a kimono left-over-right. Mitsuko used part of the obi to accent the Empire waist, and from there the dress falls to my knees. I took a square of obi fabric to make a clutch and, as a surprise, my aunt pieced together what was left to make me a matching shoulder wrap.

I invite Harumi over the next day for a preview.

"*Uwaa!* It's so gorgeous — I *love* it," she gushes when she sees it on the mannequin. "You should take one of your pictures of you wearing the kimono and frame it with one of you in the dress. Like a before and after."

I go to my desk and pick up an envelope. "I thought the same thing, except with these." I pull out two photos — a reprint of my mom wearing it first, and one of me. "See?"

Harumi walks over and gives a soft sigh. "She looks really nice," she says.

I nod. "Yeah. I think she was." Then, hoping this hasn't brought up too many feelings about her own mom, I put the photos away and turn to her. "So, you wanted to show me something about your dress?"

When I told her my *Pretty in Pink* idea, Harumi got all excited and brought over a red '50s-era dress she had that belonged to one of her aunts. Complete with layers of rustly crinoline, it echoes the vintage dress Annie Potts wore in the movie. Harumi's dress was way too big for her, but after a visit to the House of Mitsuko, it now fits her like it's custom, and she looks incredible in it.

But it turns out Harumi's not done.

"I know people might not get how my dress fits with the theme, so I had this idea." She opens up another bag and pulls out a handful of pink and white fabric bows. "What do you think about stitching these all over it? And then gluing these in the centers?" She shakes a small container of something sparkly.

I try to picture what she's suggesting. "Uhm, I'm not sure how this helps."

"These are a couple of Hello Kitty's signature colors from the '80s," she says, as if it's common knowledge. "Like, 1980? The year Yuko Yamaguchi took over as chief designer?"

"I did not know that," I say sincerely.

"Yamaguchi's the reason Hello Kitty's where she is today. I mean, Hello Kitty was this close to being canceled." She holds her thumb and index finger an inch apart. "But thanks to Yamaguchi's genius, Hello Kitty is now Queen of *Kawaii*. Like, of the world. So, I thought I could also turn this into a tribute to her AND Kitty."

I grin, picturing the finished dress in my head. "That sounds awesome. You should *totally* go for it."

Harumi beams. "I think it'll make quite the statement, don't you?"

"Absolutely." I peer into the bag. "Uhm, how many bows did you bring?"

"Eighty-eight," Harumi says. "You know, for the theme, and for good luck."

"Wow. Okay. Well, I guess this won't be any harder than sewing on a button," I say as I grab needles and thread from Mitsuko's kit.

"Eighty-eight of them!

21
Prom Night

Senior prom is now less than a week away and Harumi still doesn't have a date.

"Honestly, Emiko, I don't care," she insists. It's Sunday and Re: Gifting is quiet, so she's restocking handmade soaps, sniffing each different scented bar before putting it on the display stand. "It's such a dumb rule that tenth-graders can't go to senior prom. Otherwise, I'd totally ask Will to be my 'escort,' too" — she uses air quotes here — "but since I can't, and there's no one else, I'll just go with Arlo and the girls. You know, like, in a group."

I mull this over. A date is *totally* not a prerequisite for any dance, and I know from last year how much fun going as a group can be. But I really want her to have a memorable time, partly because it's her first Cedar Grove prom, and partly because I still feel a little twingey about Gareth and want to make it up to her.

Then, in one of those coincidences that happen sometimes, like when you think of a song right before it plays on the radio, when I walk out of the shop, an idea involving Jun comes to me just as I spot him across the street about to get into his SUV.

"Jun!" He looks around, startled, until he sees me waving at him. "Come here a sec."

He lopes over, his usual easy smile on his face. "Ms. Kimori."

"I was just thinking about you. I have a question — well, actually, maybe it's more of a favor to ask. How would you feel about — wait a minute. What are you doing here?"

"Hm?"

"I thought we weren't going to see you till Friday."

"Ah, yes. Well, I, uh — I'm almost embarrassed to admit this," he rubs the back of his neck, "but I had a sudden craving for Mitsuko's famous —"

"Never mind, it doesn't matter," I interrupt, too excited to let him finish. People come up from Vancouver all the time for Mitsuko's baking; it's no big deal, and Jun is impulsive enough to take a spur-of-the-moment trip for a raspberry swirl. I take a deep breath. "How would you feel about having *two* dates for prom?"

He looks at me for a second, his face unreadable. "I can't tell if you're joking."

"I'm not. No one's asked Harumi yet and —"

"Emiko, relax." He breaks into a grin. "How could I refuse? With you and Harumi by my side, we'll make the entire student body green with envy."

Impulsiveness must be contagious, because I'm so happy with my solution to Harumi's problem that I surprise him with a big hug. "Thank you, Jun. You're the best."

He looks around sheepishly, reminding me of where we are. "Well, I wouldn't say that."

"Well, I would. Now," I say, taking his arm, "let me tell you what Harumi's wearing."

Either Jun Morimoto lied, or he was just born to prom.

First, he shows up in a stunning chauffeured vintage Jaguar that turns Ojiichan, Seiji, and Mr. Yoshimatsu into instant fanboys.

Then, when he first sees Harumi and me, he takes us both by the hand, gives us each a flawless twirl, and tells us we look "blinding."

THEN, to caps things off, he not only brings wrist corsages that go perfectly with our dresses, but he has posies for Mitsuko, Satomi-san, and Mrs. Yoshimatsu, too.

So by the time we step out of the Jag in front of the Bayside Center, the elegant yet rustic post-and-beam venue where Cedar Grove proms have taken place for over fifty years, Harumi and I are feeling like royalty.

"My first prom!" Harumi's eyes are bright with excitement as we get our entrance bracelets.

"Mine too," Jun says, looking around the lobby.

"Wait till you see inside," I promise as I herd them along towards the main hall.

"Hang on, Emiko." Jun stops to straighten his cuffs. "Let's do this properly, shall we?" Crooking his elbows, he offers us each an arm.

Giggling, Harumi links her arm on his left while I take his

right. Then, with our free hands, she and I each grab a door handle and pull.

Harumi's jaw drops as we walk into the room. "Sugoi," she says slowly.

As the carved cedar doors shut behind us, we look up at the yards of white tulle, massive flower blossoms, and fairy lights draping down from the cathedral ceiling. Add to that the giant papier-mâché butterflies, bumblebees, and lady-bugs flying overhead or clinging to the green tulle and ivy garlands that wrap the posts — it's like walking through a Godzilla-sized bouquet.

Harumi steps away from Jun, and as she turns to take in all the decorations, the besparkled bows on her dress catch the light and shoot off tiny starbursts. The whole effect is pure Harumi and makes me laugh out loud. Jun, who's been busy checking out the rest of the room, grins at me and shakes his head.

"What?"

"You. Are. Amazing. This room — did you really come up with all this?"

I tilt my head to let Harumi know we're moving, and the three of us walk farther into the room. "It wasn't just me, a lot of people helped."

"Now you're just being modest." He stops and looks at Harumi, who still seems dazzled by everything. "Harumi, I'm going to tell you again how absolutely charming that dress is."

"Thanks, Jun. You look nice, too."

"I agree." I step back to get a better look at his all-black outfit. Jun, noticing, poses like a king to show off the short boxy jacket, the quality fabric, his baggy shirt, and his loose pants cuffed at the ankles. "Vintage?"

"Yohji Yamamoto. From my mother's collection." He straightens up and offers us his arms again. "Alright, let's find a suitable table and sit and make fun of all the boring people."

"You're bad," I say as we wind our way to the other side of the room.

While he remains standing, watching the crowd, Harumi and I sit and are soon surrounded by friends, admiring each other's ensembles and snapping pictures. I'm about to ask Jun to join us for a group shot when I glance towards the entrance and see Chisato walk in with her aunt. I assume Taka-san is here to help chaperone, something she volunteers to do often, but I'm surprised that Chisato has actually come.

Jun notices her at the same time. He sees me watching him and makes a face. "I should play dutiful son and go say hello. My mother knows their family."

"Of course."

"But," he leans in, "I'll be back before the first dance, which I expect you to save for me."

"Consider it saved," I say.

With a grin, he heads off.

The look on Chisato's face as he approaches her and Taka-san is hard to read. I have to admit, she looks nice, the delicate flowers in her hair adding an unexpected festive touch to her silvery-gray sack dress and Doc Martens. Jun, probably tired of being stonewalled by Chisato, is now talking to Taka-san, who's smiling up at him like he's Melvil Dewey, inventor of the Decimal System.

"Hi."

I turn around and find Kenzo standing there, his hands in his pockets. Like everyone, he's committed to the theme, so I don't hide the fact that I'm admiring his linen suit and pastel tee and the choice to leave his hair down in beachy waves; the *Miami Vice* vibe is complete.

I grin. "Very on point, Sanada. Well done."

"Glad you approve. I like your dress, too." He turns to Harumi, who's now standing and scanning the room. "And yours," he tells her.

"Thank you," she says, with a distracted smile.

"So, you breaking out any retro moves tonight?" I ask.

He answers with an incredulous look. "Are you?"

"Mmm, guess you'll have to wait and see."

"Yo, Kenzo!" Dev calls out. "Team photo, now!"

"Sorry," he says. "Back in a bit."

As he goes to join his friends, I wonder, again, if Jun hadn't asked, whether Kenzo and I would have ended up coming to prom together. Last year, things fell into place so much more easily.

I also try not to keep dwelling on how happy I am that Mitsuko's bombshell prediction about him and Chisato turned out to be more of a squib.

Thinking about Chisato reminds me of Jun, and I look to see if he's still with her and Taka-san when Harumi suddenly gasps.

"What's wrong?" I say.

"Over by the door," she chokes out.

There's a spotlight set up just inside the entrance that's supposed to give everyone coming into the hall a moment where they're lit up for all to see. It seemed like a good idea at the time, but now I'm not so sure, because standing there, in full Technicolor, is Gareth Tolman, posing like a swell-headed celebrity on the red carpet as Tayjon snaps photos of him. And his date.

I look at Harumi, and my heart clenches when I see that, despite purging all things Gareth from her life, she's still not fully over him. And I realize I've made another mistake by not telling her what Mitsuko mentioned weeks ago, which makes what she's seeing now a complete shock.

"Who is she?" Harumi asks as she sinks down into her seat, her skirt billowing up around her.

I sigh. "That's Kiki Shimizu-Leigh. We haven't formally met."

Kiki Shimizu-Leigh is from Vancouver via L.A. She graduated last year from some private all-girls school and told Mitsuko she's on a gap year. Since meeting Gareth in Whistler, Kiki now seems to be spending her considerable free time on the coast, living in a house with some older cousins.

Gareth, currently promenading like he's presenting Kiki at a cotillion, is wearing a shoulder-padded, pin-striped power suit, while Kiki, in her slinky black tank dress and anchor's weight of crucifixes, bracelets, and dangerous-looking belts, looks like early Madonna on steroids. Clearly, Kiki has no idea how to self-edit, and not even Coco Chanel's advice about accessories can save her.

After taking some selfies, the two continue to parade in our direction, all PDA-ing and being one of those couples you want to throw overripe produce at. They're so self-absorbed they literally have to bump into our table before they break their eye-lock. "Oopsie," Kiki says, and she giggles, while Gareth lurches backward when he sees us.

"Tolman," I say, before checking to see how Harumi's doing. Not well, it appears.

"Uhm." She pops out of her seat like a jack-in-the-box. "I need to go to the bathroom. Emiko?" Her pitch high, she doesn't wait for my response before pushing her chair back with a screech and bulldozing her way around the table.

I stand to try and stop her, or at least slow her down, because I have a sudden premonition that something unfortunate's about to happen. But it's no use, I'm too late, because things are already in motion.

So, I watch, powerless, as Harumi blindly barrels past Kiki, miscalculating how close they are, and Kiki flings her arms up like someone's tossed her a live skunk, and they both cry out in alarm as they collide and bounce against each other like they're wearing inflatable suits.

But they don't rebound back to their own corners, because, somehow, one of the bows on Harumi's dress has snagged on one of the belts snaked around Kiki's waist. And when they finally jerk apart, everyone except Harumi seems to hear the tearing sound that goes on for far too long, because Harumi, who must be in some kind of fog of embarrassment, keeps pulling away until there's a swath of overskirt hammocked behind her.

"Harumi, stop!" I grab her arm. "Your dress."

She looks so dazed, I'm afraid to break eye contact. Behind her, Gareth and Kiki stand staring with their jaws agape. Then Gareth smirks, and Kiki covers her mouth with her hand and starts shaking with laughter.

Even in the dim light, Harumi's face glows red, and, with a grimace, she turns to look behind her. "Oh, no," she whispers when she sees the ruin.

I go up to Kiki and, without a word, unhook the fabric still caught on her tacky belt and bring it back up to Harumi's waist. Thankfully, the crinoline is intact, but it's white and kind of sheer.

"It's okay," I lie. I look around, wondering how to get her out of here.

Suddenly, Kenzo appears. "What's going on?" he asks, his expression concerned.

"*Une petite* wardrobe malfunction," I say airily. "Just trying to figure out what to do."

"Here, Harumi." Kenzo takes off his jacket and places it over her shoulders. It comes down to her knees, and I breathe a huge sigh of relief.

"Hold this. I'll be right back." I give Harumi the end of the torn piece and head towards the refreshments table, in search of a responsible-looking adult. That's when I see Arlo with her friends, looking drop-dead astonishing as a punk-inspired goddess.

"Wow, Arlo."

"Hi, Emiko!" she says with her usual sunniness. "I was just coming to look for you — oh, I love what you did with your mom's kimono! Harumi told me — is she with you? I'm dying to see her dress, too."

"I'll send her right over." I take a second to appreciate her, well, everything, before gesturing to her statement safety-pin necklace. "But first, could I borrow some of those?"

A few minutes later, I find Harumi rooted in the same

spot, the fabric still clutched in her hand. Showing her the pins, I quickly explain the source before moving Kenzo's jacket aside to fasten the torn material at her waistline. "There!" I give her a big smile. "Believe me, in this light, no one will notice."

"Oh, thank you, Emiko!" Harumi turns to Kenzo, who's been acting like a human shield, and taps him on the arm. "Do you want your jacket back?"

"Only if you don't need it anymore. But if it makes you feel better, you can hang on to it."

Harumi's entire body sighs with relief. "It does," she says, and she puts it on properly.

Pursing my lips, I step back to study the whole outfit. "Let's make this look deliberate, then," I say, and I cuff the sleeves and pop the collar. "*Voilà*! Instant boyfriend blazer!"

Kenzo grins as Harumi gives me a big hug. "You're incredible!"

At some point during this fashion challenge Gareth and Kiki must have slunk away, and as I look around the crowded hall, the music volume rises steadily and the DJ starts shouting words. Prom has officially begun.

I catch sight of Jun walking towards me, a scampish grin on his face. "Miss Emiko," he says when he's within earshot. "Sorry about that . . . Taka-san, you know."

"I do. It's okay."

"But I am here now to claim the first dance." He says this playfully, and I take his offered hand, but before we head out to the floor, I turn back for one more check-in with Harumi.

Thankfully, she gives me a surreptitious thumbs-up, all smiles now, surrounded by Kenzo and some hockey mates.

I try to mouth "Thank you" to him but he looks away before I can manage it.

"Emiko?" Jun says.

I turn back to him and let him lead me out onto the dance floor, where we immediately start moving to the synth-pop classic "Bizarre Love Triangle."

"I love this song!" I shout in-between lyrics.

Jun is a fantastic dancer, like, BTS-level talented, managing to be cool and fun at the same time. I'm jumping up and down, stepping and shaking and shimmying along with Jun, arms in the air, and we don't miss a beat as the first song fades out and the next one rolls in.

"I love THIS song," Jun shouts as things get more up-tempo with Depeche Mode's "Just Can't Get Enough." And when we look at each other, I can tell he's asking the same question I am, which is: *Should we keep dancing?* And it's obvious we both want to, and it's another irresistible song, and we're warmed up, so we keep going.

We dance through one more number, Harumi bouncing in to join us, before I hold up my hand to indicate I need a drink. Harumi keeps going, finding more partners on the floor, but Jun nods and we walk back to our table, leaning against each other, tipsy with laughter. Kenzo is already there, and I'm surprised to see Chisato has joined him. She smiles tightly as I take my seat, while Kenzo barely glances at me before returning his gaze to the dance floor. Neither seems interested in chatting.

"Whooh," I say breathlessly, to break the silence.

Jun leans down. "What can I get you, Emiko?" He has to raise his voice to be heard over the music.

"Just a bubbly water, please."

Jun shakes his head so I beckon him closer and repeat my request in his ear. He gives me a thumbs-up, then straightens and looks at Kenzo and Chisato.

"Anything from the concession?" They both shake their heads.

The music really is too loud to talk, so I people-watch and spot Harumi and Arlo dancing with Jacob and Darcy. I'm glad she's having fun. It may be too soon, but the thought of finding another guy to help her properly get over Gareth skips through my mind. A short distance away, he and Kiki are slow dancing even though it's another fast song. Gag.

Jun returns and hands me a chilled can. Smiling my thanks, I press it to my cheeks before cracking it open, and I take a welcome sip as he sits down beside me. While he taps his fingers on the table, bouncing his knee in time to the music, I glance sideways at Chisato and Kenzo, trying to figure out what this murky energy I'm picking up is about.

Suddenly, Jun stands and walks over to her. "Miss Chisato," he says. At least that's what I think he says. She looks up at him, solemn-faced, and he bends down by her ear. He must have asked her to dance, because, after a moment, she nods and rises, smoothing her dress, before following him onto the floor.

He's so gentlemanly, I think. Unlike Kenzo, who's been sitting there in silent mode since the dancing started. He also seems to be more than casually observing Chisato as she leaves, but his face gives me little clue as to what he's thinking, so I toss my hair over my shoulder and wait for the next song to start.

Despite the damper that is Kenzo, the rest of the evening blurs by. I have a steady line of dance partners, including Jun several more times, and during the club remix of "Run the World (Girls)," Harumi and I join prom queen Liv Soo and her court in busting out some stage-worthy choreography. Other than short breaks to refuel, I'm on my feet, burning it up.

Jun's being great, doing the rounds and ensuring he's danced with everyone at least once, either individually or in a group. At one point, he even tries to entice Taka-san out from behind the refreshment table, but she just laughs and shoos him away.

Eventually, Kenzo decides to join in on the fun too, and dances with all of our friends — some, I notice, even twice. But so far, he hasn't asked me. I tell myself I'm not bothered by this.

As the evening winds down, and I see Harumi march off with her troop towards the refreshments, I remember I haven't thanked Kenzo for his help earlier. So, despite his odd behavior this evening, I decide to take the high road and walk around the hall till I find him, leaning against a post, watching the crowd.

"Hi." It's still too loud to have a proper conversation so I tilt my head and motion towards the patio doors.

Kenzo considers me for a second before he finally nods.

There are clusters of people already out there, but we find a spot near the pergola, overlooking the garden.

"Pretty good prom so far, don't you think?" I take in a deep breath, enjoying the cool, lilac-scented air.

"Yeah, I guess so."

"You've actually danced more than once, so I count that as a win."

"You're obviously having fun in there."

"I was. I am." Through a large window, I spot Harumi in the crowd, raising the roof. I turn and look up at Kenzo. "You were awesome with Harumi earlier."

"It's no big deal."

"It was. No one else, least of all Gareth or Kiki, did anything to help, and Harumi still gets to enjoy her first prom. So, thank you."

"I would have done it for anyone."

"Even Kiki Shimizu-Leigh?" I bat my lashes, the way she did when she introduced herself to Kenzo earlier.

"Maybe not." He's quiet for a moment, then looks at me. "Harumi's too good for Tolman, you know. So, even if this sucks for her right now, she's better off."

"Hopefully she knows that, too."

We stand there for a bit, watching everyone inside the hall, when I hear the DJ's voice; I can't make out all the words, but I can tell she's letting everyone know prom is almost over.

Kenzo clears his throat. "Do you need to go back inside? To your date?"

"Oh, Jun's not *really* my date," I tell him. "Not, like, in the traditional sense."

He looks pointedly at my wrist.

"Right," I say, acknowledging the corsage. "I mean, yes, technically, he is. But, like I told you, he just wanted to experience prom, so really, I'm more like a decorated human access pass."

Grinning as I say this, I realize I don't even know — or, TBH, really care — where Jun is right now. And though I'm sure he's probably wondering where *I* am, instead of returning to the hall to go find him, and before I can stop myself, I ask Kenzo, "How about a dance? Possibly our last one in high school?"

He looks at the hand I'm holding out but doesn't respond right away.

"Seriously, Sanada?" I say. "You're letting me hang?"

He laughs. "Come on, Kimori. Let's go."

He takes my hand and we run back into the hall. Guiding me through the crowd, he doesn't let go till we find a space, where we wait, a little awkwardly, for the next song to start.

When the air pulses with the first beats of The Cure's "Just Like Heaven," I grin and immediately start jumping and dancing around; this is one of my favorite songs, and it never fails to make me move. Kenzo's not quite as expressive or abandoned, but he keeps up, smiling as I sing out the lyrics, shaking my head in time with the music.

"What I Like About You" by the Romantics slides in next and we keep going. It feels like everyone rushes the floor for this one, and we're collectively shouting along with the hooky lyrics, hitting every "Hey!" and jumping, arms pumping, up and down, and spinning around to the irresistible beat.

At some point, Kenzo and I find ourselves surrounded by Harumi and Jun and Dev, and Chisato, Tayjon, Skye, Liv Soo, and Jeremy, and we're all dancing together, then breaking off into twos, or threes, or fours, before joining up again till we're in a circle, each of us going full tilt. And as we near the end, when the song basically just repeats the title over and over again, the girls sing a line, and the boys sing it back, and we lean in and out, back and forth, right through to the final word. It's crazy fun, and I wish the song would never end.

But it does, and as I come down from the adrenaline, the DJ says something about the last slow dance. There's more patter, she's thanking the crowd, etc., etc. I'm not listening, though, because Kenzo's standing in front of me.

He usually looks so serious, it makes him seem older than he is, but right now, he's smiling a little, and a dimple appears in his left cheek. My breath hitches as the realization of how cute he is smacks me in the face. I have a flashback to when I was six and he was seven, and he tried to steal a kiss while we built sandcastles at the beach. I punched him in the gut and ran away crying.

This present, though? This moment? It's like one of those scenes in a movie — everything around us fades away, and we're in an invisible cocoon, the only two people in the world.

"Slow dance?" he asks, and his eyes twinkle, like he's almost a hundred percent sure I'll say yes. But there's also a flicker of doubt and that, oddly, makes me feel a hundred percent confident about my answer. I feel my cheeks flush and I nod.

He steps closer. "Emiko?" he prompts.

"Yes," I say, and I give him my hand.

He takes it in one of his strong, calloused hands and rests the other one lightly on my back. I've danced a number of slow dances tonight, but this feels different. This might be a mistake.

Kenzo sways gently, shifting his weight, and I follow his lead stiffly as we wait for the song to begin. Then I hear the first notes of "True" by Spandau Ballet, and I want to melt.

I want to melt and lay my head on his chest, and I'm about to, until a quick glance around reminds me how I danced those other slow dances; most couples who aren't, like, actual couples are chatting to each other, or joking with other dancers, or even, in one case, arguing.

So, I resist melting. Because Kenzo and I aren't a couple, I remind myself. We're friends. Old friends who step, and turn, and slowly sway together on the dance floor. We don't speak, and I avoid his gaze, which I can feel on me like a feather, by looking around and pretending I'm interested in what other people are doing.

I glimpse Jun in the distance, but there are too many people around him for me to see who he's with before he disappears from view. I don't see Harumi anywhere, but I hope she's out there too, dancing with someone nice. And I see Gareth and Kiki Shimizu-Leigh, and I stumble.

"Ooh, sorry," I say, but Kenzo catches me, and when I look up at him, maybe it's the song, or just everything, but he pulls me in a little closer, and then I lean in, too. And then I do what I wanted to do earlier, and lay my head on his shoulder. I sigh, and inhale the clean scent of him, and under our hands, resting on his chest between us, his heart beats so strongly that it makes me feel calm and nervous at the same time.

We stay like this after the song fades out and a new one fades in. It's a fast one, you can tell from the intro, and as the transition beats start to quicken, the DJ invites everyone onto the floor for the final dance of the night. I lift my head and look at him, and he's about to say something, when Harumi bursts through the crowd and screams my name.

"Found you! Come on, come on! Kenzo too! This is it, the last dance, let's go!" She grabs our hands, hopping backwards, and pulls us deep into the crowd that's pulsing with the *snap-snap-snap* staccato beats of Neon Trees' "Animal" as it takes over the air.

22

Bear Aware

After a night of prom-induced insomnia, all I want to do is stay in bed until Monday. But I get up, because Harumi and I agreed to meet for lunch and a D&D — Dissection and Debriefing — of the previous evening's events.

By the time I get downstairs the house is empty, and I find a note from Ojiichan telling me he's out with a friend. I'm relieved, because I've been psyching myself up for the usual questions he asks after any school function. He's genuinely interested, which I totally appreciate. But today, I'm grateful for the reprieve and looking forward to it just being Harumi and me. I need to let last night simmer a little bit before lifting the lid.

I'm keeping it simple today, making some bucatini *aglio e olio* and a baby chard and arugula salad. I prep the garlic and red chili flakes, sautéing them gently in olive oil and salt, wash and dry the greens, and make the vinaigrette. I've only had some green tea with lemon this morning, and I'm getting quite hungry. Harumi's running late, which is unlike her, so I check my phone and find a text, but it's not from Harumi.

KENZO: You up?

I debate whether or not to answer. Kenzo is one of the reasons I had trouble sleeping last night, and the combination of sleep deprivation and hunger is making my temples throb. But I can't lie to Kenzo, so I reply.

ME: Yes. Finally.

KENZO: Busy?

I stare at his question. I'm not sure I want to see him today; I'm more than a little confused right now. I know Kenzo has no idea, but his texts are making me feel sweaty, like I'm about to write a really important test I haven't studied for.

My thumbs hover over the screen as I think about what to say. Then I drop my phone onto the counter and circle the island a few times, shaking out my hands. I fill a pot with water for the pasta, set the table, wash and dry my cup, and I'm still not ready to reply. So, I pick up my phone and send a quick text to Harumi instead, asking if she's on her way. Maybe she's too tired to come over.

I've known Kenzo my entire life. And he's always been like a brother to me. That's how I've always thought of him. I love his parents, and the twins, and I feel like a part of their family. But last night, somewhere between him lending Harumi his jacket and our slow dance, something changed.

It's like when someone takes a thing that's perfectly fine, like (I look around and see the dish soap by the sink, yes), like dish soap, and it's exactly what you want it to be, there's no need to go changing anything because it's perfect.

But then, someone decides to fool around with the formula, or redesign the label, or whatever, and it ends up, you have a different "new and improved" product. And maybe the change is subtle and you don't even notice. Or it becomes something completely strange that doesn't smell the way it used to, or suds up the way you like.

I feel like I'm losing my thread here, but my point is: don't mess with the dish soap. How do you improve what's already amazing? Why risk messing something up completely, especially when no one's asking for it? Kenzo and his family are important to me. I don't need anything to change. But it feels like things already have, without me knowing, or wanting — and it's freaking me out.

I look out the front window, hoping to see Harumi riding up the driveway, but there's still no sign of her and my phone is obnoxiously still. As I will Harumi to reply, I pace the living room and try not to obsess over whatever is going on with me and Kenzo. My phone shudders in my hand and I look down at the screen.

KENZO: Everything OK?

As I puff out my cheeks, trying to think of a non-reply reply, I hear a speeding vehicle braking and skidding on the gravel. This is an unexpected visitor, but I recognize the

SUV. Grateful for the excuse to cut things short, I send a quick text.

ME: Jun's here. Gotta go.

I rush out the front door and see that Jun has parked haphazardly near the walkway. He jumps out of the driver's seat, races around to the passenger side, and yanks the door open.

"Jun! What's going on?" He doesn't answer, and I gasp when I see him help Harumi, hugging her backpack, out of the car. She looks like she's been crying — scratch that, she IS crying, that heavy, choking kind of crying that can't mean anything good. "What happened?" I demand as I run towards them.

Jun walks beside her, holding her elbow, but she only manages two steps before her knees buckle. Lightning-fast, Jun's there to catch her and he sweeps her up, carrying her in his arms towards the house. It gives me flashbacks to how Seiji caught Mitsuko when she fell off the stool, that first day they met, in the café.

"She's not hurt, just scared," Jun grunts. He hurries into the house, not even taking off his boots, straight to the living room, where he gently sets Harumi down on one of the sofas.

"What happened?" I ask again as Harumi lies back onto the cushions, her backpack still clutched to her chest, and takes deep, juddery breaths, trying to calm herself down. "Oh my god, Harumi, are you okay?"

"She ran into a bear," Jun says.

"She *what*?"

Harumi, who's thrown an arm over her eyes, starts crying again. "It was so big," she manages. "I was ri-ri-riding my bike, and coming out of the trail, and it ju-ju-jumped out of the bushes at me!"

Jun reaches down and pats her shoulder. "You're alright now." He looks at me. "I was driving by when I saw the bear, and I slowed down to give it room to cross, and then I saw Harumi trying to stop on the pathway. So I honked my horn, and after a few blasts the bear turned and ran in the opposite direction." He turns back to Harumi and gives her a reassuring smile.

"I forgot everything you told me, Emiko," she says, still sniffling and hiccuping. "It turned to lo-look at me and I froze, I totally forgot what I was su-supposed to do, and then it-it growled at me and I thought I was going to d-die!" Reaction sets in and she bursts into fresh tears. "I've never been so-so scared in all my life."

"Oh, Harumi." I sit on the edge of the sofa beside her and take her hand, squeezing it, trying to soothe her while she turns her head and cries into a cushion. "It's okay, you're safe now. And honestly, the bear was probably just as scared of you."

After a few minutes, Harumi's breathing steadies and she sits up. She takes a tissue from the box Jun found nearby and blows her nose loudly. "Thank you, Jun." She smiles, her face swollen and red. "You saved my life."

I smile at Jun too. "Yes, he did."

Jun shrugs. "It was just good timing," he says, checking his phone. He looks up and nods towards the window. "Now, Miss Harumi, unfortunately, I do have somewhere I need to be. Have you got your mobile?"

She nods, giving him a weepy smile, and pulls her pink phone out of the front pocket of her backpack. "Here it is," she says, with a sniffle.

"Good. Now, add me to your contacts." He recites his number and, once she's tapped it in, smiles approvingly. "Alright, that's for anytime you need me, including if you decide later that you cannot bear the idea of riding home alone — pun not intended."

She giggles weakly as I stand. "Are you sure you can't stay? I've got lunch ready to go," I say.

"Very tempting. Alas . . ." He gives us a grin that is part regretful and part flirty. Seriously, what teenage boy gets away with using the word "alas" like that? Harumi's eyelids flutter and something clicks in my mind.

"You, however," Jun leans down and brushes a stray curl off Harumi's face, "are to let Emiko spoil you a little today."

I can hear her sigh as she sinks back into the sofa. "Okay," she replies, her eyes big and shimmery. "I'll see you soon?" she asks in a small voice.

"Of course."

She nods, and then her eyes drift closed.

As I walk him to the door, Jun finally notices he still has his boots on. "I'm sorry about that, Emiko."

I dismiss his apology with a wave. "Please, it's not a worry. Thank god you came along when you did, or who knows what might have happened."

"Yes, well, anyway." Jun looks embarrassed as I open the door for him.

Striding over to his SUV, he takes Harumi's bike out of the back and leans it against the front steps before getting back into his seat. Rolling down the window, he says, "You'll let me know how our little Harumi's doing?"

I nod. "I will. Thanks, Jun."

Jun starts the car and gives me a final wave.

I watch as he drives away, thinking interesting thoughts, until I see him turn onto the road and disappear.

Returning to the living room, those thoughts still percolating in my head, I check on Harumi.

"How are you feeling? Do you want something to drink?"

"Water, please," she croaks, her eyes still closed.

I go into the kitchen and return with a tray. Sitting up, she takes the glass and has a long drink. "Thank you," she says.

"Pretty exciting twenty-four hours." I take the chair beside her. "First prom, and now a run-in with a bear."

Harumi shivers and puts her glass back on the tray. "I feel like I've been on some kind of crazy carnival ride. I mean, that whole thing with Gareth and Kiki . . . But then, Kenzo — when he gave me his jacket? And then . . . you, and your blazer idea . . ."

Her voice trails off, and I feel a bump of pride remembering how I got her prom night back on track, a feeling that's reinforced when she says, "I ended up having the best time, Emiko. And I was so happy when I woke up, and excited about our lunch, and then . . . and then . . . the bear." She whispers this last part, and I know I need to distract her before she spirals out again.

"He was a real-life hero," I say. Jun and his excellent timing, honestly.

Harumi nods shyly. "He was," she says in a wistful voice. "I never expected it."

I know before that dance with Kenzo, whatever that was about, I had fleetingly entertained the idea that Jun and I had some potential to become more than friends. But if he hadn't shown up this morning, I doubt I would have thought about him at all. Not now, not with everything else occupying my mind.

But Jun and Harumi as a couple? As her eyes take on a familiar dreamy, faraway look, it confirms my earlier thought that Jun, with his dashing rescue, may have done more than simply whisk her out of harm's way.

I take a moment to consider this surprising pairing some more. As offbeat as it might appear, like wasabi-flavored ice cream, I realize it could work. And I think, *Why not?*

Out loud, I say, "It *is* unexpected. But that's what makes this interesting."

Happily, I put all the Kenzo stuff aside to focus on Harumi. If she's intrigued by Jun, maybe I could help by giving him a gentle prod? It probably wouldn't take much. After all, didn't he rush to her rescue, even remembering to grab her bike? And ask me to keep him updated on Harumi's condition? Doesn't that suggest he's worried, ergo, invested in Harumi's happiness?

I can feel excitement welling up inside me as I contemplate the possibilities. "I can totally see you two together," I say.

"You can?" she asks.

"Why not?"

She blinks. "Well . . . because? I thought you might think it was weird. I mean, you know, since he's kind of . . ."

"What are you talking about?"

"You know, the way you guys —"

I hold up my hand. "Harumi, stop. That's just how we are together — it's nothing serious."

"Really? 'Cause at the dance, you two —"

"I know. And you're not the first person to think that. But honestly, on my end, there's nothing for you to worry about. We're friends, that's all."

"So you think I might have a chance with him?"

"I do."

Harumi's face transforms, and it's clear to me, after how badly I messed up the whole Gareth situation, that it's almost my responsibility to make things right by encouraging this potential new match.

I reach out and clasp her hands in mine. "Come on," I say as I help her up and walk her to the kitchen. "You must be starving after all that adrenaline."

"I can't believe it, but I am."

During our very satisfying lunch, we laugh a lot, reliving highlights from the night (I don't know if Kenzo's a highlight yet or not, so he doesn't get a mention). And by the time Ojiichan drives Harumi and her bike home, there are no signs whatsoever that she has suffered any lasting ill effects from her ursine encounter. As I watch them leave, I grab my phone and text Jun the update he'd asked for.

ME: Hi. Harumi's homeward-bound. She seems fully recovered!

I don't get a reply immediately, so I start putting away the food. I'm almost done when I hear my phone vibrate.

JUN: Your an excellent nurse.

I frown. I get that texting is quick and shortcuts are taken, but my scalp literally tightens when people confuse *your* and *you're* like this. I'm super disappointed in Jun. I let out a deep breath and try to loosen my neck and shoulders.

I tap out another message:

ME: She called you her hero again. I'm sure she'd love it if you checked in on her later.

A minute or two goes by.

JUN: Ok.

My forehead creases at this vague response. What does he mean? Is he going to call Harumi? Or is he agreeing with me that she'd love it if he did?

ME: So you'll call her?

I wait for several minutes, but when no further texts come, I tell myself he probably got busy, maybe he's driving, and I put my phone down.

As I load the dishwasher, Kenzo pops back into my head, but I'm still not ready to deal with him. Instead, so we don't have a repeat of what happened with Gareth, I make a mental note that I should confirm that Jun isn't in love with me.

Once that's done, I'm sure everything will work out exactly as it should.

23

Decision Time

"Emiko."

I stop, silently cursing my luck, before turning to face Mx. Galloway. "Oh, hey, Mx. G. How's it going?"

"I was about to ask you the same thing. Have you seen anything from your schools yet? Most of my students have already received notifications."

I shake my head. "No, nothing." It's not a complete lie — I really haven't *seen* anything. I don't need to add that it's because I haven't yet opened any of the official-looking emails in my inbox.

"Really." Mx. G. adjusts their glasses and I brace myself for one of their patented looks.

It's not that I don't appreciate their sincere efforts to help me figure out my postsecondary plans. And I always come out of a conversation with them feeling better, sometimes even uplifted. But I need another minute before I choose the most important item from my life menu so far.

Thankfully, I'm saved by my robot-loving friend, Zera.

"Mx. G.!" Zera says, flashing me an apologetic smile. "Can I talk to you? It's, like, imperative."

"Certainly. I'll meet you in my office. Oh, Emiko," they say before I can make a clean getaway. "Let me know when you get some news."

"Absolutely, I will." And once they turn their back, I run up the stairs like I'm being chased.

Saturday morning, I'm at my desk, staring at the three unopened emails in my inbox. I really can't put this off any longer. Meeta got into Oxford, Tayjon's bound for NYU, Liv Soo and Jeremy are heading to UWBC, the Triple As each got into at least one Ivy League school, and Gareth's telling anyone who'll listen that he can't decide between McGill and "going south." I haven't asked Kenzo if he's made a decision yet, because I know, if I do, I'll have to be ready to tell him mine.

Taking a deep breath, I click on the email from Royal Victoria. "Congratulations," it starts.

From Cascadia University: "We are pleased to . . ."

And the University of Western British Columbia: "I am delighted . . ."

I shouldn't be surprised that every single school is a yes — I've worked hard to stay high on the honor roll — but by the time I've read over each acceptance, I feel like I've swallowed a bucket of concrete. I sit there for a few minutes before heading downstairs. I need to talk to Ojiichan.

I find him getting ready for a walk. "Can I come along?" I ask.

"Of course," he says, as he picks out a hat.

We start down the road, but instead of turning left at the three-way stop and going towards the café, Ojiichan turns right, which takes us to the Otter Creek Provincial Park and the pier. There are a few cars in the parking lot, and a small group of parents and their kids on the beach, but otherwise, we have the place to ourselves.

Silent and unhurried, we walk to the end of the deserted pier and sit down on one of the log benches. There's a windsurfer skimming the water way out, and we watch as she does a fancy turn and starts planing in the other direction.

I exhale loudly. "So, Ojiichan."

"Yes?" he says, eyes on the surfer.

"I got my acceptances today."

He turns to look at me, but he doesn't say anything.

"I mean, I got the emails a while ago, but I finally opened them today. And they all said yes."

"Sugoi na, Emiko-chan." He pats my knee and gives me a proud grin. "Congratulations! What a luxury to have such a big choice."

"Yeah. I guess."

"You seem troubled by this."

I nod, watching the surfer rip across the waves. "I know it's great, and I'm super lucky, but . . . it's almost TOO much choice. I mean, what if I pick the wrong school?" I don't tell him what I told Mx. G. back in September because I'm kind of hoping that feeling goes away once I make an actual decision.

"Hm. Yes. That is a possibility, I suppose. However, you could also pick exactly the right school."

"But how will I know?"

When he doesn't immediately answer, I realize this is going to be one of those times when he will not rush.

"I think you will know when you have made the correct decision, Emiko," Ojiichan says eventually.

"I knew you were going to say that." I cross my arms and slouch back against the bench. "But what if I make a decision, thinking it's the right one, and it turns out to be wrong?"

"Then you try to make another right decision."

I let out an exasperated groan. "That's not super helpful, Ojiichan."

He chuckles. "Do you really wish for me to tell you what to do?"

"No," I say, reluctantly. I track a cruise ship off in the distance for a few moments. Then, because it's easier to speak if I'm not looking at him, I say, "I think maybe I just don't know how I feel about leaving this place." When he doesn't say anything, I take a deep breath. "I mean, how do *you* feel about me leaving this place?"

Again, he doesn't respond right away, but I bury the impulse to fill the silence, because I really want to know what his answer is. So I keep my eyes focused on the cruise ship and wait.

He sighs. "That is an interesting question."

I wait some more.

"The thought of you leaving . . . Hm." He pauses. "Well. I would miss you. You brighten my life very much."

My chest tightens and my eyes suddenly get hot.

"But I would not wish for that to stop you from following your own path, Emiko. Neither would Mitsuko, nor would your parents, if they were here." I sense him looking at me but I keep my face forward, absorbing his words.

"What if I don't know what that path is?" I say after a bit, trying to keep my voice steady.

"Ah. That is another question . . . If it would help you to pick a school, we could play rock, paper, scissors?"

"Ojiichan!" I turn to look at him now. "I'm serious. I don't know what to do."

My grandfather considers me for a moment, then nods. "I am sorry, Emiko. You are right. This is serious. And I will always be happy to hear what you are thinking, and give you my opinion, if you like . . .

"But this kind of decision . . . no one else should make it for you," he continues. "Because only you know what you truly want, and only you can do the work to achieve it."

I blow out a breath. "Couldn't you at least give me a hint?"

"I just did."

"A better hint?"

Chuckling, Ojiichan stands up. "Come. I find my clearest thinking often follows after a good, long walk. And perhaps a stop later at Mitsuko's to share your news, and for some refreshments, will prove useful as well." He holds out his hand and I take it, letting him pull me onto my feet.

Normally, the year's first outdoor movie night at the Sanadas' is something I look forward to. It takes place on their spacious rear deck, which runs into a smooth outcrop that slopes gradually up the back of their property, creating a natural seating area. Historically, it's always a fun time.

This year, though, for a bunch of reasons, I'm not sure I want to go. It's Ojiichan who talks me into it.

"Everyone must be outside," I say, since the house appears empty when we arrive. Ojiichan continues out the back door while I stay in the kitchen to grab a bowl for the snack mix I've brought. I'm searching through a drawer when Kenzo comes into the room. This is the first time we've been alone since prom, and though I should be, I am not prepared.

"Hi." I hold up the bag of mix. "I made this for the twins."

"Great. They were asking if you were coming."

"Yeah, sorry, we meant to be here earlier but . . ." I trail off, not sure what else to say.

I eventually answered Kenzo's post-prom texts by keeping the tone casual, like it was friendship as usual between us. And, thankfully, he took the cue. Except, now I feel even more awkward, because *not* talking about certain things has made it hard to talk normally about anything. Words keep sticking like plain popcorn in my throat.

"It's okay. A lot of people aren't coming till later."

"Oh, that's too bad."

He shrugs, then looks at me and grins. "So, I've got some news."

"You do?"

"Yeah. I got in to all my schools."

"That's awesome, Kenzo!" I say, sincerely, because I know how hard he's worked. "Mas and Abby must be thrilled."

"They are. But not because I'm going to UWBC. I picked Cascadia."

"You did?" I look at him, confused, when he mentions my parents' alma mater. "Why?"

He opens another drawer and hands me the bowl I was looking for. "I don't know," he says. "It was tough. But, in the end, I wanted to go somewhere different from Mom and Dad. I just decided today."

"Wow."

"What about you? You must have heard by now."

"No. I mean, yes. I have. All yeses." I avoid his gaze as I fill the bowl. "But I haven't made up my mind yet."

"You're not going to Cascadia?"

"Probably? Most likely? I guess I just want to . . . consider everything."

"Oh. Well, let me know what you choose." He reaches out to grab the bowl. "Come on, the twins will be all over me for keeping this to myself."

As I follow Kenzo out of the kitchen and onto the deck, I'm struck by how . . . unfazed he seems. Like, he doesn't seem uneasy around me at all. Am I the only one feeling flustered about what happened at prom? Is it possible it really was just a dance — several dances — to him? Have I turned an egg into a soufflé?

My mind swirly, I barely notice Takeo and Tomio sitting in front of the screen with their friends and blindly turn and follow Kenzo past them, towards the outcrop end of the deck where most of the guests currently seem to be gathered. Which is how I end up sitting next to Gareth and Kiki Shimizu-Leigh, who's deep in convo with Taka-san, beside her. Mitsuko told me the two have become quite cozy, apparently as a result of Kiki discovering the photogenic little library where Taka-san works. I may have responded by saying I had trouble believing Kiki as a reader, but clearly she and Taka-san have something in common, because it sounds like they're chattering away about a book, of all things.

Anyway, if I move now, it will be too obvious, so I nod at them and at Gareth, and say hello to Mitsuko and Chisato across from me. I look around but don't see Jun or Harumi anywhere.

I never told my aunt about what went down with Gareth and me last year; it's too embarrassing. But since he still works for her, and Harumi doesn't hold a grudge, he and I have settled into an unspoken truce. Still, I'm glad to have Kenzo sitting on the other side of me.

"Sorry," he says, getting up. "I think I heard the doorbell."

As I watch him walk back into the house, I consider embracing rudeness and just going up front to join the twins and their pre-teen friends to watch *My Neighbor Totoro* for, like, the fifty-ninth time, when Kiki squawks, "I know your secret, Chi-Chi!"

"What?" Chisato's normally pale face flushes. I don't blame her — "Chi-Chi" is the worst.

"Your aunt just told me how talented you are — I can't believe you haven't performed for me yet! And — oh!" She stops suddenly and turns to Gareth. "I just had a brainstorm. Babe, I just had a brainstorm."

She takes a calming breath before returning her attention to Chisato, who looks like a field mouse staring down a screech owl.

"You have to let me pull some strings," she continues. "My family has connections at that music institute in the city, you know, the famous one."

"Oh. That's — you don't need to do that." Chisato looks uncomfortable, but Kiki waves a dismissive hand.

"Emi," Kiki says, making my teeth clench; it's like she has a tic about nicknames. "Help me —"

"Emiko," I interrupt.

"Excuse me?"

"It's Emiko, not Emi." I turn the corners of my mouth up so it looks like I'm smiling.

She barely succeeds in not rolling her eyes. "Fine. *Emiko.* What I was trying to say is that we need to join forces and convince Chi-Chi to let me do this."

She turns to Chisato. "I don't want to assume what you can or can't afford, but if you're interested, I'm sure there would be a spot for you in the gifted students program."

I have no idea what she's thinking right now, but, for the first time, I wonder what kind of plans Chisato has for herself, what she might want to do after graduation. And if, whatever it is . . . maybe Kiki's right, and it's something the Ishi family might not be able to afford.

"Well?" Kiki asks.

"*Chi-chan.*" Taka-san puts a hand on Chisato's bouncing knee, stilling it immediately. Though they don't say anything aloud, it's clear that the two of them are communicating with each other, because Chisato lets out a deep breath.

"Thank you, Kiki," she says, before looking away. "That would be really . . . that's a kind offer."

Kiki claps with glee. "Oh, I can't wait to tell them about you. You won't be sorry, Chi-Chi. Just leave it all to me."

It's not just the obnoxious nickname, it's the way Chisato sinks back and gets swallowed up in her chair that makes me feel almost sorry for her. Before I can say anything, though, she lifts herself up and, with a quick "Excuse me," heads towards the house.

She reaches the kitchen door just as Kenzo reappears, now with Harumi, and, after a brief exchange, they step aside for her before continuing out onto the deck. It's Harumi's first time here and it looks as though Kenzo's giving her a tour. She glances over to me and beams, waving, before they cut across the deck to the stairs that lead down to the gardens.

This feels like a good time to get a drink. I ask everyone if they'd like one, even Kiki, but only Mitsuko says yes.

I'm in the kitchen, filling two cups with ice, when Chisato comes around the corner, staring at her phone. "Oh," she says when she notices me, and the phone clatters to the floor. She scrabbles to grab it, then holds it to her chest, looking distressed.

"Are you okay?" I ask. "Did the screen break?"

She doesn't respond at first, which is typical; trying to have a conversation with Chisato is so painful, I wonder why I even bother. If she were a present, she'd be one of those jokey ones wrapped in like a hundred layers of paper and packing tape that you have to peel back before you reach the actual gift. Frustrating doesn't even begin to describe how I feel about that. But just as I can't NOT open a gift, I'm compelled to keep talking.

She shakes her head, but when her bottom lip quivers, I put my cups down and give her my full attention. She looks so sad, it's clear this isn't just about her phone; I reach out without thinking to touch her shoulder but stop when she flinches. "Come on," I say, and walk into the hallway, out of view of the rest of the party. I'm relieved when I turn and see that she's followed me. "What's wrong? Are you feeling sick?"

Chisato nods. "Yeah, my head . . . I think it's a migraine."

"Oh, no. My aunt gets those, too. They really knock her out sometimes. Do you take anything for them? I can ask Abby —"

"No." She keeps her eyes cast downward. "No. I just need to leave."

"What about your aunt? Do you want me to get her?"

"I'll send her a text. It's okay. I don't want to make a fuss."

"Sure, of course." I follow her to the foyer and, as she puts on her Chucks, I remember where she and Taka-san live. "Wait, you can't walk home. Not if you don't feel well."

Shaking her head, she finishes tying her shoes.

"Come on, Chisato." I look around to see if Kenzo or Abby or my aunt happens to be nearby. "I'll get you a ride."

She turns to me, and something in her normally inexpressive face stops me. "Please. Just . . . let me go. I'll be fine." She throws on her messenger bag and then disappears through the front door without a backward glance.

I stand there for a few moments, uncertain I did the right thing. Visions of another bear encounter also skitter across my mind, but I reassure myself that, other than the footpath along Kenzo's house, her route home is a populated one, so she's unlikely to run into trouble.

I go back into the kitchen and finish making my drinks, but for the rest of the evening the memory of Chisato's face keeps bothering me, like a pebble in my shoe.

By the time we're halfway through *Spirited Away*, a good crowd, including Will and Arlo, has assembled, and everyone is now seated in front of the portable screen watching it. Still too low-level perturbed to pay attention, when Jun appears in the kitchen doorway — he'd texted earlier that he wasn't sure he'd make it — I'm so grateful for a reason to move that I almost knock my chair over in my rush to meet him there.

"I'm so glad you came," I lean in and whisper.

"Let me go say hello to my father and Mitsuko. Are you seriously watching this?"

I shake my head. "Want to meet me over there?" I gesture to the far end of the deck, now empty, leaving us the outcrop to ourselves.

"Looks perfect."

Since it's the first time we've seen Jun since *bear day*, I try to catch Harumi's eye to invite her to join us. I feel like she's being less obvious with her feelings about Jun, maybe because he lives off coast, but there was no mistaking how touched she was when he did finally text her post-rescue.

So I keep trying to attract her attention, willing her to turn her head and look towards me, but I give up when it's clear she's too busy whispering something to Kenzo. Figuring I can get her at intermission, I grab an armload of cushions from a nearby stack and go set things up on the rock. I'm making myself comfortable when Jun arrives and folds himself down beside me.

"Miss Emiko," he murmurs as he surveys the crowd from behind.

"Is everything alright?" I ask when he doesn't follow up with some kind of impish compliment; not that I'm fishing, but he seems a bit subdued today.

I see him make an effort to shake off whatever's bothering him, and he flashes me one of his crooked grins. "Of course. Just decompressing." He lifts his chin towards the screen. "Hasn't everyone seen this already?"

"Not a fan?"

"Quite the opposite. I've spent many an afternoon at the Ghibli Museum."

"Show-off," I tease.

He sits up and shrugs his shoulders.

"Well, I'm glad you were able to come."

"I almost didn't." He rakes a hand through his hair and blows out a frustrated breath. "I meant to be here earlier, but . . . the ferry lineups were ridiculous. Tell me, why is it so difficult for them to stay on schedule? In all these months, I think it's been on time once. Literally, once."

"Yup, ferries — one of the joys of living on the coast."

"Well, it's maddening. I would have been here when — in time for the first film if it weren't for that." His silver hair flops in front of his eyes and he huffs it away.

"I thought you were Miyazaki-ed out from, you know, all those trips to the Ghibli?" I nudge him with my shoulder. "You probably went to, like, VIP screenings or something, didn't you?"

"What are you suggesting?" he asks in mock-outrage.

"I guess I'm surprised you'd even want to make such an *arduous* journey, just to watch some movies you've obviously seen before." I'm razzing him, but it does strike me that Jun's gone to a lot of trouble . . . unless there's another reason behind his visits?

My Spidey senses tingling, I stare at the back of Harumi's head, willing her to turn around, and wishing I had a paper-clip to toss when she doesn't budge; maybe she actually *hasn't* seen this particular movie.

"I thought twice about it, believe me," he says, in a tone I'm not expecting. And then, almost to himself, "Why anyone would want to live here is beyond me. It's such a backwater."

"Whoa." I hold up my hands to ward off the splash of attitude. "You know no one's forcing you to come here, right?"

Jun gives me a startled look, and a faint flush tints his cheekbones. I wait him out until he shakes his head and turns his dark eyes back to me. "I'm sorry."

"*Pardon?*" I say, acting like I didn't hear him.

"Ignore me." He blows out a breath. "I really did want to be here earlier." He cocks his head, his expression sheepish. "I take back what I said. There are lots of lovely things about the place. Present company included."

"Glad you think so." I try to look stern but lose it when Jun literally Betty Boops his lashes at me. "Oh my god, stop it."

"Stop what?" he says, batting some more.

"You . . ." I shake my head. After a moment, I turn to him. "I'm sure the coast is a bit of a shock after living in Tokyo or London. Or New York. I mean, obviously, we can't compete."

"It's different. But I do appreciate what you have here."

"Well, that *is* the official slogan for the Golden Coast: 'You'll appreciate what we have here.'"

Jun laughs. "I'm a prat."

"You're a *mega* prat." I whack him with an extra seat cushion to drive the point home. He picks up a cushion too, and shocks me by swatting me back. "You hit me," I say, my voice incredulous.

He seems surprised by my reaction. "I thought — but you started it!"

I whack him again, and we turn into children having a slow-mo pillow fight. Mindful of everyone watching the movie, I warn Jun to keep it down, but we clearly fail because I catch Kenzo glaring at us. Pausing, I give him an apologetic shrug and, with a shake of his head, Kenzo turns back around.

Tossing my cushion aside, I sit up, hugging my knees, while Jun fixes his hair.

"Look, I'm having a beach party next weekend," I say. "I know you're not necessarily fond of sunlight, but it'll be a true West Coast experience. Why don't you come?"

"Why would you assume I'm not fond of sunlight?" he asks.

"Let's just say I've seen salmon bellies with more color than you have."

"I don't even understand what that means."

I grin. "There will be umbrellas and shade. Lots of good food — Harumi and Mitsuko are helping with that," I throw in, casually. "And the stretch of beach below our house is one of the best in the Creek if not the whole coast."

"Consider me officially excited."

I'm not sure why I find Jun funny, but I start laughing. Jun looks at me, and then he starts laughing, too. I see Mitsuko turning around to look at us, the indulgent smile on her face telling me how pleased she is that he and I are getting on as well as we do.

But then Kenzo turns around again, too, and I think, *Uh-oh, we're being too loud,* and I clap a hand over my mouth and Jun's.

And that just makes us laugh harder.

24
Beach Party

Forget monster moth wings, graduation has transformed into a bullet train that's speeding straight towards me as I stand paralyzed on the track.

At least one thing has been crossed off the to-do list, though: I finally chose a school.

"Good for you, Emiko," Mx. G. says when I stop by their office to tell them. "May I ask what made you go with Cascadia?"

I shrug. "It seemed to make the most sense. I mean, my parents went there, and it's a little closer to the ferries. Plus, I like that the campus is smaller than the other two universities. And I think their dorms are nicer."

"Well, those are . . . all good reasons."

"Yeah," I say half-heartedly, and I wonder what Mx. G. would say if I confessed that I literally let chance decide. After ruling out Royal Victoria — double the ferries to travel between the Golden Coast and Vancouver Island just doesn't appeal — and because I didn't want Cascadia to feel like a foregone conclusion, I tossed a Toonie. And, tails, Cascadia beat UWBC fair and square.

With that big future event locked in, I've been thinking about my academic past, or, more specifically, my report cards. I've got almost thirteen years' worth saved in a box in my closet, but the only report card I remember, the only comment that I can still hear in my mind, is from my first-grade teacher, Mrs. Katz.

That year, Mrs. Katz — still one of my all-time faves — called us up one by one to her desk to receive them. When it was my turn, she told me how well I'd done, and she read out her comments, which included: "Emiko is very conscientious and mature for her age." Then she explained what "conscientious" and "mature" meant.

I realize now how much those words have influenced the way I've handled myself throughout all my years at school. It's almost like that report card became an instruction booklet for how I was supposed to operate.

It's a little scary realizing how big an impact that description had on me. It makes me wonder what kinds of things Jun or Chisato or Harumi, even Kenzo, heard about themselves when they were little. And what kind of mark, if any, that may have left.

Anyway, I'm thinking about all this while looking back on a year packed so full of what Ojiichan would refer to as "happenings" that it feels close to bursting. And if I were being my "normal" self — that is, very conscientious and mature for my age — then what I *would* be doing is studying and getting plenty of rest, eating right, and exercising regularly.

Instead, even though my plate is mounded with what most people would agree are bigger priorities, I am planning one last get-together before school ends.

Through the week leading up to it, though — especially when it turns out most people I've invited can't make it, for very responsible reasons — I swing between first and second thoughts so often, I come close to canceling the whole thing. But, convincing myself this smaller party will still be fun, and will possibly be my last shot at boosting Harumi's chances with Jun before summer, I keep it on the calendar.

The day-of starts out well enough; there's sun, it's warm, and the breeze off the water is light. I take it all as a good sign.

Mitsuko and Harumi arrive early to help get everything ready. Abby, Mas, the twins, and Seiji are all off-coast in the city today, but Jun has texted he's on his way, and Kenzo's promised to come after work with Will and Arlo. Which leaves us waiting for the mismatched set of Chisato and Taka-san and Gareth and Kiki Shimizu-Leigh (these two, this time, courtesy of my way-too-nice aunt).

Of course, Gareth and Kiki are the first to show. Even though Harumi has assured me she's completely Gareth-free, I'm glad I thought to ask Kenzo to invite Will and Arlo, too. Even though I expect Harumi to focus her energy on Jun, it can't hurt to have more people on her side of the aisle.

Anyway, after brief greetings, Gareth sets up a couple of loungers, while Kiki snaps her fingers at Mr. Yoshimatsu when he brings down firewood for the bonfire I'm planning to light at dusk.

"Oh, Mr. Y.!" she yells. "Could you bring us another umbrella? I must have complete shade." She has on enormous

Jackie O. sunnies and a hat with a brim wide enough to shelter several small children. She doesn't even wait for Mr. Yoshimatsu to reply before handing Gareth her phone. "Babe, take my picture," she says, and drops her caftan, revealing a sequined bikini that, despite the setting, still manages to feel like overkill.

Before Harumi and I can trade more than a single eyeroll, though, Mitsuko calls her over for some help, so I go back to filling the ice chest. I've just finished nestling in the last of the drinks when I hear a text come in.

JUN: Miss Emiko. Please report to the kitchen.

I smile, intrigued.

ME: Will do.

I tell Mitsuko I have to get something from the house just as Chisato and Taka-san arrive, carrying beach bags and a soft cooler. After greeting them both, Mitsuko takes Taka-san over to show her the food, leaving Chisato behind with me.

"You made it." I keep expecting Chisato to bail on things, but, aside from my birthday dinner, she keeps surprising me by showing up. I'm starting to suspect Taka-san is, like, secretly a heavy, forcing Chisato to go out and socialize, because her energy is totally dog-realizing-it's-going-to-the-vet. And in her skinny jeans, plaid shirt over band merch, and cotton beanie, she's patently more skate park than beach ready.

Nodding, she gestures to where Gareth and Kiki are posing for selfies. "Is that where you want us?"

"Sure, yeah, please. Make yourself comfortable." I wave at Harumi, who comes running over.

"Yay, you're here!" she says as Chisato gives her a small smile.

"Harumi will show you where everything is. I'll be right back." As I head up the path, I hear Kiki scream, "Chi-Chi!" and I almost feel bad for abandoning her.

But as I run up to the house, that feeling is eclipsed by my curiosity about Jun's text. Also in jeopardy: my goal to do what I can today to artfully bolster things between him and Harumi. That thought goes *poof* when he slips around the corner of the house wearing a mischievous smile. He makes a show of checking around before he turns to me and stage-whispers, "Are we alone?"

Nervous excitement ripples through me. "I think Ojiichan's in his workshop, but he should be out soon. Everyone else is at the beach. Why?"

Jun sidles over and shows me a small stoppered bottle he had hidden behind his back. It's got a striking calligraphed label on it and is full of liquid the color of sunset. "Look what I managed to find. I thought you and I could sample this together."

"What is it?"

"Umeshu — well-aged — small batch, very limited number of bottles. Clever me managed to snag this one." He dangles it in front of me like a bell.

I've never tried any other kind of alcohol, but last year one of Ojiichan's friends came to visit and he brought some plum wine as a gift. At dinner, Ojiichan let me have a taste, watered down with ice. I remember the tart-sweetness, like the fruit, but richer, with a bite from the alcohol. It wasn't awful, and I thought that one day, when it was legal for me to do so, I'd probably try some more.

But I don't mean to start now. "You are a bad influence," I say, jokingly, because I'm also sort of flattered Jun thought of me for this.

"Oh, come on, Emiko. It'll make the party bearable."

I shift back on my feet and frown. "Excuse me?"

He sighs. "Now you're upset with me, too." He pouts, before muttering, "Everyone's so touchy today."

Crossing my arms, I give him a brisk look. "Attendance is not mandatory, you know."

Jun bows his head, letting his hair flop into his eyes. "I'm sorry. Really, Miss Emiko, I am. I don't know why I said that. But I really, really think you should try some of this. It's beyond delicious *and* it's good for you."

"Of course it is."

"I'm completely serious. Look it up. It helps with exhaustion . . . and we've all been working so hard at school, haven't we?"

Maybe it's his sorry-not-sorry grin.

Maybe it's because I actually *do* feel tired . . . the party has barely begun and I already want it to be over so I can go upstairs and slip under my covers.

And, maybe, well, maybe I just don't feel like being my report card comment today.

So, with that decision made, I slide open the patio door and invite Jun inside. After grabbing a couple of red cups and filling them with ice, I let Jun pour a little of that golden liqueur and a lot more soda water into each one.

"Kampai." I tap my cup to his.

He grins. "Kampai."

The party's a complete bomb.

Other than Ojiichan, Mitsuko, and Taka-san sitting off to the side, having their usual fun-fest, no one is gelling.

Gareth and Kiki are acting like they're on their own reality show, alternately bickering and flaunting PDA all over the place.

Then there's Chisato, sitting with Harumi, Will, and Arlo, who are all gamely trying to engage her in conversation. Thankfully, unlike Will, Arlo is chatty, and, with Kiki butting in at random moments, and the well-curated playlist Jun's got on his portable speaker, at least there's some noise in the air. But I catch Chisato looking at everyone as though she doesn't understand what she's doing here.

Kenzo showed up an hour ago, freshly showered but tired, and he's barely said two words to me. I think about offering him some umeshu, too, but his vibe is kind of cloudy, so I decide against it.

Still, I'm glad he's here. Because friends show up for friends. But I'm not getting any time to talk to him because Jun's being *suuuper* attentive and I am being a terrible hostess because Jun and I keep sneaking back to the house — separately, of course, because we're not dumb — to refill our cups with umeshu and soda. It's delicious, more so than I remember from last year, and that alcoholic burn I remember from back then is barely noticeable now.

When the energy dips even lower, Jun comes up with a brilliant idea.

"What say you all to lighting the fire early?" he asks loudly. "Really get things crackling."

Arlo jumps to her feet. "I can do it. I'm the designated fire-starter in my family. Right, Will?"

Will nods, getting up as well. "Is there a bucket for water?" he asks me.

"Yes, Will," I say, a little offended that he'd even doubt it, and I wave my hand around. "We have *beaucoup* buckets. Somewhere." Jun finds the one I'm thinking about and passes it to him, giving me time to find the matchbox and toss it to Arlo.

As I settle back onto the blanket and watch her and Will get the fire going, Jun leans over.

"Miss Emiko," he whispers. "Other than these two Scouts of Canada, I believe we're the only ones here having a good time." He flashes his eyebrows up and down like a cartoon villain, and I laugh like he's the funniest thing e r, which encourages him to keep saying things that are kind of mean.

"Is it just me, or does Chisato look like a baby vampire on a day pass?" he says in my ear.

I stifle a giggle when I see Chisato giving us a look, like she heard him. Can't get mad if it's true, I think. It's also true that Kiki laughs like a donkey — pardon me, *brays*. I take another long sip of my umeshu and soda. It's sooo delicious.

"Look out, Kimori. Three o'clock," Jun mutters, doing a very bad imitation of a ventriloquist.

"Hm?"

"I believe the term is 'busted.'" His eyes shift sideways and I follow his eyeline until I land on Kenzo, who's sitting there with his arms crossed, glowering like a big fat party pooper. Jun must be reading my mind because he adds, "By the killjoy."

Jun's right, and suddenly, *I'm* mad at Kenzo. He's *totally* killing my joy. I give him a glare and, for some reason, he throws me one back. Not sure why *he's* so upset. It's not like I'm acting like the boss of him, I think to myself. I look away, ignoring him and everyone around me, and jab at the ice cubes in my drink with my straw.

As I sit there, wondering when I can leave my own party, Jun jumps onto a big log and pulls me up with him. Once we're balanced, he makes me reenact the Jack and Rose scene from *Titanic*, the one on the ship's bow. Oh, my god, that *movie*.

Anyway, it cheers me up, and we're hilarious, and I think everyone must be jealous of how much fun Jun and I are having. I look around and see Chisato watching us with her expressionless face as she pulls out her precious notebook. She clicks her pen, the same way she did in the library that day way back in the spring, and suddenly, I very much want to know what she's writing.

"Hey," I say as I step off the log. The ground is farther away than I expect and I stumble but I don't fall down. I have excellent balance. "Hey," I say again as I get closer to Chisato.

She stops writing and looks up at me, her eyes narrowing. "What are you always scribbling in there?"

I'm standing over her now, and she shrinks back, hugging the notebook to her chest. I try to grab it but all I seem to be doing is flailing my hands around her head. I accidentally hit her beanie — who wears a beanie to the beach in the summer? — and it starts to slide off, exposing the electric-blue streak in her hair.

She grabs her hat before it hits the ground, which means the cage she's made around her notebook has an opening, and I go for it. "Let me SEE!" I yell, and I manage to pull the book out of her grasp.

"NO," she yells back, which stops me for a second because it's like, wow, she can yell. But then I take in her panicked expression, and now I really can't wait to read what she's written. It's GOT to be juicy.

I step away from her, more nimbly than I think she expected, and leap onto the log, where Jun's still standing. He's watching me and Chisato, and I don't understand the look on his face, but I don't care, and I concentrate on opening the notebook.

Unfortunately, Chisato has really small writing, like, ant-sized, and I can barely make out any words. I flip through the pages but nothing stands out. Based on the way most of the writing is laid out, though, one thing seems clear.

"Well, well, well." I smile like I'm super proud of her. "I think we have a poet in our midst. Are you a poet, Chisato?"

She glares at me, silent. I try again.

"Are you, like, the Emily Dickinson of our time? Of our generation?" I'm not being snarky, I honestly want to know. I lean down, because I don't want to miss her answer, and she blinks up at me with big eyes.

And then I topple off the log.

I try to catch myself, but as I continue downward, my foot catches in the sand and I lose my balance. My arms windmill but that doesn't slow me down so I instinctively fling my hands out to brace myself and send Chisato's notebook flying. Even as I keep falling, I follow its trajectory as it sails up, up, up into the air, till it hangs for a split second like an ornament, before gravity takes over and sends it straight back down, into the fire.

Somehow, I avoid hitting my head on a log and end up on my knees, gasping as I hit the ground. "I'm okay, I'm okay," I say, trying to reassure everyone as I struggle to my feet. When I look up, however, whatever else I meant to say dies before it leaves my mouth.

Kenzo is standing across from me, holding Chisato's smoking, charred notebook by a corner, and he looks madder than I've ever seen him. Averting my eyes, I concentrate on brushing the sand off my hands and knees before I raise my head again, and I notice my aunt and grandfather are here now, too, and they don't look happy either. A quick glance around confirms that everyone is staring at me.

"What?" I say to no one in particular, and my face feels so hot, I step back from the flames. "What?" I repeat, but get nothing in response, and all I hear are the waves hitting the shoreline, the crackle of the fire, and Jun's music playing in the background.

25
The Truth

I think I'm dying.

Within seconds, I realize there is no question about it: I AM dying. I have to be, that's the only explanation for the way I feel — my skull is pounding from the chain gang trying to Shawshank their way out, while my poor eyes are squinched shut against the klieg lights that seem to be shining in my face. And my mouth. Oh, my poor, drought-stricken mouth . . .

With a groan, I attempt to get up but stop mid-turn because the room is wobbling on a Cyr wheel. Swallowing hard, a ball of nothing good heavy in my stomach, I take deep, slow breaths to try and keep things under control because I know I will not make it to the bathroom in time.

Giving up, I sink back into the mattress, letting my arm fall over my eyes. The welcome pressure keeps me tenuously weighted to the bed so I don't feel like I'm going to fall out while the room continues to spin. I hear a lowing noise and dimly recognize that it's coming from me.

I know I have, like, zero tolerance for alcohol, but I cannot believe a little bit of plum wine — *PLUM WINE* — is the reason I feel like this. I cast a mumbled string of curses on Jun Morimoto for bringing his fancy bottle of artisanal, limited edition, way-too-delicious and way-too-potent umeshu to the party.

Then I make a solemn vow not to touch the stuff again until I'm, like, thirty or something, because I do NOT enjoy the way I'm feeling. I do, however, consider recording a PSA about the perils of underage drinking because, at my core, I'm conscientious that way.

After falling back asleep, I don't wake up again for hours. Thankfully, the physical symptoms have by then subsided enough for me to roll out of bed, drag myself to the bathroom, and take a deep breath before I look at myself in the mirror. Wow. It's not good. Definitely not good.

I manage to shower, drinking as much water as I can as it streams over me. The thought of food makes my stomach clench, but a pitcher of flat ginger ale beckons me like a mirage. A sleeve of crackers wouldn't be bad, either. Plain, salty, dry crackers.

Using as little effort as possible, I pull on some sweats, a tee, and the hanten Mitsuko made me years ago, its cozy comfort exactly what I need as I lie back down again. My brain feels very, very mossy as I try to recall how I managed to get to bed last night. Moments from the beach party flash through my mind like a strobe light. I look over at the clock on my night table and stare at it in disbelief. It's past noon.

I let my feet dangle over the side of the bed and take my time standing up. As much as I'd like to stay in my room for the foreseeable future, I know I have to make an appearance before nightfall.

Creeping down the stairs, I strain to listen for signs of life. It's possible Ojiichan's gone for a walk, or is in his workshop; I'm hoping so, at least until I feel closer to human.

Unfortunately, I hear, coming from the dining table, the crinkle of the *Yomiuri Shimbun* Ojiichan has delivered every Sunday. There's no way I can avoid him. I try to clear my throat but that starts a coughing fit, and I'm hitting my chest, trying to ease it, while my grandfather slowly lowers his newspaper to give me his version of stink eye.

"Ohayou." His "good morning" sounds less than sincere, especially as we're well beyond the lunch hour.

I try smiling but, still feeling like Loki after the Hulk ragdolls him in *The Avengers*, I probably look more pained than anything, and I'm not surprised when Ojiichan gives me nothing encouraging in return.

I shuffle over to the counter. "Uhm, have you eaten?"

"Runny eggs and undercooked bacon," he says, his eyes back on his paper.

I ride out the urge to dry heave, and when I regain some control over my reflexes, I nod, murmuring, "Mm-hm, mm-hm," as I make my way to the pantry for some ginger ale and saltines. I swear I hear my grandfather shaking with suppressed laughter behind the paper.

I should mention that my grandfather has never, ever raised his voice at me, except for when I've, like, run into the street without checking both ways twice, or gone kayaking without a life jacket. So, unless life or death was at stake, his school of thought when it came to discipline was to give me fair warning, and if I chose to test the boundaries, then he usually let me do it and suffer the consequences. To his credit, when that happened, he never said, "I told you so."

So today, other than the stomach-churning breakfast mention, he just lets me wallow while leaving out a bottle of ibuprofen and an ice bag.

After filling the ice bag, I take it, along with some water and the ibuprofen, out onto the deck. My energy level is still in the red, but sitting there, breathing in the fresh air, makes me feel fractionally better.

Somewhere in the house, my phone tolls with a text, but I can't bring myself to get up and find it. As the texter tries a few more times before giving up, I knock back a couple of pills with the entire glass of water, and for the next half hour or so the most activity I can manage is balancing the ice bag on my head like a wonky beret.

I try to remember the beach party. I know it wasn't the best event I've ever hosted. In fact, it will probably go down as one of the worst, but I'm hoping no one else noticed. While I continue rooting through my recollections, in the background I hear the landline ring and Ojiichan's voice when he answers it. After a few minutes, he sticks his head out the patio slider.

"Kenzo's on his way."

I sit up. He never calls the house phone, but then I think about the unanswered texts on my cell. I stand and, feeling more clearheaded than when I woke up, I trudge upstairs to change into something more presentable.

By the time I come downstairs, Kenzo is on the deck, looking out towards the beach.

"Hi," I say as I step through the sliders.

He turns and gives me a curt nod. He's not smiling and appears to be thinking about something unpleasant. "How are you feeling?" he says eventually.

Guessing it would be a mistake to share the many un-fine things I've been feeling this morning, I simply nod, and try to smile. "Okay, thanks."

"Good. Did I wake you?" The way he says it, there's some judgment there, but I guess I kind of deserve it, so I don't reply. He looks at his feet for a few seconds before he raises his head again, and I gesture towards the kitchen.

"Do you want to come in? Get something to drink?" As soon as the offer leaves my mouth, I realize I've said the wrong thing, because Kenzo's eyebrows pinch together.

"No, thank you." His voice is cool.

"Okay, what exactly is your problem?" I say after an uneasy silence. "I didn't ask you to come over. If you've got something to say, say it."

Kenzo's eyes flare and he shakes his head, running a hand through his hair. "Do you even remember what happened at the party?"

"Yes." No, not really. I remember laughing a lot, and running back to the house, and taking turns with Jun to refill our cups with more ice and wine.

"And?"

"And, what? I'm sorry if you felt left out of the fun. Jun and I —"

"You were *drunk*, Emiko."

"I wasn't drunk, *Kenzo*." I emphasize his name to make the point clear. "I was just very relaxed."

287

"Well, if that's true, and you were sober when you did what you did to Chisato, then that makes everything worse." He turns away from me and takes a deep breath.

"What are you talking about?" I try again to replay the day in my mind, but my memory bank keeps going offline. "And why are you getting mad at me? Jun's the one who brought the wine in the first place."

Kenzo looks at me with such sheer disappointment that something withers inside me. I pretend I'm not discomforted by any of this, lifting my chin even though it feels rusted in place, and I meet his eyes. And though it makes me feel like screaming and throwing dishes, I don't break eye contact until he does.

He sighs. "The fact that Jun brought the wine doesn't matter. Because, as far as I could tell, Jun didn't force you to drink the stuff. Did he?" His expression darkens at the idea.

"No, no," I admit quickly. I can't throw Jun under the bus for that.

"Besides, what Jun does — I don't trust the guy, but this isn't about him." Kenzo stops and turns towards the garden for a moment while my heartbeat ramps up so loudly I miss the words he says next.

"Sorry, what?"

Kenzo shakes his head, and I think, maybe he's changed his mind and won't repeat himself, whatever it was. But then he looks at me. "You were so mean, Em."

My mouth drops open in shock. "What are you talking about?"

"To Chisato. You've always been a little funny about her, but what you did to her yesterday . . . it was humiliating."

"Oh my god, that is *such* an exaggeration. I was just messing around."

"*Messing around?* Did you see her face? Her aunt's face? Mitsuko's? No one except you and maybe Jun thought you were being funny."

I'm fuming, but the truth is, I don't remember much about yesterday. I mean, I do recall looking at Chisato and noticing she had her notebook out. I remember everyone arriving. I remember that first sip of plum wine, and how I didn't hate it.

I remember the flush of warmth that spread all the way to my fingers and toes, and how mellowed out I felt. Which was exactly what I needed, because the party wasn't even close to being the distraction I'd hoped it would be. I remember how Jun made me laugh. That I drank more plum wine than I'd intended.

"Chisato deserves better, Emiko. She hasn't had it easy like you —"

"Why does everyone keep saying that?" I know I sound like a brat, but honestly, it's not like she's been forced to sweep chimneys or anything.

"Because it's true and you know it."

I sputter. "I don't know anything —"

"You picked on someone smaller than you, Em. And I'm not just talking about size." He exhales loudly before turning to me. "What you did was offside. Totally offside."

My chest tight, I glare at him and draw in an unsteady breath. I try to keep my voice even. "Great," I say. "Thanks for the talk, Kenzo. Good talk." I nod, like we're having an everyday conversation and I don't feel like I've been punched in the gut.

He runs a hand over his face and his eyes are a sad, dark honey.

"What?"

He just keeps looking at me.

"What can I say? You're right. I get it, I was a mean girl. You hate me, Chisato hates me, Mitsuko probably hates me, everyone hates me. Point made. Are you happy now?"

Kenzo swallows hard, and then, in such a low voice I shouldn't be able to hear every single word as clearly as I do, he says, "I don't hate you. I could never hate you. But right now, I'm not sure if I actually like you."

His words pierce through me and I'm barely able to hold back the sob that's been building up in my chest. I turn away before the tears spill over, and I run into the house, straight up the stairs, and down the hall to my room, where I slam the door, fall onto my bed, and unravel as I cry myself to sleep.

It's dusk when I finally wake up. Disoriented and physically and mentally drained, I lie there heavy on the bed, staring out my window at the velvety blue sky. I can hear the waves retreating and surging onto the beach; comforting and constant, it's one of the best soundtracks in the world. I try to match my breathing to the ebb and flow of it until I feel some calm enter my core.

I remember everything.

Rubbing my sternum, hoping it'll ease the dull ache I feel, I recall what I said to everyone, to Chisato. What I did when

I held up her notebook and mocked it. What I did, accidentally or not, when I tossed it into a fire.

Shame overwhelms me and tears start streaming down my face and onto my pillow, but I don't try to stop them. I let myself cry, and when the tears subside, I'm left feeling empty and worn. But I know I need to get up.

I find my grandfather sitting in his chair in the living room. He's watching his favorite Hepburn in *The Philadelphia Story*, with the closed captions on and the sound low.

"Ah, Emiko-chan," he says when he sees me. He gestures to the chair beside him. "Join me."

I pad over and sit down, tucking my feet under my legs, and for a few moments we just watch the movie like it's any other Sunday night. All we're missing is the popcorn.

But I know I can't keep pretending everything is okay.

"Ojiichan," I say.

He looks at me, his face not giving away anything other than that he's listening, paying attention to me, as he always does whenever I have something to tell him.

I bow my head and take a deep breath. "I'm so sorry for my behavior yesterday. I'm so sorry I drank all that umeshu, and for getting . . ." I swallow hard.

Ojiichan waits.

"And for getting drunk and being awful to Chisato and embarrassing you and Mitsuko in front of our friends." I keep my head bowed until I'm ready to glance up at him, trying to gauge his reaction.

He doesn't respond right away. He just looks at me, and I try not to fidget or show any impatience. Finally, his mouth turns up a fraction at the corners and he holds out his warm, familiar hand. I smile and let out a breath I didn't know I was holding. Relieved, I put my hand in his and we give each other a squeeze.

"You are a good granddaughter, Emiko, and I am never not proud of you. Yesterday, I was not as proud of you as I wish to be. But today, you have made me proud once again." After a moment, he gives me a sidelong glance. "In future, though, I will ask that the next time Jun Morimoto, or anyone, shows up here with such a rare bottle of umeshu, you will remember that your grandfather is the connoisseur in the family, and that you should share such a gift."

I look at him, a little bit shocked and uncertain. "Really? That's all you're going to say about me drinking?"

"Are you planning on doing anything like that again soon?"

"No." I don't even hesitate. "I'm happy to wait a long time before I repeat that experience."

He chuckles softly, turning his attention back to the movie to watch one of his favorite scenes.

"Seriously," I continue when it's over, "you don't have anything more you want to say to me about the whole underage drinking thing?" I don't know why I keep pushing the issue, but I feel like I deserve some kind of punishment.

"Nothing is as tempting as the thing you are forbidden." He considers me thoughtfully. "You made a poor decision, yes. Jun did, too, bringing that bottle here. But I trust that you understand that, and will remember for the next time."

"Thank you, Ojiichan."

"Thank you, Emiko." He stands up and stretches his arms over his head. "I feel like some tea. I bought a new blend today. Shall I make you a cup?"

I nod, and follow my grandfather into the kitchen, taking a seat at the counter. I watch him turn on the kettle and scoop tea into a pot.

We don't talk, but it's not awkward at all. Except, just as I start to feel like myself again, I have one of these flash-forwards where I see him living here on his own. It's so brief that before I can even react I blink and see Future Me (I can tell by the clothes) sitting here with him, laughing. I blink a second time and I'm back in the present, and Ojiichan's placing my tea in front of me.

I look around the kitchen, checking that everything is as I remember.

"Are you alright?" he asks.

I focus on his face and give a tentative nod. "I think so."

He smiles reassuringly. "Then let us enjoy the tea."

I know I have some work to do to make things better with everyone; it's like I have a different kind of test coming up and I need to prepare for it. So, after a light supper and more tea, I head back to my room. Before I can change my mind, I make a couple of calls.

Afterwards, even though I've slept most of the day, I brush my teeth, turn out the lights, and climb into bed. I lie there for what feels like hours, alternating between squirming at the memories that play like a bad movie and brainstorming what I need to do next.

It's a long night.

26

Consequences

Monday morning, I look for Harumi and find her at her locker with Will and Arlo.

"Hi," I say, feeling like everything I'm wearing has shrunk two sizes.

Harumi looks at me, a worried expression on her face. "You're here . . . I wasn't sure if you would be today. Did you get my texts?"

"Uh, yeah. Sorry about that. I wasn't feeling great."

"That's okay. I mean . . ." She looks at Will and Arlo and they have some kind of silent exchange. "You know. After the . . ." Her voice trails off as she shrugs and gives me an embarrassed smile.

I let out a deep breath. "I'm really sorry I made things so uncomfortable for you all on Saturday." I look at Will and Arlo. "I don't normally do what I did. Drink like that or behave that way. And my parties are usually a lot more fun."

Will nods. "I know."

"Honestly, it's no biggie. You should see what some of my cousins do after too much sugar." Arlo's eyes grow large at the thought and I find myself laughing.

We chat a few minutes longer about Will and Arlo's plans for the summer before the siblings head for the other side of the school. I'm relieved at how easy that first apology of the day went, but as Harumi and I make our own way to class, I stop in the middle of the hall and turn to her.

"I also wanted to say sorry for, well, stealing focus and ruining any chances you might have had with —" I start, but before I can get Jun's name out, the warning bell rings and the hallway swells in sound and population.

"Aw, you're such a great friend, Emiko," she says as we pick up our pace. "It's okay . . . I haven't given up. Just keep your fingers crossed for me."

"You've got it," I say, and hold up both hands to show her.

As I'd hoped, I manage to get through the day without seeing Kenzo. And in our English Lit class, Chisato, to her credit, acts as she always does, which is to barely nod at me before finding her seat. But my luck runs out after final period, when Gareth enters my orbit.

I wasn't sure what I was going to do about him and Kiki. Obviously, I wish they hadn't witnessed me being my absolute worst. But as I stick my head in my locker and pretend I didn't see him walking down the hall towards me, I realize that, unlike him after prom, I need to do better and be better and own up to being less than my wondrous self.

So I stand up straight, come out from hiding, and turn to face him.

He stutters to a stop and his eyes ping-pong wildly in an effort to avoid mine. I swallow, my throat suddenly dry, and take a calming breath. "Gareth," I say.

"Emiko," he automatically responds.

It takes me a beat to get the words out. "I'm . . . very sorry for how my party ended. And for being a bad host. Please tell Kiki I said so. I was not myself."

"Oh. Okay."

"Great." Then, because I don't know how else to end this, I say, "Thank you. Carry on," and turn around to my locker, where I rearrange books while waiting for the sound of footsteps as he continues on down the hall.

When I don't hear any, I lean back to check on his progress, and this time, I'm the one startled into making erratic eye movements because Gareth is standing right there.

"Uhm, I'm sorry for being a jerk," he says.

"Which time?" It comes out before I can stop myself, and I clap my hand over my mouth.

Gareth, who looks like he's swallowed a bug, nods, his mouth tight. "Fair. Fair."

"No — I shouldn't have said that." I shake my head. "I'm sorry. Again."

"Well, I said stuff — did stuff — I shouldn't have, when I wasn't at my best, either."

"Okay. Thanks. I appreciate that." And I actually do.

We stand there for a moment, and then he says, staring at his feet, "So, uh, should we hug it out or something?"

"Oh, no." I retreat a step. "That's fine."

"Okay, cool. Cool." He looks at me for another second before he turns on his heel and leaves.

Four down, four to go.

Right after school, I ride over to Mitsuko and Seiji's house.

When I called to make sure they'd be home, my aunt told me that Jun and Seiji had gotten into it after the party, that there had been a lot of yelling, and that Jun had slammed his bedroom door and not come out until it was time to leave for the ferry yesterday morning. I felt sick, sure I was the reason for the argument.

So I'm taken aback when Mitsuko opens the door and pulls me into a hug. Then, with one arm around my waist, she brings me into the house where Seiji waits in the kitchen, looking uncharacteristically uncomfortable. He's usually a very self-assured, in-charge kind of guy, so something is clearly up.

They invite me to join them at the table, where a plate of still-warm mini-quiches are waiting along with my favorite teacup. Mitsuko fills it with some hojicha and we sit there, smiling awkwardly at each other.

I don't know how to start the conversation, so my aunt literally talks about the weather until I finally get up the nerve to say what I've come to say.

"I'm so, so sorry," I begin, lifting my eyes to meet theirs. "I don't know —"

Seiji puts up his hand and I stop, closing my mouth as he lowers his palm to the table. He looks at Mitsuko, who gives him a slight nod, before he turns back to me.

"We appreciate you coming to see us, Emiko," he says. "But before you go any further, I must apologize for Jun's actions." His face tightens, and while he's never been anything but kind and even-tempered around me, I can imagine how daunting he must have seemed to Jun.

"It wasn't Jun's fault," I say. "No one forced me to drink that much plum wine."

"That may be, but with both of you minors, it was irresponsible and wrong of Jun to bring it. It was simply wrong." He shakes his head, and the expression on his face keeps me mum. "I hope you can forgive me for the trouble Jun has caused."

I stare at my aunt, trying to process what is happening in front of me. I'm so mortified that Seiji feels he has to do this, I don't know how to respond, and a flicker of anger towards Jun flares up inside me. He should be here. Instead, he left his father to clean up his mess.

"Please." I lean forward, putting my clasped hands on the table. "You don't need to apologize for Jun. I'm fine. As much as I'd love to blame this whole thing on him, this was completely my own fault. I'm the one who lost control of herself.

"I feel terrible for the things I said and did, and I'm just glad you weren't there to see any of it. And I hope we can all forget this ever happened."

Mitsuko is radiating concern, and I want to reassure her, but I wait until Seiji finally nods and gives me a small smile.

I let out a big breath, but things still feel a bit tense, so I pick up a quiche and shove the entire thing into my mouth.

"Emiko!" Mitsuko gasps, but it does the job. I can see both her and Seiji relax as she shakes her head at my deliberate bad manners.

I shrug, and, after swallowing my food, raise my cooled cup of tea to them before taking a big sip. "Excellent quiche," I say with a grin.

An hour later, I'm standing on the sidewalk in front of Chisato's house, the next stop on my apology tour. I'm holding a gift bag containing a box of Mitsuko's coffee-cream éclairs, a package of *pâte de fruits*, and a tin of whole leaf tea. This is mostly for Taka-san. She's one of Ojiichan and Mitsuko's oldest friends, and I know I upset her, too, so this is a small gesture towards what I hope is forgive-and-forgetness.

I also have something for Chisato. I'm fairly positive Taka-san won't let the edible treats go to waste, but I have no sense of how Chisato will react to my gift.

As I walk up to the front door, I think about the last time I was here. It was about six or seven years ago, during the summer holidays. Chisato's birthday is December 25, which bites for obvious reasons. So that year Taka-san decided to celebrate Chisato's Christmas birthday in July; I overheard Mitsuko tell Ojiichan it was because Chisato had never had a proper birthday party before.

I'm not sure what made Taka-san think things would be better here in Otter Creek. It wasn't like any of us knew Chisato particularly well; she was this tiny, quiet, odd girl who came to visit every few years and, more often than not, kept her own company, going to the library with her aunt, where you'd find her hiding with a stack of books under a blanket-covered table. Anyway, I don't know how many kids Taka-san invited, but besides Kenzo and me, only a couple of others neither of us knew showed up. And we spent most of the party sitting on Taka-san's hard dining chairs while Chisato basically performed a piano recital.

Kenzo sat in front of me and I kept trying to kick his feet while he kept ignoring me. He was always way nicer to Chisato than I was, and he tried really hard that day to pay attention as she played everything from classical to Disney songs. Mitsuko had to pinch my leg to make me stop fidgeting. It was the most boring party I'd ever been to and I wasn't shy about telling my aunt why I thought so, later.

Now, my face heats up as I recall my behavior that day and wonder if Chisato remembers, too. At the thought that she might, that she's got these memories of when I was less than kind to her, a wave of remorse rushes through me and leaves behind something heavy in my chest. I massage it absently, trying to move it, before I ring the doorbell.

Through the sidelight, I see the shadow of someone approaching, and hear the murmur of female voices. I can't make out any words and the tone isn't encouraging, but then the door opens, revealing an unsmiling Chisato.

"Uhm, hi." I focus on her aunt looking anxious behind her. "Taka-san, thank you for letting me stop by."

"It's always nice to see you, Emiko-san," she says as Chisato angles her body to give her room in the doorway.

"This is for you." I hold out the gift bag when Taka-san remains unusually quiet.

"Oh, that's very thoughtful of you. Thank you." She takes the bag and turns to Chisato. "Why don't you take Emiko to the deck? It's quite pleasant out there in the shade," she tells me.

Chisato looks at her aunt and they do that thing where they communicate telepathically.

"My aunt and grandfather also send their regards," I say, to break the silence.

"They're always so kind. Please thank them for me." Taka-san bows her head, then retreats towards the rear of the house. "I should get these pastries into the fridge. Chisato, don't leave Emiko standing on the doorstep. Invite her in."

Chisato lets out a deep sigh and gives a half-hearted sweep of the arm to usher me inside. "This way." Her voice is flat, and she barely looks at me as I enter her house. I stop to remove my shoes, leaving them facing the door the way Mitsuko taught me. Chisato doesn't say anything when I straighten up. She just turns and marches down the hall that runs to the back of the house.

It's really more of a cottage, a cedar-shingled old-timer from when Otter Creek was a vacation spot for city dwellers wanting an escape. From what I can remember, it looks like it's been freshened up with new paint and flooring. I catch a glimpse of a piano and a guitar stand in the living room, and a kitchen bright from all the windows that line the rear wall.

We walk through a pair of French doors out onto a wooden deck where Chisato and I sit on cushioned chairs under a canvas umbrella. It's comfortable, and the view is of a back-yard filled with flowers and shrubs and raised garden beds.

Taka-san comes out with a tray filled with glasses of iced green tea, a basket of packaged senbei, and a plate of home-made cookies. "Here you go, girls," she says, placing every-thing on the table. "Now enjoy your visit. I'll just be inside." She smiles at us both before disappearing into the house.

Muttering "They're vegan," Chisato grabs a couple of the cookies and puts them on a napkin. Breaking off a piece, she pops it into her mouth, chewing slowly as she looks out at the garden.

I called Taka-san last night, not just because I wanted to apologize to her first, but to ask if I could come talk to Chisato in person.

I suppose I should have asked to speak to Chisato directly, but I'll admit I was afraid she'd hang up on me. So I asked Taka-san for help. I think it took some convincing, but late last evening she texted me the green light.

I wonder what was said to get Chisato to agree to this, because although she isn't really acting any differently than she normally does around me, she might as well be wearing warning colors, the approach-with-caution aura is so strong.

While I try to think of a way to bridge this silence, I remember my other gift and pull it from my bag. "Here. This is for you." I place the wrapped package near her glass.

"What's that for?" She doesn't touch it, leaning away like it might be booby-trapped.

I look down at my lap and take a deep breath before lift-ing my chin to face her. "I want to apologize for what I did to you at the party."

Chisato returns my gaze but her face tells me nothing.

"I wish I could say I was too —" I gulp as my throat unexpectedly closes. "Too drunk . . . to know what I was doing, but that wouldn't be true. I mean, I was not my usual self that day, but that doesn't mean I didn't know what I was doing."

Chisato breaks another piece off her cookie and inspects it before putting it back on the napkin. She lifts her eyes back to mine and waits.

"I was beyond rude, grabbing your notebook — that was completely out of order — and embarrassing you the way I did . . ." I bow my head, feeling all kinds of icky, like I've walked through some giant Australian spiderweb, invisible threads clinging to me, constant and elusive at the same time. I look up and catch her watching me, her arms crossed tightly in front of her.

"I'm really sorry for all of that." I swallow hard. "And for what happened after. I wish I could take back everything I said and did."

Moments pass. Somewhere in the cottage, a vacuum hums. Out in the neighborhood, kids are shouting after the fairground sounds of an ice cream truck.

"You threw my book into the fire." The words are colorless, monotonic, except I must be getting used to her voice, as rare as it is to hear, because I catch the slight break in the word "book" and it wrings dry something inside my chest.

I nod, my eyes hot, and I look away.

We sit like that, neither of us moving or speaking for a few moments. "Chisato . . ." I begin, but then falter.

She takes a napkin and mops the condensation off her glass.

I clear my throat and try again. "I realize how disrespectful I was, taking your book like that. How hurtful that was. For saying the things that I said. I was awful to you, and I'm sorry."

She doesn't respond in any way that I can detect, so I keep going. "And I know you'll probably never want to come to another party of mine, or hang out with me in any way, ever. But if you are willing to give me a chance to prove it, I promise nothing like that will ever happen again."

Chisato leans back in her chair and tips her head back, looking skyward as she considers my words. Eventually, she lets out a deep breath. She does this a couple more times before she tilts her chin down again.

"Okay," she says.

"Okay . . . ?"

"Yeah. Okay. I accept your apology. We're good."

"Really?" I'm glad, but also resisting the urge to look behind me in case there's someone waiting to grab me and yell "Gotcha!" I mean, she could be celebrating Opposite Day, it's hard to tell for sure.

She nods and takes a sip of her tea. Her gaze lands on the wrapped package on the table. "So what's that?"

"It's for you. You can open it if you want. Or save it, whatever."

Chisato picks it up and peels off the tape before folding back the paper to reveal a blue leather-bound notebook and a box of fancy Japanese gel pens I found at the local art supply shop. She picks up the book and fans the pages before looking up at me. "Thank you, Emiko," she says, a small but genuine smile on her face.

I smile too, relieved. "The color reminded me of your streak."

As I've come to expect, she doesn't say a whole lot more, but from the way she inspects the pens and runs her hand over the smooth cover, I'm sure it won't take long for her to start filling the book with more writing.

I know I should leave soon, but before I go, I remember something. "Oh, hey, Chisato."

She looks up. Her face is less angular than it was earlier, but that veiled expression is back in her eyes.

"I just wanted to say, I think you're really talented. Like, you're so good, I'm envious. I think you surprised us all at Jun's karaoke night."

She glances away. "Oh. Thanks." She picks up a cookie and takes a big bite. After a few seconds, it's clear she's not going to add anything more. But she pushes the basket of senbei towards me. "They're from Ueno. You should try them."

Grinning, because truthfully I had been eyeing them, I pick out a thick, craggy-looking round one. When I tear open the packaging the scent of shoyu makes my mouth water, and, after all of my earlier stress, the first bite into the salty, crispy cracker tastes extra delicious. "Oh my god," I say.

Chisato smiles. "Yeah, they're good." She pops another piece of cookie into her mouth.

I think we're both feeling more relaxed now, and I sit back, enjoying the shaded warmth. "So," I say, "have you figured out what you're doing after grad?"

She takes a long drink of her tea. "Mmm, I'm not sure yet."

"Really?" Somehow, I figured she would be very organized about things like this. "What are your choices?"

"A few different places."

I guess I shouldn't be surprised by her reluctance to share much with me. But then, remembering her reaction to Kiki's offer to help, I also realize how this could be a trickier subject for her, that she might have bigger concerns than simply trying to decide which school she wants to attend.

As I try to think of a more neutral topic, she shakes the ice in her empty glass, emphasizing the serious Greta Garbo vibes I'm now getting. Not wanting to completely overstay my welcome, I say, "I should probably head out."

"Okay," she agrees, getting up.

Following her into the house, I try not to lag as she walks to the front door too quickly for me to get a proper look at any of the photos lining the walls; it's clear, though, that most of them are of her, taken over the years.

Chisato waits, holding the door open, while I put on my shoes.

"Thanks for, uhm, listening," I say as I stand.

"Well, thanks for coming."

Her aunt comes out of a room then and rushes over when she sees me. "Emiko-san, you're leaving?"

I nod. "Thank you for everything, Taka-san."

"Oh, no, thank *you* so much, and for the thoughtful gifts." She goes to Chisato and puts a hand on her arm. "I'm sure Chisato appreciated your visit, too."

When Chisato remains silent, I pick up my backpack. "I guess I'll see you at school."

"Sure."

She doesn't say any more, so I step across the threshold and head down the pathway. When I reach the sidewalk,

I turn back to wave, but it's only Taka-san left watching me leave.

After dinner, I head straight to my room for some quiet time and space to absorb everything that's happened today. So when my phone clangs with a text, I take a few moments before checking it, and smile when I see who it's from.

HARUMI: Did you say something to Gareth?

ME: No, why?

HARUMI: I got this text from an unknown number. It was him! He said sorry for being a jerk at prom and that he wasn't his best self. How random is that?!

Shaking my head at the familiar words, I reply:

ME: Crazy random. What'd you say?

HARUMI: Just thanks with a happy face and a cupcake.

Later that night, I'm cross-legged on my bed, phone in hand, psyching myself up to do the last thing on my list, which is to apologize to Kenzo.

I exhale loudly and start typing.

ME: You were right. I remembered. I was awful to Chisato. I apologized to her today.

When he doesn't respond right away, I send a second text:

ME: I'm sorry to you, too.

Nervous about what he might say to that, I try to loosen things up by typing out a third text:

ME: And, real talk, thanks for having one of those "tough conversations" with me! 😉

Before hitting send, I reread the message.

"Nope," I say to myself, and throw my phone to the side. After a long double face-palm, embarrassed that I've stooped to a winky-face emoji, I grab my phone again and delete the whole thing.

I sit for a few moments and try again.

ME: I'm sorry for acting the way I did.

I stare at the screen, thinking, and then add:

ME: I know you didn't want to, but thanks for calling me out on it. Hope you can forgive me. Friends?

This time, his reply is instant.

KENZO: Always.

I let out such a huge sigh of relief — who knew I could hold in that much air? — that all I have left in me is enough energy to reply with an emoji. So I pick the happiest of all the happy faces and then, just to emphasize how I really feel, I add a yellow heart, for friendship.

I don't expect him to respond, not after his succinct and definitive answer. But I'm pleasantly surprised when, a few minutes later, Kenzo sends me a yellow heart, too.

27

Telling Harumi

"Here. It's just cucumber-something-infused water," Kenzo says.

I give him a look but, detecting no dig, take the glass and tap it against his. As I sip my drink, we look out over the crowd — a mix of our fellow grads, teachers, and school staff mingling, post-graduation banquet, while tables and chairs are cleared away to make room for dancing. We're back at the Bayside Center, and tonight they've opened up the loft, which is where a bunch of us have gathered to lounge after an amazing meal (my salmon was perfectly grilled, and Kenzo let me try the chicken, also delicious).

Tayjon comes up to us and he and I swap back yearbooks. "Don't read it till later," I say. "It's mushy."

He smiles. "Same, E. Same."

As Tayjon goes back to where everyone — including Liv Soo and Jeremy, Dev, and the Triple As — is talking and trading yearbooks, Kenzo leans closer so I can hear him over the increasing volume from below. "Have you seen Chisato at all?"

I shake my head. "After skipping the ceremony? I doubt we'll see her at any parties tonight."

"I just thought, you know."

Shrugging, I briefly wonder if there's anything more to Kenzo's interest, but before I can delve further, I spot Mx. G. making their way towards the exit, and I put down my glass. "I'll be right back," I tell him, and, grabbing my yearbook, I hurry down the stairs just as they walk out the doors.

"Mx. G.!" I say, following them into the lobby.

They stop and turn. "Oh, Emiko."

"You're leaving already?"

"Yes, dear George is waiting. I looked for you. I'm glad you caught me."

"Me too. I know you're going to be super busy Monday, so I was hoping you'd sign this tonight." I hold out my yearbook and a pen.

"I'd love to." As they settle at a nearby console table, I wander over to the standing display Tayjon and I put together of the year's best photos that didn't make the final cut.

"So, how are you doing?" Mx. G. asks when they find me to return my yearbook.

"I'm okay." I indicate the growing activity around us; it seems like everyone's rushing to the washrooms to freshen up before the dancing starts, and the rise in energy is palpable. "Although, I guess part of me can't believe we're here already. That we're grads now. That this is it."

Mx. G. nods. "It's just the end of one early chapter, Emiko." They pause before continuing, "I wanted to give you kudos, again, on everything you've accomplished this year. I don't pick favorites, but your class might be one of the best I've ever seen. Such good energy. So much thrilling potential. I'm truly excited for every one of you."

Any other day, compliments like this would cheer me up, but today, I feel a little awkward receiving them. I mean, I worked hard, especially after Umeshu-gate, to achieve the marks I wanted. But I'm not sure I deserve any special praise when I can't a hundred percent share their excitement about my future. Still, Mx. G.'s been there since the beginning, and gone above and beyond as a guidance counselor, so I smile, genuinely grateful.

"Thanks, Mx. Galloway, for helping me get here."

"You're welcome. Now, may I leave you with one last thing?"

"Of course. Please."

"Decisions are like outfits."

I wait, expecting a follow-up sentence. Instead, they adjust their linen stole and turn towards the front door.

"Good luck at Cascadia, Emiko. It's a wonderful university. I hope you enjoy it."

"Thanks," I reply automatically.

I stand there for a while, thinking about everything Mx. G. said. Then, laughing softly to myself, I shake my head and start flipping through my yearbook. I notice the music from inside the hall suddenly grow louder, and then I hear Jacob's voice say, "Whatcha doing there, Emi-K?"

I look up to see him and Darcy grinning at me as they hold the hall doors open. "You've been missed," Darcy says. "We volunteered to bring you back in, so come on. The night is young, and so are we — it's time to celebrate!"

Of course, without hesitation, I let them. And way into the night, we do.

The next afternoon, I wake up to the happy surprise of Mitsuko's voice floating up to my room from the kitchen. I wash up as fast as I can and, after throwing a sweatshirt over my pajamas, head downstairs, eager to see her.

"Mitsuko!" I call out. "What are you doing here?"

There isn't anything overtly wrong when I enter the kitchen, but the way Ojiichan and Mitsuko look makes me feel like I've interrupted something serious. I slow to a stop.

"*Qu'est-ce qui se passe?*" I ask cheerily in an effort to diffuse the tension.

Mitsuko hops off her stool and heads straight to the fridge. "How were your grad parties? Did you get enough sleep? You're probably starving," she says as she pokes around among the contents.

"They were great." I watch them carefully. "Is everything okay?"

"When is Harumi coming over?" Ojiichan asks.

"After dinner."

"I see some labneh," Mitsuko tells me. "And . . . baby carrots?" She turns and shakes a glass container and a small bag like they're full of cat treats.

I give both my aunt and my grandfather a firm look.

"Tea?" He holds up the electric kettle.

I sigh loudly and put my hands on my hips, striking the classic *I'm-not-kidding* pose. "No, thank you. I'm fine. Seriously, what's going on? You two are acting really funky."

Mitsuko looks at Ojiichan, and something passes between them, before she turns her attention back to me, her expression anxious. "This was a shock to us all, Emiko."

I slide onto a stool and sit back, trying to stay calm.

"It's Jun . . ." she continues.

"Is he alright?"

She nods. "Yes, yes, he's fine. It's just — oh, Emiko, we had no idea." She trades another look with Ojiichan before turning back to me. "Jun's gone. To Toronto."

"Oh-kay." So far, I'm surprised, but I still don't understand why this seems to be such a big deal. "Is it because of his mom?" Kana, from what Mitsuko's told me, doesn't stay put in one place for long, so it wouldn't surprise me to hear that she's moved again.

Mitsuko shakes her head. "No," she says slowly. "She's gone to London."

"London. But not with Jun?"

"No. He left. With Chisato."

"Chisato?"

"Yes."

I look at my grandfather, who shrugs. I turn back to my aunt. "Chisato *Ishi*?" I say, like there could be another Chisato we all know.

"None of us knew a thing, not his mother, not her aunt. Seiji's so upset. We don't understand it. I mean, we actually thought you and he might —" She stops, her lips pressed thin.

As I sit there letting this percolate, I try to recall the last time I actually saw Chisato at school. It would have been during finals last week, because, outside of English Lit, the girl really walked the halls like a ghost.

Jun and Chisato. Jun and Chisato? "They went to Toronto together? Like a couple?"

"Yes."

I stare at my aunt as I digest this news. "Wow." I run through all the times I've seen them together, which is maybe, what, a half dozen times since they arrived? If that? I sit up as a light goes on. "They met in Tokyo."

Mitsuko nods, frowning as she fixes a pot of tea. We wait in silence until she pours a cup and pushes it towards me. "Taka-san doesn't know the details, but she did learn that they met at a concert last summer. I gather they got serious quite quickly, but her other aunt and uncle — they're very strict, apparently — disapproved, so she was sent here.

"Jun . . . well, you know he had some trouble in school before, and so he acted up until they kicked him out. He convinced his mother he needed a new start, and so she brought him to Vancouver. He told her he wanted to spend more time with Seiji. Meet me."

At this, her face flushes, and I feel my own temperature spike on her behalf.

"Well, that was convenient. He used you guys."

"No, I don't think he meant —"

"Of course he did. He used you, he used Seiji. He used us all." I flash back to last summer, out in the pavilion, and something Kenzo said.

"Like, he couldn't be bothered to come to your wedding, but he throws a fit so he can move closer to a girl?" I shake my head. "Nice."

"I'm sorry, Emiko," she says.

I frown. "You do not need to apologize for Jun — *he's* the one who should be here apologizing. He's the one who needs to explain." I step off the stool and walk over to my aunt. "Please don't feel bad about this. This is all on him." Bending my knees so I'm eye level with her, I hold her gaze until she nods.

Ojiichan clears his throat. "So, you . . ."

I straighten up and toss my ponytail back over my shoulder. "I'm fine." My grandfather and aunt trade glances. "What? Honestly, I'm fine. Doesn't mean I'm not mad, and not just for myself, either. He basically lied to everyone the whole time he was here, if you think about it.

"I'm going to get dressed," I add abruptly, and I start heading back to my room, but then I stop. "Why Toronto? Did Taka-san say?"

"Chisato applied to a music program without telling Taka-san and got a full scholarship. And Jun's apparently going to take acting classes. With his mother's support." Mitsuko's face tells me what she thinks of that parental decision.

I take this in. "Hm. That's almost funny." Nodding, more to myself than anyone, I turn to go upstairs when I feel two pairs of eyes boring into my back. "I'm fine," I yell over my shoulder.

I hold it together until I get to my room. Then, not caring what's on my streaming service, I hit play and turn up the volume, thankful when loud, thumping bass beats fill the air. I need some privacy.

I fall face first into my pillow and scream as loud as I can. It feels really good, and even though I'm pretty sure my grandfather and aunt can hear what's happening, I do it again.

Then I get up, turn down the music a little, and grab my phone.

"Jun," I type as I try to organize all the thoughts flying through my head. But there's too much to say, so I forget about order and start texting whatever comes to mind first, a storm-swollen river of consciousness.

As I fill the first bubble, though, I realize that shouting at anyone this way — even Jun — is ugly and, ultimately, counterproductive. So I take a few breaths, remind myself that the first rule of angry texting is *just don't*, and delete everything.

No, I need to be cool about this. What I want to say to Jun deserves to be a proper document, complete with proper punctuation and spelling. Laid out in a way that's thoughtful. Structured. Irrefutable. Once it's sent, I'll text him and demand he check his email. And if he doesn't reply, I'll print out a hard copy, track him down, crumple it up, and throw it really hard at the back of his head.

Happy with my plan of attack, I sit at my desk, turn the music down to a less aggressive volume, and bring up my account. And after an album's worth of songs, I hit compose and start typing.

Jun —
YOU HAVE GOT TO BE KIDDING ME.

I pause, then delete everything back to the em dash.

I CANNOT BELIEVE YOU . . .

I sit, watching the cursor blink for a minute, before backspacing to the beginning.

No. Probably not.

Turning off the caps lock button, I swivel around in my chair to look out the window and try to let my emotional dust settle.

At times like this, I wish we could unfold our brains like old-school paper maps and spread them out on a table. So we could see where we've been, figure out the best routes to where we want to go. Understand how we ended up where we are. It might help me to see the big picture of my life so far if I could, to understand the scale of things in relation to each other.

I get up and pace the room.

Stare at myself in the bathroom mirror.

Lie with my head hanging off the edge of the bed.

Eventually, I sit back down at my desk and turn around and around and around in my chair slowly, thinking.

I haven't heard from Jun since the beach party, other than a quick "Sorry" text a few days after. I have to say, even though I don't blame him for the umeshu incident, I did expect a little more from him. So, I haven't been clamoring to see him, and I definitely had no intention of participating in any more jokey-flirty behavior.

Then a little voice reminds me that I DID participate in a lot of jokey-flirty behavior with Jun, pretty much from the get-go; that there was also that very short period there when I thought we might be destined to become more than just friends.

Then up pops an image of Harumi, and her face when she told me she was starting to have feelings for Jun — I keep that in the back of my mind as I work through all the things I want to say to him.

I mean, if I were to compile a list of all the qualities a potential boyfriend should have, for *anyone*, Jun Morimoto would tick a lot of boxes. But thinking back on the time we spent together, as charming and cute and cheeky as he was, I realize now that I was only getting the junk food version of Jun. Flashy, fun, and not entirely good for me in the long run; eventually, too much of it makes you crave something more substantial. Although, that *accent* — it's almost criminal how easy it is for him to get away with half the stuff he says.

Then I remember, I was just the distraction.

I can feel myself bristling as I think about how he used his charmy no-good ways to cover up whatever was going on with Chisato. The memory of him asking me to take him to prom makes me snort in disbelief, as do all the other times I was his perfect excuse to come up to the coast to see her.

But as I consider Chisato, and the way she acted around me, I realize . . . she *must* have believed Jun's charade. Which would explain why it seemed she was always wanting to avoid me. *I'd* have wanted to avoid me if our positions had been reversed.

I stand and start pacing the floor again, and I'm sure I'm close to getting my ten thousand steps when my eye catches on a photo on the wall; it's one of Mitsuko and me on her wedding day. When she got married to Seiji — a.k.a. Jun's dad. That happy image acts like an antidote to the ick in my system, and after several long moments I can feel it all flush away. Because even though I still want to shave his eyebrows off in his sleep — one for me, one for Harumi, and, if he had a third, one for Chisato — I'm reminded that Jun is literally family now. Like, forever.

I sit back down at my desk and start typing.

Dear Jun —

When I'm done, I read it over. It's definitely a lot less ALL CAPS than my first attempts. I'd even go as far as saying it's *très* mature. I still tell him off, because what he did — using us, lying to us, bailing without a word — was all (as he would have to agree) extremely bad form. And given our recent history of jokey-flirtiness, there's no way he could have known that I didn't have any feelings for him. Or that he hadn't broken my heart.

But the fact is, he hasn't. Not even close. My heart is intact.

As I consider what this all means, I hit "Save Draft" before going into my closet to change. There, I see my kimono-dress hanging in its dry cleaner bag. Harumi and Jun flash through my mind again, along with moments from prom, and the day after with Jun and the bear, and oh, how I wish I'd kept my meddling mouth shut.

I close my eyes as it hits me that, once again, I'm going to be the bearer of bad news for Harumi.

When I open the front door and see Harumi's cheerful face, I feel like I'm about to punt a kitten.

"Hi!" She holds up a bag. "I brought movie mix."

With both of us so busy with finals and school these past

few weeks, we planned this post-exams-and-grad get-together to watch movies and catch up. Now, instead of looking forward to a chill evening hanging out, all I can think about is how I'm going to tell her about Jun.

"Awesome. Come in," I say.

"Hi, Fuji-san!" She waves as we pass the living room, where Ojiichan's watching *Jeopardy!*

"Oh, Harumi-chan. It has been awhile. How nice to see you."

"You too."

Normally, I'd stop and let Harumi and Ojiichan visit, but I'm too nervous to dawdle so I keep walking until we get to the kitchen. I grab a bowl for her mix, adding it to my tray of savories. "Can you manage the drinks and blondies?" I ask.

"Sure." If she thinks I'm acting odd, rushing us like this, she doesn't say anything. She just grabs the second tray and follows me downstairs to the family room.

"So, what are we watching?" she asks as we settle into our seats.

I hand her the remote. "Whatever you want."

"Really? Horror?"

"Anything but that."

As she clicks through all the options, I sip my iced hibiscus tea, trying to come up with the best way to broach the subject. And just then she says, in a distracted voice, "Hey, did you hear about Jun and Chisato?"

I cough as some tea goes down the wrong way. "What?" I manage without sputtering.

She nods, still perusing the newest releases. "Yeah. Everyone's talking about it. Wild, right?"

"Wild?" I turn my head to look at her, not sure what to make of this . . . nonchalance while talking about the guy she told me she likes. "I guess that's one way to describe it." Harumi sighs. "I mean, it's sort of romantic, too. Jun and Chisato, having a secret relationship? And having to hide it from everyone because her family disapproves? It's like Romeo and Juliet, except without all the death." Her eyes take on a far-away glazed look for a few seconds before she shakes her head and focuses on me again. "Sorry," she says with a giggle.

"You're not upset by this?" My eyebrows knit as I try to take in her reaction.

"Why would I be upset? I think it's kind of cool, and super exciting." She pauses and finally seems to notice my expression. "Are *you* upset by this?" She looks at me quizzically before her mouth suddenly drops open. "Oh my god, Emiko. I'm sorry, I didn't even think."

"What?"

"You liked Jun!"

"No." I stare at her. "YOU liked Jun."

"I *what*?"

"You liked Jun. You told me so. After the bear scare."

"Uhm, no, I never . . ." She stops, a thoughtful look on her face, as if she's trying to remember that day. "Oh no. No. No. No, I did not — DO NOT like Jun like that."

"I'm quite sure you told me you did."

"I didn't say his name, Emiko. I didn't."

She smiles, her expression bashful, while I wrack my overtaxed brain, turning over every bit of conversation I can recall. But when I come up empty, I have to admit she's right. She never did say his name.

"So, if you weren't talking about Jun, who did you think I meant when I said *he* was a hero? I mean, Jun literally saved your life."

Harumi clicks through more movie options before putting the remote down. "Kenzo," she says finally, and looks up at me, literally starry-eyed. "I like Kenzo."

"Kenzo." I don't understand why it feels like someone's just shoved me hard in the chest, but I fall back into my chair and stare at Harumi.

"Remember how he gave me his jacket when my dress . . . ?" She stops, and her smile drops for a moment.

"Yeah, I do." I swallow hard because my voice sounds strange and croaky.

"He was so nice to me, like, the nicest any boy has ever been to me. But I never, ever imagined I had any chance with him until you said I shouldn't put myself down like that. That I was good enough for anyone."

"I did say that." I'm internally kicking myself, but I have to be honest, even if it hurts. "I meant it, Harumi. I still mean it. It's just that . . . I really thought you meant Jun. I had no idea you were talking about Kenzo. I mean, has he . . . have you . . . have either of you even, you know, talked about this?"

I realize I'm babbling so I stop and try to regroup. But I'm struggling. Kenzo. And Harumi.

"No." She shakes her head, but the smile is back. "I haven't said anything, but every time I see him, he stops to talk to me, and at movie night, he showed me around the garden and all the things he's done to it. He's really talented, and he knows so much about plants. I can't even keep a succulent alive."

"Okay, but . . ." I stop, because — and I'm really being objective here — I cannot imagine Kenzo and Harumi as a couple. I mean, they're just too different. And not in an "opposites attract" kind of way, but different, like pairing pickles with red velvet cake. No one would ever choose that if they saw it on a menu. Because it's wrong. It's just wrong.

"But what?" she says.

I take a deep breath. "I just . . . I'm just surprised. I wasn't expecting you to say Kenzo. That's all."

"Well, nothing's happened yet. I mean, he hasn't asked me out or anything." She blinks. "Do you know if he's ever had a girlfriend?"

I shake my head. "Not as far as I know."

"How is that even possible? I mean, he's so handsome and so nice." She sighs before grabbing some chips.

I can't say anything to her. I have no clue if Kenzo likes her that way, but how would I know, really? I haven't been trying to avoid him, but since the beach party — actually, it probably goes back to prom — we haven't spent a ton of time together. And last night, with my focus on celebrating grad with all my friends, there was no repeat of our dances at prom. I feel completely unmoored.

But as I look at Harumi sitting there, all moony about Kenzo, I know I have to find my way and support her in this. She's not wrong in thinking he's awesome; he is. The fact that she figured it out before I did, that's on me.

"Ooh, how about this one?" She points to the screen. "I heard it's really good."

"Sure," I say, though I barely register what she's chosen.

As she holds up the remote to press play, Harumi turns to me. "So, what should I do?"

"About what?"

"Me and Kenzo! I mean, I know he'll be gone in the fall, but he's here all summer, right?"

"Oh. Yeah. I guess so."

Thankfully, the movie starts, distracting Harumi, so I'm able to sit there, mostly uninterrupted, wondering what kind of summer I have ahead of me.

28
Consolation

After another sleepless night, I'm down at the beach sitting on a lounger, staring out at the water. I ended our evening early, after telling Harumi truthfully that I had a headache, and I've spent the hours since ruminating about her and Gareth and Jun and Chisato, and basically everything that's happened over the past year. Trying to understand how it is that I got so much so wrong.

I think about Kenzo, too. Wondering if he knows, what he thinks of it all, what he thinks about Harumi. If she's right in thinking he likes her the way she likes him.

I sigh and rub my eyes, tired and confused by the badly edited montage of key moments I keep playing on a loop in my mind.

I'm so immersed in my own virtual reality that I don't hear Kenzo approaching until he's standing right beside me.

"What are you doing here?" I say, surprise making me sound unfriendly. He's wearing a soft, faded denim shirt and old khaki shorts. Worn canvas sneakers, no socks. It's really unfair how good he looks.

He gestures towards the house. "I had something I wanted to talk to your grandfather about. He told me where you were."

"Oh." We both stare at our feet, and then suddenly start talking at the same time.

"How are you —?" he says.

"How's —?" I stutter.

We stop, and, after an awkward pause, I laugh, despite how supremely unfunny I'm finding this.

Kenzo shakes his head. Most of the time his hair is tied up or back. But today he's wearing it loose, and I notice how thick and wavy it is, so different from my own. In the sun, it's quite hypnotic. If I were checking off a box, I'd call it brown, but that doesn't begin to cover the variations in it — silky chocolates and shiny caramels with bronze and even coppery highlights.

My hands flex involuntarily as I imagine what it would feel like to run my fingers through it, which I suddenly really, really want to do. Instead, I swallow and try to smile like I'm calm, having a normal conversation with a person I have normal feelings for.

"You first," he says.

"Hm?"

His mouth quirks and he brushes some of that very touchable-looking hair off his face. (The word "locks" flashes through my mind; if anyone's hair fits the word "locks," it's Kenzo Sanada's. "Flowing" works, too.)

"You first," he repeats. "What were you going to say?"

What was I going to say? I can't remember, so I blurt out the first thing that comes to mind. "How're the twins?"

"They're fine."

"Oh, good." This is a safe topic, I decide. "What are they up to these days? I haven't seen them in ages."

Kenzo gives me a patient smile and sits down at the end of my lounger, making me scooch up and hug my knees to my chest. "Well, they've signed up for a bunch of different camps, and they keep asking Mom and Dad for a goat."

"A goat?"

"Apparently, goats will eat anything, and some people are using them to clear brush and yard waste, so they want a goat to start their own business and partner up with me. They wanted to call it *Toats Ma Goat Will Eat Everything Service*. I managed to convince them that that was too long *and* stupid." He grins.

I laugh, for real this time, and the tension slips off me like a heavy coat.

He laughs too, and shakes his head. "I'm not sure if Mom and Dad will do it, but I almost wish they would, just so I can witness Takeo and Tomio trying to wrangle a goat."

"I would totally watch that show," I say.

Another silence falls between us; it's less uneasy than earlier, but it's not the same comfy silence we used to share. I don't know what to do with this tangled ball of feelings, so I put it aside and try to bluff my way through this, whatever. Because no matter what happens, I don't want Kenzo to feel differently about me.

So, I put on a smile and keep lobbing questions that get sillier and sillier, to put off hearing what he's come to tell me, in case it's what I'm afraid of — that he's fallen for Harumi, and out of some sense of loyalty for all our years of friendship he feels the need to share this news with me first.

When I finally run out of questions, I get up and take a few steps towards the water.

Standing, Kenzo clears his throat and walks up beside me. "So, uhm, I guess you've heard about Jun and Chisato." He doesn't look at me, facing the water as well.

"Yeah. Who knew? Not us, obviously," I say as lightly as I can.

"How're Mitsuko and Seiji taking it?"

I shrug. "I think they'll be okay — I mean, Mitsuko was upset at first because she . . ." I stop, remembering this is a topic I want to avoid.

"She what?"

I sense Kenzo looking at me, but rather than reply right away, I bend down to pick up a small handful of rocks. "Oh, nothing." I start slinging them into the water, one after another. When I run out, I glance over and see his face, and, sighing, I decide I might as well dive in and come out clean.

"She just — you know, saw how things were between Jun and me and thought maybe . . ." I pause, and blow out another loud breath. "I guess she, and Seiji, had hopes. That's all."

Kenzo doesn't say anything, but he shoves his hands into his pockets and lets out a long exhale.

I sneak another peek at his face; he looks thoughtful.

"So, are you okay?" he asks. His eyes meet mine briefly. "I mean, I think *everyone* thought you and Jun were, you know, close."

"Oh, no." I shake my head. "No." But as I say that, all the times Jun and I were together, the way we joked around, teased each other, the whole plum wine disaster — there's no way I can deny how things looked, and I feel my cheeks flush. "Okay, I know it seemed that way, and of course Jun's a fun guy, and he's got that whole model slash whatever thing going for him. But honestly, as much as I liked being with him, I never, ever LIKED him that way."

Kenzo's looking at me again, and there's something about his expression I don't understand. He looks like he's holding something back. "You never liked Jun that way," he says, almost to himself.

I nod. "Honest." I take a few steps closer to him and touch his arm. "Honest."

His gaze drops to my hand so I pull it away and retreat a step. There are a lot of words logjamming inside me, and if I don't let them out soon, I'm going to start choking. I swallow hard and try to take in a deep breath. "Although it's possible . . . I might have enjoyed all the attention Jun paid me," I admit.

Kenzo doesn't react. He just keeps looking at me, his face as still as a sculpture. I try not to get distracted by all these things I can't believe I've never noticed before — I mean, I've been looking at him for years, and it's never been like this. I see a muscle tic in his jaw, but otherwise he doesn't move.

"But it was never serious or anything," I continue. "And now, it turns out Jun was just using me as cover. So, for that, if I ever get the chance, I might hide a dead fish in his car. But I'm fine otherwise."

"Because you never liked Jun that way."

I purse my mouth, thinking. "Maybe at first, for, like, a nanosecond. But then, at prom, I realized I just liked him as a friend. A flirty friend, for sure, but just a friend, and . . ." I pause, not sure if I should mention how I'd also thought Jun and Harumi might make a perfect pair. Which, of course, reminds me how wrong I was about *that*, and how Harumi told me she's crushing on Kenzo. And that she thinks Kenzo might like her back. Oh god, I'm so jumbled up right now. Without thinking, I start heading down the beach.

"Emiko," Kenzo calls out as I walk away. "Wait."

I ignore him and keep going.

"So that's it?" he says as he catches up to me.

It's low tide, and the large rocks that normally hide underwater now dominate the beach. Most of them are covered in barnacles and mussels, but there's a range of smooth outcrops that are irresistible. I climb onto the nearest one and start traveling along the top; it's like walking on a sleeping dragon, the flowing ridges going up and down.

Kenzo steps onto the rocks beside me and, without having to say it, we get ready to play a game of beach parkour. I give a shriek of laughter when I wobble, almost losing my footing on a peak, and stick my arms out to regain my balance.

"First one to fall before we reach the end," I point to the huge rock that juts into the water at the far end of the beach, "is a rotten egg!"

I take off as fast as I can without looking to see if Kenzo's behind me. We've played this game forever, trying to scramble across the natural obstacle course without falling.

There are spots where it gets challenging, where you have to jump from one rock to another. But I grew up on this beach, and even though something changes every day, I know every permanent boulder, every heavy log above the tide line, and I know the best ways to get from one end to the other without touching the ground.

Kenzo grew up here too, though, and he's taller and more athletic, so even with my head start, he overtakes me easily and is waiting, standing on what we call "home rock" because it's where all our races end. It's a huge granite outcrop, monolithic and flat enough that when we were younger we pretended it was an island and pretty much lived on it all summer.

I leap up, instinctively reaching a hand out to Kenzo. He grabs it and pulls me towards him, and I just manage to stop myself from colliding into him, taking my hand back and walking away, pretending I need to catch my breath. Which is kind of true.

"No one touched the sand," I say eventually. "No rotten eggs here."

"So that's it?" he asks again.

"What do you mean?"

"All's forgiven? Jun lied to everyone and, just like that, everyone's happy and Jun gets away with it?" Kenzo shakes his head. "Man, I feel sorry for Chisato."

"Chisato?"

"He's so not worthy." Walking over to the edge of the rock, he stands with his hands clasped on top of his head. I know this pose; he does this when he's trying to figure something out.

"He's not *completely* terrible," I say.

Kenzo mumbles something but it gets lost in the breeze.

He turns to me. "I don't want to talk about Jun or Chisato anymore."

"Okay."

He takes a deep breath. "So, here's the thing . . ."

I feel a moment of panic. He's going to say something about Harumi. I can feel it in my gut, and I shiver, wrapping my arms around myself. "No, wait," I say.

He stops.

"You're my oldest friend."

Kenzo nods slowly as his eyes narrow, a faint furrow appearing on his brow. "And?"

I shrug, throwing up my hands. "That's it. That's all." I take a step back and try to pull myself together.

"You're my oldest friend, too," he says in a serious voice.

"And I would hate to lose that friendship," I blurt out.

Kenzo's eyes widen, and I don't know why, but he looks almost hurt by what I just said. "Oh. Okay. Right." He turns and jumps down onto the sand, and without a backward glance starts walking home.

He's a third of the way there before my brain wakes up and I yell his name. I have to yell it a couple of times before he stops and slowly turns around.

Something like a shock surges through me, and with a quick hop, I'm on the ground running. "I'm sorry," I yell, but the wind tosses the words back in my face. Shaking my head, I concentrate on getting to Kenzo as fast as I can, except I can't gain any traction because my feet keep sinking and slipping in the sand. Thankfully, by the time I reach him, I'm not too winded, so I manage to sound coherent when I repeat myself.

He looks at me, his eyes guarded. "What are you sorry for, Emiko?"

"For interrupting you like that. That was not a good friend move. I'm sorry. It's just that — well, this year's . . . And you and I lately — and all this change, and . . . and . . ."

Pausing to gather myself, I add, "I don't know why I'm being bizarro, but I'll try to get a grip, okay?"

I hold my breath as Kenzo takes in my apology and exhale when he offers back a smile, although it doesn't really reach his eyes.

"So, what did you want to tell me?" I ask.

He considers me for a moment before shaking his head. "Nothing. It doesn't matter." He turns and starts walking.

"Is it about Harumi?" I can't help it, I have to know.

He stops and turns back, a confused look on his face. "Harumi?"

I nod.

He walks towards me. "Why would you think I want to talk to you about Harumi?"

"Because I'm her friend."

"I know that."

I nod. I don't know what else I can, or should, say. So, I wait.

Kenzo looks at the ground and rakes a hand through his hair before he turns towards the water. His arms go up and he clasps his hands on top of his head again, shaking his head as he seems to be thinking hard about whatever it is he wants to say.

"Kenzo."

He doesn't respond, but I can tell he heard me.

I feel an obi-sized knot forming in my stomach, but I can't

let this go. I have to know. "If you wanted to tell me something about Harumi, or anyone," I add when I see his neck stiffen, "you know you can talk to me, right? About anything?"

It feels like it takes forever for him to respond, but finally, his arms drop to his sides and he turns to face me. He takes a deep breath, while I can't seem to get any air into my lungs.

"Here's the thing," he says again. "I need to talk to you . . . about you."

I stare at him, and my heart starts pounding like it's trying to break out of my rib cage, which suddenly feels two sizes too small.

"And me." Kenzo takes a step closer as he says this, and I blink up at him, and without even thinking about it, I step forward too, and we're standing senior-prom-slow-dance close.

"You? And me?" It's hard to even get those few words out, but I manage somehow.

Kenzo nods, and a dimple appears in his left cheek as the corners of his mouth turn up into a half-smile.

But he doesn't speak.

And, I realize three things as I continue to look up into his face.

One, that I have loved Kenzo Sanada my entire life, from the day we met, and no matter what happens after this, no matter where we end up, I always will.

Two, that this beautiful, kind boy, my oldest friend, who's growing up to be a beautiful and kind man, will always tell me the truth, no matter how hard it may be for him to say, or how hard it may be for me to hear.

And, holy Keanu. Three . . . he's going to kiss me.

29
The Kiss

My heart is beating so hard and fast, I'm sure it's leaving a bruise.

Kenzo reaches out and cups my face in his strong hands, looking into my eyes, a question in his. I wonder which of us is trembling; maybe we both are.

"Is this okay?" he asks softly.

His mouth is so near mine I'm not even sure I hear him; I could be reading his lips. I nod twice, as my eyes drift closed, trying to tamp down the fizziness I'm feeling, as if it's sparkling water, not blood, coursing through my veins. If he weren't holding my face, even as tenderly as he is, I feel like I could float away, float away, and keep going up and up until I find my place in the sky as a sun, or a star, a celestial being made of shimmering light and joy.

"Yes," I breathe.

And then the world and my life stops. When his lips touch mine, I know in that blink of time that I will now and forever be thinking of my life in two parts, the before, and the after, of this kiss.

He tastes like mint with a hint of sweetness. I love mint. His lips are soft, warm, and feel perfect against mine. My eyes flutter open as we slowly part, and I smile as I stare into his amber eyes, warm and glowing. I love his eyes. I tilt my mouth up towards him and, this time, I kiss him. I can feel him smiling and I smile and we laugh softly as our foreheads meet.

"Hi." He tucks my hair behind my ears, which feels so good, my eyes fall shut again. He strokes a thumb over each eyebrow, trails a finger down my nose, then traces my top lip, back and forth.

I'm having trouble breathing, I'm feeling too many things, all good, but I'm also kind of dying and I bite my bottom lip because I don't want this to end. When he stops, my heavy eyelids lift in slow motion; it's hard because I feel almost mesmerized, and, blinking, I try to focus on his gorgeous, handsome beauty.

I haven't been this close to Kenzo in a long time, and I take advantage of it to study every inch of his face. I want to trace my fingertips over his strong eyebrows, too, loving how they feather off like a brushstroke. His eyelashes are ridiculous, and I smile when I see all the freckles sprinkled like cinnamon on his tanned skin, especially the ones across the strong, straight bridge of his nose. I want to bite his jawline.

"Wow," I whisper, and then my eyes meet his.

There's a glint in Kenzo's eye, and the corners of his mouth twitch like he's trying not to laugh; he's been watching me, and I can feel laughter bubbling up inside me, too. I'm not sure what he thinks is so funny about this but, for me, I suddenly feel a little embarrassed, and it's like I need to release this tension I didn't know I was carrying.

So I start giggling, and once I start, I can't stop, and it builds and builds, and then he starts, and we both get to where we're holding our stomachs, we're laughing so hard. When I can finally take a breath, I wipe the tears from my eyes and he smiles as he replaces my hand with his. Then, we're somehow thinking the same thing at the same time and we lean in towards each other and kiss.

We kiss.

We kiss.

We kiss.

And it's like nothing I could have ever imagined.

I'm breathless when we finally break apart. And I swear I don't mean to, but I start giggling again. Kenzo looks at me, a quizzical frown on his face.

"I'm sorry," I manage as the fits of laughter keep increasing in intensity until I have to back away and lean over, one hand holding my aching stomach while the other grips Kenzo's for balance.

"What's so funny?" he asks.

"It's not you. It's not you." The giggles are simmering down, and I take deep breaths until I'm able to stand up. "I'm sorry, I don't know what came over me, but while we were, you know, kissing, I suddenly thought, wow, this totally doesn't feel like I'm kissing my brother." I look up at him, and I can see he's not sure where I'm going with this. "I mean, you know, for years, I've considered you like a brother."

He leans down until our foreheads are almost touching. "Listen to me very carefully, Emiko Kimori," he says, his voice almost growly. "You are definitely not my sister, and my feelings for you are anything but brotherly."

"Oh-kay." I can feel my face heating up again, and the inside of my head is like a bingo machine full of bouncing colored balls. I keep my eyes downcast, hyper-aware of Kenzo's strong hands holding my waist and the fact that he's looking at me so intently. I'm in so much trouble.

"Emiko," he says softly.

I look up at him and, just like that, the tender expression in his eyes makes any nerves I'm feeling dissolve like a snow-flake on my tongue.

"Kenzo," I say, and a smile curves my mouth as I lean in to kiss him again.

You find a lot of interesting things on the beach. I think that's the attraction, because there's constant change, from the rocks and the logs, the shells and the debris, the seaweed and the helpless creatures who are at the mercy of the always moving waters and shifting tides; it's a lottery, what washes up on shore.

I've found shells, of course; glass tumbled smooth and frosty; sanded driftwood that makes my imagination fire; and rocks disguised as eggs, one of the perfect shapes in nature.

Once, Kenzo and I found a lidless chest freezer sitting empty, an abandoned alien ship against the stripped logs. We played in and around that thing for weeks until, one day, we ran to the beach only to find it had been taken back by the sea.

But the most exciting thing I've ever found was a skull. I tell Kenzo the story.

One fall afternoon, when I was about six years old, Ojiichan and I went beachcombing after a big storm. The sky was brilliant, the way it is after it's been washed by a hard rain, and the light made everything look extra — extra clear, extra bright, extra real.

I was exploring a large rock outcrop that becomes visible only during extreme tides. It held dozens of pools that demanded inspection, and I had just climbed over a ridge when I spotted the skull at the bottom of a particularly deep one.

I nearly fell over with fright, as it seemed to be looking up at me with its empty eyes. But then, recognizing it as an animal's, I continued to stare at it, fascinated, and it quickly transformed into something cheerful and friendly. Any fear I had of it turned into mist and evaporated in the warmth of the sun.

I stood up and called Ojiichan from where he was collecting seaweed for the garden. I must have been sparking with some kind of energy because he scrambled over to me as fast as he could.

"What is it, Emiko-chan?" he asked, a touch of worry in his voice.

I pointed to the skull, not yet brave enough to touch it. "Look."

Ojiichan squatted down and carefully lifted it out of the water, clean and white. "Uwaahh, sugoi. What a wonder." As I'd expected, he was as excited by my find as I was.

"What do you think it is?" I asked as I crouched beside him.

He turned it over in his hands and studied it from several angles before he spoke. My grandfather knows a lot of things, and I was certain he would know what kind of animal this was.

"It could be a seal, maybe," he said.

My eyes widened. "Or an otter?"

He chuckled, nodding, as he considered the idea. "Yes, possibly an otter."

I let out a breath, feeling even luckier that I had found such a treasure.

Ojiichan showed me how the jaw worked and carefully let me run my fingers over the few remaining teeth, and the forehead, and the bone above the eye sockets.

Eventually, I got comfortable enough to hold it in my own hands. I turned it over and around and couldn't stop staring at it. With its missing teeth, it reminded me of a jack-o'-lantern, which made me laugh.

"It's smiling," I said. "Don't you think so, Ojiichan?"

Then, I noticed a distinct, thin, Y-shaped indentation running along one side of the skull, but couldn't find a matching indentation on the other. When I asked Ojiichan about it, he held it up to examine it closely.

"Hm, that is a good question." He peered at the depression, which was about as wide as bakery twine. "I do not know for sure, little one, but my guess is that perhaps this was caused by a blood vessel of some kind."

He explained what veins and arteries were before continuing, saying, "I think, as the animal grew, the bone was pressed against it and, over time, the vein or artery left its impression." He turned to smile at me.

I thought about this, the idea that something I knew had to be softer than bone could, over time, leave that kind of mark. "Like a fossil?" I asked.

Ojiichan considered this for a moment. "Yes, I suppose it is a little bit like a fossil."

"Wow."

Ojiichan nodded. "Yes, exactly. Wow."

Eventually, it was time for us to return home, and I asked Ojiichan if we could keep the skull.

He looked at me and shook his head. "I am sorry, Emiko-chan, but I do not think we can. I believe there are very strict rules about taking such things. Do you not also think the spirit of this creature would be unhappy if it were taken away from its home?"

I wrestled with this, and while a part of me wanted to argue with Ojiichan, another part understood exactly what he was saying and agreed with him.

So, we held a burial. I didn't want to leave it where it was, in case someone else came along and took it with them as a souvenir.

Because the tide was at its lowest, Ojiichan and I were able to walk quite a way before hitting the water's edge. There, with my little shovel and bucket, we dug a deep hole in the heavy, wet sand.

I held the skull in my hands for one last time and looked at it head-on. Chuckling again at its expression, I patted it gently on the snout before placing it at the bottom of the hole.

We took turns filling it back in with sand, and when the skull was buried, Ojiichan said a few words to wish it well on the next leg of its journey, and I offered my thank-you for letting me find it.

It didn't take long for the waves to lap at our feet, and for the sand to settle, erasing all signs that it had ever been disturbed.

"Sate, Emiko-chan," Ojiichan said, holding out his hand. "Mou kaerou ka? Shall we go home?"

I nodded and put my hand in his.

I don't know why, but this detail on the skull obsessed me for years. The idea that, inside all of us, things could be marking our bones without us even knowing it, let alone feeling it. That our bones can yield to something that's not hard. That our skulls and bones are not perfectly smooth.

And is it possible, I wonder, for feelings or emotions to impress themselves on our bones as well? Because I'm starting to believe that's what's happened to me with Kenzo.

He's been in my life, in my soul, for so long, but I didn't think about it, the way I don't consider what my veins and arteries are doing in my body — I ignore the fact that it's a miracle that I'm alive, and take for granted that things are working the way they should.

Kenzo doesn't interrupt me as I tell him about the skull, and everything, but I can sense he's curious where I'm headed. I'm not sure I'm explaining myself as well as I could. I need a table.

"I'm telling you this because I feel like that's you, over all these years. Somehow, you've left an imprint on my bones and I didn't know it until now. And it's an impression that's permanent and that I'll carry with me always."

Then I shock us both by bursting into tears. But they're happy tears, and after wiping them away and sharing one more kiss, I put my hand in Kenzo's.

And we sit there, talking and not talking, for a while longer.

So, it turns out Kenzo might be a bit of a romantic.

Before we head home, he holds up his phone and tells me he wants to take a selfie, so that we have something to remind us of today. I don't tell him there's no way I'll ever forget any of this, because I have a feeling he already knows.

Instead, I laugh, and we snuggle close, the water behind us our backdrop, and Kenzo reaches out to snap the picture. We take a slew of them and get a little silly, making faces, laying big smoochy kisses on each other's cheeks, rubbing noses, that sort of thing.

I never thought I'd be part of one of those couples — the idea has always made me a bit squeamish — but it feels easy and right with Kenzo, like neither of us is trying too hard. And, well, it's not like I haven't been wrong about this sort of thing before.

For our last selfie, Kenzo wants a proper one, with the two us looking into the camera. He raises his arm so we get a good angle and I say *cheese* and he taps the button.

For a few seconds, we just sit there, absorbing everything. And then I turn to him, and I'm so happy I don't know if I can even stand it.

"Let's see," I say, and he hands me his phone. I hit the gallery icon and start swiping as I lean against him, my back to his front. Kenzo nestles his head on my shoulder so he can view the photos too.

We smile at most of them, they're already a good memory; almost die laughing at a couple of phenomenally bad ones; and then come to the final photo, which is kind of perfect. Kenzo's managed to get it so there's the sea and horizon in the background with our smiling faces filling two-thirds of the frame.

"Oh my god." I sit up so quickly I almost give Kenzo whiplash.

"What is it?" he asks, as I zoom into the background. Blinking rapidly, I whirl around so that I'm facing the sea.

"Em, what is it?" he repeats, his voice concerned.

Squinting, I scan the water, but other than a tugboat in the distance there's nothing of note. I turn to look at him, and I'm not sure if I want to start laughing or crying.

Kenzo's brow creases as he tries to read me.

"We were photobombed," I tell him.

"We were?" He looks out towards the sea, but I know he won't find the culprit.

I nod, showing him the blurry image on his phone, and point to the unmistakable, awe-inspiring creature breaching the water. "By a whale."

30
Changes

We tell Ojiichan, Mitsuko, Mas and Abby, and Takeo and Tomio pretty much right away, because there doesn't feel like any reason not to. And, funnily enough, no one seems overly surprised, not even the twins.

Unfortunately, I can't fully bask in our new couple-glow because, though Kenzo has no idea, there's a Harumi-shaped shadow following me around, a constant reminder of who I need to tell next.

Still, certain her reaction will not be positive, I avoid her for days, barely sleeping as I brood over how to deliver the news and explain my part in it. Knowing I can't put it off forever, I finally invite her over for afternoon tea, hoping finger sandwiches, scones, and tiny pastries will make things easier.

They do not.

"You *what?*" Harumi's eyes flare with shock and bewilderment as her teaspoon drops to the table with a spattering of sugary tea.

"I'm sorry, Harumi —"

"I literally just told you I liked Kenzo!" Red blotches her cheeks, and, looking close to tears, she turns her face away from me.

"I know," I say, feeling everything grow hot.

"Then why didn't you just say you liked him too?" When I don't answer right away, she shakes her head, muttering, "You never tell me anything."

"What?" I look at her. "Yes, I do."

"No, you don't, not really. And if you had, I never, ever, would have dreamed I had any kind of chance with Kenzo. Never. But you let me think I did." She quickly brushes away the tears now spilling down her face, visibly trying to keep her composure.

I let out a deep breath, trying to ease the band tightening around my chest. "I'm so sorry for that. I never meant . . . But I didn't realize . . . until you said his name out loud. And then . . . I knew, but I didn't see the point in saying anything because I didn't know if he felt the same way."

"Obviously, he does." She stares past me. "OBVIOUSLY, Kenzo would like you more than me. Everyone does. Why wouldn't he?"

"Harumi —"

Standing up, she shoves her chair back. "You should have told me."

"Wait. I know. Can I explain —?"

"There's nothing to explain — you like Kenzo, he likes you. I'm not stupid."

"I know you're not stupid."

"I just feel stupid." Her voice cracks a little, and the sinkhole in my stomach grows bigger. Her gaze averted, she asks, "Did you tell him about me?"

"No. Of course not."

Harumi thinks about this for a moment, then lets out a deep breath before picking up her backpack and hugging it to her chest. "I'm going home."

"Please, can I —?"

She shakes her head, again, avoiding my eyes. "I know you were only trying to be nice . . . with everything. But I don't . . . I don't want your help anymore, Emiko, with anything."

"Oh," I say.

"And I think . . . I can't be friends with you right now," she continues, her voice unnaturally high.

"Okay." I try to swallow the hard lump in my throat. "I . . . I understand."

She nods stiffly, and for a brief moment I think she might say something more. But then, without another word, she runs off the deck, grabs her bike, and rides away.

"Still nothing?" Kenzo asks when I check my phone again.

I shake my head as I stare at the screen. I didn't tell Kenzo the reason Harumi's not talking to me, other than to confess that I've been a bad friend and I need to make things right. He didn't press, of course.

"It's been over a week," I say, looking over my apologetic texts again, the ones asking how she's doing, if we can meet to talk and clear things up. But she hasn't replied to a single one. "I haven't even seen her at the café, or the shop, or anything."

Kenzo looks thoughtful, and then he tells me she's not working at Re: Gifting anymore. "Will told me Arlo got her a job as a junior camp counselor."

"Oh. Well, maybe she's gone, like, full campcore and is living tech-free for a bit." I say this hopefully, but inside, I'm wondering if she's swung from not interested in being friends "right now" all the way over to "ever again."

"She'll come around."

I sigh. "We'll see." We're at Senior Dogs, even though I'm not on shift. Safiye had told me about a couple of new arrivals, which was the perfect excuse to bring Kenzo and show him around.

I'm cuddling a sweet old girl named Scout, and Kenzo has Stumpy, a scruffy-faced mutt, asleep on his lap.

"I get why you like volunteering here," he says as Stumpy snores away. "This is pretty relaxing."

"It's the best perk." I lower Scout onto my lap, too, and give her ears a reassuring rub. After a few minutes of letting the dogs calm me, I exhale loudly. "So, I wanted to talk to you about something."

Kenzo looks up.

"It's something I've been thinking about for a while now."

"Okay."

"Like, seriously. This isn't a spur-of-the-moment idea."

"Shoot."

"And just to be clear, this is just an *idea*, so be honest and tell me what you think. No pressure. I haven't even said this out loud to anyone so maybe it's going to sound crazy."

"Em." He says my name in a way that always stops me in my tracks, and I look up at him. He smiles. "Tell me."

So, I do.

We follow the advice Ojiichan gave me that day at the pier and go on a lot of long walks to talk things through, figure things out, because, amazingly, Kenzo loves my idea; he even says it was something he'd briefly considered himself.

"You're not just saying that?" I ask when he tells me this. We're seated facing each other, cross-legged, on home rock after a productive trek to the west end of the beach and back.

"I can prove it to you. I wrote it down."

"Why did you stop considering it?" I ask, curious.

He gives me a half-embarrassed grin. "No particular reason."

I scramble to my knees, which isn't fun on the hard surface. "Ow." I place a hand on his shoulder and lean in towards him. "Come on, Sanada. What was the reason?" Looking into his eyes, I give him a coaxing smile.

"Nothing. I came up with something else."

I respond by refusing to let him break eye contact; when I literally go nose-to-nose with him, he finally caves and laughs. "Okay. Okay."

I sit back on my heels, trying not to grin too broadly.

"Don't let this go to your head, Kimori," he says in a mock-stern voice.

"I won't," I say in the same tone.

Kenzo looks downward and traces a line in the rock. "You." He lifts his eyes to meet mine, and my breath catches at the expression in them; thankfully, he looks away again before I spontaneously combust. "The reason was you," he says.

Of course I have to kiss him after that.

The two of us do our homework, and when we've finally solidified our plan, we present it to both our families at my house. After Kenzo passes around the handouts, I run through what I feel is a very thorough and compelling PowerPoint slideshow.

The response is underwhelming.

No one says anything for so long, I break out in a nervous sweat. Ojiichan makes noises like he's about to speak, but then falls silent, while Abby and Mas exchange looks and Mitsuko folds and refolds her napkin.

"Well, what do you think?" I say when I can no longer stand the silence.

Mas sighs as he looks at Kenzo. "You know your mom and I will support anything you want to pursue. But giving up a spot at university —"

"Deferring, Dad," Kenzo corrects. "It's just a deferral."

Abby speaks. "I guess what we're concerned about is this deferral becoming permanent. And then what? What will you do?"

"I don't know, Mom. I can't predict the future. But right now, I plan to go to university. Just not right away."

"It's one year." I look at my grandfather and aunt. "After that, our hope," here, I turn and smile at Kenzo, "is that we'll have a better idea of what we really want to do, and we can go to university and pick our courses with intention, not just for the sake of it. Which is what it would feel like if we went this fall."

"Why can't you do the same thing at school?" Mitsuko asks. "I thought the point of university was to go and try anything that interests you, explore different subjects."

"It still feels too structured, too limiting." I'm not sure how else to explain it, but both Kenzo and I feel like university isn't what we need right now. "The things that really interest us aren't things we've seen in a course catalog."

My grandfather leafs through the papers in front of him. After a few minutes, he stands up, causing Kenzo and I to trade worried glances.

"Ojiichan?" I say.

"I think this is best contemplated for at least one night." He looks at Kenzo, a fond smile on his face. "Kenzo, I trust that is acceptable to you?"

"Of course," he says. "Thank you."

"Emiko?"

"Yes, of course." I mean, what else am I going to say?

Ojiichan and I walk everyone, including Kenzo, to the foyer. It's not the most boisterous farewell scene we've ever had, because everyone's clearly preoccupied, but Mas, Abby, and Mitsuko all give me hugs before they head out the door.

Kenzo's the last to leave and he leans in close. "Text you later," he whispers before he says good night to Ojiichan and runs to catch up with his parents.

I shut the door quietly behind him.

"Emiko."

I spin around to face my grandfather. "Yes, Ojiichan?"

"You have thought about this carefully."

I'm not sure if he's asking me or telling me, so I just nod.

"It is quite an undertaking," he says.

"I know. And . . ." I hesitate for a moment, then realize I should have said this to him earlier, ". . . and part of me is scared about leaving you, and going away for such a long time. And I might get so homesick I run back before you even have a chance to miss me. But another part of me is *really* excited about this idea." Remembering something else he told me at the pier, I add, "It feels like the path I'm supposed to take."

Ojiichan doesn't respond right away, though he's definitely thinking. "Mm-hm," he says eventually. "It is almost uncanny."

"What is?" I ask.

"How much you remind me of your mother right now." He smiles softly, then straightens up. "Thank you, Emiko. I will see you in the morning. Oyasuminasai."

"Oyasuminasai, Ojiichan." I watch him head down the hall to his study, a little miffed, I have to say, that he's leaving me hanging like this.

By the time I reach my bedroom, though, I'm feeling . . . okay. I check my phone and, as promised, there's a text waiting.

KENZO: Anything?

ME: Nope. But I'm cautiously optimistic. You?

KENZO: They sent me to my room.

ME: What?!

KENZO: Kidding. I left to give them privacy. They're talking.

ME: OK.

I gnaw on my thumbnail for a second, thinking.

ME: What happens if they don't all agree?

There's a pause before he answers.

KENZO: Then we go with Plan B.

ME: We have a Plan B?

KENZO: Not yet. But we'll come up with one if we need to. It'll be OK, M.

I smile down at my phone. Kenzo's quiet confidence is one of his many attractive qualities.

ME: OK, K.

KENZO: See you tomorrow?

ME: Can't wait.

KENZO: Night. 🖤

ME: Oyasuminasai.

* * *

As hoped, Plan A gets a big boost when Ojiichan agrees that what I want to do falls under education and he signs off on allowing me to access my trust fund for the trip. A couple more discussions assure Mitsuko and Mas and Abby that Kenzo and I have way more in mind than a yearlong holiday traveling through the U.K. and Japan.

And once they accept that, they are full-on committed and give us way more support than either of us expected.

Ojiichan, Mitsuko, Seiji, and Mas and Abby all have friends and family in England and Scotland, and by reaching out to them, Kenzo is able to arrange meetings, short internships, and special access to more than a dozen world-renowned gardens, including Kew in London and the Royal Botanic in Abby's hometown of Edinburgh.

I'd already talked to Meeta, and in addition to hosting us for a visit in Oxford, my amazing friend has gone above and beyond and provided us with even more leads. Combined with our families' extensive contacts, I now have a growing itinerary of private cooking and baking lessons at a mouthwatering list of high- and low-end eateries and bakery-cafés, short-term classes at a variety of cooking schools, and behind the scenes tours at London's famous food halls and markets, like Borough and Billingsgate Fish.

Once word gets out to the entire network, Kenzo and I also have no shortage of places to stay, which is so incredible, we don't know how to express how grateful we are to everyone.

It's the same story for Japan, with the added bonus of finally meeting my great-aunt in Kyoto—she of the gorgeous calendars—and a bunch of Kenzo's relatives, for the first time.

Truly, if it weren't for Harumi's conspicuous absence during all this, I would feel like the happiest, luckiest girl in this universe.

"Is this really happening?"

We're taking a break from our marathon planning sessions to stargaze on the back deck with the twins. While Takeo and Tomio argue over whose half of the sky has more fireballs, I turn to Kenzo on the lounger beside me and repeat my question.

"Is this *really happening*?"

"Are you talking about the meteor shower?" It's a cloudless, pitchy night so it's easy to spot the Perseids shooting every which way across the sky, but the dark means I can barely make out his face; still, I can tell he's teasing.

"No." I smile. "Our trip. Are we really doing this?"

"I've seen some plane tickets with our names on them."

"Wow," I say, falling onto my back again.

"Wow," he agrees.

And as we continue to watch for shooting stars, his hand finds its way into mine.

31
All the Endings

A couple of days later, I'm clearing tables at the café while Gareth raves about his and Kiki's fave new indie band.

He's still kind of annoying, but since he stepped up back when I apologized for the beach party, I try to listen as he goes on and on . . . until the café door swings opens and Chisato Ishi walks in. It's like that scene in an old Western, when the stranger enters the saloon and everyone, from the piano player to the barkeep, stops whatever they're doing to check them out.

But it's not a movie; she's really here. And when she sees me, she freezes for a moment, like she's changed her mind and wants to bolt. Then, she lifts her chin, straightens her spine, and walks over to where I'm standing.

"Gareth. Emiko." She greets us both, but it's obvious who she's here for.

"Howdy," Gareth replies, tipping an invisible hat. Thankfully, he keeps quiet after that and pretends to be absorbed in tidying up the display case.

Chisato barely acknowledges him, tugging on the sleeves of her hoodie as she scans the nearly empty café before looking at me. "Can we talk outside?"

"Sure." I pick up my tray. "Let me get rid of this first, though." Chisato nods and leaves.

"Huh. I wonder what she's doing back," Gareth says as he refills a plate of Bakewell tarts.

"I have no idea."

"I should tell Kiki. She'll want to know."

I bite my tongue and finish cleaning up as Gareth pulls out his phone to send his text. Despite the lowlights of our history, I might actually miss him a little after he moves to California for school. Jury's still out on Kiki Shimizu-Leigh.

"You okay if I take a break?" I ask as he tucks his phone away.

"Go, I got this." He gives me one of his trademark winks.

"Still with the winking, Tolman? We talked about this."

"I told you, I can't help it," he says, chuckling as I head out the door.

Chisato's on the bench in front of the café so I sit down beside her. She's staring at the road and doesn't say anything right away, but since she's the one who called this meeting, I just wait.

Eventually, she sighs and glances over at me. "This is weird."

"Yeah," I agree. "Is Jun with you?"

"He is."

"Mitsuko didn't mention anything."

"We didn't tell anyone we were coming, just my aunt. He's at his dad and your aunt's house now." After another silence, she says, "I was pretty overwhelmed by him. When we met. You know how he is."

"I do." And if the level of attention Jun paid me was any indication, I imagine for Chisato it must have compared to being followed by a spotlight.

"But I liked it. Liked him. Liked how he made me feel."

I nod, even though she's not looking at me.

"But then all this drama happened, back in Tokyo, with my aunt and uncle — and they threatened to cut me off if I kept seeing him. Because they thought he was a distraction. A bad influence." Chisato's voice trails off, and I wonder if she's flashing back to the beach party, too.

After a few moments, she continues. "My aunt and uncle — everything comes with strings. They gave me an ultimatum, basically — their money, their rules. I didn't have much choice, not if I wanted to continue my studies. But I wanted to get away from them, and from Jun, so I asked Aunt Taka if I could come to the coast to finish school. All I wanted to do was earn the biggest scholarship I could so I could tell my aunt and uncle thanks but no thanks and go study music without anyone's help."

She stops, and sighs. "It probably wasn't a good idea, but Jun and I stayed in touch. I told myself that we could just be friends. Then, he went and followed me across an ocean. And then, he kept coming up here."

Looking down at her hands, she flexes her fingers. "I tried to resist, you know. We had a couple of huge fights and I'd be like, no, I don't need this . . . complication. But then he'd do something sweet. And when I found out about my scholarship, he was so excited for me, he was like, let's just go, let's get off the coast, let's get started on our life together." She blows out a long, slow, breath.

"That's a lot," I say.

"It is," she says eventually. "And I'm really not an impulsive person, normally. But it turns out, I'm crazy for him. So, I said yes."

"Wow."

She sits up. "But we shouldn't have left like that. I mean, I told Aunt Taka what we were doing, but it was a shock to her. We could have handled things better. We should have."

I'm moving the puzzle pieces around in my head when something hits me. "Whose idea was the hair?"

Chisato looks at me, surprised, as her hand goes up to her blue streak. "Uhm, mine."

I nod. "Cool. It suits you both."

After much internal debate, I did finally send Jun that email, followed by a text telling him to "CHECK YOUR INBOX NOW." I think about the surprisingly decent response I got back.

"Did you help him write his reply to me?" I ask.

"No. That was a hundred percent Jun." She turns to me. "But I owe you an apology, too. Not just for hiding the truth . . . I knew what he was doing with you, too, pretending. And I didn't like it, but until I knew what I was doing after grad, I couldn't say anything. So I didn't stop it. I'm sorry for that. For all of it."

I shake my head, trying to imagine what she's gone through. "You don't owe me anything, Chisato. Our Oscar hopeful, though? While he's here, he should probably sleep with one eye open."

Chisato actually laughs. "I'll tell him."

We sit there for a few more minutes, taking in the laid-back bustle of summer in the Creek, until a large group of tourists wanders into the café.

I stand up. "I should get back to work."

Chisato rises, too. "Okay. Thanks, Emiko."

"When are you two heading out?"

"In a week."

"Well, I'll be shocked if Mitsuko and Seiji don't plan something. So, I guess I'll see you soon."

She gives me an easy smile. "Definitely."

Like magic, the day of our farewell party arrives.

Tomorrow, we've got reservations for the first ferry out, and Mas and Abby will be driving us to the airport. Today, everyone still on the coast that we wanted to see before leaving Otter Creek is either here already or on their way.

Except Harumi. She eventually answered me, and after an exchange of more reserved yet friendly texts, I invited her to come. When she replied that she wasn't sure she could, it made me sad, but I don't blame her; if she had been right about Kenzo, and this was their party, then it'd be hard for me, too.

I take a breath to clear my head and focus on what's happening on the lawn in front of me — Takeo and Tomio trying to impress the Triple As with their new card tricks; Kenzo laughing with Jacob and Darcy and Liv Soo's Jeremy; and Liv and some of her squad teaching Kenzo's teammates moves to use when they score on the ice.

Over on the water side of the yard, Ojiichan and Mitsuko have joined the circle of grown-ups, which includes Safiye and her partner, Pablo. And entertaining them all is a pair of dogs that Safi and Pab brought with them, for some extra socialization time. That's what I tell people, anyway.

I watch the dogs for a few moments more before clearing the empty dishes from the potluck table. I'm halfway up the stairs to the kitchen with a stack of them when I sense movement to my right, and I turn to see Harumi standing on the deck, flanked by Arlo and Will.

"Hi," I say, climbing the last few steps to meet them.

"Hi," Harumi says.

An uncomfortably long pause follows until Arlo jumps in. "Sorry we're late. Kenzo said any time after lunch. We brought spinach pie." She holds up a large foil-covered pan. "Homemade."

"That sounds delicious, thank you. I'm so glad you could all come," I tell them.

Will coughs and lifts up a heavy-looking bag. "I brought you a watermelon. To replace the one I broke last year."

I stare at him, not sure if he's for real, and he looks back at me, straight-faced and innocent. He manages to hold it briefly before breaking into a shy grin.

"Good one, Will," I say, impressed. "You had me there for a second."

"Rivers!" We all turn and see Kenzo approaching the house. "Come and join us," he calls up. "You too, Arlo."

Arlo turns to Harumi and touches her arm. "I'll see you down there, okay?"

Harumi smiles, nodding.

I watch Arlo and Will go down the stairs to meet Kenzo before continuing into the kitchen.

Harumi follows and sits at the island, and, after putting the dishes in the sink, I turn to face her. "It's great to see you. How have you been?"

"Good. Really good," she says.

"I'm glad." And then, "I've really missed you."

Harumi's barely-there smile crumples. "Me too," she says, swallowing hard. "Me too." She lets out a loud breath before continuing. "So, you're really going?"

"We are. Although I won't believe it until we land at Heathrow."

"Well . . . I'm excited for you." She straightens up. "For the both of you."

"Honestly?"

She looks at me, nodding, and finally — *finally* — a proper Harumi smile takes over her face and makes my heart glow. "Honestly," she says. Then she steps off her stool and we both go in for a hug. "I'm sorry it took me this long to get here."

I shake my head. "I'm just happy that you did," I say as we pull away. "Oh no," I add when her bottom lip starts to quiver.

"And now you're leaving —"

"Which is why you can't start with this!" Blowing air, I fan my eyes to stave off the tears. "Not yet, anyway. It's too early."

"Okay. Okay. I'll save it for later." She wipes her cheeks, and then giggles, and just like that, I feel like we're back to ourselves.

"Come on," I say as I head out the slider. "Let's go catch up outside. Are you hungry?"

"Uhm, actually . . ."

I turn back as Harumi stalls on the threshold.

She looks serious, and nervous. "There *is* something else I want to tell you."

"Alright." I keep my voice calm as various possibilities fly through my head.

We walk out onto the deck together and she stands beside me. "Remember how you didn't think Will was a good match for me?"

"Yes." I cringe recalling the things I said to her, and so many of the things I said and thought about Will. "I'm sorry, Harumi. I was totally out of line and unbelievably idiotic about everything. Will's really —"

"No. You were right."

I stop short. "I was?"

She nods. "I mean, I do like Will. A lot. We've gotten to know each other really well this summer and he's such a good friend. But I figured out he's not the right one for me, either."

"Okay," I say slowly.

"It turns out, Arlo is." She doesn't look at me when she says this, which gives me a chance to repeat her words in my head and process the meaning.

"Arlo?" I blink a few times, and then, "Oh my GOD, Harumi!"

She turns and starts giggling when she sees the expression on my face.

"*Arlo.*" I play back all the times I saw the two of them together, searching for that moment when this pairing should have been obvious to me. "Arlo," I repeat. Because now that I know — she and Harumi — well. I grab Harumi and give her a long hug. "Arlo is perfect for you!"

She laughs. "I know."

"Wow. You and Arlo . . . I can't believe I never —" Harumi pulls back, cocking an eyebrow, and I shut my mouth. "Never mind. I'm just . . . so happy for you."

"I'm so happy for me too, Emiko."

"This couldn't be more awesome," I say as we step apart. "I mean, wow. Wow." Then I frown as I remember something. "But . . . what about Will? I mean, I'm pretty sure he had a crush on you."

Harumi sighs, though her smile lingers. "Yeah. He did. And at first, Arlo and I were just friends. It was so easy, like we'd been friends forever. Which I guess is kind of true? And then, after our . . . you know, the last time I was here, I told Arlo about everything, and then, I got the job at the same camp we met at, and one day, I looked at her and realized I wanted to be more than friends. So I told her, and she said she did too.

"We told Will right away, but he said he kind of already knew. He's really sensitive that way. And he and Arlo love each other so much, he couldn't be mad."

At that moment, Arlo, who's holding Lucy Maud — a Norwich Terrier who may be my most favorite shelter resident ever — turns and looks up towards the house. And the way she beams at Harumi as she waves one of Lucy Maud's paws at us, it makes my heart squeeze in the very best way.

As Harumi waves back, I take her other hand. "Come on," I say as we head down the steps. "We have a lot to celebrate."

All our friends have arrived and the party's still going strong, but I sneak away for a few minutes to myself. I head to my spot of choice, the viewing pavilion, and lean against a corner pillar.

As I take more mental snapshots of the people and the moments I want to carry with me, I start thinking about the things that happened this year and how they helped bring me here. And recalling Mx. G.'s last words of guidance, I understand now how they weren't kidding.

Because not every decision works; many definitely need tailoring; a few will make you look bad; while others might be worth saving for the future. And some, thankfully, are going to fit exactly right. But you'll never really know until you try them on.

Before I can continue to ride this train of thought, a small bark attracts my attention, and I turn to see my grandfather chatting with Safiye and Pablo.

Throughout the day, I would catch Ojiichan joining them while trying hard to be super casual and not show any particular interest in either Jem the Cavapoo, or sweet, feisty Lucy Maud. But I know what to look for, and even though Jem is love in a dog suit, it's Miss Lucy Maud who sits in front of Ojiichan at every opportunity, tongue lolling, tail thumping. She's made her preference clear. And he's managed to resist. Until now.

I suppress the squeal that bubbles up inside me when Pablo picks up Lucy Maud as he says something to Ojiichan. Lucy Maud is a wriggler, but when she looks up at

Ojiichan, she settles immediately, and after a few moments, her mouth drops open into an adorable canine smile. Even from here, it's irresistible.

"Come on, girl," I say under my breath.

As I'd hoped, Ojiichan says something to Pablo before reaching out to rub one of Lucy Maud's ears. Then Pablo hands her over, and it takes a few seconds for Ojiichan to get comfortable, but before long he's cradling the tiny bundle of a dog in his arms like a pro. Things could still go either way, but then I see my grandfather say something to her, and though I'm too far away to hear the words, I can tell he's calling her "little one." And I know my work here is done.

Kenzo finds me then, and notices the pleased grin on my face. "What are you up to, Kimori?" he asks.

I shrug, giving him my best wide-eyed "Who, me?" look.

Am I a matchmaking genius?

When I review my less than successful attempts over the past year, I'm willing to concede that I'm probably not . . . *if* we're only considering matches between people.

But as I watch Ojiichan falling in love in real time with Lucy Maud, I have to think — if it involves a dog — then, maybe?

And when I remember George and Mx. G., and Frisby and his biker lady, and I realize that I am now THREE FOR THREE pairing dogs with their humans, I'm sure we can all agree that the answer is *yes*.

Yes, I am.

Most definitely, yes.

"Emiko."

I look up, eager to tell Kenzo about my last matchmaking attempt for a while, only to forget pretty much everything I was going to say when I see him smiling at me in this way he has that's reserved just for me. So I reach up to give him a quick kiss instead.

And then he pulls me in for a longer one.

The End

Acknowledgments

It would take a book much thicker than this one to list every single person (and dog) who has influenced and shaped the way I view the world. Thank you all for the gifts and lessons that helped get me here.

An extra-large thank you goes to the entire team at CookeMcDermid Literary, most especially to my wonderful and wise agent, Rachel Letofsky. Thank you for your early belief in *Emiko*, and for the editorial guidance that made all the difference in finding her a home. I wish every writer might find someone so kind, who cares for their work as much as you do.

A giant hamper of gratitude and an endless supply of yummy things goes to my editor and publisher, Tara Walker, assistant editor Ashley Rhamey, and the editorial team at Tundra and Penguin Random House Canada. Tara, having you shepherd me through two book "firsts" is an unbelievable bit of serendipity. Thanks to you and Ashley both for making this whole journey an absolute joy. I could not have gotten Emiko's story to where it is without you.

Lynne Missen, thank you for being there at the beginning, and starting me down this path with your insightful comments and helpful feedback. And also, for the perfect vacation read!

To Catherine Marjoribanks and Eugénie Szwalek, many thanks for the thoughtful and thought-provoking copy edit and equity/authenticity review. Your help with the final sand and polish of this manuscript was invaluable.

To Gigi Lau, the design and production teams at Tundra, and Jacqueline Li, thank you for creating SUCH a gorgeous book! Every element, from the artwork on the cover to the choices on the pages in between, has come together so beautifully. I'm beyond proud to display the final result on my shelf.

To Sam Devotta and the marketing and publicity, sales, and rights teams at Tundra, thank you for all the enthusiasm, creativity, and hard work you put in to give *Emiko* the best launch into the world, and the highest chance possible to find her readers.

I'm blessed and grateful to have so many friends and family members who have, over the years, supported my goal to be a writer. I appreciate every kind deed and encouraging word they've ever done or shared. On this project in particular, though, I wish especially to thank:

Jas Uppal, for her unwavering faith and friendship, and for being my biggest cheerleader since our Franklin days; and Dave, for being so awesome, and Jacquelyn and Alexa, for their observations and opinions (and being awesome, too);

Alice Matsumoto, for her buoying reaction to an early draft coupled with her perceptive feedback, and for having that vision three decades ago which has now, amazingly, come true;

Wendy Cummings, ever my unofficial "publicist," for being so steadfast, and for insisting on waiting "for the book to come out" before she'd read it;

Carol Humphries, for the years of laughing till we cried, for cheerfully championing my work, and for all those extra jars of antipasto;

Camryn Zayshley, for letting me pick her brain and answering all my questions about high school and teen life on the coast, and for my favorite little bowl;

Barbara Dylla, for taking the time to read the manuscript with her expert eye and introducing me to spicy bucatini aglio e olio when we were both a lot younger;

Anne Klok, for sharing her love of YA novels and S19, and for laughing in the right spots of an early draft;

Andy Cook, for unknowingly providing the kickstart I needed to stop just thinking about writing a novel;

Every teacher and staff member who made my time at Templeton Senior Secondary so memorable;

Dr. Deborah Pope and the Ezra Jack Keats Foundation, for the early validation and support, and for continuing to celebrate the kinds of children's books that help make possible YA books like this;

The Mears, Mann, Cummer, and Ruta family members in Winnipeg, Manitoba, and Atlanta, Georgia, for all their support and encouragement (and meals!) over the years;

Yosh and Masami (and Mimi-chan, gunning for World's Oldest Dog) in PoCo, British Colombia, for showing up and always being so supportive;

Team KAAS (Kimi, Aiko, Alexander, and Sander), for cheering all the way from the Netherlands and for letting me be a cool aunt (!);

Maki and Mike in St. Catharines, Ontario, for the gratifying reactions to the early drafts, and Mike, for the grammar-schooling and high school insider knowledge;

My mom, who is always so proud of everything I do, and my late father, who was a guiding presence in so many scenes;

Paul, who has given me so much, including his whole heart and soul in support of my dreams. I could not and would not be here without him.

Finally, the fictional setting of this story was inspired by British Columbia's lower Sunshine Coast, the traditional territories of the shíshálh and S̲kwx̲wú7mesh Nations. I am grateful to have called the area home for over twenty years; the beauty of that place, along with the very wonderful people I met there — many of whom still live there — will always hold a special place in my heart.